# PRAISE FOR THE GUILD HUNTER NOVELS OF NALINI SINGH

## Archangel's Kiss

"Everything that urban fantasy romance fans could ask for—sexy thrills, compelling characters, and an original mythology combined with more than a dash of horror. Paranormal romance doesn't get better than this."  —*Love Vampires*

"The world is heartbreakingly original . . . The characters . . . are mesmerizing . . . Sizzling hot."  —*Errant Dreams Reviews*

"The mystifying world of angels beckons in the second installment of Singh's remarkable urban fantasy series . . . Better clear off more space on your keeper shelf!"
—*Romantic Times* (Top Pick)

"In the mood for a dark,  that may have you gaspin this in ways you can't ima already anxious to read [th

"I'm so intrigued by this w cannot wait until the next Angel book."  —*Dear Author*

"Nalini Singh has really outdone herself with *Archangel's Kiss*. I could not put this book down and continued to read well into the night . . . Nalini Singh is a master at her craft. I can't wait for the next book."  —*Night Owl Reviews*

"Ms. Singh's books never fail to draw me in and keep me enthralled until the very end . . . Utterly fascinating. The Guild Hunter series is one that will not disappoint and will keep readers invested until the very end."  —*Romance Junkies*

"Terrific . . . [It] grips the audience."  —*Midwest Book Review*

*continued . . .*

# Angels' Blood

"Terrifyingly, passionately awesome . . . You'll love it."
—Patricia Briggs, #1 *New York Times* bestselling author

"I loved every word, could picture every scene, and cannot recommend this book highly enough. It is amazing in every way!" —Gena Showalter, *New York Times* bestselling author

"This is probably one of the best stories I have ever read and will be one that I will rave about for quite a while."
—*Fallen Angel Reviews*

"Amazing. Fantastic. Simmering with both violence and sexual tension, and with vivid worldbuilding that blew my socks off." —Meljean Brook, national bestselling author

"A refreshing twist on vampire and angel lore combined with sizzling sexual tension make this paranormal romance a winner." —*Monsters and Critics*

"With the launch of a second paranormal series, Singh provides incontrovertible evidence that she's an unrivaled storyteller . . . Tremendous!" —*Romantic Times* (Top Pick)

"Nalini Singh should take a bow! *Angels' Blood* is going to leave you hungering for more instantly." —*Romance Junkies*

## FURTHER PRAISE FOR THE NOVELS OF NALINI SINGH

### Blaze of Memory

"*Blaze of Memory* is another incredibly strong entry in the Psy-Changeling series, my very favorite in paranormal romance."
—*Romance Novel TV*

"This is a keeper . . . A definite classic."
—*A Romance Review*

## Branded by Fire

"An emotional masterpiece."                    —*Romance Junkies*

"[Singh] grabs the reader . . . and leaves them begging for more."                    —*Night Owl Reviews*

## Hostage to Pleasure

"Singh is on the fast track to becoming a genre giant!"
                    —*Romantic Times* (Top Pick)

"A thrilling read with action, danger, passion, and drama."
                    —*Romance Junkies*

"An intriguing world that's sure to keep readers coming back for more."                    —*Darque Reviews*

## Mine to Possess

"Fierce . . . Paranormal romance at its best."
                    —*Publishers Weekly*

"If you've been looking for a book that will entice and entrance, look no further."                    —*Romance Reviews Today*

## Caressed by Ice

"A fast-paced, edge-of-your-seat romantic paranormal that will pull you straight into the story and into the amazing Psy-Changeling world!"                    —*Romance Reader at Heart*

"The paranormal romance of the year."                    —*Romance Junkies*

"Craving the passionate and electrifying world created by the mega-talented Singh? Your next fix is here! . . . Mind-blowing!"                    —*Romantic Times* (4½ stars, Top Pick)

*continued...*

## Visions of Heat

"Breathtaking blend of passion, adventure, and the paranormal." —Gena Showalter, *New York Times* bestselling author

"This author just moved to the top of my auto-buy list."
—*All About Romance*

"Will set all your senses ablaze and leave your fingers singed with each turn of the page. *Visions of Heat* is that intense!"
—*Romance Junkies*

## Slave to Sensation

"I LOVE this book! It's a must read for all of my fans. Nalini Singh is a major new talent."
—Christine Feehan, #1 *New York Times* bestselling author

"An electrifying . . . volcanic start to a new series that'll leave you craving more." —*Romance Junkies*

"AWESOME! . . . A purely mesmerizing book that surely stands out among the other paranormal books out there."
—*Romance Reader at Heart*

# Archangel's Consort

## Nalini Singh

BERKLEY SENSATION, NEW YORK

**THE BERKLEY PUBLISHING GROUP**
**Published by the Penguin Group**
**Penguin Group (USA) Inc.**
**375 Hudson Street, New York, New York 10014, USA**
Penguin Group (Canada), 90 Eglinton Avenue East, Suite 700, Toronto, Ontario M4P 2Y3, Canada
(a division of Pearson Penguin Canada Inc.)
Penguin Books Ltd., 80 Strand, London WC2R 0RL, England
Penguin Group Ireland, 25 St. Stephen's Green, Dublin 2, Ireland (a division of Penguin Books Ltd.)
Penguin Group (Australia), 250 Camberwell Road, Camberwell, Victoria 3124, Australia
(a division of Pearson Australia Group Pty. Ltd.)
Penguin Books India Pvt. Ltd., 11 Community Centre, Panchsheel Park, New Delhi—110 017, India
Penguin Group (NZ), 67 Apollo Drive, Rosedale, North Shore 0632, New Zealand
(a division of Pearson New Zealand Ltd.)
Penguin Books (South Africa) (Pty.) Ltd., 24 Sturdee Avenue, Rosebank, Johannesburg 2196,
South Africa

Penguin Books Ltd., Registered Offices: 80 Strand, London WC2R 0RL, England

This is a work of fiction. Names, characters, places, and incidents either are the product of the author's imagination or are used fictitiously, and any resemblance to actual persons, living or dead, business establishments, events, or locales is entirely coincidental. The publisher does not have any control over and does not assume any responsibility for author or third-party websites or their content.

ARCHANGEL'S CONSORT

A Berkley Sensation Book / published by arrangement with the author

PRINTING HISTORY
Berkley Sensation mass-market edition / February 2011

Copyright © 2011 by Nalini Singh.
Excerpt from *Kiss of Snow* by Nalini Singh copyright © by Nalini Singh.
Cover art by Tony Mauro.
Cover design by George Long.
Cover hand lettering by Ron Zinn.
Interior text design by Kristin del Rosario.

ISBN: 978-0-425-24013-7

BERKLEY® SENSATION
Berkley Sensation Books are published by The Berkley Publishing Group,
a division of Penguin Group (USA) Inc.,
375 Hudson Street, New York, New York 10014.
BERKLEY® SENSATION and the "B" design are trademarks of Penguin Group (USA) Inc.

PRINTED IN THE UNITED STATES OF AMERICA

10  9  8  7  6  5  4  3  2  1

*To everyone who has ever dreamed of flying and to all of you who have flown with me.*

# 1

Swathed in the silken shadows of deepest night, New York was the same . . . and altered beyond compare. Once Elena had watched angels take flight from the light-filled column of the Tower as she sat in front of the distant window of her cherished apartment. Now, she was one of those angels, perched high atop a balcony that had no railing, nothing to prevent a deadly fall.

Except of course, she would no longer fall.

Her wings were stronger now. She was stronger.

Flaring out those wings, she took a deep breath of the air of home. A fusion of scents—spice and smoke, human and vampire, earthy and sophisticated—hit her with the wild fever of a welcoming rainstorm. Her chest, tight for so long, relaxed, and she stretched her wings out to their greatest width. It was time to explore this familiar place that had become foreign, this home that was suddenly new again.

Diving down from the balcony, she swept across Manhattan on air currents kissed by the cool bite of spring. The bright green season had thawed the snows that had kept the

city in thrall this winter, and now held court, summer not even
a peach-colored blush on the horizon. This was the time of
rebirth, of blooming things and baby birds, bright and young
and fragile even in the frenetic rush of a city that never slept.

*Home. I'm home.*

Letting the air currents sweep her where they would above
the diamond-studded lights of the city, she tested her wings,
tested her strength.

Stronger.

But still weak. An immortal barely-Made.

One whose heart remained painfully mortal.

So it was no surprise when she found herself trying to
hover outside the plate-glass window of her apartment. She
didn't yet have the skill to execute the maneuver, and she
kept dropping, then having to pull herself back up with fast
wingbeats. Still, she saw enough in those fleeting glimpses to
know that while the once-shattered glass had been flawlessly
repaired, the rooms were empty.

There wasn't even a bloodstain on the carpet to mark the
spot where she'd spilled Raphael's blood, where she'd tried
to staunch the crimson river until her fingers were the same
murderous shade.

*Elena.*

The scent of the wind and the rain, fresh and wild, around
her, inside her, and then strong hands on her hips as Raphael
held her effortlessly in position so she could look her fill
through the window, her hands flat on the glass.

Emptiness.

No sign remained of the home she'd created piece by precious piece.

"You must teach me how to hover," she said, forcing herself to speak past the knot of loss. It was just a place. Just
things. "It'll be a very good way to spy on potential targets."

"I intend to teach you many things." Tugging her back
against his body, her wings trapped in between, the Archangel
of New York pressed his lips to the tip of her ear. "You are full
of sorrow."

It was instinct to lie, to protect herself, but they'd gone beyond that, she and her archangel. "I guess I somehow expected my apartment to still be here. Sara didn't say anything when she sent me my things." And her best friend had never lied to her.

"It was as you left it when Sara visited," Raphael said, drawing back enough that she could flare out her wings and angle her body into the air currents once again. *Come, I have something to show you.*

The words were in her mind, along with the wind and the rain. She didn't order him to get out—because she knew he wasn't in it. This, the way she could sense him so deeply, speak to him with such ease, was part of whatever it was that tied them to one another . . . that taut, twisting emotion that ripped away old scars and created new vulnerabilities in a whip of fire across the soul.

But as she watched him fly through the lush black of the sky high over the glittering city, her archangel with his wings of white-gold and eyes of endless, relentless blue, she wasn't sorry. She didn't want to turn back the clock, didn't want to return to a life in which she'd never been held in the arms of an archangel, never felt her heart tear open and reform into something stronger, capable of such furies of emotion that it scared her at times. *Where are you taking me, Archangel?*

*Patience, Guild Hunter.*

She smiled, her grief at the loss of her apartment buried under a wave of amusement. No matter how many times he decreed that her loyalty was now to the angels and not to the Hunters' Guild, he kept betraying how he saw her—as a hunter, as a warrior. Shooting down below him, she dove then rose through the biting freshness of the air with hard, strong wingbeats. Her back and shoulder muscles protested the acrobatics, but she was having too much fun to worry—she'd pay for it in a few hours, no doubt about it, but for now, she felt free and protected in the dark.

"Do you think anyone is watching?" she asked, breathless from the exertion, once they were side by side once more.

"Perhaps. But the darkness will conceal your identity for the moment."

Tomorrow, she knew, when light broke, the circus would begin. An angel-Made . . . Even the oldest of vampires and the angels themselves found her a curiosity. She had no doubts about how the human population would react. "Can't you do your scary thing and make them keep their distance?" However, even as she spoke, she knew it wasn't the reaction of the general population that worried her.

Her father . . . No. She wouldn't think about Jeffrey. Not tonight.

As she forced away thoughts of the man who had repudiated her when she'd been barely eighteen, Raphael swept out over the Hudson, dropping so hard and fast that she yelped before she could catch herself. The Archangel of New York was one hell of a flier—he skimmed along the water until he could've trailed his fingers in its rushing cold, before pulling himself up in a steep ascent. Showing off.

For her.

It made her heart lighten, her lips curve.

Dipping down to join him at a lower altitude, she watched the night winds whip that sleek ebony hair across his face, as if they could not resist touching him.

*It will do no good.*

"What?" Fascinated by the almost cruel beauty of him, this male she dared call her lover, she'd forgotten what she'd asked him.

*For me to scare them away—you are not a woman to stay in seclusion.*

"Damn. You're right." Feeling her shoulder muscles begin to pull in ominous warning, she winced. "I think I need to set down soon." Her body had been damaged in the fight against Lijuan. Not much—and the injuries had healed, but the enforced rest period meant she'd lost some of the muscle she'd built up prior to the battle that had turned Beijing into a crater, its voice the silent cry of the dead.

*We're almost home.*

Concentrating on keeping herself going in a straight line, she realized he'd shifted position so she was effectively riding his wake—meaning she no longer had to make as much effort to hold herself aloft. Pride had her scrunching her face into a scowl, but contrasting with that was a deep warmth that came from knowing she was important, more than important, to Raphael.

And then she saw it, the sprawling mansion that was Raphael's clifftop home on the other side of the river. Though the land backed up against the Hudson, the place was hidden from casual view by a thick verge of trees. However, they were coming at it from above, and from up there it looked like a jewel set in the velvet darkness, warm golden light in every window—turning into pulses of color where it hit the clean lines of the stained glass on one side of the building. The rose bushes weren't visible from this angle, but she knew they were there, their leaves luxuriant and glossy against the elegant white of the house, hundreds of buds ready to bloom in a profusion of color as the weather grew warmer.

She followed Raphael down as he landed in the yard, the light from the stained glass turning his wings into a kaleidoscope of wild blue, crystalline green, and ruby red. *You could've landed on one of the balconies*, she said, too focused on ensuring a good landing to speak the words aloud.

Raphael didn't disagree, waiting until she was on the ground beside him to say, "I could have." Reaching out as she folded away her wings, he gripped her gently at the curve where her neck flowed into her shoulder, his fingers pressing into the sensitive inner seam of her right wing. "But then your lips would not have been so very close to mine."

Her toes curled as he tugged her forward, pleasure blooming in her stomach. "Not here," she murmured, voice husky. "I don't want to shock Jeeves."

Raphael kissed away her words with a slow thoroughness that had her forgetting all about his butler, her body warming with a slow, luscious sense of anticipation. *Raphael.*

*You tremble, Elena. You are tired.*

*Never too tired for your touch.* It terrified her how addicted she'd become to him. The only thing that made it bearable was that his hunger, too, was a raw, near-violent craving.

A lick of storm against her senses before he drew back with a hotly sexual promise. *Later.* A slow, intimate stroke along the upper curve of her wing. *I would take my time with you.* His lips parted, his spoken words far less incendiary. "Montgomery will like having you for his mistress, Elena."

She licked her lips, tried to breathe—and heard the rapid tattoo of her heart against her ribs. Yeah, the archangel knew how to kiss. "Why?" she finally managed to say, falling into step beside him as he walked to the door.

"You're likely to get dirty and destroy your clothes on a regular basis." Raphael's humor was dry, his voice an exquisite caress in the night. "It is the same reason he likes it when Illium occasionally stays here. You both give him plenty to do."

She made a face at him, but her lips kicked up at the corners. "Is Illium coming to join us?" The blue-winged angel was part of Raphael's Seven, the vampires and angels who had given their loyalty to the Archangel of New York—even to the extent of placing his life before their own. Illium was the only one of the Seven who saw her human heart not as a weakness, but as a gift. And in him, she saw a kind of innocence that had been lost in the other immortals.

The door opened at that moment to expose the beaming face of Raphael's butler. "Sire," he said in a plummy English accent she was certain could turn cold and intimidating on command. "It is good to have you home."

"Montgomery." Raphael placed a hand on the vampire's shoulder as he passed.

Elena smiled at the butler, delighted by him all over again. "Hello."

"Mistress."

She blinked. "Elena," she said firmly. "I'm no one's mistress but my own." Then there was the fact that though he chose to work in the service of an archangel, Montgomery was a strong vampire, hundreds of years old.

The butler's spine went stiff as a board, his eyes shooting to Raphael—who gave a languid smile. "You must not shock Montgomery so, Elena." Reaching out to take her hand, he tugged her to his side. "Perhaps you will allow him to call you Guild Hunter?"

Elena looked up, certain the archangel was laughing. But his expression was clear, his lips set with their familiar sensual grace. "Um, yes, okay." She nodded at Montgomery, then felt compelled to ask, "Will that do?"

"Of course, Guild Hunter." He gave a small bow. "I was not sure if you would wish a meal, Sire, but I have sent a small tray up to your rooms."

"That will be all for tonight, Montgomery."

As the butler whispered away, Elena looked with growing suspicion at a large Chinese vase in one corner of the hall, opposite the stained-glass wall beside the door. It was decorated with a pattern of sunflowers that seemed oddly familiar. Letting go of Raphael's hand, she stepped closer . . . closer. Her eyes went wide. "This is mine!" Given as a gift by an angel in China after Elena completed a particularly dangerous hunt, one that had taken her into the bowels of the Shanghai underworld.

Raphael touched his fingers to the small of her back, a searing brand. "All of your things are here." He waited until she looked up before saying, "They were moved to this house for safekeeping until your return.

"However," he continued when she remained silent, her throat a knot of emotion, "it seems Montgomery could not help himself when it came to this vase. I'm afraid he has a weakness for beautiful things and has been known to relocate an item if he feels it is not being accorded the proper appreciation. Once, he 'relocated' an ancient sculpture from the home of another archangel."

Elena stared down the corridor where the butler had disappeared in refined silence. "I don't believe you. He's too prim and proper." It was easier to say that, to focus on the humor, than to accept the tightness in her chest, the feelings locking up her throat.

"You would be surprised." Touching her lower back again, he nudged her down the hall and up a flight of stairs. "Come, you can look at your belongings in the morning."

She dragged her feet at the top of the staircase. "No."

Raphael measured her expression with those eyes no mortal would ever possess, a silent visual reminder that he had never been human, would never be anything close to mortal. "Such will." Leading her to a room that flowed off what she knew to be the master bedroom, he opened the door.

Everything from her apartment lay neatly stacked, slipcovers over the furnishings, her knickknacks in boxes.

She froze on the doorstep, uncertain how she felt—relief and anger and joy all battled for space inside of her. She'd known she could never go back to the apartment that had been her haven and more, a furious rebuttal against her father's abandonment. The place wasn't built for a being with wings—but the loss had hurt. So much.

Now . . . "Why?"

His hand closed around her nape with no attempt to hide the possession inherent in the act. "You are mine, Elena. If you choose to sleep in another bed, I will simply pick you up and bring you home."

Arrogant words. But he was an archangel. And she'd made a claim of her own. "As long as you remember that goes both ways."

*Acknowledged, Guild Hunter.* A kiss pressed to the curve of her shoulder, his fingers tightening on her nape just a fraction. *Come to bed.*

Arousal kicked her hard, her body knowing full well what pleasure awaited her at those strong, lethal hands. "So we can talk knives and sheaths?"

Sensual male laughter, another kiss, the caress of teeth. But he released his hold, watching in silence as she stepped into the room and lifted a slipcover to run her fingers over the delicately embroidered comforter on the bed that had been her own, then she moved to explore the vanity with its store of pretty glass bottles and brushes set tidily inside a small box.

She felt like a child, wanting to reassure herself that everything was here, the need visceral enough to hurt.

As she gave in to the emotional hunger, her mind disgorged images of another homecoming, of the shock and humiliation that had burned her throat when she'd found her things piled up like so much garbage on the street. Nothing would ever erase that hurt, the pain of the knowledge that that was exactly what she was to her father, but tonight, Raphael had crushed the memory under the weight of a far more powerful act.

She had no illusions about her archangel, knew he'd done it in part precisely for the reason he'd given her—so she wouldn't be tempted to treat her apartment as a bolt-hole. But had that been his sole motivation, he could as easily have sent her stuff to the dump. Instead, every single piece had been packed with care and moved here. Some of it had been exposed to the elements when her window shattered that night, and yet now everything looked pristine, speaking of meticulous restoration.

Heart aching at the wonder of being so cherished, she said, "We can go now." She'd come back later, decide what to do with everything. "Raphael—thank you."

The brush of his wing against her own was a silent tenderness as they entered the master suite. No one else ever saw this part of him, she thought, eyes on her archangel as he moved closer to the bed and began to strip without flicking on the lights. His shirt fell off his body, revealing that magnificent chest she'd kissed her way across more than once. Suddenly, the overwhelming weight of her emotions was gone, buried under an avalanche of gut-wrenching need.

Raphael looked up at that moment, his gaze glittering with an earthy hunger that said he'd sensed her arousal. Deciding to save the talking for later, she was raising her fingers to tug off her own top when rain—no, *hail*—hit the windows in staccato bullets that made her jump. She'd have ignored it, except the hard little pellets of ice kept smashing into the glass over and over again. "Must be a storm." Dropping her hands, she walked to one of the windows after glancing over to ensure the French doors to the balcony were secure.

Lighting flashed in vicious spikes in front of her as savage winds began to pound the house with unremitting fury, the hail turning to torrential rain between one blink and the next. "I've never seen it come in this hard, this fast."

Raphael walked to stand beside her, his naked upper body patterned with the image of the raindrops against the window. She looked up when he didn't say anything, saw the shadows that had turned his gaze turbulent in an unexpected reflection of the storm. "What is it? What am I not seeing?" Because that look in his eyes . . .

"What do you know of recent weather patterns across the world?"

Elena traced a raindrop with her gaze as it tunneled across the glass. "I caught a weather update while we were at the Tower. The reporter said a tsunami had just hit the east coast of New Zealand, and that the floods in China are getting worse." Sri Lanka and the Maldives had apparently already been evacuated, but they were starting to run out of places to put people.

"Earthquakes have been rocking Elijah's territory," Raphael told her, speaking of the South American archangel, "and he fears that at least one major volcano is about to erupt. That is not all. Michaela tells me most of Europe is shuddering in the grip of an unseasonable ice storm so vicious, it threatens to kill thousands."

Elena's shoulder muscles went stiff at the mention of the most beautiful—and most venomous—of archangels. "The Middle East, at least," she said, forcing herself to relax, "seems to have escaped major catastrophe from what I saw on the news."

"Yes. Favashi is helping Neha deal with the disasters in her region."

The Archangel of Persia and the Archangel of India, Elena knew, had worked together on previous occasions. And now, when Neha hated almost everyone else in the Cadre, she seemed to be able to tolerate Favashi—perhaps because the other archangel was so much younger. "It means something, doesn't it?" she said, turning to place her hand on the wild heat of Raphael's chest, the shadowy raindrops whispering over her skin. "All this extreme weather."

"There is a legend," Raphael murmured, his wings flaring out as he tugged her into the curve of his body—as if he would protect her. "That mountains will shake and rivers overflow, while ice creeps across the world and fields drown in rain." He looked down her at, his eyes that impossible, inhuman chrome blue. "All this will come to pass . . . when an Ancient awakens."

The chill in his tone raised every hair on her body.

# 2

Shaking off the bone-deep cold, she said, "The ones who Sleep?" Raphael had told her about those of his race who were so old they grew weary of immortality. So they lay down and closed their eyes, falling into a deep slumber that would break only when something compelled them to consciousness.

"Yes." A single word that held a thousand unsaid things.

She leaned deeper into him, sliding her arms around his waist. The backs of her hands brushed against the raw silk of his feathers, and it was a quiet, stunning intimacy between an archangel and a hunter. "This kind of a disruption can't happen every time. There must be a few who Sleep?"

"Yes." His voice grew distant in a way that was the mask of an immortal who'd lived centuries beyond a millennium. "What we may be witnessing is the rebirth of an archangel."

She sucked in a breath, understanding flickering at the corners of her mind. "How many archangels Sleep?"

"No one knows, but there have been disappearances throughout our history. Antonicus, Qin, Zanaya. And . . ."

"Caliane," she completed for him, shifting so that she

could see his face without craning her neck. He was so good at hiding his emotions, her archangel, but she was learning to read the minute shifts in those eyes that had seen more dawns than she could ever imagine, witnessed the birth and fall of civilizations.

Now, her back against the glassy cold of the window, she didn't protest as he leaned in to place one hand palm-down beside her head. Instead, she ran her fingers down the muscled planes of his chest to rest at his hips, anchoring him to the present, to *her* as she asked him about a nightmare. "Will you know if your mother wakes?"

"When I was a child"—skin touched with heat, but his eyes, they remained that inhuman metallic shade—"we had a mental bond. But it burned away as I grew, and as she fell into madness." His gaze looked past her, to the pitch-black of the night.

Elena was used to fighting for what she needed, what she wanted. She'd had to become that way to survive. It had toughened her. But what she felt for this male, this archangel, it was a stronger, more powerful need, one that gave her an insight the hunter alone would've never had. "Stop it."

A silent glance rimmed with a thin frost made up of the myriad dark echoes that lingered in an archangel's memories.

"If you let the memory of her spoil this," she said, refusing to back down, "spoil *us*, then it doesn't matter if she is the Sleeper. The damage will have been done—by you."

A long, still instant, but his attention was very much on her now. "You," he said, his wings spreading out to block the rest of the room from her view, "manipulate me."

"I take care of you," she corrected. "Just like you took care of me by not letting me answer my father's call earlier today." At the time, she'd gotten snippy—because she'd been afraid. And she hated being afraid. Especially of the hurt that Jeffrey Deveraux meted out with such cruel ease. "That's the deal, so learn to handle it."

Raphael brushed his thumb across her cheekbone. "If I do not?" A cool question.

"Stop trying to pick a fight with me." She knew what haunted him—that his parents' madnesses would one day manifest in his own mind, turning him monstrous. Except Elena would never allow that to happen. "We fall, we fall together." A soft reminder, a solemn promise.

*Elena.* One hand going down to curve around her ribs, just below her breasts, as he moved his other thumb over her lips, shaping and stroking her.

"If your mother does wake," she murmured, her top suddenly abrasive against her nipples, "what will happen to her?"

"Some say a long Sleep cures the madness of age, so she could once more become Cadre." Yet Raphael's voice said that he didn't believe such a thing possible.

"Will the others on the Cadre try to locate her, kill her beforehand?"

"Those who Sleep are sacrosanct," Raphael told her. "To harm a Sleeper is to break a law so ancient, it is part of our racial memory. But there is no law that bars a search."

She knew without asking that he'd be undertaking such a search, could only hope what he discovered wasn't a nightmare made flesh.

"I'll speak to Jason," he added, "see if he has heard any rumblings on this subject that I have not."

"Is he healed?" Raphael's spymaster had been injured in the same violent explosion of power that had leveled a city and smashed Elena to the earth. "Is Aodhan?" Both angels had refused to leave her and fly to safety, though they were far stronger and faster. Even as they fell to the unforgiving earth, the two males had attempted to shield her body with their own.

"If you are," Raphael said, stroking his hand down to rest at her waist, "then of course they walk without injury."

Because she was an immortal new-Made, while Jason was hundreds of years old. Aodhan, she wasn't sure about—he was so very *other*, it was hard to judge—but the fact that he was one of Raphael's Seven spoke for itself. "Beijing . . . are there any signs of recovery?" The city had ceased to exist in anything but memory after the events of that bloody night, so many dead that Elena couldn't think about it without a sense of crushing weight on her chest, heavy and black and flavored with the taste of old death.

"No." An absolute statement. "It may take centuries for life to take root there once more."

The punishing might of power implied by that observation was staggering. It made her viscerally aware of the strength of the man who held her in an embrace she'd never be able to break if he decided to keep her prisoner. It should've scared her. But if there was one thing she knew, it was that with Raphael, any fight would be no-holds-barred. There would be no stilettos in the dark, no hurtful blades hidden behind a civilized facade . . . unlike the cutting words of another man who'd once claimed to love her.

Her soul pinched in hurt. "I can't avoid my father forever," she said, leaning back against the window again, the cold of the glass almost painful against her wings. "What do you think he'll say when he sees me?" As far as Jeffrey knew, Raphael had saved her broken and dying body by Making her a vampire.

Raphael gripped his hunter's jaw with one hand, placing the other beside her head. "He will see you as an opportunity." Honest words, for he would not lie to her. "A way to gain entry into the corridors of angelic power." If Raphael had his way, Jeffrey Deveraux would even now be rotting in a forgotten grave, but Elena loved her father in spite of his cruelty.

Now, she wrapped her arms around herself, and her words, when they came, were jagged pieces of pain. "I knew that before I asked . . . but part of me can't help hoping that maybe this time, he'll love me."

"As I can't help hoping that my mother will rise, and will once again be the woman who sang me such lullabies that the world stood still." Pulling her into a crushing embrace, he pressed his lips to her temple. "We are both fools."

Thunder crashed at that moment, lightning flashing brilliant in the dark gloom of the world beyond the windowpane.

It turned Elena's hair to glittering silver, her eyes to mercury. Those eyes, he thought as he lowered his head, as he took her lips, would change over the centuries, until they might very well become what they appeared under storm-light. *Come, Guild Hunter. It is late.*

"Raphael." An intimate murmur against his lips. "I'm so cold."

He kissed her again, moving one hand down to close over her breast. Then he took them into the heart of a tempest far more demanding in its wrenching hunger than the winds that raged outside.


The nightmare came again that night. She should've expected it, but it pulled her into the bloody ruins of what had once been her family home with such speed that she had no chance to fight.

"No, no, no." She closed her eyes in childlike defiance.

But the dream forced them open. What she saw made her freeze, her pulse pounding beat after panicked beat at the back of her throat.

There were no broken bodies on the floor slicked by a dark, dark red. *Blood.* Everywhere she looked, there was blood. More blood than she'd ever seen.

That was when she realized she wasn't in the kitchen where Ari and Belle had been murdered after all. She was in the kitchen of the Big House, the house her father had bought after her sisters . . . *After.* Gleaming pots hung on hooks above a long stone bench, while a massive fridge stood humming quietly in the corner. The stove was a shiny steel edifice that had always terrified her into keeping her distance.

Tonight, however, that steel was dulled with a rust-red coating that made her gorge rise, made her stumble to look away. At the knives. They lay everywhere. On the floor, on the counters, in the walls. All dripping thick, heavy gobs of deepest red . . . and other, fleshier things. "No, no, no." Clutching her arms around herself, her thin, fragile body that of a child, she skittered her gaze across the nightmare room in search of a safe harbor.

The blood, the knives had vanished.

The kitchen lay pristine once more. And cold. So cold. Always so cold in the Big House, no matter how much she cranked up the heat.

A shift in the dream—she'd been wrong, she thought. This cold place wasn't pristine after all. There was a single high-heeled shoe on the dazzling white of the tile.

Then she saw the shadow on the wall, swinging to and fro. *"No!"*

"Elena." Hands gripping her upper arms tight, the clean bright scent of the sea in her mind. "Guild Hunter."

The snapped words cut through the remnants of the dream, wrenching her back into the present. "I'm okay. I'm okay." The words came out jerky, disconnected. "I'm okay."

He pulled her into his arms when she would've jumped out of bed. To do what, she didn't know, but sleep never came easy after the memories hit her with such brutal force. "I need to—"

He shifted until she was half under him, his wings rising to encase them in lush, dark privacy. "Hush, *hbeebti.*" His body, heavy on her own, formed a hard shield against the softly swinging shadow that had chased her across time.

When he dropped his head and murmured more quiet, passionate words in the language that was part of her mother's legacy, she lifted her arms and wrapped them around his neck, trying to pull him down. Trying to drown herself in him. But he squeezed her thigh and raised himself up on one arm so he could look down at her. "Tell me."

Elena had always made sure to hug Beth after the day their family shattered, to ensure her younger sister didn't ever feel the chill, but she'd never had anyone to hold her in turn, never had anyone to smash apart the block of ice that encased her organs for hours after a nightmare. So, the words took time to come, but he was an immortal. Patience was a lesson he'd learned long ago.

"It didn't make sense," she said at last, her voice raw—as if she'd been screaming. "None of it made sense." Her mother hadn't done what she had in the kitchen. No, Marguerite Deveraux had very carefully tied the rope to the strong railing that went around the mezzanine. Her pretty, shiny high heel had dropped onto the gleaming checkerboard tile of the hallway that was the grand entrance to the Big House.

A glossy cherry red, that shoe had made Elena's heart fill with hope for a fractured second. She'd thought her mother had finally come back to them, finally stopped crying . . . finally stopped screaming. Then she'd looked up. Seen something that could never be erased from the wall of her mind. "It was all just a big jumble."

Raphael said nothing, but she had not a single doubt that she was the complete and total center of his attention.

"I thought," she said, clenching her hands on his shoulders, "that the nightmares would stop after I killed Slater. He'll never again hurt anyone I love. Why won't they stop?" It came out shaky, not with fear, but with a tight, helpless rage.

"Our memories make us, Elena," Raphael answered, in an echo of something she'd once said to him. "Even the darkest of them all."

Hand splayed out on his chest, she listened to the beat of his heart, strong, steady, always. "I won't ever forget," she whispered. "But I wish they'd stop haunting me." It made her feel like a traitor to say those words, to dare to wish for such a thing when Ari and Belle had lived the nightmare. When her mother had been unable to escape it.

"They will." Knowledge in his tone. "I promise you."

And because he'd never broken a promise to her, she let him hold her through what remained of the night. Dawn was pushing its way into the room on slender fingers of gold and pink when the sweet nothingness of sleep took her under.

But the peace only lasted for what felt like a mere blink of time.

*Elena.* A wave crashing into her head, a fresh bite of storm. Groggy with sleep, she blinked open her eyes to see that she was alone in the sun-kissed bed, the rain having cleared away to leave the sky beyond the windows a startling azure. "Raphael." A glance at the bedside clock showed her it was midmorning. Rubbing at her eyes, she sat up. "What is it?"

*Something has occurred that requires your skill.*

Her senses stretched awake in anticipation, her mental muscles seeming to pop with the same pleasure-pain as her physical ones when she lifted her arms and arched her body. *Where do you need me?*

*A school upstate. It is named the Eleanor Vand—*

She dropped her arms, abdomen heavy with dread. *I know what it's called. My sisters go there.*

# 3

Ten-year-old Evelyn saw Elena first. Evelyn's eyes went wide as Elena said good-bye to the angel who'd escorted her to the location via the quickest route, and flared out her wings to come to a steady landing in the front yard of the tony prep school, the velvet green perfection marred only by a number of errant leaves. Miniature twisters of spring green and crisp brown, small dervishes full of irritation, rose up in the wind created by her descent.

Folding away her wings, Elena gave her youngest half sister a nod of acknowledgment. Evelyn went to raise a hand in a tentative hello, but Amethyst, three years older than her sister, grabbed that hand to pull Evelyn to her side. Her dark blue eyes, so like her mother, Gwendolyn's, warned Elena to keep her distance.

Elena understood the reaction.

Jeffrey and Elena hadn't spoken for a decade after he threw her out—until just before the violent events that had led to her waking with wings of midnight and dawn. And prior to being disowned, Elena had been banished to boarding school for some time. As a result, she'd had no real contact with either of her half siblings. She knew of them, as they knew of her, but beyond that, they might as well have been strangers.

There wasn't even a surface resemblance to compel the recognition of familial ties—unlike Elena's pale, near-white hair and skin touched with the sunset of Morocco, not to mention her height, the girls had their mother's exquisite raven hair and petite build, their skin a rich cream that wouldn't have looked out of place on an English rose. Evelyn still carried a layer of baby fat, but her bones were Gwendolyn's, delicate and aristocratic.

Both of Jeffrey's wives had left their marks on his children.

Looking away from the two small faces that watched her with a combination of wariness and a tight, cool accusation, she took in the rest of the people on the porch. Several other girls clustered together just beyond Evelyn and Amethyst, all dressed in the maroon and white of the school, along with a number of adults who had to be teachers. Nowhere did Elena see any sign of Raphael, which meant he was either inside the heavy building of cream-colored brick or behind its ivy-covered walls in the large inner courtyard where the girls ate lunch, sat on the grass, played games.

Elena knew that because she'd made it a point to find out. It didn't matter that the three of them were only connected by the frigid ties of Jeffrey's blood—Evelyn and Amethyst were still her sisters, still hers to watch over. If they ever needed her, she would be there . . . as she hadn't been able to be there for Ari and Belle.

Heart encircled by a thousand shards of metal, each a stabbing blade, she began to head for the entrance. That was when she saw Evelyn shake off her older sister's hold and run down the front steps toward her. "You're not a vampire."

Rocking back on her heels at the challenge in that small, rebellious face, in those bunched fists, Elena said, "No."

An instant of searing eye contact, gray to gray, and Elena had the feeling she was being sized up. "Do you want to know what happened?" Evelyn asked at last.

Elena frowned, glanced at the porch—to see no one else making a move to come forward, the adults appearing as shell-shocked as the majority of the girls. Returning her attention to her sister, she fought the urge to touch her, hold her close. "Is there something you want to tell me?"

"It was awful." A whisper, nothing but horror on that soft face that was of a child's yet, not of the woman she would one day become. "I went into the dorm and there was blood every-where and Celia wasn't there even though we were supposed to meet. And I can't find Bets—"

"You discovered this?" Feral protectiveness bared its teeth. No, she thought, *no*. The monsters wouldn't steal another one of her sisters from her. "What did you see?" Her gut knotted, bile rising in her throat.

"Nothing after that," Evelyn confessed, and the relief threatened to send Elena to her knees. "Mrs. Hill heard me scream, and she dragged me out the door almost straightaway. Then they made us all stand out here, and I heard wings . . . but I didn't see your archangel."

At that instant, Elena glimpsed a shrewdness in those gray eyes that reminded her of Jeffrey's. It caused a painful twist-ing in her chest—because she, too, was her father's daughter, at least in some part of her soul. "I'll take care of things," she promised. "But I need you to go back up and stay with Am-ethyst until I figure out what's going on." It could only be a vampire gone rogue if Raphael had called for her.

Evelyn turned and ran back up to the porch, sidling up to her older sister's stiff form.

*Raphael.*

For an instant, the only thing she heard was infinite silence. No deep voice laced with the arrogance of more than a thou-sand years of living. No rush of the wind, the rain in her head. Then it thundered, until she almost staggered under the un-leashed power of it. Of him.

*Fly over the first building and—*

*I can't. I landed already.* She wasn't yet strong enough to achieve a vertical takeoff, something that required not only considerable muscle strength, but a great deal of skill.

*Come in through the front door. You will find your way.*

His certainty—knowing the only thing that could've caused it—made her stomach clench, her spine go stiff. It took conscious effort to sweep aside the sensations and narrow her focus to the upcoming hunt. Contracting her wings as close to her back as possible so they wouldn't inadvertently brush against those huddled on the porch, she walked up the stairs and across aged but solid brick identical to that of the building itself.

Whispers surrounded her on every side.

"Thought she was dead—"

"—vampire—"

"I didn't know they Made angels!"

Then came the secretive clicks that announced cell phone cameras in operation. Those pictures would hit the Web in minutes if not seconds, and the news media wouldn't hesitate to pounce the instant after that. "Well," she muttered under her breath, "at least that takes care of announcing my presence." Now all she'd have to deal with was the media scrum that was sure to hit like a freaking tornado.

*Whispers of iron in the air.*

She jerked up her head, her senses honing in on that thread that spoke of blood and violence. Following it, she made her way down the deserted hallway carpeted in burgundy, its walls lined with class photographs spanning decades past, the students starched and pressed, and to a staircase that curved sinuously up from her left.

In spite of the fact that the building was old, its bones heavy, the corridor was filled with light. She saw the reason why when she stopped on the first step, glanced up—a magnificent glass skylight, domed and gilded with gold, and caressed by a few errant strands of ivy. The leaves looked like emeralds scattered against the glass. But that wasn't what caught her attention.

*Iron again, so rich and potent and thick that it sighed of only one thing.*

Death.

"Upstairs."

Startled, Elena turned to find herself facing a skeletal-thin woman garbed in an elegant suit that straddled the border between pale olive and deep gray. The color appeared almost harsh against skin of a pale, papery white. "I'm Adrienne Liscombe, the principal," the stranger said at Elena's questioning look. "I was checking to make sure all the girls got out."

Having noticed the signs on the doors that opened off the right side of the corridor, Elena said, "This is the office building?"

"This floor," Ms. Liscombe said, her words crisp, correct. "The second floor houses the library and work spaces for the girls. Above that are a number of dorm rooms, with further facilities on the fourth floor. We function as a home to many of our students—and the staff offices are set up as studies since a significant proportion of us also live in. A girl can come down from her room at any stage to talk to a member of the staff."

Elena realized that notwithstanding her clear-cut enunciation, her immaculate suit, and her precise gold jewelry, the principal was rambling. Gut-wrenchingly conscious of what might have reduced a woman who gave every indication of having an almost austere toughness of spirit to such a state, she said, "Thank you, Ms. Liscombe." Drowning as she was in the acrid scent of blood—and of thicker, more viscous fluids—it took conscious effort to make her voice gentle. "I think the girls could use your guidance outside."

A sharp nod, light glinting off the sleek silver of her hair. "Yes, yes, I should go."

"Wait." The question had to be asked. "How many of your pupils are unaccounted for?"

"A full roll call hasn't yet been taken. I'll do it now." Shoulders being squared, professional calm reasserting itself in response to the concrete task. "Some of the girls are away on a field trip, and we have the usual number of absences, so I'll have to cross-check the list."

"Please get it to us as soon as you're able."

"Of course." A pause. "Celia . . . she should be here."

"I understand." Walking up the varnished wooden stairs that spoke of another time to the muted sounds of the principal's retreating footsteps, Elena reminded herself to keep her wings raised. It wasn't quite second nature yet, but she was far more adept at it than when she'd first awakened. Her original motivation had come from not wanting to have them dragging through the dust and dirt of Manhattan's streets.

Today, she needed the reminder for a far more sinister reason.

Entering the third-floor hallway, she ignored the exquisite oil paintings that spoke of money and class to follow the stench of iron and fear to the room at the very end, a room that held an archangel with eyes of pitiless blue. "Raphael."

She halted, tried to breathe. The cloying richness of the smell threatened to choke her as she took in the blood-drenched sheets, the pool of dark liquid edged with red on the floor, splattered on the walls, the most unspeakable graffiti. "Where's the body?" Because there would be a body. A human being couldn't lose this much blood and survive.

"In the woods," he said in a tone that made the hairs on the back of her neck rise, it was so very, very, *very* calm. "He dragged her there to feast on her, though he spilled most of her blood here."

Elena stiffened her spine against the flood of pity. It would do no good to Celia now—and would get in the way of what Elena *could* do, the justice she could help attain. "Why did you ask me to come inside?" If she was to track the vampire, her best bet would be to begin at his last known position.

"The body was discovered floating in a small pond. It's likely he bathed in it before he left."

Elena jerked up her head. "You're telling me he's *thinking*?" Because water was the sole factor that could confuse the bloodhound senses of the hunter-born. Vampires caught in the grip of bloodlust—the only thing that could explain the savagery of this attack—did not think. They rampaged with unstoppable violence, were most often caught while they gorged on the blood of their victims. "Is it"—*another Uram*? she finished, conscious that the darkest of angelic secrets could not be spoken aloud, not here.

"No." Raphael's voice was, if possible, even more gentle.

Cruelty wrapped in velvet, she thought. He was riding the razor's edge of rage.

"Find his scent, Elena. This is the place where it will be strongest."

He was right. Anything she got near the pond would be diluted. Here, he'd killed, perhaps shed some of his own blood if the victim had been able to claw at him as she fought for her life. Taking a deep breath, Elena shut out everything—including the icy knowledge that this could have been one of her sisters—and focused on the rich strokes of scent that saturated the room.

The easiest to identify was Raphael, her anchor.

Then the metallic kiss of blood. And . . . *a stormy scent licked with fire.*

Her eyes snapped open. "Jason was here?" Her ability to track angels continued to be wildly erratic, more often off than on, but she knew that combination of notes, knew also that it was rare for the black-winged angel to make a daylight appearance.

*Yes.*

Chilled by the way Raphael stared unblinking at the pool of blood, she pushed aside the question of why Raphael's spymaster had passed through here—why, indeed, the Archangel of New York was on a scene that should've been filled with cops and hunters—and focused her senses once more. It was startling, what little effort it took to isolate the vampiric thread. Unlike most places in the state, this school was apparently free of vampiric employees, a humans-only zone.

No wonder Jeffrey had chosen it for his daughters.

But one vampire had invaded this sanctum, a vampire with a sickly sweet edge to his smell.

*Burnt treacle . . . and slivers of glass, heavier notes of oak underneath.*

Tugging on that thread, she angled her head toward the window. "That's how he got out." But she left the room through the door, knowing she'd never be able to squeeze out the same way, given her wings. She was aware of Raphael at her back as she found an exit and stepped outside, rounding ivy-covered walls until she stood below the window.

That particular section of wall was clear of the dark green vine. "Place has high ceilings." Which, since the room was on the third floor, equaled the window being a considerable distance off the ground. "How did he get up?" Most vamps wouldn't have been able to jump that high. However . . . She pressed her nose to the wall, drew in a breath.

*Crushed glass, oak leaves.*

Then she saw the streak of red by where she'd placed her right hand, palm-down.

Dropping it, she looked around her feet as she spoke. "He climbed up and down like a fucking spider." There was only a subset of vampires who could pull off that particular trick. "Should help narrow down his identity."

"His name is Ignatius," Raphael said to her surprise—just as she glimpsed droplets of dark liquid on the grass. "I felt his mind turn bloodred when I touched it."

Elena wasn't sure of Raphael's range, but if he'd touched Ignatius's mind, then there was something wrong here. "You weren't able to execute him." She followed the trail across the manicured green of the inner lawn, through the heavy archway carved out in the middle of the long school building at the other end, and into the woods that normally provided a serene backdrop—but today seemed an ominous mass, the leaves dull beneath a sky that had shifted from azure to dirty gray in the minutes she'd been inside.

Not answering her implied question, Raphael rose into the air as she tracked Ignatius through the woods, her wings catching on branches and thorny bushes. Wincing at the uncomfortable sensations, she tucked them even tighter to her body but didn't slow her progress through the trees. She hesitated at one point, certain she felt the tug of something to her right, but the trail of oak and glass was vivid straight ahead.

Shaking off the impulse to turn, explore, she continued the track. Jason's black-winged form appeared out of the looming dark of the woods less than five minutes later—he stood unmoving as stone, guarding a body that lay beside the placid waters of a small pond.

The girl was still wearing her school uniform, her entire frame soaked. Her blouse should've been white. It was a nauseating salmon pink, and shredded as Elena knew her flesh would've been shredded. Strangling the pity that threatened to derail her, Elena didn't move toward the body—her priority was to track the killer, to make certain no other girl would end up a broken doll beside a pond that should've been a place of play, not a macabre bath flavored with death and horror.

*You were right*, she sent to Raphael, *he washed in the pond, cut off the scent trail*. But he would have had to get out at some point. So, leaving Jason to continue his silent vigil, she began walking across the moss-laden stones that rimmed the water gone murky with churned up silt . . . and other, darker things.

It only took a minute to find him again. The scent trail was weaker, drenched in water until the oak alone remained, but that was all she needed. Drawing the crisp forest air into her lungs, she began to run, determined to hunt the vampire to ground. He was fast, she realized almost at once, glimpsing the tracks he'd left behind in the damp patches of earth caused by last night's storm. In contrast, she was no longer as quick and agile as she'd once been, unused to running with wings.

But it wasn't a disadvantage, not today. The vampire had slowed down maybe five hundred yards into his escape, probably figuring the water had erased his scent. It would have if he'd taken a bit more care. Then again, Raphael had said the girl's body had been in the water, too. Her murderer had likely dragged her in there with him because he couldn't stop feeding.

The end result was that given the small size of the pond, the blood and death had polluted it, destroying its ability to wash the vampire clean of his sickening acts of violence. *Good girl*, she thought, speaking to the child who lay so motionless under wings of midnight black. *You marked the bastard even in death*. Elena would hunt him down using that mark.

Half an hour into the run—through twisting paths that tried to muddy the trail and confirmed the vampire was rational—the sun weak and sluggish overhead, she began to feel a stitch in her side. "Damn it." She didn't need Raphael's sadist of a weapons-master, Galen, to pound at her to know she wasn't in full hunting shape.

Breathing past the stabbing pain, she snapped up her head as the shadow of wings swept along the ground in front of her—to see Raphael flying to a location just beyond the rise, his speed breathtaking.

*Archangel, what do you see?*

# 4

There was no answer, only the painful bite of ice in her veins.

*Rage.*

Pure and violent and cold, so cold.

"Shit." She pushed up her pace, cursing the fact that she couldn't do a vertical takeoff for the billionth time. It could take years to master, she'd been told—perhaps longer seeing as she hadn't had wings since childhood. Well, fuck it, she thought. If she had to ask Galen to come to New York to torture her again every single day for the next year, she was going to learn.

Raphael dived in front of her and by the time she crested the rise, her chest heaving, he had his hand clamped around the neck of a vampire whose clothing remained damp enough to stick to his skin. The Archangel of New York was holding the panicked creature at least two feet off the ground with no visible effort. The vampire's eyes bulged, blood vessels popping as he scrabbled at the hand around his throat, his legs kicking at the air in a futile attempt to escape.

"You are not in bloodlust," she heard Raphael say in a voice so clear, it was a blade, slicing and brutalizing without mercy.

Instinct, paired with what she'd learned of Raphael in the time they'd been together, had a very bad feeling forming in the pit of her stomach. Scrambling down the rise without caring about the mud that streaked her jeans and wings both, she looked into the vampire's face. The male's reddened eyes were lucid . . . but for the terror in their depths. His mouth was another matter. Rimmed with dried blood that had survived his impromptu bath, it turned his face into a grotesque mask.

"Why?" Elena asked, knives in hand though she had no memory of drawing them from the sheaths strapped to her forearms. "Why did you do it?" The image of the girl's ravaged body played over and over on the screen of her mind. That could've been Evelyn, could've been Amethyst. Her sisters. *Again.* The thought echoed until it was almost all she could hear.

Raphael began to squeeze the vampire's throat. "It matters little why." Blood trickled from one of the vampire's eyes, a macabre tear.

"Wait." She put her hand on the corded strength of Raphael's forearm. "Your vampires don't disobey you. Not like this." They were too aware of the brutal justice of his punishments. The fact that this Ignatius had done what he had in spite of that . . .

The vampire began to claw at Raphael's hand with the last of his strength, as if conscious that after crushing his throat, the Archangel of New York would almost certainly rip off his head and have his entire body burned. Raphael shook off the clawing hands as if they were less than flies, his expression so calm it was terrifying.

*Raphael*, she tried again, using their mental connection in the hope it would penetrate the ice that was his rage. *We need to know why.*

Raphael glanced at her. "All right." And before her horrified eyes, the vampire began to bleed . . . everywhere, his very pores seeming to erupt under extreme pressure. She knew what Raphael had done, knew he'd shredded the killer's mind like so much confetti. That task complete, he tore off the vampire's head with a single efficient wrench and burned both pieces to ash with the vivid blue of angelfire. The pulse of raw power could kill an archangel—the vampire's body didn't even survive a full second.

It all happened so fast that she was still staring at the place where the vampire had been when Raphael turned to her, a slight glow to his wings that augured nothing good. The primal part of her brain, more animal than human in its determination to survive, fired a surge of fear-laced adrenaline through her system. *Run*, it said, *run*! Because when an archangel glowed, people died.

But Raphael wasn't simply an archangel. He was hers.

She stood her ground as he stepped closer, bent to speak with his mouth brushing her ear. "Someone whispered to him that I was dead"—cool tone, quiet words that made her nerves skitter—"that there was no longer any need for him to leash his desires." Moving back a step, he lifted a finger to tuck a flyaway strand of her hair behind her ear.

The gentleness of the act didn't reassure her—not when his anger kissed a knife blade against her throat. "That doesn't make sense." It took effort to keep her voice steady—yes, he was hers, but she'd only scratched the surface of him. "Even if he did think that, why come here, to this place?" She wasn't egotistical enough to think it had anything to do with her. No, Raphael was the target, but *she* was the weak point in his defenses. "It's too far out of the city to be anything but a specific location."

Raphael's eyes shone with that dangerous metallic tinge, a look to him she couldn't read. He'd been alive for over a thousand years and had so many facets to his personality that she knew it would take an eternity to see them all. Right now, it was obvious that reasoning with him would be akin to banging her head against thousands of rapier-sharp blades.

It would only make her bleed.

Taking a deep breath, she gestured back to where she'd

seen Jason. "I need to examine the body, make sure there wasn't anything weird about the kill." It appeared to have been a simple feeding gone feral, but after the past year and a half, she wasn't much on taking things at face value.

Raphael flared out his wings, their glow painful in the dull, cloudy light. "You can report back to me later today. Dmitri is almost here—he'll deal with the school."

He was gone in a sweep of wind an instant later, leaving her staring up at him. She didn't mind the order—he was her lover, but at this moment, she was acting as a hunter and he'd treated her as one. Since she had no intention of giving up her position with the Guild, that worked for her.

What worried her was the distance he'd put between them, a distance that had returned her to the rooftop where they'd first met, when Raphael hadn't been a man who wore her claim of amber, but only an immortal who could crush her with a single thought. An immortal who'd made her close her hand over the cutting edge of steel, until her blood spilled dark and wet onto the tiles.

"We're not going back to that, Archangel," she murmured, hand clenching in sensory memory. "If you think we are, you're going to get one hell of a surprise."

Turning on her heel, she made her way back to Jason through the leaf-littered ground, the wooded area eerie in its silence. It was as if the birds themselves were mourning the loss of a young, vibrant life. Anger was a fist in her throat by the time she reached the body—it didn't matter that the monster who'd stolen Celia's young life had been executed, justice done. She was still dead, her dreams forever ended.

Jason stood in the same position where she'd last seen him, a stone guardian, and now that Elena knew to look for it, she was able to make out the pommel of the black sword he wore strapped to his back, hidden against the sooty black of his wings. "I didn't expect to see you here," she said, trying to distance herself from what she had to do next.

Jason stepped back to allow her closer to the body. The move threw the tribal tattoo on the left-hand side of his face momentarily into the light before he angled his head toward the shadows he wore like a cloak once more, until even though his hair was pulled off his face in a neat queue, she could only just glean his eyes. "I was meeting with the Sire when the message came through."

Kneeling beside Celia's body, her wings pressed against pine needles and innumerable crushed leaves that scented the air in a green perfume soaked with last night's rain, Elena frowned. "Why did it come to the Tower? It should've been directed to the Guild."

"The Guild Director herself called Raphael when she realized your sisters might be involved." Jason's tone was calm, so calm she'd have thought him unaffected if she hadn't seen the black flames in his eyes before he used the shadows to his advantage. "We were able to get here faster than any of the hunters who might've been called."

*Thank you, Sara.* With that, Elena put everything else aside. Celia deserved her full attention. "You pulled her out of the water?"

"Yes. I thought I glimpsed a sign of life."

But the young girl was gone, her face holding the horror of her last moments on this earth. Her skin might've been a vibrant caramel shade in life, but in death, it was a dull gray brown, the blood that pumped through her veins having spilled out of the ripped and torn flesh of her neck, her chest.

"Has the M.E. been called?" Since hunters were often the first people to find a vampire's victim or victims, they were trained in basic crime-scene protocols during their years at Guild Academy and authorized to inspect bodies—but it was always a good political measure for the Guild to keep the authorities in the loop.

"The Guild Director stated she would take care of it."

Leaning in, she examined the neck, trying to see only the pieces, not the whole. Not Celia, the girl who had been, but simply the brutalized flesh of a neck. And lower down, the ground meat of a chest that was still as flat as a boy's. "He was feeding in a frenzy," she murmured, "tore through her skin, ripped it up badly enough that he exposed bone." Nothing unusual there, except that Ignatius hadn't been in bloodlust. "Do you know why he'd feed like this if he was lucid?"

"Most vampires are neat." Jason's wings rustled slightly as he resettled them, and the sound was a welcome reminder that the painful silence of these woods wasn't the only reality. "It's a matter of pride—tearing up a body not only denotes lack of control, it means a vampire loses his or her willing partners very fast. Pain isn't why most humans take a vampiric lover."

A flash of memory, Dmitri's dark head bending over the arched neck of a woman who'd been all but purring for his blood kiss. And later, in the Refuge, Naasir with his eyes of silver and scent of a tiger on the hunt, a woman's shuddering moan. "Yeah." She sat up on her haunches, her wings spread out on the forest floor. "Can you help me turn her?"

Jason did so in silence.

The girl's back was unmarked from what Elena could see. "That's fine for now. I'll attend the autopsy, make sure I didn't miss anything."

Noises came from within the woods as they turned Celia gently onto her back once again—the murmur of voices, footsteps. It didn't surprise her when Jason melted into the shadows until she could only see him because she knew he was there—unlike Illium, Raphael's spymaster didn't like the spotlight. Even tight-mouthed Galen had friends, a woman he appeared to love, but Elena had never seen Jason with anyone when it didn't involve his duties.

"I heard a rumor you were back"—a familiar male voice—"didn't believe it."

Elena looked up to see death-scene investigator Luca Aczél doing a pretty good job of keeping his surprise at her wings to himself. With his silver-touched black hair, patrician features, and long pianist's fingers, she'd always thought Luca would look more at home in a boardroom than surrounded by violence, but there was no question that he was brilliant at what he did. Celia would be in good hands.

"Luca." Rising to her feet, she stepped aside and gave him

a quick rundown of what she'd seen and done since her arrival on the scene.

Luca crouched down beside the body, his skin appearing darker than its usual honey brown in this light. "Is the vamp dead?" There was a hardness in his eyes that would've surprised many.

Elena had known Luca too long, seen him at too many crime scenes, understood that he'd always walked a fine line when it came to separating his emotions from the often heart-rending reality of his work. "Yes."

"Good." A pause. "Hell of a welcome back, Ellie."

Elena touched her hand to Luca's shoulder as she passed, intending to check out the primary scene one more time.

"Hey, Ellie." When she glanced back, he said, "It's good to have you back, notwithstanding the circumstances."

The words, the quiet acceptance, meant everything. "I haven't forgotten I owe you a drink."

"It's two now—interest's a bitch."

Five minutes later, the light exchange felt as if it had taken place in another lifetime. A lifetime in which she wasn't standing in the middle of a room saturated with violence while the crime-scene techs worked with calm industriousness around her. It didn't matter that the killer had been caught and punished, the scene still needed to be documented for both the Guild's archives and the M.E.'s.

If, one day in the future, Celia's parents demanded to know what had been done to gain justice for their little girl, there would be some answers for them. Nothing that would lessen the hurt, nothing that would bring their daughter's laughter back into their lives, but answers all the same.

Just like Elena had had a file to read after she grew old enough to request it.

Shoving aside the jagged edge of memory, she looked around the room, her eyes skimming over the blue-overalled forms of the two techs. She knew one of them, but the other was a stranger. Both had nearly swallowed their tongues when she walked in, but Wesley had lightened the mood by saying, "Can I take a photo of you?" A flash of white teeth against night-dark skin. "Then I can sell it to the reporters as an exclusive and make enough money to pay my as yet nonexistent kids' college tuitions."

"Hate to dash your hopes, but I'm probably already on the air by now. The students," she'd said in explanation when confusion colored those pale brown eyes.

"Aw, shit."

That had been the extent of their conversation. Wesley and his colleague, Dee, went about their business with an efficiency that told her they'd been working as a team long enough to have developed a rhythm, while Elena stood in the center of the room, drowning in the echoes of violence. One of the bunk beds had sheets drenched with red turning to a dull brown that failed to mute the evil that had been done here, while more blood—arterial from the pattern of the spray— splattered the wall to its right, closest to the door.

Wesley was standing there staring at that wall. "Ellie, do you see?"

"Yes." She turned in a circle, found the blood drips on the floor and wall near the window, felt her hand clench. "Dee, could you do me a favor for a second?"

The petite blonde rose to her feet, fingerprint brush in hand. "Sure, what do you need?"

"If you'd stand by the door." Elena waited until she'd done so. "Bend down a little. That's it." Heading over, she looked at the spray. "That's how tall Celia would've been while standing."

Straightening, the tech looked behind her, her bones sharp against skin that hadn't yet thrown off the pallor of winter. "Bastard took her out here, sprayed the wall."

"Then who bled out on the bed?" Having moved to the bunk, Wesley lifted up the mattress with careful hands. "It's soaked through. No way the girl had enough in her after splattering the wall that bad."

*Damn it.* "Call your people, tell them the pond needs to be searched." A vampire of Ignatius's age—he'd appeared sixty at least—could've carried the slight weight of two young girls without a problem. Or . . . he'd discarded one in the woods where the angels hadn't spotted it from above, and Elena had bypassed because she'd been focused on the murderer.

Wesley was already taking out his cell phone. "You going to check the trail?"

"Yes, but someone needs to talk to the principal, find out—" A new scent curved into the room, erotic and luscious and flavored with sensual decadence. It was a lure, that scent, a trap that caught only the hunter-born in its jaws, and Dmitri knew how to use it to its greatest advantage.

# 5

Instinct had her stepping out to meet the leader of Raphael's Seven in the corridor. The vampire with his chocolate-dark eyes and black hair was dressed in what looked like a ten-thousand-dollar suit from some fancy store like Zegna's, the ensemble black on black with an amber-colored tie that threw the tanned color of his skin into sharp relief. Except as she knew all too well, that color wasn't a tan.

"I heard," he said when she reached him, and for once, his voice carried no hint of the double-edged blade of sex. He sounded as she'd once imagined him—a battle-hardened warrior with scimitar in hand, ancient runes carved onto the weapon's very surface. His scent, too, she realized, was being held in fierce check.

He spoke again before she could say a word. "You need to return to the Tower."

Elena scowled—the day she let Dmitri give her orders was the day ice-skating became a regular activity in hell. Part of it was simple contrariness because he'd made it crystal clear he considered her a weakness in Raphael's armor, but part of it was self-preservation. Because the instant Dmitri decided she wasn't only a weakness, but actually *weak*, he'd stop fencing with her and come at her full tilt.

Raphael would kill him for it, but as Dmitri had once said to her, she'd still be dead. So she folded her arms, braced her legs. "The second body could—"

He sliced out a hand, cutting off her words. "Raphael isn't acting right."

Their eyes met in dangerous understanding. "Has he gone Quiet?" The terrifying emotionless state that had once turned Raphael into a monster, driven her to shoot him in violent self-defense, scared Elena even now.

"No." A single precise word. "But he is not acting himself."

"No," Elena agreed. Raphael was an archangel, could be merciless in his punishments, but he was also piercingly intelligent. He shouldn't have needed her to remind him that they needed to know why Ignatius had done what he had. That was something the Raphael she knew would've considered long before it got to the point of execution—but today, it was as if he'd been driven by untrammeled rage. "Have you seen him like this before?"

"No. And I have known him near to a thousand years."

Elena sucked in a breath. In spite of the fact that he was almost impossibly good at hiding the sheer *power* within him, she'd known Dmitri was old, but even then, she hadn't come close to guessing the depth of his age. "Does this place have a balcony I can use as a launch point?" She'd pursue the mystery of Dmitri later. Right now, she had to go to her archangel.

"A small one upstairs. If you stand on the railing, you should have just enough lift to rise." He pointed to a staircase she hadn't seen till that moment. "I'll organize a search for the second body," he said as she took the first step up, "ensure the medical examiner knows you'll need to look at the remains."

Elena's hand clenched on the balustrade. The lives of two innocent families were about to be smashed to splinters that would never again form a complete whole. "My sisters?" she asked, fighting her mind's attempt to shove her back into the horror-filled past of another family, one that had broken forever in a small suburban kitchen almost two decades in the past. "The other girls?"

"Being sent home. Your father dispatched a car to pick up your sisters—they left fifteen minutes ago." Still no sarcasm, no attempt to unsettle her with that scent of his.

Dmitri's restraint worried her more than anything he could've said.

Leaving him the task of locating the second body, she made her way to what proved to be some kind of an art studio surrounded by huge windows designed to catch endless sunlight. But there was no luxuriant warmth, no shimmering gold today. The world outside was a sullen gray, the atmosphere suffocating in its heaviness.

Shaking off the thought that nothing could fly in such leaden air, she made her way onto the attached balcony. Dmitri had told the unadulterated truth when he'd termed it small. It took all of her balancing skills to get herself onto the tiny railing, and even then, the ground looked far too close.

Sucking in a breath, she flared out her wings . . . and dove.

The ground rushed up at blazing speed as she beat her wings hard and fast, muscles straining to painful levels. In the end, she could've skimmed her fingers over the grass, but she got airborne, pulling herself up until she was high enough to ride the air currents. Her shoulders ached from the unaccustomed amount and type of flying she'd done today, but not enough to make her worry about falling out of the sky.

Having caught her breath on a fast current, she stroked her way even higher—so that no one looking up would immediately recognize the unusual colors of her wings. The wind whipped her hair off her face, threatened to lay frost on her skin. The cold distracted her enough that she almost ignored the fleeting glimpse of black high above.

*Jason.*

Watching over her.

It would've annoyed her on a normal day, but today, she was too concerned about Raphael to bother. Instead, she made a mental note to ask the other angel to teach her some tricks about blending into the sky—she loved her wings with mad passion, but unlike Illium's distinctive silver-edged blue, they didn't blend into daylight skies. As with Jason, her wings were fashioned for the rich black of night, and perhaps most of all, for the hue of twilight.

Finding a thermal, she surfed it like a young fledgling, giving her muscles a break in the process. The thought conjured up images of Sam, the child angel who'd been caught in the middle of a narcissistic adult's attempt to grab at power. Elena couldn't think about how she'd found him—his small body curled in on itself, his wings broken—without feeling a chaotic mix of rage and pain. The only thing that made it bearable was that he was well on the way to being healed.

A rush of wind had her blinking furiously. When it passed, she saw Archangel Tower rising out of Manhattan, a proud, uncompromising structure that dwarfed the tallest of skyscrapers. Even on a day like this, with the sky a menacing slate gray blanket, it pierced the skyline, a gleaming column of light. She arrowed her way toward it using the last vestiges of her strength, certain Raphael would have headed to what was effectively the place from which he ruled his territory.

The wide landing space of the Tower roof appeared moments later, seeming to float above the clouds. It was a stunning sight, but she didn't have time to appreciate it—because she'd miscalculated the speed of her descent, and it was too late to rein it back. "No pain, no glory," she muttered under her breath and, teeth bared in what her fellow hunter and sometimes-friend Ransom called her "kamikaze smile," angled in for landing.

She remembered to flare out her wings in short, sharp beats as her feet touched the ground, having learned from excruciating experience that kamikaze ways or not, she did not like crashing to her knees. Even with her increased healing abilities, it still hurt like a bitch. The end result was that she ended up racing across the roof even after landing.

*Think parachute, Ellie.*

Recalling Illium's words of advice, she cupped her primaries inward, no longer riding the air but gathering it. Her body slowed. Slowed further . . . until she was finally able to snap her wings to her back. "Well," she said to the transparent wall half an inch from her nose, "that went well." She'd ended up almost plastering herself against the glass cage that housed the elevator.

Adrenaline continuing to pump through her veins, she pulled open the door and pushed the button to bring up the elevator. Of course, she could've attempted to land directly on the balcony outside Raphael's office and suite, but she'd probably have broken more than a few bones in the process, given the limited landing area. And she'd had quite enough broken bones in the past year and a half, thank you very much.

The elevator whisked her to Raphael's private level in a split second. Getting out, she looked up and down the gleaming white corridor decorated with accents of gold—tiny, almost microscopic flecks in the paint, gold threads in the deep white pile of the carpet. It was the coldest elegance—her feathers sleeked against the tinge of ice in the air, a chill that was already neutralizing the adrenaline as it burned through to her very bones.

Shaking off the frigid sensation, she walked into the large study that flowed through to the bedroom suite. Clouds caressed the glass that was the back wall, blocking out the rest of the world—and making her feel cocooned in nothingness. It was a disorienting sensation. "Raphael?"

Silence.

Absolute.

Endless.

No scent of the wind and the rain on the periphery of her senses. No whisper of wings. No hint of power in the air. Nothing whatsoever to tell her that Raphael was in the vicinity. Yet she knew he was.

Taking a deep breath, she reached out with her mind.

*Raphael?* She couldn't control her thoughts like he could, couldn't sense whether she'd reached him until he answered.

This time, her only answer was more silence.

Uneasy, she crossed the plush carpet of the study to enter the attached suite—rooms she'd glimpsed briefly when they'd first arrived. The suite occupied just under half the floor—the other half being set up with rooms for the Seven—and functioned as another home for Raphael. Stepping into the huge living area, she called out his name, but it echoed hollowly against the emptiness of a space that bore the masculine stamp of her archangel.

There was no over-the-top decorating, nothing ornate. The furniture was an elegant black, strong and with sleek, simple lines that suited Raphael. However, it wasn't a soulless place. In contrast to the relatively modern furniture, a tapestry depicting the rich hues of some ancient court adorned the living room, while when she pushed open the door to the sprawling bedroom, she glimpsed a painting on the wall to the left and—

She whipped her head around.

The painting was a full-length portrait of her, knives in hand, wings spread, and feet planted in a combat-ready stance as her hair flew off her face in a playful wind. The artist had captured her with her head tilted slightly to the side, a smile of mingled challenge and desire on her face, laughter in her eyes. Behind her lay the mountainous beauty of the Refuge, and in front of her . . . That wasn't in the portrait but she knew. It could only have been Raphael in front of her. She looked at no other that way.

Her fingers lifted of their own accord, touched the thick strokes of oil paint, vibrant with color. She had no idea when it had been painted, was unbearably curious about it, but that curiosity, she thought, dropping her hand, would have to wait. The strange chill pervading these rooms only intensified her need to find Raphael.

Pulling out her cell phone, she called their home over the

water. "Montgomery," she said when the butler answered, "is Raphael there?"

"No, Guild Hunter. The Sire has not returned home as of yet."

"If he does, can you call—"

*Keeping tabs on me?*

Shivers running up her spine, Elena closed her cell phone and turned to the bedroom doorway . . . to see an archangel with eyes of liquid metal and wings outlined by the lethal stroke of power. His hair, black as the heart of midnight, was wind-tousled, his body magnificent, but it was his eyes that held her.

In those eyes, she saw age, cruelty, and pain.

So much pain.

"Raphael." She closed the distance between them, ignoring the cold that raised every hair on her body. "I was worried about you."

*I am an archangel.*

Unsaid were the words that he found the worry of a woman who'd been mortal not long ago—who was still not a true immortal—laughable.

She refused to let him intimidate her. They'd made promises to each other, she and her archangel. She wasn't about to stumble at the first hurdle—even if her pulse thudded hard and uneven in her throat, the animal part of her brain recognizing that this predator had no mercy in him.

Reaching him, she tilted back her head, met the intensity of his gaze. The metallic shade was so inhuman it hurt, her eyes tearing up in instinctive defense. Blinking, she looked away.

*You give in so easily.*

The weight of the cold confidence she heard in him was daunting, but she'd always known he'd never be an easy man to love. "If you think I've given in, Archangel, you don't know me at all." Flicking away the tears, she stepped close enough that her breasts brushed his chest.

Electricity arced between them, a white-hot whip.

And the archangel came to life. Thrusting a hand into her hair, he tugged back her head to take her mouth in a kiss that was both a claiming and a warning. He was in no temper to play.

Neither was she.

Twisting her arms around his neck, she kissed him back with the same raw passion, stroking her tongue against his in deliberate provocation—because no matter how hot he burned, Raphael's hunger she could handle. It was when he went cold, cloaking himself in the arrogance of power beyond mortal ken, that she thought she might lose him. Even as the thought passed through her mind, she sensed a change in his kiss, a subtle but unmistakable control. Not happening, Archangel, she thought and bit down hard on his lower lip, knowing it would set him off in this mood.

His hand tightened in her hair, wrenching back her head. *Do you think you are safe?* He pushed his free hand up under her tank top at the same time, long, strong fingers closing over her breast in blatant possession.

"Safe?" Gasping in a breath, she ran her own fingers along the part of his right wing she could reach. "Maybe not." *But I've always wanted to dance with you anyway.*

He squeezed and molded her sensitive flesh. *Then dance.*

Her top was suddenly gone, torn off her body to leave her upper half bare. Spreading her unfettered wings, she tugged at his shirt. It disintegrated off him the next instant, and she found herself skin to skin with an archangel burning with a cold white flame.

Real fear spiked for the first time.

She'd never tangled with him when he was like this, never been so close to the deadly strength of him that she could feel the icy burn of it against her flesh. The sensation was both exhilarating and terrifying. Ignoring the fear, she moved closer . . . and rubbed the softness of her belly against the hard ridge of his erection.

Raphael shifted their positions without warning, slamming her back against the wall, her wings spread out on either side of her. She sucked in a breath and then he was taking it from her in the most primal of kisses as he tore off her remaining clothes, leaving her naked and vulnerable. When he put his hands under her thighs and lifted, it was instinct to wrap her legs around his waist.

The cold, cold burn of his power kissed her in her most sensitive place.

# 6

Shuddering, she broke the kiss. He refused to let her go, pulling her mouth back to his with the hand he had fisted in her hair. It should've scared her, but all it did was make her more determined to win this battle, to bring Raphael back from the abyss she could see in the wintry black of his eyes. She'd seen many colors in those eyes, but never that vast, forsaken darkness.

*Archangel*, she whispered into his mind, trying to keep her sanity as he plucked at the taut peak of her nipple with fingers that knew her every weakness. *Raphael*.

No response, the icy caress of his power so strong that she couldn't keep her eyes open any longer. She shoved her hands into his hair as her world became dark, squeezing her thighs around him at the same time. Something was very, very wrong, but she wasn't about to be scared away, even if fear was a tickle at the back of her throat, a jangling accent to the hunger that turned her body damp and ready.

Because lethal as he was, he was still hers, and her body knew him, knew the pleasure he could give. Today, however, that pleasure might well be spiced with a little sensual cruelty. It was tempting to surrender, to allow him to play her body with consummate skill, but instinct told her that that would be the quickest way to lose this battle. To lose *him*—to the demons that had turned the agonizing blue of his eyes to a harsh, unforgiving midnight.

*My lovers have always been warrior women.*

He'd said that to her at the start.

Ripping away her lips from his with force, she turned her head to the side, gasping for air. He took a firmer grip on her hair, threatening to wrench her back. She blocked his arm with her own.

A blaze of arctic white around them, so potent and blinding it felt as if her eyes were open, not closed. "Raphael," she said, fighting to breathe past the press of it, so pure, so cutting, "either turn off the power, or give me my weapons."

A pause.

*Why would I give you your weapons?* A silken whisper in her mind.

"Because," she said, feeling as if her lungs were being squeezed to emptiness, "you don't get off on women who can't fight back. You like warriors, remember?"

Laughter in her head, tinged with a kind of ruthlessness that made her fear turn knife-edged. *There is, I find, something exquisitely pleasurable in having a warrior helpless and spread before me.*

It was dread that licked through her veins now. There wasn't any hint of the lover she knew in him at this moment, nothing she could reach or touch or reason with. "It's hardly a challenge, though, is it?" she murmured, fighting the hunter within her, the part that told her to claw at those amazing eyes, rip at his wings, anything to get away. "I walked into your arms."

Lips along her neck, the fist in her hair tugging her head farther to the side. She felt teeth . . . and lower, the rigid push of his erection. That, she understood. It was real and earthy and wild. Making a snap decision, she whispered, "Take me,

Raphael. Take your warrior." The words were deliberate, a reminder of the bonds between them.

He froze against her. *Giving in after all?*

Pulling up his head with the hands she'd clenched in his
hair, she kissed him her way. All wet heat and wild passion . . .
and a love that was becoming ever more intertwined in her
heart. *This power stuff is sexy, but I want you inside me, thick
and hard and now.*

Raphael squeezed her thigh. *Elena.*

Her heart skipped a beat. Because that voice, that tone, she
knew it. *Raphael. I need you.* He was the only man she'd ever
said that to in her adult life, the only man who'd won that trust
from her. "I need you."

A shudder in the big body that held her pinned to the wall,
the frigid bite of his power turning into a molten caress that
was a thousand featherlight kisses over her skin, and then the
blunt tip of his erection nudging against the entrance to her
body. Sucking in a breath before he reclaimed her lips, she
held on tight as he pushed into her with a slow, measured intensity, not stopping until he was buried to the hilt within her.

Her body arched at the near-violent shock of pleasure.
He took advantage of her position to play with her breasts,
to bite and lick and suck until she rolled her hips in urgent
movements, nails biting into his shoulders. "Stop teasing,
Archangel."

Another pause, and suddenly he was pure male demand,
his body slick and hard and very, very physical under her
hands. Opening her eyes, she looked into his . . . and saw endless, relentless blue right before he ground against her with
the sexual experience of a being who had lived centuries upon
centuries, and he sent her hurtling to the stars.

Crying out, she gripped him with her body, claiming him,
taking him with her.

She came to lying on the bed on her front, with Raphael
leaning on his side beside her, his gaze focused inward. "Hey."

She reached over to touch his thigh. "Don't go away again." It came out huskier than she'd intended, tangled with the fears of the child who'd been abandoned long before she'd been thrown out of the hollow elegance of the Big House.

His thigh flexed under her touch. "Did I cause you any bodily injury?"

She remembered what he'd said once. About breaking her. Knew that she had the power to savage him—but that wasn't who she was. Who they were. "No. You just scared me a little."

*Apologies, Elena.* He ran his hand over the arch of her wing. *I was not . . . myself.*

It was an admission she'd never expected, because though they'd been together this long, they were still learning each other. And the Archangel of New York had long ago learned to keep secrets—his own, his race's, his Seven's.

And now, his consort's.

"I know." Shifting up onto her elbow, she closed her hand over the muscle of his shoulder, needing the raw physicality of the connection. "Something is wrong, Raphael. That vampire might've appeared sane, but he didn't act in any way rational when he attacked the school, and you should've seen that. But you didn't."

"I remember little of my actions during that time." A question without being a question as he nudged her down onto her back, one big hand warm on her abdomen.

Knowing the loss of control had to be a vicious beast tearing him apart, she recapped the events. "Do you remember executing Ignatius?"

"Yes." He dipped his head a fraction, and she took the invitation to stroke her fingers through his hair. "When you speak of the events, I do recall them—but there is a red haze over it all."

Thick and silky, the vivid black strands of his hair kissed a cool caress over her skin. "If I had to put a name to what I saw in your expression, I'd call it rage."

"Yes." Moving his hand over her stomach, he settled it low

on her hip. "But I have lived long enough that I can handle rage. This was . . . other."

She went motionless, worried by his choice of words. "Outside of yourself?"

His eyes gleamed adamantine blue beneath lowered lashes. "Impossible to confirm."

Elena wasn't about to let it go at that. "Talk to me." She knew what he was, understood that he held more power in his body than she would probably ever know, even if she lived ten thousand years. Equals, they weren't. Not on that playing field—but when it came to the emotions that could tear a heart apart . . . "Raphael."

*Nadiel,* he said into her mind, *exhibited such extreme rage.*

His father had also gone inexorably insane.

"No," she said, not even needing an instant to evaluate the thought. "You're not going insane."

"So certain, Guild Hunter." Formal words, a tone that told her he considered her statement nothing but a platitude.

Lifting up her head, she nipped at his lower lip. "The taste of you is ingrained into my very cells. You're the rain and the wind and at times the clean, wild bite of the sea. I'd know the instant something changed."

He rose off her, allowing her to sit up as he shifted to sit with his legs over the side of the bed, his back to her, his magnificent wings spread out. Each filament of each feather was tipped in gold, glittering even in the dull light whispering through the windows. A lethal temptation to mortals—and former mortals.

Elena was reaching out to indulge her desire to touch when he said, "You lie to both of us."

Frowning, she wrapped the sheet around herself—letting it gape low at the back to accommodate her wings—and scrambled off the bed to stand in front of him. "What are you talking about?"

He raised his head, his face so very clear of emotion that the pristine beauty of it felt as if it should draw blood, it was so sharp, so pure. "Did Uram's scent change?"

*Acid and blood and . . . sunlight.*

She shivered at the memory of the bloodlust-driven archangel, her ankle aching in sympathetic memory where Uram had crushed it—simply to hear her scream. "I only met him after he'd already crossed the line into insanity," she said, knowing this conversation was beyond important. "I have no way of knowing what he would've been to my senses beforehand— it's possible that the blood, the acid in his scent was because of what he became, not what he once was."

Raphael didn't look convinced. However, neither did he dismiss her argument as he rose to his feet and pulled on his pants. "It can no longer be avoided. I must speak to Lijuan—"

An eerie cold in the room, a prickle of fear along the back of Elena's neck. "It's almost as if she can hear it when you speak her name."

Raphael didn't tell her she was being a superstitious twit. *Yes*, he said instead, *we have no way of knowing what Lijuan hears on the winds now.* "I cannot disregard the fact that my . . . rage comes at a time when an Ancient appears to be stirring to wakefulness. As the oldest among us, Lijuan is the only one who may have some kind of an answer."

"I'll come with you." Not long ago, as Beijing trembled around her, Elena had stood face-to-face with the shambling empty-eyed shells who provided irrefutable proof of the dark heart of Lijuan's strength. The Archangel of China had bought the dead back to life—whether they wished to return or not.

They'd been monsters, feasting on the flesh of those Lijuan did not favor to clothe their own emaciated forms. But they'd also been victims, mute and unable to scream. Elena had heard them all the same, and everything in her rebelled at the idea of Raphael alone in the presence of the being who'd created those "reborn." "It's—"

A brush of strong fingers against her jaw. "She does not see you yet, not truly. I would keep it that way."

Elena set that jaw. "My safety isn't enough to compromise yours." Lijuan was a nightmare, and her power came from the same dark place. There was nothing remotely human in her, nothing that even hinted of a conscience.

Raphael shook his head. "She will not kill me, Hunter."

"No but she wants to . . ." Had Lijuan been another woman, it would've been a simple equation. But the oldest of the archangels had no desires of the flesh—she didn't even eat, much less take lovers. "Possess you," she completed.

A look that made her feel as if she'd been stripped to the skin, laid out before him like a feast. "But I wish to possess you, *hbeebti*. The two desires are not compatible."

*Hbeebti.*

A beautiful word from the Moroccan half of her mother's lost heritage. "I'm not letting you sweet-talk me."

A curve to his lips, her archangel finding dangerous humor in her stubbornness. "Then let logic persuade you. She is as apt to take offense at your presence as ignore it. If I am to do this, I want to get something out of it."

Her hand scrunched the fabric of the sheet. "Damn it." She knew he was right. Lijuan was unpredictable—she *might* decide to take the presence of Raphael's "pet" as an insult. "Do it fast. Don't let her get her hooks into you."

A nod that sent his hair sliding across his forehead in a wash of gleaming midnight. "You asked me once what you should call me."

Elena scowled. "I think you said something like 'master,' but I've decided I had to be hearing things."

"What would you like to call me?"

That made her pause. "Husband" was too human, "partner" factually wrong for a being as powerful as an archangel, "mate" . . . perhaps. But none of it was quite right. "Mine," she said at last.

He blinked, and when he raised his lashes again, the blue was liquid fire. *Yes, that will do.* "But for public consumption, you are my consort."

"Consort," she murmured, tasting the word, feeling its shape. "Yes, that fits." A consort was more than a lover, more than a wife. She was . . . someone with whom an archangel could discuss the darkest of secrets, someone he could trust to speak only the truth, even if it wasn't something he wanted to hear. "If that crazy-ass bitch tries anything," she said, referring to Lijuan, "and being in my mind would help anchor you, then do it."

Raphael closed his hand over her bare shoulder, stroking to curve his fingers around her nape, his thumb playing over her pulse. "You fight so hard for your independence, and yet you would give me such entry?"

"I know you won't abuse it." Not now, not when he knew how very important it was to her that her mind be her own.

"I thank you for the offer, Elena." It was an oddly formal statement, almost as if he was making a vow, his expression so intent she could do nothing but wrap her arms around him. The sheet slid to the floor at the same moment that he moved his free hand down her spine to her lower back, pressing her against him, his wings rising to curve slightly around her.

"The painting," she said, stealing a moment to simply be with her archangel. "When was it done?"

"During the time you trained with Galen." He answered her next question before she could ask it. "It is Aodhan's work, done at my request."

Elena thought of the angel with his eyes of shattered glass and wings that glittered diamond bright in the sun. "I never saw him."

"He is adept at being unseen."

"Most men would choose a painting of a nude for the bedroom," she teased. "You chose a hunter with knives."

"You are the only woman allowed in my bedroom, Elena."

That she was loved . . . it was wonder enough. That she was loved by this man, it was beyond wonder. And it gave her the will to step back into the darkness. "I need to tell you what I found at the school."

He listened in quiet. "You plan to liaise with Dmitri, confirm if they located the second body?"

"Yes." Frustrated anger had her fisting her hand against his back. "It wasn't a coincidence that the vampire picked that school was it, Raphael?"

His answer destroyed her final ephemeral hopes. "No. It cannot be."

# 7

Less than an hour later, Elena found herself at the city morgue, looking down at the heartbreaking evidence of why Ignatius had spilled innocent blood. The girl who lay on the slab had been named Betsy, an old-fashioned name for someone so young. But maybe she'd liked it. Elena would never know. Because Betsy's throat had been torn out, coloring the bed where she'd gone to lie down a violent crimson.

They'd found her discarded in the woods not far from the pond, a bare few feet from where Elena had hesitated during the tracking.

"She was a day student, didn't have a bed at the school," Dmitri told her from where he stood on the other side of the body. "Her teacher sent her to the infirmary after she complained of a stomachache, but Betsy's best friend had a room at the school. It looks like she snuck in there instead. In the confusion, everyone thought the nurse had sent her home."

"Evelyn," Elena said, as she took in the small heart-shaped face surrounded by hair of a brown so dark it could be mistaken for black. According to the file, Betsy's eyes had been a deep gray before death had stolen a film of dullness over them. "She looks like my youngest sister." And the bed saturated with Betsy's lifeblood had been Evelyn's.

That was why Betsy was dead.

"I need to make a call." She fisted her hand against the urge to touch Betsy's pale skin in futile hope—there was no longer any warmth there, no longer any life. It had been irrevocably stolen.

As she watched, Dmitri reached out to tug the sheet over Betsy's face with a tenderness that made a knot form in Elena's throat. "I'll organize discreet surveillance on your sisters," he said, his tone so very even that she knew it was a mask.

Nodding, she stepped out into the cold, crisp light of the corridor, and collapsed against the wall. The shakes took time to pass. "I'm sorry," she whispered to the girl who would never again laugh or cry or run . . . and to the one who would soon be told that her best friend was dead.

Then she stiffened her spine and used her cell phone to call a number she'd avoided since waking from the coma. Her father picked up on the first ring. "Yes?" A curt demand.

"Hello, Jeffrey."

His silence was eloquent. He didn't like it when she used his name—but he'd lost the right to any familial address the day he'd told her she was an "abomination," a pollutant in the illustrious Deveraux family tree. "Elieanora," he said, his tone pure frost. "May I assume the unpleasantness at the girls' school today had something to do with you?"

Guilt twisted her stomach into knots. "Evelyn may have been the target." Hand pressed hard against the chipped paint of the wall, she told him the rest. "Her best friend, Betsy, was murdered. You must know how alike they look . . . looked."

"Yes."

"Evelyn needs to be told. The names will leak to the media soon enough."

"I'll have her mother speak to her." Another pause. "The girls will be tutored at home until you sort out whatever mess you've created this time."

It was a direct hit, and she took it. Because he was right. The two youngest Deveraux girls were in the line of fire because of her. "That's probably for the best." She didn't know what else to say, how to speak to this man who had once been her father and was now a stranger who seemed to want only to hurt her.

In the days after she'd woken from the coma, she'd remembered forgotten pieces of her childhood, remembered the father she'd loved all those years ago. Jeffrey had held her hand in the hospital after her two older sisters had been murdered in that blood-soaked kitchen, led her down to the basement in spite of bitter opposition so she could see Ari and Belle again—she'd needed to be certain that her sisters really did rest in peace, that the monster hadn't made them like him. He'd cried that day. Her father, the man with a stone-cold heart, had cried. Because he'd been a different man.

As she'd been a different girl.

"From your silence," Jeffrey said with cutting impatience, "I take it the Guild Director didn't pass on my message."

Jeffrey had never liked Sara, being as she was part of Elena's "filthy" profession. Elena's hand tightened on the phone, until she was sure she could feel her bones crunching against one another. "I wasn't able to meet Sara this morning." They'd been meant to have coffee, catch up. Elena had been looking forward to kissing her goddaughter, Zoe, seeing how big she'd grown.

"Of course. You were at the school." Rigid and unbending as granite. "I need to speak to you face-to-face. Be here tomorrow morning, or lose your right to take part in the decision."

"What decision?" Jeffrey and she hadn't had anything to say to each other for ten years before Uram invaded the city. Even now, the only words they exchanged were well-honed weapons, designed to inflict maximum damage.

"All you need to know is that it's a family matter." He hung up, and though it frustrated Elena until tears—stupid, unwanted—pricked at her eyes, she knew she'd turn up at his

office as ordered. Because the family he spoke of might be
splintered, but it included not only Amethyst and Evelyn, but
also Marguerite's youngest daughter, Beth.

None of the three deserved to be caught in the crossfire of
the endless war that raged between Jeffrey and Elena.


Having spent two hours in the Tower with Jason, talking through the information that had brought the black-winged
angel to the city, Raphael now came in for a silent landing in
the woods that separated his estate from the home Michaela
used while in his territory. As he walked to take a position in
front of the small pool his gardener had created in a grotto
he'd shaded with vines and tucked in among the solid bulk
of the larger trees, Raphael wondered if Elena saw more than
he did.

He knew he was arrogant. It was inevitable, given the years
he'd lived, the power at his command. But he'd never been
stupid. So he heeded his hunter's words, augmenting his mental shields with care before he stared down at the placid waters
of the darkened pool and said, *Lijuan*, "pushing" the thought
across the world.

There was a chance he'd fail to reach her, for he had no
intention of undertaking a true sending. The price demanded
was too high. In the Quiet, he became monstrous, stripped
down to the lethal cold of power without conscience. It was
during such a state that he'd terrified Elena so much she'd shot
him, the scar on his wing a stunning reminder to never again
walk that road.

If this did not succeed, he would have to send Lijuan a
handwritten message—the oldest of the archangels eschewed
modern conveniences like the phone. However, the water rippled an instant later, far faster than he'd expected. He'd known
Lijuan's strength had grown exponentially, but the rapid response, coupled with the fact that he'd used a minute amount
of his own power, argued for a strength beyond anything the
rest of the Cadre had imagined.

"Raphael." She appeared of the flesh as her image formed on the water, her face as ageless as always. Only the pure white of her hair, the pearlescent glow of her pale, pale eyes betrayed what she was, what she was becoming. "So you return to me after all."

He didn't react except to say, "Do you think to make me a pet, Lijuan?"

A tinkling laugh, girlish and all the more disturbing for it. "What a thought. I think you would be a most troublesome one."

Raphael inclined his head. "You are home?" Lijuan's palace lay in the heart of China, deep in mountainous territory Raphael had never traversed, though Jason had managed to work his way inside before Lijuan's "evolution." Raphael's spymaster had returned from the clandestine visit with half his face torn off.

"Yes." The other archangel's hair whispered back in a breeze that he was certain affected nothing else in the vicinity. "I find," she continued, "that there are certain pleasures of the flesh I do still enjoy after all, and where best to partake of them than in my palace?"

Raphael didn't make the mistake of thinking she spoke of sex. Lijuan hadn't been a sexual being for thousands of years . . . or not sexual in the accepted sense. "Are your toys surviving the experience?"

A finger rose up until he could see it, waved at him. "Such a question, Raphael. You would call me a monster."

"You would take it as a compliment."

Another laugh, those eerie, near-colorless eyes filling with a surge of power that turned them wholly white, without pupil or iris. "An Ancient rises to consciousness."

He wasn't surprised she'd guessed at the reason behind this contact. Despite the nightmare she'd become, he'd never doubted Lijuan's intelligence. "Yes."

"Do you know how old your mother was when she disappeared?" she asked without warning.

An image of startling blue eyes, a voice that made the

heavens weep, and a madness so deep and true it mimicked sanity. "Just over a thousand years older than you."

Lijuan's lips curved in a smile that held a strange amusement. "She was vain, was Caliane. She liked to tell people that because it made her almost the same age as her mate."

Raphael felt ice form in his chest, spread outward in jagged branches, threatening to pierce his veins. "How much older was she?"

Lijuan's answer shattered the ice, turned it into shards of glass that spliced through his system, causing massive damage. "Fifty thousand years. Even that may have been a lie. It was whispered that she was twice that age when I was born."

"Impossible," he said at last, knowing he could betray none of his shock. To do so would be to tempt the predator that lived within Lijuan. "No archangel that old would have chosen to remain awake." A hundred thousand years was an impossible eternity. Yes, they had old ones in their world, but except for a few notable exceptions, most of them chose to go into the Sleep for eons at a time, awakening only for brief periods to taste the changing world.

Lijuan's smile faded, her voice echoing with a thousand ghostly whispers. "They say Caliane Slept before, more than once. But when she woke the final time, she found Nadiel."

"Then I was born." He thought of his laughing, singing mother, thought, too, of her descent into a madness that had seemed to come out of nowhere. But if she'd been alive for so many millennia . . . "Do you lie to me, Lijuan?"

"I have no need to lie. I have evolved beyond even Caliane."

On the surface, that certainly appeared true. Age had never been the arbiter of power among their kind. Raphael had become an archangel at an age unheard of among angelkind. And at just over five hundred years old, Illium was already far stronger than angels ten times his age. But that wasn't why he'd contacted Lijuan. "Is it my mother who wakes?" he asked, holding that "blind" gaze.

"There is no way to know." The whispers in her voice sounded almost like screams. "However, the magnitude of the disruption, the strength of the quakes and the storms, says that the one who wakes is the most ancient of Ancients."

Raphael wondered what it was Lijuan saw with those eyes, if it was worth the sacrifice of a city . . . of what remained of her soul. "If this Ancient wakes without sanity, will you execute him or her?" Not before. Never before. To murder an angel in Sleep was to face automatic execution—no one was immune to that law. Even Lijuan, invulnerable though she might be to death, would find herself shunned by the entire angelic race if she crossed that line. Not something a goddess would enjoy.

Another girlish laugh, this one a giggle that was more disturbing than her appearance. "You disappoint me, Raphael. What need do I have to execute an old one? They can do nothing to me . . . and perhaps they can teach me secrets I do not yet know."

It was then Raphael realized that if one monster came to waking life, it might well strengthen another.


The conversation with Jeffrey, coming as it did on top of the painful visit to the morgue, left Elena feeling as if she'd been beaten by stone fists. It was tempting, so tempting, to go home and hide, just pretend that everything would be okay when she came out again.

Except, of course, that was a child's ploy. Elena hadn't had the luxury of believing in hopeless dreams since she'd been a scared ten-year-old slipping and falling in a family kitchen turned abattoir. "Do you know where Jason is?" she asked Dmitri when they exited the morgue.

Dmitri pressed the car remote to unlock the flame red Ferrari parked in the employees-only lot. "Tired of your Bluebell already?" A tendril of champagne circled around her senses, cut with something far harder.

Never had she felt that harsh edge in Dmitri's scent. She pitied the woman he took to his bed today. "Yeah, that's it. I'm building a harem."

Opening the door to the Ferrari, Dmitri braced one arm on top. For a moment, his expression turned probing, and she had the feeling he was about to say something important. But then he shook his head, his hair lifting slightly in the dull breeze, and pulled out his cell phone, checked something. "He's at the Tower."

Surprised by the straight answer, she fought off the wickedness of champagne to say, "Can you ask if he'd mind meeting me at the house?"

Dmitri made the call. "He's leaving now," he said, snapping the phone closed. "Nowhere for you to take off from here."

Elena looked up. "Hospital building is high enough. I'll head up to the roof." Suiting action to words, she made her way back into the building and up. It was an interesting journey. There were only a few hospital staff in the lower corridors, and the ones who did see her seemed to lose the ability to speak.

Deeply bothered by that reaction from the people of a city she considered home, she found her way to the elevator and pushed the button. Because the staff used it to move beds from floor to floor, the cage was plenty big enough for wings. Then the doors opened on the first floor.

Two nurses, chattering to each other, looked up. Froze.

Elena stepped back. "Plenty of room."

Neither woman said a word as the doors closed on their stunned faces. Variations of the scene were repeated on the next four floors. It was funny . . . except it felt wrong. This was New York. She needed to belong here—though she knew she would never again fit in the same way.

"Hmph."

She glanced up at that sound to see that the doors had opened on the fifth floor to reveal an elderly man leaning on a cane. "Going up?"

He nodded and stepped in, making no effort to hide the fact that he was staring at her wings as he used his cane to push the button for his floor. "You're a new one."

"Very." She stretched out her wings for him, the knots in her soul unraveling a little. "What do you think?"

He took his time replying. "Why are you taking the elevator?"

Smart man. "Felt like it."

He laughed as the doors opened on his floor. "You sure sound like a New Yorker!"

Elena was smiling when the doors closed, something she would've never predicted minutes ago as she stood beside Dmitri. When the doors finally opened on the last level, she got out and made her way to the roof with firm steps, no longer feeling as if she'd been pummeled to screaming point.

The flight across the Hudson, assisted as she was by strong winds, went by fast. Jason was waiting for her in the front yard, his wings folded neatly back, his hair in its usual queue. It was the first time she'd seen his tattoo in full light, and the detail and intricacy of it made her suck in a breath.

Damaged by Lijuan's reborn before Elena woke from her coma, the ink had been redone with such perfection after Jason healed that no one would ever know the difference. All curves and swirling lines, it spoke of the winds of the Pacific and the soaring beauty of the skies at the same time. "Where were you born?" she found herself asking, not expecting an answer.

# 8

"A small Pacific atoll that no longer exists." There was nothing in that statement. No pain, no sorrow, no anger. Nothing.

The very lack of emotion was another answer.

Letting Jason's secrets lie, she said, "I was hoping you could teach me some tricks about flying in daylight without making myself too big a target."

Jason narrowed his eyes, his attention going to her wings. "There are a few techniques you can use straight away, but for the rest, you'll need to practice until you can pull yourself high above the cloud layer in a burst of speed."

"Do you have time to give me a lesson now?"

A small nod.

"I flew a longer distance than usual today," she admitted, "so I might be off the pace."

"We'll be moving slowly—it's not about speed below the cloud layer, but about utilizing light and shadow to your advantage."

Nodding, she fell into step beside him as he led her toward the cliffs. Evening shadows had fallen by the time he pronounced her proficient enough to continue the drills on her own. "I leave Manhattan tonight."

"Take care, Jason." As Raphael's spymaster, he walked dangerous roads.

He looked at her straight on with those eyes as dark as the blade he carried along his spine. "What is it like to be mortal?"

Startled, she took a second to think, to consider. "Life is much more immediate. When you have a time limit, every moment gains an importance that an immortal will never know."

Jason spread those amazing wings designed to blend into the night. "What you call a time limit, some might call an escape." He was rising into the sky before she could answer; he was a shadowy silhouette against the first wash of night.

But his weren't the only wings she spotted. *Does Jason want escape so very much, Archangel?*

*Yes. His sole tie to the living world is through his service to me.*

"Was it a woman, like with Illium?" she whispered as he came in to land with a rush of wind that blew the hair off her face.

"No. Jason has never loved." Closing his arms and his wings around her, he turned his head to look out over the Manhattan skyline as it flickered to glittering life. "It would be better if he had—then he may have had some good memories to fight the dark."

Elena tried to hold on to that thought as she fell into sleep that night, tried to tell herself to remember the laughter and the joy. But it was a nightmare that came after her, choking her with the smell of rancid blood and the gurgling whispers of a dead child lying on a morgue slab, the sounds shaped as fine, sticky strands that were very much real. The cobwebby filaments wrapped around her until she lashed out in panic, tearing herself awake to jerk up into a sitting position.

Her hand, she realized after long moments, was clenched tight around the hilt of the knife she'd hidden under the mattress on her side of the bed, the metal cold against her palm.

Adrenaline pumping, she turned her head—to see Raphael awake and rising from the bed.

"Come, Elena."

It took conscious effort to release the knife from her white-knuckled grip. Placing it beside Destiny's Rose, the diamond sculpture that was a priceless work of art . . . and a gift from her archangel, she took the hand he held out, let him tug her to a standing position. "Are we going flying?" Skin jittery, heart pounding double-time, she felt as if she would break apart.

Raphael gave her wings a critical appraisal. "No. You strained them today." A glance at the wall clock. "Yesterday."

It was five a.m.; the world was still cloaked in night when Raphael led her outside. He'd dressed only in a pair of flowing pants that moved like black water over his form, while she'd pulled on sweatpants and a white silk shirt much too large for her frame. Raphael had said nothing when she'd taken it from his closet, simply sealed the wing slots with a minute flicker of energy so they wouldn't flap around her.

It was crisp out, making her cheeks tingle. "Where are we going?" she asked as Raphael led her to the woods on the opposite side to the one that separated his home from Michaela's.

*Patience.*

Looking around the area she hadn't yet explored, she realized two things at once. One—Raphael's estate was huge. And two—they were on a delicately constructed path designed to meld into its surroundings.

Curiosity fought the remnants of anger and fear. Won. "How about a clue?"

Raphael brushed his wing over her own. "Guess."

"Well, it's black as pitch, and we're in the woods. Hmm, not sounding too good . . ." She was tapping her lower lip with a finger when the path curved—to bring them to within ten feet of a small greenhouse lit from within with what looked like three yellow orange heat lamps.

"Oh." Pleasure rolled through her. "Oh!"

Releasing Raphael's hand, she covered the remaining distance at a run to push through the door and into the humid embrace of a place clearly built to accommodate wings. She was aware of Raphael entering behind her, but her attention was on the luxuriant ferns that hung from the ceiling baskets, their fronds curled and fine; on the sleepy plum-colored blooms of the petunias to her right; and—"Begonias." Back before Uram, she'd babied her own until they bloomed proud and lush. These sported brown leaves, pitiful flowers. "They need care."

"Then you must do what is necessary."

She shot him a glance, her fingers itching to pick up the gardening implements she could see sitting on a small bench in the corner. "You have a gardener."

"This is not his territory—he was instructed only to ensure the plants did not die in the interim. It was built for you."

She couldn't speak, her chest too tight, too full. Instead, as the Archangel of New York watched with endless patience, she explored the gift he'd given her, something infinitely more precious than the most exclusive clothes, the most expensive jewels. If he hadn't already owned her heart, she'd have handed it to him right then and there.

Some time later, Montgomery appeared with a steaming carafe of coffee, buttered slices of toast, small bowls of fruit salad, and a selection of tiny pastries. The butler, dressed with his usual attention to detail, was seemingly not the least nonplused at finding one of the most powerful beings in the world holding up a branch while she trimmed the deadheads. "Good morning, Sire, Guild Hunter."

"Good morning, Montgomery." Raphael took the coffee the butler held out, and it struck her then.

Home.

She was home.

Two hours later, her heart overflowing with a quiet, intense happiness, she was on her way to see Sara prior to her meeting with Jeffrey when her cell phone rang. Landing on the nearest flat roof, she answered it to hear her father's voice.

"We'll have to meet tomorrow," he said at once. "I have an unexpected business situation to deal with today."

She should've let it go, but the abandoned teenager in her struck out. "Family always takes second place, doesn't it, Jeffrey?"

A sucked in breath, and for an instant, she had the disorientating sensation that she'd wounded him. But when he spoke, it was to thrust the knife into her own heart. "Family is hardly your specialty, Elieanora."

No—because he'd made sure of it.

Snapping the phone shut, she took off again, her mood shattered. To top it off, Sara wasn't at the Guild. Frustrated and needing to *do* something, she decided to head to Ignatius's apartment. It was unlikely she'd find anything there to explain his bizarre behavior, but—

A feather of heavenly blue edged with silver tumbled down in front of her.

Delight had her shrugging off the lingering echoes of Jeffrey's taunt. Grabbing at the feather, she craned her neck to search for its owner. But on this field, he had her at a massive disadvantage, her ability to hover and turn nowhere near fast enough to catch the angel Galen had called Butterfly.

Sliding the feather into her pocket to add to the collection she planned to give Zoe, she continued on her way. She glimpsed a whisper of blue with her peripheral vision moments later. "When did you get in?"

For an answer, Illium arrowed his body, his feathers sleek against his back, and dropped toward the skyscrapers as if he was made of stone. She just barely bit back her cry and was pretty sure she was doing a good job of acting nonchalant when he missed a peaked roof by what looked like a millimeter at best and flew back up to hover in front of her, his upper body bare.

"Aw, Ellie." Eyes like ancient gold coins, even more startling against those incredible black lashes tipped with blue. "No screaming? You stole all my fun."

"That's me. A nasty ole fun stealer." But her lips wanted to quirk, her heart ridiculously soft where it concerned the only one of Raphael's Seven she considered a friend. "You get stuck with bodyguard duty already?" She and Raphael were going to have to have a talk about his habit of ordering people to shadow her, but she wasn't going to refuse the protection right this second—because much as it galled, she was a big fat media target at this point, if nothing else.

She'd already had to detour well out of her way to lose a news chopper that had threatened to send her tumbling down into the steel forest of Manhattan. Unlike Illium, she wouldn't have been able to pull up in time to avoid massive injury. The idiot reporters didn't realize she wasn't as strong as other angels—she couldn't hold her own against the disruption caused by chopper blades as they sliced through the air.

Illium, with his wings of silver-kissed blue and a face de-signed to seduce both males and females, not to mention his ability to do the most impossible acrobatics in the air, would provide a worthy diversion. The fact that he'd decided to ditch half his clothing was just icing on the cake.

Having shifted position to fly beside her, he now said, "I asked," answering her earlier question. "I know I'm your fa-vorite." He brushed his wing over hers when she didn't reply.

"I swear to God," she muttered, fighting a laugh, "if you've dusted me with blue, I'll tie your balls in a knot and hang you up by them on the nearest sharp object I see." The last time he'd glittered blue angel-dust over her wings, Raphael had—eventually—seen the humor in the situation. She couldn't guarantee Illium's health if it happened a second time.

Illium dipped low, stroking back up with movements that looked lazy but took considerable muscle strength. "Be nice to me or I won't give you your present."

"Idiot." But he *was* her favorite of the Seven. How could he not be when he saw her human heart not as a curse, but as a gift? When he would lay down his life for the archangel who was Elena's? When he laughed with the same easy joy as the chil-dren in the Refuge? "Sam," she murmured, her throat thickening at the thought of the boy who'd been so terribly hurt. "Is he—"

"He's well, Ellie. We watch over him." A quiet reminder that for all his laughter and beauty, Illium, too, was a member of Raphael's Seven. And that he had no qualms over issuing the bloodiest of punishments. She would never forget the sight of him standing in that strange, blooming winter garden, skin bloody and sword flashing lightning-bright as he sliced the wings off angels who'd come to do harm.

"He misses you."

A silly, happy smile erased the shadow of memory. "I've only been gone a couple of days."

"I made a solemn promise that I would tell you to call him every night. Don't make me a liar."

"Never." Elena adored little Sam, had spent hours with him when she'd been confined to the Medica during her recovery after Beijing. "What about Noel?" The adult victim of the archangel Neha's daughter, Anoushka's, vicious craving for power had healed of his physical injuries weeks ago. But those weren't the deepest hurts.

"He is . . ." Illium paused for a long time. "Broken. Inside, he is broken."

Elena knew about being broken. But she also knew about survival. "The man who survived what was done to him"—blood and meat, that's all he'd been when they'd found him—"will survive that, too."

"He'll have to," Illium said. "Raphael has assigned him to Nimra's court. She doesn't play overt games of power—but even Nazarach does not dare step foot in her territory without invitation."

Elena frowned, making a mental note to ask Raphael why he'd sent the damaged vampire into what sounded like a deadly field. Nimra had to be both brutal and cruel if she managed to hold Nazarach at bay, and Noel needed to heal, not fight for his next breath.

*A chopping-slicing sound. Distinct. Unwelcome.*

"Is that—" Her eyes widened at the black dot growing larger on the horizon with every slap of sound. "Damn it to hell!" It was the same news crew that had been hounding her the entire morning.

Illium zipped in front of her. "They dare do this?" His

voice was suddenly that of the man who'd amputated angelic wings in cold, clear-eyed retribution. "I will ensure it doesn't happen again."

"No, Illium." She managed to grip the muscular warmth of his upper arm. "No blood, not here. This is my home."

That incredible hair—ebony dipped in crushed sapphires, startling and impossible—blew back in the increasing turbulence caused by the chopper. "If you don't teach them a lesson now," he said as she tightened her hold on him to help maintain her position, "the vultures will see you as weak. You cannot be seen as weak, Ellie."

*Because she was Raphael's consort.*

And weakness in an archangel could be fatal.

"Shit." Strengthening her hold, she screamed against the wind. "How strong are you?" He was five hundred years old, had survived a deathly plunge into the Hudson, and once glowed with power to her naked eye. But she had no idea what that translated to in terms of physical might.

"Strong enough to break that machine in half."

*Oh.* "How about you turn it upside down and land it that way instead?" She squeezed his arm, felt muscle and tendon shift under her touch as he took more of her weight. "No fatalities, Bluebell."

Illium blinked, met her gaze . . . then gave a slow, wicked smile. "Where do you go?" When she told him, he said, "I'll meet you there."

She released his arm and dropped below the turbulence as fast as possible, clearing off in a direction that would take her out of the path of any activity. But she wasn't so distant that she missed the sight of Illium flying above the machine.

Her throat dried up, and if he'd been close enough to hear her, she'd have told him to stop. Dear God, those blades would shred his wings if he made a single error of judgment. But then Illium—laughing, playful, *powerful* Illium, did something and the blades just . . . stopped. He let the chopper free-fall for two stomach-churning seconds before catching it from below and flipping it over.

She realized the fiend was having fun.

Shaking her head, she carried on toward Ignatius's apartment, which ended up being very close to the Tower. Thankfully, the high-rise had a flat roof, so she didn't have to make a tight landing. Skidding across the rough surface, she took a minute to catch her breath before searching for and finding the entrance to the building. It was locked.

"Ash, thank you again." The other hunter had not only taught Elena how to pick locks with the skill of a master jewel thief—and didn't that just bring up all sorts of intriguing questions—she'd given Elena a set of slim lock-pick tools that she carried in a special pocket built into the knife sheath on her thigh.

Pulling out the pick she needed, she went to work. "Too easy." She squeezed through the tiny metal door, a hiss escaping her mouth as her right wing scraped along the rusty edges.

Glancing back, she saw that while a few deep blue feathers bore flecks of metal, there was no blood. Probably the best she could've hoped for, she thought, deciding against the elevator at the end of the service corridor—who knew how tiny that would be. Instead, she took the stairs down three levels to the floor where Ignatius had had his apartment.

She scented him the moment she opened the stairwell door and stepped into the corridor—the burnt treacle of his scent was imprinted in the walls, in the carpet. But not only his. There were, in fact, so many vampiric scents threaded through the air that she wondered if this wasn't an "overflow" building, used by vampires who weren't high enough in the hierarchy to rate a room in the Tower, but needed to be close to it.

A door opened down the hall as she stopped in front of Ignatius's apartment.

*Crushed diamonds in aged brandy, decadent chocolate stroking over her breasts, fur sumptuous and thick against her most intimate flesh.*

# 9

"What are you doing here?" She got the question out between gritted teeth, fighting the hotly sexual need aroused by Dmitri's insidious scent—a need that was a compulsion disguised as seduction. It made her wonder just how many hunter-born had fallen prey to that snare. And what Dmitri had done to them.

"I had business with another resident." The vampire strolled over, his hands in the pockets of his stone gray suit pants. He'd discarded the jacket and the open collar of his white shirt exposed a triangle of skin the shade of sun gold honey.

Rich, dark eyes met hers . . . right as another wave of scent—luscious and primal in its erotic promise—crashed over her senses. Her knees threatened to crumple. "So," she managed to get out through a throat gone husky with driving hunger, "the truce is over?"

"Wouldn't want you to think we were friends." It was the kind of thing she was used to hearing from Dmitri, but there was a thrumming anger beneath the words today, the same anger she'd sensed as they stood looking down at Betsy's desecrated body.

She didn't take it personally. She'd stood over too many broken and mutilated victims, knew what it was to want to strike out, make someone pay. The desire was a quiet, unremitting fury that could destroy. If her friends in the Guild hadn't pulled her back when she'd gotten too close, hadn't taught her the brutal necessity of emotional distance, she'd have fallen into the abyss long ago. So yes, she understood—but that didn't mean she was about to allow Dmitri to use her as his whipping boy.

He was so close now that the heat of him caressed her body in long, languid strokes, his scent twining around her like a thousand silken strands. Breathing through her mouth, she put one hand on his heavily muscled shoulder, leaned in close as if she planned to whisper in his ear . . . and bit down on his earlobe.

HARD.

"Fuck!" He wrenched away with preternatural speed.

"Game over?" she asked with poisonous sweetness as she struggled to catch her breath. "Or do you want a matching set?"

"Bitch." A slow, sensual smile that no longer held the raw edge of rage. "Always liked that about you."

Sliding back the dagger she'd pulled the same instant that she bit him, she said, "I can't do this with you here." Even muted as it was now, his scent blinded her to anything else in the vicinity. It was a drug, that scent, addictive and toxic. "Get out or I'll kill you."

Her flat statement made him blink, rock back on his heels. "You sound as if you really mean that."

At that instant, she did. Allowing the knowledge to seep into her expression, she met those eyes filled with a confident, potent sexuality. Slater had touched her with his scent, nearly broken the mind of the child she'd been—a child who didn't understand why her body *liked* what the monster was doing to her. Her horror of compulsion ran deep, deep enough to drive her to the most primitive savagery in a bid to survive.

Dmitri inclined his head, withdrawing all but a final taunting tendril of scent. "I think you might want this." A slender metal key dangled from his finger.

She stepped aside.

To her surprise, he prowled forward and inserted the key into the lock without further jerking her chain. Her eyes were drawn to the droplets of blood on his shoulder. "You bring out the worst in me."

Nudging open the door, he turned, a faint smile on that face meant for silk-sheeted bedrooms and blood-soaked fields of battle. "Thanks."

"Did you come inside before I got here?"

"No." He leaned in the doorway while she walked through and into the living room. "I hear your Bluebell is here." A pregnant pause.

Neck prickling in warning, she shifted to keep him in her line of sight. "What?"

"Be careful with Illium, Elena." A soft caution. "He's vulnerable to the humanity you carry within." He was gone the next instant.

Frozen by the impact of the unexpected words, she started when she heard the whisper of angelic wings. "Stay there." She kept her back to Illium as she spoke. "I want to do a walk-through first."

"Your wish. My command."

His unruffled agreement cut the taut rope of tension running up her spine. Glancing over at him, she saw that he was playing a carved silver knife in and around his fingers, each flick blindingly fast. Her friend, she thought. He was her friend, just like Ransom, just like Sara, and she wouldn't damage that friendship with false worries.

*He has a fascination with mortals.*

Raphael had said that to her before she'd woken with wings of midnight and dawn.

"Why are you staring at me, Ellie?" Illium said without taking his eyes from the blade dancing around his fingers.

The words were instinctive, something she might as easily have said to rib Ransom. "You're so pretty, it's difficult to resist."

A flashing grin, a hint of that aristocratic English accent in his response. "It's hard to be me, it's true."

Snorting, but with her composure restored, she began to inspect the apartment. It was much as she'd expected. Ignatius had been neat enough, but not obsessive about it. She could see a glass in the sink, a sweater thrown over the sofa, and the bed, though made, was done so in a way that said he was more worried about comfort than anything else. There was even a flower in a vase on the bedside table—a bit exotic for her taste, but vampires tended to go for the dark and lush.

Returning to the living area, she nodded Illium inside. "There's nothing weird here. No scents that shouldn't belong, no signs that he was losing his mind." Vampires in bloodlust often destroyed their homes during the first surge. "Supports what we saw at the scene—that he was in control of his faculties when—"

"Elena." Illium's voice was as lethal as the sword he wore along his spine.

Guard up, she walked to where he stood in the bedroom doorway, followed his gaze to the glossy black of the hothouse orchid that stood on the bedside table. "Tell me what that means."

He didn't reply, his gaze focused inward.

An instant later, the wind and the rain, crisp and clean, filled her mind. *Illium tells me it is a pale, scentless facsimile of the original, but it is nonetheless her symbol.* Raphael's voice was so strong, she knew he had to be in the Tower. *My mother is waking.*

Sucking in a breath, she stared at the luxuriant black of the petals, a color so deep and rich she'd never before seen its like. *She was controlling Ignatius?*

*Perhaps. It's more likely she simply took advantage of urges he would have otherwise kept contained.*

Elena blew out a breath, biting down on her lower lip. *It's a little pat, don't you think, Archangel?*

A pause. *Wait there. I will join you.*

Turning to Illium, Elena raised an eyebrow. "How did you know about the orchid? You weren't born until hundreds of years after Caliane's disappearance."

"I did read some of my history books in school." A disgruntled look. "Jessamy used to threaten to tie me to a desk unless I did my homework."

She could just see him, a blue-winged boy with eyes of gold and a smile full of mischief. But tempting as it was to follow that thought, she focused on the death that seemed to be stalking those closest to her. While she wasn't convinced that Caliane had anything to do with this, about one thing she had no doubts whatsoever. "Raphael is the ultimate target."

Everyone else was collateral damage.

Her hands fisted against the cold-blooded malice of that truth just as Raphael walked into the room. Brushing his wing over her own, he moved past her to pick up the orchid. "Illium," he said, "leave us."

"Sire."

Only after Illium was gone did Elena walk over to put her hand on Raphael's arm, her eye on the flower that had seemed an innocent decoration minutes earlier. "Even if your mother is waking," she said, having had time to think things through, "the turmoil around the world says that that awakening is hardly a calm, ordered thing. But going after my half sisters? That was very much a calculated act—a *conscious* act."

Raphael dropped the orchid onto the clear glass of the bedside table. "You are forgetting my rage."

"No, I'm not. That came out of nowhere, like the ice storms and other disasters. Who's to say the rest of the Cadre isn't feeling the same impact?"

Raphael went motionless. "You are right, Elena. I will speak to my people, find out if any of the other archangels have acted unlike themselves of late." Lifting his hand, he stroked his fingers along the sensitive arch of her wing.

She shivered. "You ask me—someone is using the disruption caused by the waking of an Ancient to his or her own advantage. Everyone knows the possibilities, knows that the one who wakes might well be your mother." And that even an archangel could be blinded by the black crush of memory. "They're trying to rattle you."

"They harm what is mine," Raphael murmured, "by harming those you love." His hand fisted in her hair. "It is a coward's game."

Hearing the cold condemnation in that statement, she knew the architect—or architects—of this vicious game would soon find themselves in the crosshairs of the Archangel of New York.

They were about to take off a few minutes later when Elena mentioned she was heading over to see if Sara had returned to the office.

"Illium will go with you."

Elena blew out a breath, ready for battle. *"Raphael."*

"I do not have time for this, Guild Hunter."

She went to snap back a demand that he make time, but one look at his expression and annoyance was swept aside by a deeper, far more intense emotion. "Raphael, you look . . ." Cruel. Heartless. "What are you going to do?"

His answer was austere. "A vampire thought to betray me. Now I must punish him."

Ice trailed up her spine. Closing the small distance between them, she put her hand on the tip of his wing, holding him to her. His responding glance was that of the immortal he was—someone for whom mercy was a weakness. "Would you stop me, Elena?" A question asked without intonation as she moved to face him.

Spreading out her own wings to keep her balance on the edge of the roof, she narrowed her eyes. "I'm no innocent. You damn well know that."

Midnight strands of hair danced over his face as the wind stroked through them, possessive as a lover. "Yet you stand in my way."

"I know you need to control your vampires." Every hunter knew the truth—that the almost-immortals were predators under the skin. Given free reign, they'd drown Manhattan in crimson, turn it into an abattoir devoid of life. "You have to deal with transgressions hard and fast to ensure no repeats."

Raphael continued to watch her with that quiet, remote patience.

Frustrated, she growled low in her throat and grabbing at the white linen of his shirt, pulled him down toward her. She knew she'd startled him, but his hands locked tight around her hips to keep her from overbalancing on the ledge.

"*You*," she said against those perfectly shaped lips that could turn cruel without warning. "*You're* my priority. Punish who you must, but don't do anything so terrible that it pushes you into the Quiet." She hadn't known him in that inhuman, emotionless state, was terrified of losing him to it even now. "Not that. Never again, Raphael."

A shudder passed through him, his hands flexing on her hips as he tugged her to his body. "You hold me to the earth, Elena."

Able to feel the heated strength of him against her abdomen, she nipped at his lower lip with her teeth, relief a whisper of rain against her senses. "Don't you forget it." Moving her hand down to play over the amber he wore on the ring finger of his left hand, she used those same teeth on his jaw. "You belong to me, Archangel. And I look after what's mine."

An hour after he'd watched Elena's wings sweep out toward the Guild in a play of midnight and dawn, Raphael turned his attention to the vampire who huddled in a chair in front of the black granite of his desk, a weak, whimpering creature who'd sought to steal from an archangel. The stupidity of the act aside, the fact that he'd even considered he might get away with it argued to a greater rot. Raphael intended to excise that rot from existence before this day was done.

"Do you know what I'm going to do with you?" he asked

softly from where he stood by the huge window that looked out over Manhattan. He'd punished and executed many over the centuries that he had ruled, but he had not expected betrayal in the heart of his territory and that honed his anger into a gleaming blade.

"Sire, I didn't—I—" Blubbering words running together in an unintelligible babble.

Raphael let him speak until he ran out of words. "Tell me why," he said, turning to watch for his hunter in the skies as he had a habit of doing.

A sniffle, a sucking in of air. "She said you would never know."

Raphael swiveled to face the vampire. "Who?"

Compulsively rubbing together his hands, he said, "One of the head accountants."

"I want a name." How deep did this treachery run?

"Oleander Graves."

Raphael knew all of his senior people, and that name wasn't on the list.

"She said you'd never know," the vampire blubbered again, bringing Raphael's mind back to the unpleasant task at hand. "She was so beautiful."

Weak, Raphael thought in disgust. The male was so weak, he should've never made it into the Tower, but even immortals sometimes made mistakes. Without further words, Raphael reached out with his power and crushed the vampire's rib cage into his chest, piercing his internal organs.

As blood bubbled out of the man's mouth, Raphael knew that to those outside the Tower the punishment would appear barbaric. They knew nothing of the bloodlust that lurked near the surface of so many vampiric minds, how easy it would be for the monsters to roam free. And this damage would heal in a day at most. The real punishment was yet to come. "You are to go to ground for the next decade."

Panic in those eyes, a plea that Raphael could not heed, not if he intended to keep the Hudson from running a dark ruby red. He was an archangel—even if every vampire in the city surrendered to bloodlust, he'd gain control within hours at most, but to do so, he'd have to slaughter hundreds of the Made. "Go."

As the vampire left, clutching broken ribs and fighting not to dribble blood on the pristine white of the carpet, Raphael turned back to the window. The sentence was just, but it would likely break a mind as weak as the one that had just scuttled out of his office. *Any other punishment would've given encouragement to others who might seek to betray me.* Reaching out to speak to Elena was not a conscious decision.

*Raphael?*

*I sentenced him to be buried alive in a coffin-sized box,* he told his hunter with the heart of a mortal. *He will be fed enough to be kept alive and whole, but he will remain in that box for ten years.*

Shock, worry, pain, he felt the cascade of her emotions like blows.

*I'm sorry, Raphael. I'm sorry he put you in a position where you had to make that choice.*

In spite of her earlier words, he'd expected her to be horrified by what he'd done, for this was not something she could have expected. It was not a human punishment. But he'd forgotten that she was a woman who'd survived a monster, who understood that sometimes there were no easy choices. *Come to me after your talk with Sara. I would hold you.*

Fifteen minutes later, there was a flicker of midnight and dawn on the horizon as his consort dropped down from the clouds not far from the Tower; Illium's distinctive wings remained in shadow. The blue-winged angel had an open affection for Raphael's hunter, and he'd let it go—would continue to let it go . . . so long as Illium never forgot that Elena was mate to an archangel. *I have her.*

*Sire.* The angel cut away in another direction.

*Wait. I received a message for you earlier today.*

A questioning silence.

*The Hummingbird wishes to see her son.*

Quiet, such quiet. *I will go to her.*

*No. She is coming to New York.*

He felt Illium's shock. The Hummingbird seldom left her secluded mountain home, and even then, it was only to go to the Refuge. *We will watch over her, Illium. Have no fear of that.*

The Hummingbird had saved Raphael from excruciating pain when she'd found him on that forsaken field where Caliane had shattered his body like so much glass, and for such would've earned his loyalty. But Illium's mother had gone beyond that—she'd shown a broken young boy incredible kindness at a time when his whole world was falling apart. There was little Raphael would not do for the Hummingbird.

*Sire, I must—*

*Go*, Raphael said, knowing the angel needed time to get his mind around the news. *She arrives in a week's time.* He was walking out onto his private balcony as he spoke, switching the mental connection. *Come, Elena.*

*I can't land there. I'll brain myself.*

He almost laughed, and he had not thought he could do that after the sentence he'd just delivered. *I will catch you.*

That she didn't question him after that, simply changed trajectory so that she flew into his arms . . . it broke him. Then it reformed him anew. "Elena," he whispered into her hair as he crushed her to him.

She wrapped her arms around him, his fragile consort with her incredible will and her refusal to surrender. "Tell me," she whispered.

And he, an archangel used to keeping a thousand secrets, told her.

# 10

Evening shadows lay heavy on the horizon when Elena walked out across the lawn behind Raphael's—their—home, heading for the edge of the cliff beyond the trees. After leaving the Tower earlier that afternoon, the intimacy of those moments on the balcony a tight warmth in her chest, she'd called a delighted Sam using the Web link in the library.

"Ellie!" His grin had stretched from ear to ear. "You didn't forget me!"

"Of course not." Laughing as he bounced in his seat, those wings that looked too big for his body rising and falling in excitement as loose black curls tumbled over his forehead, she'd asked him how his day had gone.

"Father took me flying again!"

Since Sam had been forbidden from using his wings for another month, his father had begun to carry him up into the sky in his arms, his love for Sam a fierce thing no one could miss, in spite of the fact that he was a man of few words. "Was it fun?"

An enthusiastic nod. "He can go so *fast*."

Their conversation had lasted half an hour, with Elena exchanging a few words with Sam's mother as well. The tiny angel with hair of the same lustrous blue black and wings of dusty brown streaked with white, still touched her baby with protective care, but she smiled just as often—and for the first time, Elena truly believed that the small family would be okay.

She'd spent the remaining time doing flying drills, all of them geared to build up her muscles, with an oddly subdued Illium. Having discussed it with Keir, Raphael had told her that she wouldn't be able to achieve a true vertical takeoff without wing strength of a kind she simply did not have. It was a physical impossibility.

"Your immortality," he'd murmured as they stood on the balcony, "has not yet grown deep enough into your cells. But," he'd added, "given your hunter strength, you may well be able to learn to do a bastardized version that relies not on the power of your wings, but on sheer muscle."

It'd be a much harder road and each takeoff would hurt like a bitch even after she mastered it, but Elena wasn't about to be a sitting duck, not if she could do something about it. Maybe she was an immortal new-Made, she thought now, trying to see through the straggling clouds, but she would not be easy prey.

*There.*

The magnificent breadth of Raphael's wings came into view as he descended to join her on the clifftop, the tips flaming as they caught the last vestiges of a sun that had finally made an appearance late that afternoon. "You go to visit the Guild Director and her family?"

Pushing off strands of hair that had escaped her braid, she said, "Come with me."

A slow blink. "They are your closest friends, Elena. They wish to have you to themselves for this night."

"I'm becoming part of your world—come become part of mine." She saw the surprise on his face, saw, too, that he'd very much not expected the invitation.

His body was a hard wall of muscle against her as he pulled

her close, until her breasts pressed against his chest. "What will Sara and Deacon say to that?"

She ran her hands down the wings he spread for her, indulging in the ability to touch him as she pleased. "Not scared of a couple of hunters are you, Archangel?"

A flare of absolute blue as his lashes lifted. *They may choose to sever their friendship with you rather than welcome me into their home. You cannot forget the actions I took in the Quiet.*

"No." But she also knew something else beyond any shadow of a doubt. "You have your Seven. I have my friends—they'd cut off their right arms before they'd shove me out into the cold."

Such loyalty, Raphael thought. He wouldn't have believed mortals capable of it except that he had known Dmitri when he was human . . . and he had known Elena. "The invitation is very welcome," he said. "I will accept it another day. Tonight, I must remain here."

Pale gray eyes sparked with intelligence. "What's happening?"

"I have a meeting with Aodhan."

"Here? In New York?"

"I, too, am surprised." Aodhan preferred the seclusion of the Refuge. "We meet at the Tower."

Tucking back another flyaway strand of hair, his consort looked him full in the face. "I want to talk to you about something else, too."

"What would you have of me, Guild Hunter?"

"I don't need a bodyguard anymore—Illium's trick today with the helicopter seems to have gotten the message across to the media hounds."

*You are my heart, Elena.* He would not allow anything to happen to her.

She took a step back. "No chains, Raphael."

He closed his hand around her nape, refusing to permit her to distance herself. "I have allowed you much freedom, but on this I will not budge."

Temper sparked off her. "It's not up to you to allow me anything. I'm your consort. Treat me as one!"

Yet she was so very mortal still—even the Angel-born remained vulnerable for over a hundred years, and Elena had started out mortal. Immortality had barely kissed her blood, had had no real chance to intertwine with her cells. *You will not win this argument, Hunter.*

"Fine, but it's one we'll continue to have every single day till you start acting reasonable."

Until her, no one had challenged him on this level. Until her, no one had loved him with all the strength in this hunter's soul. "According to Dmitri, the most sensible act would have been to kill you the instant we met."

Her eyes narrowed. "Stop trying to distract me." Breaking his hold with a move he hadn't expected, she picked up the small bag he'd noticed at her feet. "Raphael?"

Catching the suddenly somber note in her voice, he lifted his eyes to the changeable mists of her eyes. "Hunter."

"Don't clip my wings. It'll destroy both of us."

With those disturbing words, she dove down across the Hudson. As he watched her disappear toward Manhattan, aware that Illium would trail her to the Guild Director's home—where another of his Seven had stood watch for hours to ensure no unwelcome surprises—he knew she was right. She would never be happy in a cage. But after the events that had almost stolen her from him not once, but twice, he wasn't sure he had the ability to set her free.

Elena shoved the argument—and the reason behind it—to the back of her mind as she came to a smooth landing in front of the brownstone that was Sara and Deacon's. Her best friend dragged her inside an instant later . . . where Elena got a welcome surprise. "You bought the neighboring town house!" They'd taken out the facing walls of both homes, then closed the small gap between the two buildings by extending one of the houses.

Since Elena hadn't noticed anything from the outside, they had to have recycled the materials removed during the demolition of the walls to build a seamless exterior over the extension. Fantastic as that was, it didn't compare to the inside—the entire first floor was a massive open-plan space that flowed into the kitchen.

"Yep." Sara beamed, her rich coffee-colored skin all but glowing. "With the way Deacon's business is going, we could afford it so we decided why not." A pause. "More important, I wanted my best friend to feel welcome in my home."

Swallowing the knot of emotion in her throat, Elena put down her bag to wander over the gleaming wooden floors covered with Navajo rugs that matched the warm, earth-toned color scheme of the house. "It's gorgeous, Sara."

"Deacon did most of the renovation himself—Zoe and I just held boards, took him the occasional nail, and generally supervised." A big grin.

"I know you chose the colors." Feeling totally at ease, she spread her wings. "It's—"

"Oh, God, Ellie," Sara said on a gasp, clutching the back of the sofa. "Each time you do that, I start to feel faint."

Elena was laughing at the look on her friend's face when a big, bad-ass man with deep green eyes, golden skin, and dark hair walked into the room, a little girl cradled in the crook of his arm. "Deacon." Smiling, Elena moved close enough that he could tug her into a one-armed embrace.

He held her for several long seconds. "It's good to see you, Ellie." Quiet, powerful words.

Looking up, she met the eyes of the child who'd tucked her head shyly against her father's neck. "Hello, Zoe," she whispered, amazed at how big Sara's baby had become in the year and a half since Elena had last seen her.

Sara came over then, picking up one tiny hand and pressing a kiss on Zoe's palm. "This is Auntie Ellie, Zoe."

That was when a massive hellhound of a dog came around the corner, heading straight for Elena. "Slayer!" Laughing as he jumped on her, intent on loving her to death, she looked up to see Zoe giggling.

It made her want to tug the girl into her arms and pepper that precious face with kisses, but she was a stranger to Zoe right now. A stranger with bribes. "I have presents for you," she said after Deacon pulled Slayer off with one hand.

Eyes the same dark color as Sara's went wide with interest.

Giving Slayer a final scratch that had his tail wagging triple-time, Elena went to her bag and took out the handcrafted doll she'd bought from one of the artisans at the Refuge. Zoe took it with careful hands, rising away from her father's shoulder to pat at the doll's thick curls.

"What do you say, baby girl?" Deacon prompted.

Zoe's "Thank you" was shy.

Elena said, "You're welcome," and retrieved the collection of angel feathers she'd been saving since she woke from the coma. Startling gold and white, blue edged with silver, midnight and dawn, shimmering gray, a sweet, beautiful brown, and an incredible crystalline white, they made Zoe hold her breath. When Elena lifted her hand, her goddaughter stared in wonder . . . then closed one fist gently around the feathers. "Papa. Down."

Obeying the order, Deacon bent to put her on the floor. Feathers in hand, Zoe toddled over to the coffee table and put her treasures on the glass so she could admire them one by one, the doll held close to her side. Slayer, having been banished to sit by the mantel, sidled around to stand next to his favorite human being.

Sara touched her hand to Deacon's heart when he wrapped a heavily muscled arm around her shoulders. "Didn't you have something for Ellie?"

"Let me go grab it." Kissing his wife on the nose, the former bogeyman of the Guild prowled out of the room after ruffling Zoe's tiny curls.

"I got you and Deacon gifts as well," Elena said. "From the Refuge. Found a gorgeous collar for your monster dog, too."

Sara took her hands, squeezed. "The best gift is you, here. I missed you so much."

Elena had to look down for a second to blink away the surge of emotion. Sara wasn't her blood, but she was her sister in every other way that mattered. "I had a run-in with Jeffrey." It spilled out, the one subject she hadn't been able to talk about when they'd met earlier, the wound too raw. "He's furious that the girls have been targeted because of me, and I can't blame him."

Sara's jaw tensed. "That's—"

"He's right this time, Sara." Guilt twisted through her, a hard, abrasive rope. "But at least that's something I understand. What I don't know is why he wants to meet me tomorrow."

"Do you want me to come with you?"

"No, I—" That was when she felt a small, baby-soft hand patting at her feathers with unhidden wonder. "Hey, sweetheart." Looking down into that adorable face, she decided to push Jeffrey, the murders, her frustration with Raphael's protectiveness, out of her mind and just enjoy spending time with the family of a friend who'd opened her heart to Elena when she'd been nothing but a scared girl without home or hope.

*I'll watch over you*, she promised Zoe silently, though the thought of surviving her best friend was an aching sorrow in her heart. *Over you and all who come after you.* Sara's blood.

Having received the message of Aodhan's arrival, Raphael swept down across the sparkling nightscape of Manhattan to land on the wide Tower balcony outside his office—where the angel stood waiting. Unlike Illium, who even with his remarkable wings and eyes of gold, managed to walk among mortals, Aodhan would never fit easily into this world. He was cut in sparkling ice, his wings so bright as to almost hurt human eyes, his face and his skin seeming to be created from marble overlaid with white-gold.

Michaela, that devourer of men, had once said of Aodhan, "Beautiful—but so very cold, that one. Still, I would like to keep him as I would a precious gem. There is no other like Aodhan in the world."

But Michaela saw only the surface.

Raphael walked to the edge of the space that had no railing, running his eyes over his city. "What did you discover?"

Aodhan tightened his wings to avoid any contact as he came to stand on Raphael's left. "I cannot understand," he said instead of answering, "how you can live surrounded by so many lives." A stark curiosity underlay his every word.

"Many cannot understand your preference for solitude." He watched as a number of angels came in for landings on lower balconies, their wings silhouetted against the night sky. "You surprise me with this visit, Aodhan." The angel was one of Raphael's Seven for a reason, but he was also damaged.

"It is . . . difficult." Aodhan's expression was haunted in a way that not many would've understood. "But your hunter . . . She is so weak, and yet she fought the reborn with unflinching courage."

"Elena will find it amusing that she is an inspiration." Yet she would also understand what it meant for Aodhan to take this step, his hunter with her mortal heart.

Aodhan was silent for another long moment. "East," he said at last. "Naasir and I both believe the Ancient Sleeps in the Far East."

With Galen in charge at the Refuge, Raphael had set Aodhan and Naasir the task of searching for clues as to the location of the Sleeper who might well be his mother. However, he hadn't expected any kind of an answer so soon. "Why?"

"Jessamy tells me that when an Ancient awakens, it is not a process of a few days or even weeks. It can take up to a year." His crystalline eyes, fractured outward from the pupil, reflected a thousand shards of light as he spoke. "Yet not one of the Cadre sensed this."

Raphael understood at once. "Because the region falls in Lijuan's shadow." Any fluctuations in power in that area had been attributed to Lijuan's evolution. "Keep searching." The temptation to join the hunt was strong, but after having been absent from his Tower for so long, he couldn't leave it for what might turn out to be weeks—too many covetous eyes were trained on his domain.

Aodhan bent his head. "Sire."

As the angel began to expand his wings in preparation for flight, Raphael stopped him with a single touch on the shoulder. Aodhan froze.

"Talk to Sam." Knowing the demons that tormented the angel, Raphael broke the contact. "Elena gave him a dagger. Legend says the ruby in the dagger was a gift from a sleeping dragon. It may be nothing—"

"But it may denote knowledge of an Ancient." Aodhan's wings glittered in a stray shaft of moonlight as he hesitated. "Sire, I would come to this city again."

"Are you certain?"

"I have acted the coward for centuries. No more."

Raphael had been there when Aodhan was found, had carried the other angel in his arms the hours it took to reach the Medica and Keir. "You are no coward, Aodhan. You are one of my Seven."

Aodhan glanced back toward the office, in the direction of the wide shelves of deep ebony that lined one wall. "Why do you not display one of my feathers? My wings are as unusual as Bluebell's."

Raphael raised an eyebrow. "Illium is a performer." While Aodhan, like Jason, preferred the shadows.

As he watched, Aodhan pulled out a perfect, glittering feather and walked inside to place it beside the heavenly blue that was Illium's. Raphael inclined his head when the angel returned. "After this task is done, you will move here." Manhattan was still reeling from Elena's return—Aodhan's presence might just bring the city to a standstill. But that was a problem for another day. "If you and Naasir are able to narrow the search area to a specific locality, call and wait for me. Do not approach."

"If it is her . . . you believe she will kill."

"My mother is the specter in the dark, Aodhan, the nightmare that whispers in the hindbrain." And he was her son . . . the son of two archangels gone insane.

# 11

It was after Zoe had been put to bed, and the adults had finished dinner that Elena opened the box Deacon had brought down and saw the weapon he'd created for a hunter with wings.

"Ooooh." Delirious with pleasure, she picked up what seemed to be a modified crossbow, so small and light that— "It's meant to be strapped to my leg?"

"Yeah." Deacon grabbed the harness and got her to stand so he could buckle it around her thigh. "I decided it would be problematic on the shoulder—your wings would be too close, too easy to damage."

Nodding in agreement, Elena checked the weapon. "Balance shouldn't be an issue in flight, given its weight. But what the heck is this?" She pulled out a small, circular blade, its serrated edges razor-sharp and felt her eyes widen. "It shoots these things? Like the weapon you've got?" The weapon she'd lusted after since the day she'd first seen it, in the middle of a junkyard crawling with vampires.

"Yep. It's also designed so you can use it one-handed if required." He tightened the harness. "Slot it in."

Flipping the safety, Elena did so, then took a few steps. "Light, portable."

"He tested it on me," Sara said from where she was curled up on the couch, bowl of strawberry ice cream in hand. "Since I'm shorter and not as strong, I thought you'd have no problem."

Elena stroked the weapon, felt her hunter instincts sigh. "It's perfect. Deacon, come here."

When he stepped close, she reached up and smacked a kiss on his beautiful lips. "You're wonderful."

"Hey," Sara said from the couch, waving a spoon in the air. "Mine."

Grinning, Elena shifted the harness a fraction higher as Deacon went to sit beside Sara and steal her ice cream. The moment was so *normal* that for an instant, she could almost believe she'd never left New York, never fallen into the arms of an archangel.

Then her cell phone rang.

Having followed Illium to the location, Deacon's gift strapped to her thigh, Elena took extreme care as she angled in to land—tired, she was liable to make mistakes, and this was not the time for a broken arm or leg. Below her, the green heart of Manhattan lay swathed in darkness but for the old-fashioned lamps along the pathways that meandered through the park.

*"Oof."* Coming down hard, with a power that made her knees ache, she closed the distance to where another one of Raphael's Seven stood beside an indistinct lump on the ground.

*Poison, the pungent stink of bowels evacuated, viscera . . . and below it, the whisper of violets dipped in ice.*

Gorge rising, she nonetheless made herself look at the body. The male—a vampire from his scent—had been beheaded, but that had been done last if she was any judge, after his organs had been ripped out then thrust back into his body *in the wrong places*. As far as brutality went, it wasn't as bad as anything Uram had done, but the bloodborn archangel had made a vicious art form out of murder.

"Who is he?" she asked Venom.

The male had been at death's door not long ago, but you couldn't tell that from his current appearance. Dressed in his usual black on black suit, his reptilian eyes shaded by wraparound sunglasses even in the darkness, he looked like he'd stepped out of the pages of some exclusive magazine. "The accountant Raphael sentenced to go to ground."

Elena didn't need him to spell out the fact that someone was playing games here. "Where's Raphael?"

Venom continued to give her straight answers for once. "At the site where this man was supposed to be buried tonight. Since this murder is unlikely to be a chance event, the killer may have staked out the other location. But this site is your best bet of catching a scent."

"Yes." From the pattern of blood, the churned up dirt and grass, this was where the victim had been murdered, which meant the killer's scent should be a violent stain across the entire area.

Filtering out Venom's vampiric signature, she picked up the scent of violets and crushed ice again . . . but with this much carnage, there was no way to be certain it was the victim's at a distance. Girding her stomach, she went to her knees—careful to avoid the splatter—and bent. But she couldn't reach the body without placing her hands in blood-soaked evidence. "Venom, hold me at the waist."

Strong, cool hands around her waist an instant later. She fought the instinctive urge to throw off the intimate hold and, trusting him to keep her from falling on the body—and yeah, that trust came hard—leaned in close enough to sniff at a patch of unravaged skin.

*Violets. Ice. And a hereto hidden undertone of something light, fruity. Watermelon?*

"Enough."

The vampire's hands tightened for an instant, and she almost hoped he'd attempt to drop her. But he behaved, and she was on her feet moments later. "I have his scent," she said, gesturing to the body, "and I've weeded out yours. Anyone else been on the scene?"

He pointed up. "Just Illium and he hasn't landed."

Good, she thought, that meant the caress of poison had to belong to the killer. Focusing on that element, she began to pull apart the notes to create a more detailed profile.

*Oleanders, rich and sweet, with a thread of darkest resin humming a discordant note, and below that a touch of juicy red berries bursting open. But the scent of oleanders in full bloom overwhelmed, it was so very, very intoxicating.*

She was following the trail even as the thought passed through her head, barely aware of Venom remaining beside the body while Illium flew overhead. The scent meandered through Central Park, as if the killer had taken a stroll. Given his confidence, she more than half expected to lose him as soon as she hit the pond, but surprisingly, he hadn't gone into the water.

Instead, she found herself following him to the edge of Fifth Avenue. Where the sensual whisper of oleanders snapped off with such suddenness that she knew he'd gotten into a cab. Blowing out a breath, she waved Illium down. "Trail's cold," she said when he landed. "Might as well lead me to the other site just in case he did scope that out."

It was only as they were flying over the Hudson that she realized they were heading toward Raphael's estate. Figuring the burial site had to be somewhere beyond, she found herself deeply shaken when Illium dove down to land on the edge of the wood that separated the mansion from Michaela's U.S. home. He stayed in position as she walked in. *Archangel?*

*Slightly to your right, about fifty meters ahead.*

Raphael held out a hand when she reached him, but she didn't take it, staring at the rectangular coffin-sized hole in the earth. "When exactly," she said, "were you going to tell me he was going to be buried on the grounds of our *home*?" She understood that he had to control his vampires in ways that might seem cruel to her, but this . . .

A chrome blue gaze met hers, vivid even in the night shadows. "I needed him close enough that I could maintain a mental watch."

"How many others?" she whispered, feeling sick to her

stomach. She'd walked these woods before, might well have stepped over them.

"None, Guild Hunter."

The ice in his voice should've scared her, but she was too furious. "You know this is wrong, Raphael, keeping this from me. Yet you did it intentionally." His expression didn't change, but she knew without a doubt that she was right. "Why?"

"Because you have a mortal heart." A pitiless statement.

She shook under the verbal blow. "Is that so wrong?"

"It is not a matter of right or wrong"—metallic blue, so very, very inhuman—"but of fact. This would have disturbed you to an extent that would've made it impossible for you to live here."

It was the absolute truth, made no less so by the fact that he'd seen it with such cold clarity. Anger battled with other, deeper emotions, and it took her almost half a minute to find the control to say, "I want to ask you for something, Archangel." He'd given her his heart, given her power over him, but until now, she'd never gambled anything on that power.

"What would you have, Guild Hunter?" So formal, so distant.

The part of her that was still the child abandoned by mother and father both was terrified of pushing him too far, until he left her, too. It was a nauseating sensation—but this was a stand she had to take. "Strike this punishment from the books. Surely there are other ways?"

Raphael was as unmoving as stone in front of her for a long, long moment. "Is it a boon you ask, Hunter?"

"No," she said with slow deliberation. "I ask this as your consort. This . . . it's not worth tainting the relationship between us."

The Archangel of New York closed his fingers gently around her throat—not a threat, but a mark of possession. "Is our relationship so weak?"

"No." She would fight to the death for it . . . for him. "It's something extraordinary—and it deserves to be protected against all the crap the world is going to throw at us."

The metal receded as she watched, replaced by a penetrating, piercing shade akin to the mountain sky at noon. "Ah, Elena. So eloquent."

"I mean it." Her stomach was so tight, a thousand knots within.

"I will have Dmitri think of another suitable punishment."

Air rushed into her lungs as she took a true breath. "I'm sure he'll have no problems." Dmitri was one of the oldest vampires she'd ever met—and he had a thing for pain. "There's nothing here, scentwise."

"I didn't truly expect it. He was meant to be transported here later tonight, after having had time to put his affairs in order." Raphael stroked his thumb over his consort's pulse. "What is it I sense in you, Elena?" Fear, an insidious intruder, one that would steal her from him.

She gave a slight shake of her head. "Not you." A pause. "Me. I'm a little messed up. Sometimes it all just roars back to the surface."

Stroking his hand along the back of her neck, he tugged her close, took her lips in a slow, deep caress that reminded her the nightmares had no claim on her now—she belonged to an archangel.

His hunter lifted her fingers to her kiss-wet lips when they parted, eyes huge in the darkness. "*Shokran*, Archangel."

"You are welcome, Guild Hunter." Wings brushing over his consort's, he turned to walk back to the house with her. "This murder is a message. It can be nothing else."

"The question is who—" Elena froze. "The killer's scent was heady with oleander. It's a flower, but it's also a toxic poison."

"Neha."

Leaving an exhausted Elena to her bath—though the idea of joining her was a much more pleasurable thought— Raphael walked down to the library and put through a call to Neha. The Archangel of India took her time answering, and her visage, when it appeared on the screen, was pure arctic chill. "Raphael." With her hair pulled off her face into a tight bun and her features free of artifice, she had a pure, unadorned beauty.

The impression was furthered by the folds of the white silk sari set neatly over her shoulder, the stark shade bearing only the thinnest border of small faceted beads. Around her throat lay a necklace shaped to mimic a slender black serpent, its hissing mouth open. But of course, Raphael knew that was no necklace.

"Neha," he said, watching as she allowed a cobra to twine its way around her arm. "You know why we're having this conversation." Vampires, Elena had told him as she sank into the bath, had strange, unexpected scents, so the potency of poison could mean nothing. However, as evidenced by Venom, Neha had a way of marking those she Made.

Now the Queen of Snakes, of Poisons, curved her lips into a smile that held an amusement as cold as that of the blood that flowed through her favored creatures. "It is but a game, Raphael."

A mortal may have attempted to appeal to her conscience, tried to make her feel guilt for the senseless death—most likely *deaths*—she'd engineered, but he spoke to her pride. "It is beneath you, Neha, to act through such pathetic fools."

Titus would've exploded at the insult, Michaela would've hissed in anger, but Neha . . . Neha sighed and reached up to pinch closed the mouth of the snake at her neck, holding it shut until the creature started to struggle before releasing it. And still it stayed curled around her throat. "You are right," she murmured. "But you helped take something I love from me, Raphael."

"So you would take what I love from me?" So smart, so vicious, he thought, so like the snakes she kept as pets.

"I'm sure your hunter is none too pleased to discover that by becoming yours, she has placed everyone she loves in mortal danger." Stroking her fingers along the cobra's gleaming skin as she confirmed her part in the murders at the school, she met his gaze with eyes of darkest brown, eyes that were very much sane. "As for the other . . . betrayal is always a hard pill to swallow. He was weak, ridiculously easy to break and control."

Raphael had already set Dmitri and Venom the task of ensuring Neha had planted no more snakes in their midst. "Why kill him?"

Neha lifted a shoulder in an elegant shrug. "He may have known something, though the point is moot now. As a tool, he wasn't the most useful one—and I'm sure he considered it a mercy. He would've never survived his punishment with his mind intact."

Perhaps. But Raphael was quite certain the man would not have chosen to die by having his internal organs ripped from his living flesh. "You know what Anoushka did was anathema." Neha's daughter had been party to the brutalization of a child. It was one of the greatest taboos of their race.

"I am a mother, Raphael." A pause, an instant of piercing sorrow. "I was a mother."

"Now you would make other mothers feel the same pain?" Neha was one of the few in the Cadre who had always treated mortal children as precious.

A slow blink, cold and dark, as she stared at him with a gaze that had been known to ensnare lesser angels. "I think you will soon have far bigger problems to worry about than my modest games."

Raphael said nothing.

Smiling, Neha reached out of the shot, and when her hand returned, those elegant fingers held a black orchid. "I thought this was a nice touch on my part." She ran the ebony petals over the cobra's skin. "It'll amuse me to watch you when she rises. She left you to die broken on a field far from civilization, did she not?"

Having expected the taunt, he didn't react. "Neha," he said softly. "I will, if not forgive, not retaliate against these trespasses because you lost a child—but do not play games in my territory again."

Neha laughed, a bitter hiss of sound. "What would you do to me, Raphael? I have lost that which matters most."

"A lie," he murmured, waiting until her laughter died to deliver his coup de grace. "You would not like to lose your power."

Neha's expression went flat, hard. "You are arrogant enough to think you have the strength to affect my rule?"

"Never forget that I was the one who executed Uram when it needed to be done." It had taken something from him to end the life of another archangel, but Uram had turned monster and could not be allowed to savage the world. "Never forget what and who I am, Neha."

The Archangel of India held his gaze for a long, long moment. "Perhaps your mortal has not changed you after all."

Raphael said nothing to that, ending the call, but as he turned to walk up to join his hunter, he knew Neha was wrong. Elena had changed something fundamental in him. *Do you wait for me, hbeebti*? he asked, touching her mind, finding her awake.

*The bed's cold without you.*

As he opened the bedroom door, he knew he would never again be able to return to the life he'd led before her—where hardness of the heart was nurtured and love termed a weakness. "Are you tired, Elena?"

Rising up into a sitting position, his hunter allowed the sheet to slide down to pool at her waist.

# 12

Elena's throat went dry under the unwavering focus of Raphael's gaze, the skin over her breasts suddenly too tight. Her need for him was a deep, aching hunger fueled by a day that had stirred hidden fears, painful secrets. She wanted his mouth on her, his hands on her—but there was a dangerous look to him tonight. Nothing akin to the rage that had made him burn so cold after the events at the girls' school, nothing that scared her . . . except in the most sensual of ways.

"Planning to come over here, Archangel?" she asked when he continued to caress her only with those eyes of inhuman blue, the ache inside her transforming into something darker, hotter.

He leaned against the closed door to the bedroom. "First, I intend to savor the view."

She was a hunter, had never been a prude, but he made her skin flush, her nipples bead to urgent points. "At least take off your shirt," she said, rubbing her feet against the sheets. "Make it fair."

"Why would I wish to do that when I have a naked hunter in my bed, ready to submit to my every whim?"

Her toes curled, because right now, that look in his eyes—it was that of a conqueror, a man used to surrender. But that wasn't the only thing she saw on his face. The faintest of smiles tugged at those lips that knew her every hidden pleasure point; his shoulders were relaxed in a way that told her he was playing with her. Oh, not all of it. A large part of him *was*, in all probability, experiencing the same arrogant satisfaction as any conqueror faced with a woman clothed only in her skin, a woman who had no intention of denying him anything . . . but this particular one had given her the right to make her own demands.

Eyes on him, she ran her hands down her rib cage, then back up to palm her breasts. Liquid heat in that gaze, but he didn't move from the doorway. "More, Elena." It was a command, given in the tone she only ever heard in bed, sexual and demanding and, sometimes, without mercy.

"Always with the orders," she whispered, rolling and tugging at nipples that begged for a harder, bolder touch, yet so unbearably sensitive that she thought she might shatter if he so much as put those strong hands on her. "Maybe I want to be the one giving orders in bed."

"What order would you give?" An intimate question, his gaze lingering on her lips with unhidden intent before dropping to the hand she slid provocatively under the sheet.

Breasts flushing under the sexual kiss of those eyes, she took in the hard power of the magnificent body braced against the door. "I'd say come here"—stroking her fingers between her legs in sinful emphasis—"so I can show you how very ready and willing I am." The physical connection . . . they both needed it on the deepest level tonight—to burn away the cold, dark places in the soul, to lock them together in an earthy glide of flesh.

"I," Raphael said, "do like it when you do wicked things to me," and it was an echo of something she'd said to him once.

The memories of the velvet heat of his cock against her tongue made her thighs clench around the intrusion of her hand. "Then why," she asked, fisting her free hand on the sheets, "aren't you moving?" He hadn't touched her, and she was liquid-soft with welcome.

"Because tonight, Guild Hunter, I have wicked things of my own in mind."

She stopped breathing. When he skimmed his eyes down to linger where the sheets pooled at her waist, the command might as well have been spoken, it was so very direct, so very male. Taking a jerky breath, she used one hand to push the sheet to the top of her thighs, where the bunched material continued to hide her from his view . . . and stopped.

*Elena.*

She shook her head. "The shirt has to go." When dancing with an archangel, a girl had to play dirty.

Pushing off the door, he raised his fingers to the buttons of the black shirt, undoing them with a quick efficiency that made her mouth water. Those fingers, they knew her body so well, had touched her both with exquisite tenderness and in dark possession. It was clear what she'd be getting tonight, she thought as he shrugged off the shirt to the floor and raised an eyebrow.

God but he was beautiful, his shoulders and chest heavy with muscle, his skin a gold that invited her mouth, her touch. But that wasn't the bargain they'd made. Removing her fingers from her desire-slick flesh, she brought her knees to her chest before sliding the sheet up and over her thighs to gather at her feet. "There you go."

The archangel folded his arms. "Legs down."

Shaking her head, she focused on the proud push of his erection against pants the same shade as his shirt. Tiny internal muscles clenched. "I want something in return."

"No."

She went to protest the flat refusal, but he'd already crossed the room to close his hand around her nape. His mouth, that lethal, knowing mouth, was on hers a fraction of a second later. Raising her hands to grab at his waist as he leaned above her, she gasped when he moved his other hand down to cover her breast with a confidence that said she was his and he knew it.

The squeeze was proprietary, his skin just rough enough to tantalize her nipples.

That was when she realized she'd dropped her knees. "I guess you think you've won." A husky whisper as he lifted his head and pushed her back onto the bed with a hand splayed on her breastbone. Maybe she should've resisted, but she wanted him on top of her, inside her, his cock parting her wet, passion-swollen tissues in hard demand.

"This round, yes." Raphael simply stood there for long seconds, indulging in the sight of his consort. She had the body of a warrior. Strong, sleek with muscle. Pleasing to his every sense.

The eyes that watched him were hazy with desire, her lips curved in the slight smile of a woman who knew her lover would satisfy her, one leg cocked up at the knee as she lay languorous and warm and aroused in their bed. When she turned over onto her front, her extraordinary wings spreading out on either side, he didn't stop her. Instead, climbing onto the mattress, he straddled her on his knees before sweeping the silken threads of her hair off her back, to run his finger down the line of her spine.

She shivered. "Archangel."

He liked the way she said that, the sound a throaty pleasure on its own. Leaning to place his hands palms down on either side of her head, he kissed the back of her neck, felt her lower body rise toward him. As he continued to lave kisses along her spine, stroking his fingers along the sensitive inner edges of her wings at the same time, her breathing got choppier, the small shifts of her body more and more insistent . . . the earthy scent of her arousal infusing the air.

His cock jerked, but he wasn't done yet.

Caressing the base of her spine with a swirl of his tongue, he lifted himself up again and said, "It is time for the first wicked thing, Elena." He slid his hands under her hips and pushed upward.

"Not from where I'm lying." Her voice was breathless but she heeded his silent request to bring herself up onto her knees and elbows, spread her thighs.

Unable to resist, he moved both hands down the sensitive insides of her thighs, heard her make a quintessentially feminine sound of pleasure. In this position, she was open to him—luscious and flushed, her plump folds pure erotic invitation. Not giving her any warning, he put his mouth on her. She would've jerked away in sensual shock except that he had a firm grip on her thighs.

A shudder rippled over her as he took his first taste. He needed this, needed her. The day had taken a brutal toll, but here there was only his consort who had not shied at witnessing the ruthless reality of what it took to keep the Hudson from running bloodred, who had come into his arms though her anger at him had been a harsh whip.

"Raphael, please." A sensual plea.

Lifting his mouth from her, he reached down to tease a single finger through her damp heat. It caused her hand to clench on the sheets, her heartbeat to accelerate . . . but she was a hunter, a warrior. Making an unexpected move, she pulled away and onto her back with a grace that had one of her wings shimmering above him for a single second. The first thing she did was clear away the tangle of her hair. The second was to rise up onto her knees and claim his mouth in a kiss that tasted of a feminine possession he had no intention of denying.

Using the opportunity to caress the lush weight of her breasts, the sensitive peaks of her nipples, he halted her when she went to push him to his back. "No, Guild Hunter. Not tonight." He had never been loved with such fierceness as his hunter lavished on him. But the instant she put her hands, her mouth on him, he would be undone—and tonight, he wanted something else. *I would pleasure you.*

"Torture me you mean." In spite of the soft complaint, she lay back, let him come over her, stroke her from shoulder to breast to hip. He plucked at her nipple, rubbed his thumb over her collarbone, ran his lips over the curve of her hip. Started again. Her mouth was a kiss-wet enticement, the pulse in her neck an inducement to suck, to mark, the leg she curled over his hip sleek temptation.

When she rose up toward him, he rocked his clothed lower body against her.

*Oh.* The friction of Raphael's pants, the press of the zipper . . . It had Elena digging her nails into his shoulders. "I ache for you," she whispered, her need a wide-open gash in her heart.

Raphael stopped his languid strokes to reach up and push back the sweat-damp strands of hair off her forehead, cup the side of her face. "You have me, Elena. Always." His kiss was a dark claiming that had her gasping for breath, the taste of him in her every cell.

"Now."

"No." Shifting to slide his fingers between her legs, he pressed down on her clitoris, making her cry out. "Tell me," he said, gliding his fingers through her quivering flesh to the slick entrance of her body, "if I move too fast."

"You," she said, hands clenching on his shoulders as he pushed two of his fingers inside her with blunt deliberation, "are a tease."

Firmly embedded in her, he began to spread his fingers, causing her inner muscles to spasm . . . but he stopped just before she would've gone over, keeping her balanced on that finest of edges. "Not a tease"—his fingers coming together, spreading again—"but there is something to be said for patience." A single hard, fast withdrawal and thrust.

*Raphael.* Gripping at his biceps, she rolled her hips in an attempt to urge him to finish it, but he returned to the tormenting indolence of his movements even as he dipped his head to suck one of her nipples into his mouth, tasting her with that same leisurely pleasure.

Her entire body hovered on the brink. "You're in a devil of a mood."

A smile against her breast as he released her nipple with a wet sound to kiss the skin around it. "I wish to enjoy my consort. You will allow it."

Thrusting her hand into his hair, she pulled up his head.

"This consort has a knife under the mattress that she won't hesitate to use if you don't give her an orgasm soon."

He smiled. A brilliant, blinding thing. So rare were smiles such as these from her archangel that her heart stopped for a second. *Mine*, she thought, *you are mine.*

That smile grew wider. *Yes.*

It was only then that she realized she'd sent the thought to him. That he hadn't hesitated for an instant . . . it vanquished the ugliness that had awoken in her earlier, the painful echo of rejection and loneliness. She knew it would rise again—the scar was too deep, too vicious not to—but this man, her archangel, he kept hold of his own; his possessive will was her shield.

"Why are you smiling?" Her own lips curving, she stole a kiss.

"Because I have my warrior in bed, so tight"—two teasing pumps with his fingers—"hot"—teeth on her jaw—"and wet." Dipping his head, he lavished her neglected nipple with attention. The long, deep tugs pulled at things low in her abdomen, making her squirm, squeeze down on his fingers. Reaching up with his thumb in response, he circled around . . . then finally rubbed at the pulsing nub of her clitoris with the firm touch that he knew drove her crazy.

So close. *So* close.

He lifted his thumb.

"I am never going down on you again," she threatened, chest heaving.

Laughter against her skin. *What if I ask very nicely?* With that, he began to move those knowing fingers in a rapid rhythm, bending his head to suck hard at her nipple at the same time . . . before biting down with his teeth.

The orgasm rocked her so hard, she didn't only see stars, she saw whole constellations exploding in a flash of white-gold. It was glorious, leaving her a wreck. When she was able to lift her heavy eyelids at last, she found Raphael rising to strip off the rest of his clothes. The beauty of him struck her anew. That body—powerful and dangerous, his cock a heavy thickness. Eyes of a blue as vivid as the mountain sky at noon. Wings that could take him above the clouds in an unrivaled burst of speed; the breadth of those wings was exceptional.

As she watched, he reached down, fisted his cock. Pumped once. Twice.

The embers in her body flared to smoldering life. This time, when she raised her arms in silent invitation, he came. No more teasing, no more words. Her archangel pushed her thighs apart and took her with a hard, hot thrust that was an exquisite burn through flesh already swollen from the force of her first orgasm.

"Your mouth," he said, and then he was taking that mouth as he moved his cock in and out of her in a demanding rhythm that had a rich, dark heat rolling up over her body. This pleasure, it was primal and thick and visceral. It curled her toes, made her breasts swell, and the delicate flesh between her legs flush anew with a rush of blood.

She'd never felt so possessed, so indulged. The orgasm built slower, lasted longer, hit harder. But this time, she felt the scalding rush of Raphael's own pleasure, heard her archangel's powerful wings snap wide above her as the muscles in his back flexed and bunched.

Her thoughts splintered.

# 13

There was only pleasure, no assault of nightmare that night, but Elena was still in no mood to speak to Jeffrey the next morning. "When am I ever in the mood?" she muttered as she landed in front of the tony town house guarded by metal gates on the eastern side of Central Park. She'd expected the meeting to be at his office at Deveraux Enterprises but had received a message an hour earlier moving things to this location.

It was a lovely home, as genteel and elegant as the woman who was Jeffrey's second wife. The small area of greenery around it—an incredible luxury in the middle of Manhattan—was landscaped with a graceful perfection that somehow didn't cross the line into severity. Elena couldn't fault Gwendolyn's taste, for all that some small part of her resented the woman for taking Marguerite's place at Jeffrey's side. But then, Marguerite wouldn't have recognized the man her husband had become, so it was just as well.

Walking up three shallow marble steps with that hollow realization ringing in her skull, she pressed the doorbell to her father's home, a home she'd never been invited to, never been welcome in, until this moment. The bell echoed inside, as if the house was empty. A minute, then two, passed without footsteps. Fully capable of believing Jeffrey had decided to leave her standing on the doorstep, she'd turned to head back down when the door was pulled open.

She glanced over her shoulder, a cutting retort ready on her lips. It died the instant she met the composed blue eyes of the society beauty twenty years his junior whom her father had married one fall while Elena had been at boarding school. "Gwendolyn," she said with a politeness Marguerite had drummed into her. She'd run into her father's second wife once or twice over the years, but neither of them had made the effort to strengthen the relationship beyond a cool formality.

"Elena. Come in."

Glad that Gwendolyn at least didn't seem to insist on using her full name, Elena walked in, conscious of the fact the other woman was studiously *not* staring at her wings. "I expected a maid," she said, looking down the long foyer lined with small, softly lighted cubbies that held what were no doubt priceless objects d'art.

"This is family business," Gwendolyn said, tugging at the sleeve of her jewel green silk shirt.

Elena frowned, not at the words, but at the restless movement—Gwendolyn was one of the most "together" people Elena had ever come across. But now that she was paying attention, she saw that the other woman's eyes were shadowed, smudges of purple marring the rich cream of her skin. "What's wrong?" she asked, suddenly realizing this might not be about Jeffrey playing power games after all.

Gwendolyn glanced down the corridor, stepped closer. "I know you don't think of them as your sisters," she said in a low, intense tone, "but I need you to stand up for my baby."

Elena went to ask what the hell was going on when a door opened down the hall. Jeffrey's tall form appeared a moment later. Dressed in charcoal pants bearing a faint navy pinstripe paired with a white shirt, the buttons undone at the collar, he was as casual as she'd seen him in the years of her adulthood.

Before . . . She remembered the dreams, remembered the laughing paint-covered man who'd thrown her into the air and caught her on a sunny day flavored with the mingled scents of freshly cut grass, ice cream, and burgers. Long before the blood, before the death. Before the silence . . . and the shadow on the wall.

Steeling her spine against the devastating impact of the memories, she met his gaze, shielded as always by the clear glass of his metal-rimmed spectacles. "Why am I here, Jeffrey?" She knew Gwendolyn would say nothing now. Having seen them in public, she understood very well who held the reins.

It was nothing like the marriage Jeffrey had had with Elena's mother—a woman who'd teased her husband as often as she'd kissed him. A woman whose body might have survived, but whose spirit had broken under the hands of the serial killer drawn to their small family home because of Elena. That was a guilt that threatened to turn her feet to lead, leave her defenseless in the face of what was almost certainly going to be a knock-down, drag-out confrontation—her meetings with her father never ended any other way.

"I'm glad to see you have some sense of family obligation," Jeffrey said in that razor blade of a voice. "I suppose you have had more important people to visit in the days since your return to the city."

Anger, wild and hurting, slammed through the guilt. "They cared when you threw me out onto the street," she said, glad to see him flinch. "I wouldn't expect you to understand that kind of loyalty." She didn't know what she'd expected—that her father would be taken aback by her wings to the extent of dropping that glacial mask? That he'd look at her with wonder and awe? If she had, she was a fool.

"Jeffrey." Gwendolyn's mellifluous voice.

Jeffrey's jaw was tight, his eyes glittering behind those thin metal frames, but he gave a jerky nod, said, "Come into the study. The girls?" The latter words were directed at his wife.

"In Amy's room, with strict instructions not to come out."

The tendons along Jeffrey's neck went white with strain, but he said nothing as he walked into the study. Elena followed at a slower pace, wondering at the undercurrents she could sense. Maybe she'd been wrong about Gwendolyn. It certainly seemed like the other woman was flexing her claws.

Chewing on that, she found herself in a large room with mahogany bookshelves lined with leather-bound tomes, a solid desk of the same wood taking center stage. That still left plenty of room for the deep armchairs set to one side, near the French doors. It wasn't only a masculine room, it was devoid of even the slightest feminine touch.

*Snick.*

The sound of the lock clicking into place as Gwendolyn closed the door was loud in the silence. Needing space, Elena walked to the French doors and swung them open, shifting to lean against the doorjamb, one of her wings exposed to the crisp spring air, the other to the emotional chill inside the library.

Jeffrey stood on the other side of the room, against a bookshelf, his arms folded. "So, you're an angel."

"I'm afraid asking me to whore myself for you isn't going to work any better this time than it did the last," Elena snapped out, her calm disappearing in the face of that judgmental gaze.

White lines bracketed Jeffrey's mouth. "You're my daughter. I shouldn't have had to go through your Guild to find out if you were alive."

"Please." Elena gave a bitter laugh. "When have you cared whether I lived or died?" Not once in the ten years of their estrangement had he bothered to check up on her, even when she'd been badly injured in a hunt, hospitalized for weeks. "Just tell me why I'm here so I can get back to my life."

It was Gwendolyn who spoke from her position by the door, her body held in a way Elena would've never expected from Jeffrey's perfect society wife. "It's Evelyn," she said in a quiet, determined tone. "She's like you."

*"No."* The single word was gritted out by Jeffrey.

"Stop it." Gwendolyn turned on her husband. "Denying it won't make it any less true!"

Jeffrey's response was lost in the buzz of noise inside Elena's head as she tried to make sense of the curveball Gwendolyn had just thrown her. "Like me? How?" She wasn't going to make any assumptions, not here.

Gwendolyn's lips pursed tight, her hands fisted at her sides as she stared at her husband. When Jeffrey didn't speak, the black-haired woman turned to Elena. "Hunter-born," she said. "My baby is hunter-born."

If Elena hadn't been braced against the doorjamb, she'd have collapsed—her body felt as if it had taken a tremendous blow. Disbelief had her saying, "That's not possible." Hunter-born were rare, very rare, being birthed with the ability to scent-track vampires. However, it did run in families—Elena had always believed her ability came from her mother's unknown bloodline.

"We've run tests," Jeffrey snapped out. "Using Harrison and some of his friends. She can track them."

Harrison was a vampire, and Elena's brother-in-law, married to Marguerite's only other surviving daughter—Beth. The fact that Evelyn could track him . . . "You," Elena whispered, staring at Jeffrey. "It comes from *you*." He'd known, she thought, glimpsing the flash of some unnamable emotion in his eyes. All this time, when he'd been rejecting her for her "base, inhuman" occupation, he'd known it was his blood that had given it to her.

A muscle pulsed along Jeffrey's temple, his skin pulled taut over that aristocratic bone structure. "That has no place in this conversation."

Elena laughed. Harsh, jagged. She couldn't help it. "You hypocrite."

His head snapped toward her. "Be quiet, Elieanora. I'm still your father."

The hell of it was that part of her was still the little girl who'd once adored him, and that part wanted to obey. Fighting the urge, she was about to retort when she glimpsed Gwendolyn's face. The other woman looked shattered, and all at once, Elena's anger with her father, his fury at her, wasn't the most important thing. It would keep. It had kept for over a decade.

"She'll need training," she said, speaking to Gwendolyn. "Without it, she'll find it difficult to focus and concentrate." The cacophony of scents in the air, especially in a city as full of vampires as New York, could severely impact one of the hunter-born. Elena had taught herself to filter out the endless "noise" in the years before she grew old enough to join the Guild without parental permission, but it had been a painful, lonely road. One Evelyn didn't have to take. "You need to register her at Guild Academ—"

"No!" Jeffrey's voice was rigid with withheld rage. "I will not have another daughter of mine tainted by that place."

"It's a school," Elena said, keeping a white-knuckled grip on a temper that pulled aggressively at the reins. "It has specialized teachers."

"She *will not* be a hunter."

"She already is, you bastard!" Elena yelled, the reasoned adult falling apart under the echoes of childhood. "If you're not careful, you'll lose her the same way you lost me!"

The blow hit. She saw it.

For herself, she wouldn't have fought. But for Evelyn, she pushed forward, using the advantage. "Being hunter-born isn't a choice. It's part of our very makeup. If you ask her to make a choice, she'll probably choose you." Before Jeffrey could pounce on that, she added, "And she'll go mad if not in the next few years, then in the next decade." The urge to hunt was a pulse in the blood, a hunger that could consume if caged.

Gwendolyn gave a short, choked cry. "Jeffrey, I won't lose my daughter. You might be able to walk away from your child, but I won't." Turning to Elena, she said, "Can you send me the information about the Academy? Perhaps . . . would you speak to Eve?"

Shaken by the maternal love that had turned cool, composed Gwendolyn into a lioness, Elena nodded. "I'll be out in the garden if you want to bring her down." Suiting action to words, she stepped out into the small backyard and breathed in deep lungfuls of the open air. This close to Central Park, it held hints of fir and water and horses, but below that was the constant hum of the city, a touch of smoke and metal, the active press of humanity.

Rubbing at her eyes with one of her hands, she froze when she felt Jeffrey in the doorway at her back. "Is it possible the vampire who murdered the girls at the school was drawn to Evelyn?"

The question threw ice water across her senses. Because it meant he *knew*. Jeffrey knew Slater Patalis had been drawn to their small family home because of Elena. Part of her, the part that held the lost, hurt girl she'd once been, had hoped he didn't, that there might yet be hope for a relationship between them, but if he knew . . . "No," she said in a hoarse whisper. "We caught the vampire who murdered Celia and Betsy. He wasn't like Slater."

"We don't mention that name, Elieanora." Words so steady, they were steel. "Do you understand?"

Elena turned this time. "Yes." If he wanted to forget the monster, she couldn't blame him. What she could blame him for was that he'd forgotten his daughters, his wife, as well. "Evelyn needs to be trained as fast as possible. Her skills will provide a defense against attack." Pausing, she went to thrust a hand through her hair before remembering she'd braided it. "Amy should also be tutored in basic self-defense."

"Because you've made them targets."

She flinched, but didn't back down. "They're your daughters, Jeffrey," she whispered, hitting back because that was what she did with Jeffrey. That was their endless cycle of pain and recrimination. "Unless you've turned over a new leaf, there's more than one competitor out there who'd love to get his hands on your child."

Jeffrey opened his mouth, closed it without speaking. A

moment later, Evelyn squeezed past her father. She didn't get far before Jeffrey's hand came down on her shoulder. "Evelyn."

The ten-year-old, her eyes an echo of the man who towered above her, lifted up her face. "Yes, Father?"

"Remember who you are. A Deveraux." A stern reminder.

Elena wanted to say that there was no question about the fact that Eve damn well was a true Deveraux—since hunting seemed to run in the blood—but restrained herself in the face of the anxiety the girl was trying so hard to mask. "Come on, Eve," she said instead. "Let's talk."

Raphael met Jason in the skies above Staten Island, the cloud layer a thick white foam below them. "I thought you'd left the country." His spymaster was meant to be on the way to Europe.

"I had an unexpected meeting come up." Jason didn't explain further, and Raphael didn't ask. Jason would have been no good to him as a spymaster if he didn't think for himself—like the others in the Seven, the male served Raphael not out of obligation, but out of choice.

"I returned to the Tower before dawn this morning to pick up something," Jason continued. "It is as well—I can confirm the name of the one who murdered your man last night. She calls herself Belladonna, though she has also used the name Oleander Graves."

That name was no surprise. Neither was the gender of the killer—female vampires bore the same bloodlust as males—but the speed with which Jason had tracked her down was. "How did you find her?"

Jason braced his wings against the push of the wind. "Elena will be able to verify from the scent, but Neha's assassin is not as clever as she believes. She said some indiscreet things to the dancers at Erotique that made it child's play to tie the murder to her."

Raphael raised an eyebrow. "I did not know you patronized

Erotique, Jason." The club of choice for the more high-ranked vampires, its dancers and hostesses were considered to be both accomplished and sophisticated.

"Illium," Jason said in short explanation. "He spent some time there after helping Venom take care of the scene. When he saw me come in this morning, he asked if I could corroborate his suspicions using my contacts—I was also able to pinpoint her current residence." He named the apartment building and number.

Making a mental note of it, Raphael put aside the matter of Neha's pet vampire for the present. The assassin would be uncomplicated enough to dispatch now that she'd been located. "Tell me about Illium." The visit to Erotique could've been nothing, a diversion to take his mind off the upcoming visit by the Hummingbird, but given the blue-winged angel's fascination with mortals, it could augur something far more dangerous.

"There is no need for concern," Jason said at once. "Galen would've warned us if there was."

Raphael agreed on that point. The two angels were fast friends and had been for centuries. "And you, Jason? Who will warn me about you?"

# 14

His spymaster turned so that his tattoo fell in direct sunlight, striking and speaking of a dedication beyond pain. "I will, Sire. Then you will execute me as you promised when I became one of your Seven."

Raphael met Jason's eyes. "The promise was made and will be kept if necessary, but I prefer you alive. You're the best spymaster in the Cadre."

Jason's lips curved in the faintest of smiles, a rare sight. "They've all tried to recruit me—Charisemnon and Favashi in particular."

"I would expect nothing else." But he knew Jason would not betray him. The black-winged angel had sworn allegiance to Raphael on a field carpeted with a wash of blood. None of it had been Jason's. But his blade had run slick with it. The next target would've been his own body if Raphael hadn't stepped in.

Bonds forged in such black fire didn't easily break.

Turning back to the matter at hand, he said, "I'll speak to Elena about the scent." His instinct was to protect her from the harsher aspects of his world, but she was hunter-born.

*Don't you dare stop me from being what I am. Don't you dare.*

She'd been weak, unable to fly when she'd said that, but he'd never forget the look in her eyes. If he crossed that line, if he denied that part of her, he would shatter her. He knew he was capable of such cruelty, but he also knew he'd break if Elena broke.

"Sire," Jason said, cutting into his thoughts, "there is another reason why I returned to the city. You asked me to keep my ears open for any reports of disquieting behavior by the other archangels."

Raphael flashed back to the red haze that had clouded his vision, the rage that had all but stolen his will. "Who?"

"Astaad." Jason named the Archangel of the Pacific Isles as a gust shoved at them from the left. "It's difficult to get spies into his inner circle. In their own way, his people are as loyal to him as the Seven are to you."

Raphael adjusted his wings without thought, holding his position above the clouds. "He rules with an alternately beneficent and bloody hand."

"He also treats his women as precious."

Astaad's harem was composed of the most exquisitely beautiful vampires in the world, women he cosseted and protected. It was a well-known aspect of his character, but for Jason to remark on it . . . "He has done something to his women."

A nod that made Jason's hair gleam blue black in the light. "The operative I managed to get into his court is a low-class servant, but she's been listening to the women who tend to the harem and word is that Astaad beat one of his favorite concubines almost to a pulp."

"Astaad would consider such an act a stain on his honor." Raphael thought again of the way he'd executed Ignatius, knew that if Astaad had been in the grip of the same fury, then the concubine was lucky to be alive. "Continue to keep an eye on the situation. Send word as soon as you have any further information."

Leaving Jason, Raphael made his way back toward Manhattan, flying low enough to see other angels going about their tasks above the gleaming steel and glass of the high-rises. The sun was bright today, and his city glittered like a faceted gem beneath the dazzling light—it was no wonder others in the Cadre watched it with covetous eyes. What they did not understand was that to hold this city, you could not hold humanity in contempt.

*Archangel.*

Angling his head at the brush of that voice kissed by spring and steel, he saw the distinctive shine of Elena's hair sweeping around the side of the Tower. He watched his consort fly to him with slow, deep sweeps of her wings—she had been awake only months, and already, she flew with such grace and strength. *Come, Guild Hunter.*

She changed direction to follow the path he took over the high-rises and the rush of the East River to the roof of a small apartment building. Landing beside the translucent blue waters of the pool in the center, he turned to watch her as she backwinged to a smooth landing not far from where he stood, the tips of her wings a shimmering dawn-edged gold. "You have been practicing your landings."

"Illium wouldn't let me break yesterday afternoon until I got it right nine attempts out of ten. And Montgomery had brought out fresh *peach pie.*" The attempt at humor couldn't quite hide the hurt in her eyes.

Anger twisted through his veins, a cold, remorseless thing that saw nothing wrong with pain, with death. "What did your father say to you?"

Pushing a hand through her hair, she strode past the large planters and to the edge of the pool, hunkering down to dip her fingers desultorily in the water. "Nothing. Just . . . the usual crap." Then she told him about her youngest half sister, her voice hot with naked anger. "It fucking destroys his moral high ground, doesn't it?"

"Your father doesn't strike me as the kind of man who would ever admit to being at fault." No, Jeffrey Deveraux was far too determined to win at any cost.

Rising, she flicked off the water. "Yeah." Then she did something he would've never expected. Stepping forward, she buried her face in his chest.

Trust, he thought, as he enclosed her within the protection of his arms, his wings; there was such trust in what she had done. "I have a task for you, Guild Hunter," he said, weaving the fingers of one hand through the pale silk of her hair, unraveling her braid.

"Good." A rough statement.

"The vampire who spilled blood last night may be in this building. You must hunt."

A hum of energy in the body under his hands and then she was pulling away to head for the rooftop entrance to the building. "The scent was rich, distinctive, the notes unusual. I should be able to narrow it down very fast if he is—or was—anywhere in the vicinity."

*She, Elena*, he corrected, remembering the once tested her with two barely-Made vampires. Sh shocked by their skittering, animalistic appearance but ha faltered in her task. *Neha's assassin is a woman.*

"Figures." Opening the door, she hesitated. "This place is too narrow for wings. Not a good tactical move to be trapped in there—and not necessary. The scent of oleanders in bloom . . . I can almost touch it. Too strong for her not to be inside."

"It won't be difficult to draw her out," he said once she returned to his side. However, when he flew down to the window that looked into the vampire's room, what he saw had him calling off the hunt. *She's dead. There is a noose wrapped around her throat—I'm fairly certain it will turn out to be a snake.*

Elena dropped down beside him. *Neha decided to clean up her mess.*

*So it would seem. Dmitri will organize the body retrieval.*

*Once it's out of there, I want a chance to double-check the scent. Just in case.* Flying down below him and then back up with an awkward grace that did nothing to hide the potential of what she would one day become, Elena brushed silky strands of hair out of her eyes. *Do you have time to come spar with me?*

*Missing Galen?*

A dark word. *Bastard was good. But you're meaner when you're in the mood.*

Raphael wasn't sure he liked that. *I would never hurt you, Elena.*

*Of course not.* She waved at a young blond angel sitting with his legs hanging off one of the high balconies of the Tower as they passed. The male beamed, waved back. *But you also don't have to worry about an archangel zapping you if you put a bruise on me. We can go at it full tilt, and I really need some no-holds-barred sessions.*

Only she could speak to him thus. Only she could make him feel young in a way he had not felt for over a thousand years. *We'll train at the house.* Bypassing a group of angels coming in to land on the Tower roof, he took them toward the Hudson. *Afterward*, he said as they hit the airspace above the water, *you may thank your trainer in the most age-old of ways.*

Warmth uncurling in her abdomen at the sensual order, Elena went to tease Raphael when a roaring wind came out of nowhere, crumpling her wings and threatening to send her slamming into the suddenly raging waters below. *Raphael!* The mental cry was instinctive, tearing out of her even as a strange, exotic scent wrapped a suffocating blanket around her senses.

The rain and the wind in her mind, a drenching storm that shoved away all other impressions. *My apologies, Elena.* He took control, overwhelming her will with his own as he twisted her body in a way she would've never done herself, allowing her to spread out her wings and find stability moments before she would've hit the water.

Her mind was her own again a split second afterward.

The whole thing had happened so fast she hadn't had time to feel much beyond the adrenaline pumping through her body, but now, as she winged herself to a balanced position, she blew out a breath. Once, when they'd first met, Raphael had said something to her.

*I could make you crawl, Elena. Do you really want me to force you onto your hands and knees?*

"I thought you couldn't do that anymore," she whispered out loud, knowing he remained connected to her. "I thought I had shields now."

*You do, but you must focus to hold them. Panic throws you wide open.*

"Hell." She knew he was right. She *had* panicked. Flight was still new to her—and the terror of falling was one so visceral, it was hard to hold on to logical thought in the face of it.

Dropping down to join her at the lower altitude she was just managing to maintain, her muscles taut with shock, Raphael flew by her side as she pushed herself home. It felt like it took forever, but she came to a staggering stop on the grounds below their bedroom at last. Raphael swept down in front of her an instant later, catching her shaky form with a hold on her upper arms.

"Thanks," she said, bracing herself with her palms on her thighs when he released her. "Not just for now." She looked up. "For before."

His eyes pulsed with surprise. "I expected your anger."

"I'm not stupid. Stubborn, but not stupid." Rising to her full height, she blew out a breath. "I don't like the fact that I'm still so vulnerable to you, but fact is, that isn't going to change overnight." She'd taken an archangel as a lover knowing the disparity of strength between them.

"You know I'd fight you to my last breath if you attempted to coerce me in a normal situation. What happened over the water"—her heart raced in remembered shock—"was in no way a normal situation." A blast of wind crashed into them right then, ripping the last words from her lips, clawing at her wings as if it would tear them off.

Raphael tugged her into the protection of his body, spreading his wings over them as the wind punched again and again. *Do you sense it?*

She went motionless at his question. The wind . . . it carried a scent. Faint. So, so faint. And so unusual that she couldn't pinpoint it—except she knew it was the same thing she'd scented the instant her wings crumpled. *What is that?*

*A rare black orchid found in a rain forest deep in the Amazon.*

She shivered. "It truly is her?"

*So it would seem.*

When the rage of wind finally died away with a last cutting whip, she looked up and brushed midnight strands of hair off Raphael's face, revealing the incredible masculine beauty that had the power to make mortals weep. "She isn't that strong yet." The entire thing had only lasted a minute at most.

"No." *But it appears she has noticed my consort.*

"God, I'm slow today." That blast of wind on the Hudson hadn't been a chance gust. It had been an arrow meant to shatter her bones when she hit the water at high velocity. "So she's conscious?"

Raphael shook his head. "I've had Jessamy doing some research," he said, mentioning the woman who was the repository of angelic knowledge, the keeper of their histories . . . and one of the kindest angels Elena had ever met. "Come, we will speak of it inside."

They walked into the house, turning in the direction of the library, a room that sang to the curious heart of her nature. The first time she'd entered it, she'd noticed only the books arranged on the wall-to-wall shelves on the ground level, the fireplace to the left, the gorgeous wooden table and chairs set below the window.

But like all angelic rooms, this one had a soaring ceiling—and that ceiling was a work of art, the wooden beams carved with painstaking attention to detail and inlaid with darker pieces that were perfectly contoured to fit. "Aodhan?"

"No," Raphael said, following her gaze. "That was done by a human, a master at his craft."

"Amazing." She wondered at the pride the man must've felt to build such a room for an archangel.

Raphael stroked his hand down her hair, his touch oddly tender.

"Archangel?"

"I'm far more powerful than when Caliane disappeared." His words held a haunting sense of pain, of memory. "But I am still her son, Elena. Thousands upon thousands of years younger."

Elena shook her head. "You were younger than Uram, too. Yet you won."

"My mother is beyond Uram, beyond Lijuan." Raphael's words sent a chill down Elena's spine. "She lived as an archangel for tens of thousands of years. There is no knowing what she has become."

Thinking of what Lijuan had done to Beijing, the stench of smoke and death that was said to linger over the empty crater than had once been a vibrant, living city, Elena felt fear attempt to take a clawhold on her heart. She refused to allow it, her love for this archangel far stronger than any imagined foe. "She doesn't know what you've become either, Raphael."

Her archangel's expression didn't change, but she knew he'd heard her. "Jessamy," he said, "tells me that Caliane is likely in a half-dream state at present. She has some semblance of consciousness but may have no real knowledge of the acts she's committing."

"She could think this is all a dream?"

Closing his hand around the back of her neck, he tugged her closer. "Yes." His kiss was more than a little dangerous. *But we did not come here to talk about Caliane.*

She pressed her lips to the hard angle of his jaw, anticipation burning away the last vestiges of the fear she'd felt as she fell. "Let's get sweaty."

# 15

An hour later, Elena was a hell of a lot more than sweaty. Raphael had given her the no-holds-barred combat she'd asked for—and more. "You know what makes me really mad?" she said, hands on her knees on the other side of the rough practice circle they'd set out on the lawn.

Raphael, shirtless chest gleaming with the lightest film of perspiration, pushed back his hair. "Enough talking," he ordered. "Up."

She bared her teeth at him. "It's the fact that you're not even breathing hard while I feel like I got done over by a pack of vamps." But she rose to her full height, because if she could learn to hold her own against Raphael for so much as a second, she'd be unbeatable against most vampires and humans.

He came at her without warning, a blur of speed. She wrenched out of the way and went down hard. Galen's earlier training kept her from landing awkwardly on her wings, but they got crushed into the grass nonetheless as Raphael swept down to pin her. "Galen didn't teach me that," she said, chest heaving underneath him as he pinioned her hands above her head.

"What?" Heat blazed off him, his eyes glittering in a way she usually only ever saw in bed.

She couldn't help it. Arching up, she kissed him, flicking out her tongue to taste the aggressive maleness pumping through his body. "The thing you do with your wings." Instead of answering, he kicked her legs wider and suddenly the position was a hell of a lot more intimate. "Raphael"—a husky censure—"Montgomery is probably keeping an eye on us."

"He would never be so ill-bred." A hot wet kiss against her neck. "The wings?"

She forced her brain into gear. "You use them. Galen taught me to keep them out of the way, so I wouldn't nick them with knives or the short sword, but you use your wings for balance, and you even go slightly airborne to avoid blows." She'd never seen anyone move with that kind of lethal grace. Galen was a different kind of a fighter—more brutal, harsher in his movements.

Another kiss, the feel of teeth. She hissed, went to hook her leg over him when he rose off her, extending a hand to help her up. "Galen taught you what was necessary for survival," he said once she was back on her feet. "He had to focus on tactics he knew you could master in the timeframe we had before Lijuan's ball."

Reaching up to redo her ponytail, Elena nodded. "I figured. I'm guessing using wings like you do will take me considerably longer to learn."

"At this stage," Raphael said, walking over to pick up two short swords from where she'd left them on the edge of the practice circle, "your wings are more of a liability in combat."

She caught the swords by the hilts and watched him pick up a set of much smaller knives. "Giving me the advantage?"

A smile with more than a hint of arrogance. "You are but a babe in arms yet, Elena." Knives held to either side, gaze focused on her. "It would hardly be fair to take you down again so soon."

She settled into a crouch, wings pinned tightly to her back. "Come on then, angel boy." She kept her eyes on the muscles in his shoulders, saw the instant one tensed.

A split second later, they were moving in a wicked, dangerous dance of steel and bodies. She'd never really had a chance
to spar with Raphael like this, and damn if it wasn't the most
fun she'd ever had. The archangel was good. Better than good.
Not that that should've come as a surprise, she thought, blocking his blades and striking out with her own as she spun away.
None of the Seven would have given their allegiance over to
an archangel they didn't respect on the battlefield.

A lick of iron in the air.

"Stop."

"Damn it." She dropped her hands, glancing at the fine
hairline scratch on her left arm. "Would that have cost me my
arm in real combat?"

Raphael saw the disgusted look on Elena's face and had
to bite back a smile of pride. Hair pulled off her face with
warrior-like practicality and sweat sheening her body, her
musculature fluid and graceful, this was his consort. "That
was a tactical error," he said, knowing she had the ability to
become unbeatable with those blades. All she needed was a
little more time to grow into her immortality—and further
skilled instruction.

"You took a chance," he pointed out, "and dropped your
guard on the left because you thought I couldn't turn that
fast, but don't ever judge another angel's—or even an older
vampire's—agility by your own." She'd only been angel-Made
for less than half a year. The fact that she was already blindingly
good, her hunter instincts coming to the fore, was no reason to
go easy on her. If anything, she needed to be pushed harder.

She raised her blades. "Once more through."

"Go."

The clash of steel, the sweaty, slippery slide of bodies,
the wild *life* of it all exhilarated Raphael. He sparred with his
Seven once in a while, but it had always been a practical exer-
cise to keep his physical skills sharp. Elena fought like it was
part of her very self, and her joy in it infected him until it was
a pulse beneath his skin.

*Then she will kill you. She will make you mortal.*

Lijuan knew nothing, he thought as he dodged the blade of one short sword and flicked his knife under the strap of Elena's tank top, cutting it in a single swipe. He might heal slower, might injure easier, but he was alive in a way Lijuan had never been and never would be—because she had killed the human who had once, long ago, threatened to make her mortal.

Ignoring the strap he'd cut, Elena swung back and . . . threw both blades. Taken by surprise, he bent backward, crushing his wings into the grass—one blade passed a bare inch from his face. The other nicked his cheek as it thunked into the earth behind him.

"Goddamn it, Raphael!" Elena was cupping his face in her hands before he could remind her it was never a good idea to throw away her weapons. "You're not supposed to get injured. That's the only reason we're using real blades."

For the first time in forever, he was stunned to silence. Not by her words, but by the tenderness in her hands, the worry in her eyes. He was an archangel. He'd been wounded far, far worse and shrugged it off. But then, there had been no woman with skin kissed by the sunset and eyes of storm gray to tear into him for daring to get himself hurt.

"Are you listening to me? I could've hurt you!" *Again.*

He shook off his stunned bemusement to answer her assertion, hearing the unspoken word. "I could've deflected the blades using my power. But that would not make this in any way a fair fight." *It is nothing similar to when you shot me, Elena. I was dangerous to you that night.*

In answer, she angled his face to the light, stood on tiptoe to examine the cut. "It's much deeper than the insect bites you've given me when I make a mistake."

Moving his knives to one hand, he cupped her cheek. "This is less than an insect bite to me. Do not worry that you will have to seek another consort."

"Don't even joke about that." But she relaxed, her hands falling to rest on her hips. "So how did I do?"

"You threw away your weapons. Galen taught you better than that."

"You were about to get me. It was meant to distract you so I could go for my knives—or in a real fight, for my gun." Her gaze dipped to his left wing, making it clear she was referring to the weapon designed to disable angelic wings.

Raphael didn't like the fact that he'd forced her to defend herself with such violence that night, but he did not regret the starburst pattern of golden feathers that was the scar he wore on his wing. As far as he was concerned, it was as much a mark of Elena's claim on him as the amber ring he wore on his finger. "It may be a good strategy in certain situations," he said, looking at things from her point of view. "We'll work on it."

When she moved as if to pick up the swords, he shook his head. "Not today. You're starting to lag."

She made a face. "You're right. I'll cool down, shower, then I have an errand to run." The slightest pause that he only caught because he was looking right at her. "I might ask Illium for some low-key flying lessons later—the vertical take-off thing is kicking my ass, but I'm not giving up."

He said nothing until they'd stowed their weapons and were stripping for the shower. "What is this errand that puts such sorrow in your eyes, Elena?"

Her naked back tensed, then shuddered. "I haven't told you something," she said in a rush of words as he curved his fingers around her nape, stroking his thumb gently across her skin. "Remember the first time you sent Illium to watch over me?"

"Yes. It was after a meeting with your father—you went to a bank."

"There was a safety deposit box there for me. Jeffrey . . . I don't know why, but he kept . . ." It was hard to speak, to think about her father's baffling actions. He'd thrown her out of his home, called her an abomination, and couldn't speak to her without bitter anger flowing between them like so much spilled wine. But . . .

"My mother's things," she whispered, turning to face Raphael. "He kept my mother's things. They're in a storage unit out in Brooklyn." She'd flown over the facility early that morning but hadn't been able to make herself land. "I'm so scared to go there. Because when I do . . . I have to admit all over again that she left me, that she didn't love me enough to stay."

Tears burned at the backs of her eyes, but she refused to let them fall—she'd cried so much for her mom, but then she'd gotten angry. "Sometimes, I hate her." That was her biggest secret and biggest sin.

Raphael leaned across to touch his forehead to hers. *What I feel for Caliane is beyond hate at times—for what she did, the atrocities she committed. And yet . . .*

"Yes." She buried her face in his neck. "And yet . . ."


As it turned out, she didn't have to tear the scab off that particular wound that day. Her cell phone was beeping with a message when she came out of the shower. Grabbing it, she frowned. "It's from the Guild." Guilty relief curled down her spine when she called back and was told to suit up for a hunt. "I'll be there as soon as I can."

Raphael finished buttoning his shirt, the slots for his wings flowing with smooth perfection over his back. "What does the Guild need from you?"

She began to dress. "There's a bloodlust-ridden vampire in Boston."

"The senior angel in that territory should have sent me a report." Walking over, he picked up his own cell phone, found a message. "Two people are already dead."

Boots on, Elena began strapping on her weapons, including Deacon's gift to her. She had no control-chip-embedded weapons, but since Ransom—already close to Boston—would've been issued one, that wasn't a problem. The control chips effectively knocked out a vampire's will for a short period, giving a hunter the chance to restrain the target—because under normal circumstances, the Guild's people did not kill.

Execution was an angel's job.

However, since bloodlust was involved in this case, they'd

been given the go-ahead to execute if retrieval proved too dangerous. "Ransom's almost there but he's got no backup." She called the other hunter her "almost friend" because they had a tendency to irritate each other as often as they made one another laugh, but she'd spill blood for him in a heartbeat. As he would for her.

"I see."

Elena set her jaw at that cool statement and finished strapping the miniature flamethrower to her other thigh. "I let it go before, but I can't anymore." Walking to the vanity, she began to plait her damp hair with practiced quickness so that it would stay out of her way. The fine, silky stuff had a tendency to escape even the tightest braid, but the damp should help keep it contained. "You took a hunter as your consort, Raphael."

"That is no longer the only factor." An answer made in the tone of an immortal used to getting what he wanted. "More than one archangel would like your head as a trophy."

"Is it life if you live it in a cage?" A taut question as, braid done, she began to strap on her knife sheaths over her forearms. "I won't live like that."

Twisting her braid around his hand as he came to stand behind her, Raphael pressed his mouth to the exposed skin of her nape. "Take the chopper. You don't have the endurance to fly that far."

Emotionally vulnerable to him in a way that scared her at times like this, she pulled away, turned. "Who'll be piloting the chopper?"

"Venom."

"That's your final offer?"

When the archangel merely looked at her with those eyes of pitiless blue, she had her answer. "Fine." Frustration turned her muscles rigid. "But make sure he keeps out of my way."

Elena made a call to Sara once they were in the air, stiffly conscious of the vampire at the chopper controls beside her.

God, she was so mad at Raphael. She'd known this fight was coming, but that made it no easier to handle—especially when Raphael simply refused to give ground.

No negotiation. Nothing but an archangel's expectation of obedience.

If he thought that was the end of—

"Ellie?" Sara's voice sounded as if it was coming from the moon. "Where are you?"

"Approximately halfway to Boston," she said, then got straight to the reason why she'd called. "Why did you pull me in?" Not that she wasn't happy to be back in the field, but the Guild had any number of hunters at its disposal.

Sara's voice dropped out for a second, came back. ". . . all over the place. We need everyone we've got."

"What?" Elena pressed on the headphones. "Repeat that."

"Vampires breaking their Contracts all over the place," Sara said. "It's like some weird—" A crackle of noise and the call dropped completely. But Elena had heard enough—chaos on this scale could only be connected to one thing . . . only one being.

Caliane.

# 16

Ransom was waiting near the deserted concrete pier in Boston where he'd asked her and Venom to land when she'd made contact as they came into the city. Lifting her off her feet as soon as she reached him, he planted a smacking kiss on her laughing lips. "Ellie, those wings sure are sexy."

God, it was good to see him. "Put me down, gorgeous."

"Archangel the jealous type?" He continued to hold her, which argued to his strength—her muscle mass was high to begin with and her wings only added to that.

Pushing at his shoulders, she freed herself. "I thought we had a vampire to catch?"

"Yeah, come on." His face—a stunning mix of Native American skin and bone structure, and eyes of Irish green—was suddenly all business. "The trail leads to a particular section of warehouses about five minutes away on foot. That's why I asked you to land here."

"If you're so close," she said, "why did you wait for me?" Pretty as he was, Ransom was also one of the Guild's top hunters, someone she'd have at her back anytime.

"It's not just one, Ellie." He began to lead her past a huge boathouse and toward a number of warehouses she could see in the distance. "And they're helping each other."

"Shit." It was rare, very rare, for vampires to hunt together—but when they did . . . "What's the body count?"

"Twenty-two, last I heard." Ransom's long hair, a sleek tail down his back, shifted in the breeze as he gave her the update. "But that was half an hour ago."

"They can't be feeding if they're moving that fast." Which meant they were killing for the hell of it, and that made them a plague. "You said they're helping each other—are they acting like they're thinking?"

"Not on a complex level, but someone's definitely home upstairs. Weird, huh?"

Elena thought of Ignatius, wondered if Neha hadn't gotten the message after all.

*Iron in the air, thick, fresh.*

Ransom brought up a hand at the same instant that she caught the scent.

Raising her wings and tucking them tight to her body—something she'd finally learned to do on command—she took a long, quiet breath.

*Motor oil and fish.*

*Blood, rancid fat, effluent.*

*Blueberries bursting open, their juices staining the earth.*

Any and all of them could be vampiric scents, but Ransom didn't need her nose today. He needed good old-fashioned backup. Pulling out the weapon Deacon had designed for her, the one she'd taken to calling her "blade-bow," she fell in behind him as the other hunter led her and Venom through the labyrinthine passageways between the warehouses.

The day had turned dull about an hour ago, clouds racing to cover the sun, and now, a fat pellet of rain hit Elena's cheek. She bit back a curse. If the vampires decided to run, the rain would be their willing accomplice in washing away the trail. Which meant they had to neutralize the targets here—retrieval was simply not on the table, not if the vampires were hunting in a pack.

Her wing brushed against something sharp, snagged. She bit down on her lower lip to quiet her gasp and stopped just long enough to unhook her wing from the rusty nail. Blood darkened the midnight blue feathers near the center of her right wing, but she was more worried about tetanus. An instant later, she remembered she was no longer vulnerable to disease—she still wasn't going to be punching corroded nails into her body anytime soon.

Continuing to hug one side of the thin alleyway as Ransom took the other, she glanced back at Venom. The vampire was sticking to her but keeping enough of a distance that he wouldn't be a liability in a fight—in fact, given what she'd seen of his skills, he'd be an asset.

*Blueberries, ripe, ripe blueberries.*

She hissed under her breath at Ransom. When he turned, she motioned toward a warehouse about three down from where they currently stood. She saw him nod just before the skies opened and rain sleeted down like some great faucet had been turned on in the heavens.

"Fuck," she muttered, and abandoning all ideas of subtlety, ran toward the back of the warehouse as Ransom circled around to the front. She was only two feet from the wooden door when she caught a hint of sharp, astringent mint in the air, and then she was being slammed down onto the wet asphalt. Skin tore off her cheek, and her right hand landed awkwardly enough that she might have broken her wrist if she hadn't begun to half roll at the instant of contact. As it was, one of her wings crumpled under her with a searing pain that she hoped like hell didn't mean she'd broken one of the fine bones within.

The weight on her back was gone the next moment, and she didn't have to look to know that Venom was dealing with the vampire who'd attacked. She took one glance to make sure he had the upper hand—oh, yeah—before leaving him to it and closing the distance to the door. She could hear the hard, thudding sounds of fighting now, as well as a wave of eerie laughter from within, which meant they'd ambushed Ransom as well.

Her hand tightened on the blade-bow.

"Wait." Venom's breath at her ear, his hand on her arm. "Go up, come in through the roof—from the state of this place, it's probably half rotten anyway."

That would be a huge advantage but—"Can't do a vertical takeoff."

Venom went down on one knee, his eyes preternaturally vivid in the rain, his sunglasses having been lost in the fight. When he cupped his hands, she realized what he intended and slung the blade-bow over her shoulder. "Ready?" She put one foot in his cupped hands, rested her hands on his muscled shoulders. At his nod, she said, "Go."

He lowered his hands and then he *pushed*. Vampires were fast and strong, but she'd never have expected the power he put behind his assist. Twisting in midair, she managed to grip the lip of the roof, feeling the metal cut into her palms deep enough that blood gushed warm and thick. But that mattered nothing while Ransom was down there alone.

Using the muscle that made her hunter-born, she managed to get herself over and onto the roof—and though one of her wings complained a little, it didn't appear broken. It was obvious Venom had been right about the condition of the roof. Knowing Ransom didn't have much time, she retrieved her bow, then ran across the cracked and rotting structure until she came to a part that caved in, taking her with it.

She allowed herself to fall, spreading out her wings to slow her momentum as she hit the warmer air inside the warehouse. Startled bloodstained faces lifted up to hers, male and female both, red swirling in those eyes. *Bloodlust.* That confirmed, she didn't give them any warning, just started firing. The little spinning blades cut through necks, sliced through brains, blew through hearts . . . Jesus, she thought. Deacon was *good*.

Feet hitting the floor with a jarring *thump*, she yelled, "Ransom!"

"Not dead yet!" came the response from within a tangle of vampires.

That was when she saw the eyes in the walls, the vampires crouching up on ledges, ready to pounce. She turned just in time to take out two behind her. Christ, how many of them were there? Then there was no more time to think—her wings made her so vulnerable on the ground that she couldn't afford to let them get close. Using the blade-bow one-handedly, she began firing the miniature flamethrower with the other. Not so useful a weapon when in flight, but it did a hell of a job in close combat.

Screams, high and shrill, filled the warehouse as flesh sizzled and charred, the smell nauseatingly akin to a backyard barbeque. And it wasn't only her and Ransom doing the damage. She glimpsed Venom with the wicked curved knives he liked—where in the blazes had he pulled those from?—slicing off vampiric heads with that reptilian speed that both repelled and fascinated her. Blood fountained as he executed a stacked blonde vampire about to claw at his face, spraying his cinnamon skin with ruby red droplets.

"Ransom, look out!" she yelled as she saw one of the crouchers go for her friend.

Ransom lifted a gun, shot, even as she drilled one of her blades into the vampire's skull. The male fell, his body twitching as if he was fighting to rise in spite of the fact his brains were leaking down his temples. But, he was damaged enough that they didn't have to worry about him for a while.

Fingers, slick and cold on the tip of her wing.

*No.* Her wings were highly sensitive and she hated having them touched by evil. The urge to spin, to act without thought was almost blinding, but she fought it and instead turned Deacon's blade-bow backward, calculating the location of the vamp from the scent of honey and marigolds so thick in her nose.

A gurgling sound, fingers spasming then slipping away told her she'd hit her mark. Firing the flamethrower at a vamp who was running toward her in a fucking four-legged lope, she fried the petite brunette midjump before swiveling on her heel to turn the flames on the vampire who'd touched her wing . . . and who was trying to clamp his bloodstained teeth onto her feathers.

When he met her eyes, he smiled. "She wakes." It was a near-sibilant whisper, his throat almost destroyed by her blade—and still his eyes, they gleamed with an unholy joy. "She wakes."

Shaking off the shiver crawling up her spine, Elena said, "Yeah, well, it's goodnight for you." With that, she turned the flamethrower on the sucker.

When she swiveled back around, it was to a scene of carnage . . . with only two other people left upright. Ransom held two smoking big-ass guns, one on either side of his body, his legs spread as he stood checking to see if any of the vamps near him still breathed. His face was bloody with claw marks, his black T-shirt almost shredded off him, and his hair, having come loose in the struggle, ran a silky black rain down his back.

By the door near where she'd been attacked stood Venom, blades swiveling in his hands, his suit jacket and tie gone, his white shirt splattered with blood. His hair, for once, wasn't GQ-perfect. Instead, it tumbled over his forehead, and paired with his feral smile, it turned him shockingly attractive in a very disturbing way.

His eyes, slitted and inhuman, met hers at that moment. "I can't hear any pulses."

"We'll check one by one to be sure," she said, chest rising and falling in short, sharp breaths like the two men. "This group was far too organized—we don't want any of them waking up."

Silently, they did exactly that, covering every inch of the warehouse. "I count fifteen," Ransom said, when they met in the middle.

"Yeah, that's what I got," Venom added. "There's one outside, too, so sixteen in total."

Ransom really looked at the other man for the first time, shook his head, stared again. "Holy hell, your eyes are like a fucking viper's."

Venom raised an eyebrow. "You have hair prettier than one of Astaad's concubines."

Ransom gave the vampire the finger. Venom grinned.

Certain that all was now well in the male world, Elena reached into her pocket and pulled out a spare hair tie, throwing it to Ransom. "I'd say this was impossible if I wasn't standing in the middle of it. We have what, maybe three rogue vamps in the state in a year?"

"Rogues, yes," Ransom pointed out, pulling his hair back in that rough way men had of doing. "Bloodlust? We'd get maybe one that was totally whackjob."

"The Sire keeps a tight control on his vampires," Venom said, going down on his haunches to wipe off his bloody blades using the shirt of a fallen vamp. "This simply shouldn't have happened."

Remembering what that last vampire had said, Elena knew there was a high chance Caliane was behind this, but she kept her mouth shut. Much as it pained her to keep a secret from Ransom and the Guild, she'd agreed to be Raphael's consort. He had her first loyalty. She wouldn't betray that trust—more, she wouldn't share the shreds of information she had when nothing could be done about it.

"We need to ID the vampires," she said, bending to strap the blade-bow to one thigh and the miniature flamethrower to the other, "notify the authorities."

"I'll do the authorities," Ransom said, pulling out his cell. "They know I was on this track."

"I know at least two of the vampires from sight," Venom said, disappearing his blades into the crisscrossing black sheaths on his back that she could see now that he wasn't wearing his jacket. "Give me a few minutes to see how many others I can ID."

As Venom did that, Elena went around checking for wallets where they hadn't been fried by her flames or otherwise destroyed. She ended up finding seven pieces. Venom ID'ed four others from sight, which left them with five unknowns, most of them either charred beyond recognition or missing a face courtesy of Ransom's gun.

"The angel in charge of this region is on his way with the authorities," Ransom told them, closing his cell phone. "He'll take care of the rest of the IDs. Looks like he's going to need to break out the DNA kit for a few."

Elena looked toward the hole in the roof where she'd entered the warehouse and found rain still pouring in. "I think we all need a shower."

The men didn't say anything as they followed her out of the warehouse and into the torrential downpour. The water around them turned to rust, then a pale orange, then sepia, until finally, it ran clear. Blinking the rain from her eyes, she walked back to the door.

"Ellie." Ransom's voice. "Our job is done. We just hold the scene until the cops arrive."

Elena nodded. "I know, but I want to check their scents. This kind of a mass outbreak . . . for all we know, it could be a mutant virus."

Of course both men fell into step beside her, though they'd already verified that every single one of the vampires was well and truly dead. Vampires weren't true immortals. They could be killed not only by other vampires and angels, but also by humans—beheading and fire were the best methods, though removal of the heart also worked if you then cut or, in Ransom's case, blew off the head to make certain.

Leaving the two men to talk in quiet tones near the doorway, she went from body to body, searching, searching . . .

*Dark, lyrical, lush.*

There it was again, that haunting, intricate scent beneath the more brash smells of the fallen vampires. She was almost certain she'd scented the same thing when the wind threatened to crash her into the Hudson . . . except something niggled at her, some "off" note she couldn't quite identify. "Damn." She knew for certain she'd be tracking down the essence of this particular black orchid as soon as she got back to the city.

Deep in the heart of Manhattan, Raphael snapped the neck of a bloodlust-ridden vampire after blazing through his mind to take what he needed to know. That information proved both sickening and . . . sad. Some would have said the Archangel of New York had no mercy in him, but he didn't enjoy the waste of life. Most of these vampires had gone mad beyond any hope of recovery.

An insane vampire could not be allowed to continue to live, because driven by the urge to consume blood far beyond that which was necessary for life, that vampire would kill hundreds of innocents. "Under five decades old," he said to Dmitri as the leader of his Seven came to stand beside him after dispatching his own prey. Around them, the city lay wrapped in a cloak of fear and danger, the lights in the high-rises fragile bulwarks against the dark that had fallen an hour earlier.

"Mine, too," Dmitri replied, the edge of his long black coat lifting slightly in the breeze. "Venom just sent me a message— all the ones he recognized in Boston were young. No one over six decades old."

"She is not yet conscious in truth, her strength weak," Raphael said. "Yet she can do this." Cause carnage on a scale unseen for centuries, turning formerly sane vampires into killing machines.

"Sire . . . Aodhan and Naasir, how close are they to finding her?"

Raphael looked up at the sliver of moon visible in the cloud-heavy sky. "My mother," he said to one of the very few men he trusted, "was intelligent even in her final madness. She has not been found for over a thousand revolutions of the earth around the sun. Even if we do manage that, it will be no easy task to contain her." But he must attempt it.

For she lived because he had failed.

*"Shh, my darling, shh."*

The final words she'd spoken to him as she walked away, her delicate feet getting ever smaller as she almost danced over the dew-laden grass. Dew glimmering with droplets of crimson, a sudden burst of color that had sprayed the meadow when he fell from so high; his wings crumpled, his body hitting the earth at a velocity that had torn off parts, left his mouth overflowing with blood, his ribs crushed into his heart and lungs, the leg that had remained attached to his body smashed into at least fifteen different fragments.

As he'd lain there, vulnerable in a way he hadn't been since childhood, she'd crouched down beside him, her fingers gentle and maternal as she pushed back blood-soaked strands of his hair.

*"Oh, my poor darling. My poor Raphael. It hurts now, but it had to be done." Her blue, blue eyes awash in tenderness. "You will not die, Raphael. You cannot die. You are immortal." A kiss on his broken cheekbone, light as a butterfly. "You are the son of two archangels."*

*He said nothing, couldn't speak, his throat crushed. But she understood what was in his eyes—immortals could die. He'd watched his father die. At his mother's hand.*

*"He had to die, my love. If he had not, hell would have reigned on earth." A slow smile when he continued to stare up at her, saying a thousand things even in his silence. "And so must I—that is why you came to kill me, is it not?" Laughter, soft and full of a mother's delight in her son. "You can't kill me, my sweet Raphael. Only another of the Cadre of Ten can destroy an archangel. And they will never find me."*

*Her feet moving light and graceful across the grass, the soles of her feet tinged with the red of his lifeblood. Angel-dust trailing from her wings, sparkling and glittering with a purity that mocked.*

"Come, Dmitri," he said, shoving the memories back into the shadows where they had remained for most of his adult life. "We must continue." Not since he'd first taken the city as his own had he had to help run such a patrol—he was an archangel, his focus on larger matters.

But today, as evening turned to night, he needed to fly, to sweep across his city and clear it of the evil that Caliane had unleashed. His mother would not take his territory. And he would not fail again—even if it meant killing the woman who had once cradled him in her arms with such infinite love that the echo of it haunted him even now.

# 17

Elena and Venom helped Ransom sweep the rain-slick streets of Boston after the authorities cleared them to leave the warehouse site. They found only one other vampire—but he was so deep in bloodlust he didn't even look up from nuzzling his victim's mutilated neck when Ransom walked up behind him. His head rolled off his neck an instant later, spraying Ransom with blood once again.

"Fuck," he muttered tiredly as the drizzle soaked the blood farther into his clothing, no longer strong enough to wash him clean. "Call the cops." He threw her his phone, and she redialed the number he'd used earlier.

That done, she sat down on the steps of one of the gracious old homes that lined this quiet stretch. All of them were now locked, lights blazing through every window. The word had apparently gone out in the media about a surge of bloodlust-ridden vamps, and anyone with a brain had hunkered down to wait out the violence.

To her surprise, Venom sat down beside her, leaving enough of a gap between them that he wouldn't brush her wings by accident. She was sure it wasn't a courtesy directed at her, but habit, given how much time he spent around angels. Still, she was grateful.

From Ransom, she'd accept that kind of contact. But Venom? They might work together, and he'd proven he had a heart behind those disturbing eyes when he'd put his life on the line to protect the children in the Medica not long ago, but when it came to her, he held far less charitable views. "Pity about your suit," she said, glancing at the rolled-up sleeves of his bloodstained white shirt.

"It was one of my favorites." Slitted green eyes looking directly at her.

But she'd learned her lesson. She shifted her gaze forward to Ransom. Venom's laugh was soft, taunting, but she didn't fall for the bait. If he entranced her, she'd be easy prey—and she wasn't sure the creature that lived in Venom would be able to resist taking advantage. "Can I ask you a question?"

"You can ask." He leaned back with his elbows on the step behind him as they watched Ransom check the victim and her killer for ID.

"Those eyes," she said, "how long did they take to develop after you were Made?" Every vampire had once been human, even Venom.

A rippling shrug that made her aware of the fluid, muscular grace that lurked beneath those fancy suits he liked to wear. "Jury's out on that. Neha says it began the moment of my Making, that she glimpsed the pupils start to change shape."

Every hair on Elena's body stood up straight at the sound of that name. The Archangel of India had never been Miss Congeniality, but as the murders of Celia and Betsy evidenced, she was now one scary nightmare intent only on vengeance for the death of her daughter. "You don't agree?" she asked, shaking off the reaction.

Venom looked up at the cloudy night sky, fine droplets of rain shimmering on his lashes. "I noticed a change perhaps a year after my Making. It was slight, but I could see that my irises were no longer true brown at the edges but were shifting to a dark, dark green."

Elena wondered how that had affected the young male Venom must've been—she wanted to ask if he'd been scared, but knew he wouldn't answer that. "How many years did the entire process take?" she asked instead, figuring he'd be far more liable to answer that question.

"Ten," he said, continuing to stare up at the sky, the rain having all but ceased. "I remain the only one of Neha's Making to show such an extreme change—I think she was disappointed it stopped with the eyes."

Remembering the way he'd moved the one and only time they'd sparred with each other, she shook her head. "But it didn't, did it?"

A lazy smile that she caught out of the corner of her eye.

"Ellie," Ransom said at that moment, coming to lean against the decorative metal railing that ran alongside the steps. "You need a place to stay tonight?"

"No. Venom's going to fly us back to New York." To her archangel. Argument or not, she couldn't deny that she missed him. For the first time in her life, she had someone who was *hers*, and somewhat to her surprise, she was discovering she was possessive as hell.

Ransom's face lit up with wicked glee. "Living the high life, Ellie. You'll be forgetting your friends soon."

"I've already crossed you off my party invite list."

He laughed, throwing back his head. "I can't wait to see you as the hostess with the mostess."

"You'll be waiting an eternity." The idea of being a hostess of any kind gave her hives.

"You are consort to an archangel," Venom said, rising to his feet with a sensual grace that came from the same place as his eyes. "You'll have to learn at least the rudiments of civilized behavior."

Gripping the wet iron of the railing, she pulled herself up just as two cop cars turned the corner. "Yeah? Being a dick doesn't seem to have stopped you from working for Raphael."

Venom grinned, flashing those canines she'd seen weep poison. "I can be charming. Didn't seem worth the effort with you."

"Oh, he's just asking for an ass-kicking," Ransom drawled. "Too bad the bloodbath's going to have to wait." Turning, he headed toward the police officers, with Elena and Venom following.

It took only fifteen minutes to get the formalities sorted— the cops were ready to give them medals after the night the city had had—and then they were away. Ransom had left his bike near where they'd landed the chopper, and she hugged him as they reached it. "How's your librarian?" she whispered in his ear.

His lips curved against the skin of her neck. "She makes my brain melt."

Continuing to be amazed by the fact that Ransom was in a stable relationship, she pulled back. "When do I get to meet her?"

"I don't want to scare her off just yet." Joking words, but they held a grain of truth—hunters often had trouble holding on to the men and women they loved for the same reason as cops. The endless fear of picking up the phone or opening the door to the worst kind of news wore away at emotional ties until they were burned through.

Elena hugged him again. "If she's stuck this long, I think the foundation is set."

"Yeah, I like to think so." Ransom squeezed her tight. "But I'm not taking us, or Nyree, for granted."

She'd never heard him sound so serious about a woman. Hoping like hell this Nyree didn't break his heart, she left him straddling the bike and headed over to the chopper, Venom at her side. It startled her to realize that not only had she and Venom had a fairly reasonable conversation tonight, they hadn't threatened to kill each other once. *Huh.* Probably a side effect of the adrenaline, the camaraderie that came from being in a bloody bat—

The earth moved beneath her feet.

Hard.

She clamped her wings tight to her back as the movement threw her sideways onto the concrete . . . on the same side where she'd gone down in front of the warehouse. More skin peeled off her face, her palms suffering further damage as well.

Hands clamping around her ankles.

Looking down, she saw that Venom had her in a powerful grip, his own feet braced against the base of the chopper. "What the—" Following the direction of his gaze, she felt the air whoosh out of her lungs. The other side of the concrete pier was just . . . gone, a gaping hole in the earth with jagged insides that would tear apart her wings—and she was a bare two inches from the edge. Nodding at Venom, she let him pull her toward him as the earth continued to roll.

In any other situation, it would've felt disturbingly intimate to have his hands on her calves, her thighs, her hips as he pulled her down until she could brace her own feet against their transport, her wings spread over them both. "The chopper might tip!" she said in his ear, fighting to be heard over the roar of the quake.

His hair whipped off his face. "I've been in other quakes! This one feels like it should be over soon!" Under her wing, his hand dug into her hip as another wave struck.

With it came a whisper of scent that was darkly familiar.

Then, as suddenly as it had begun, the quake was over, taking the scent with it before she could even begin to break it down. But she knew she'd sensed it above the Hudson.

Scrambling away as fast as she could—her wings were screaming with sensation—she got to her feet.

Venom flowed to a standing position with that strange reptilian grace an instant later, not commenting on her jerky escape. "We need to get away before another tremor strikes." He was already reaching for the cockpit door.

"Wait." Her blood turning cold, she was running even as

she yelled out instructions over her shoulder. "Start the engine! I need to find Ransom!"

Venom was by her side before she finished speaking. She didn't bother to curse. Following Ransom's familiar scent, which though not as clear to her as a vampiric trail, was more so than it would've been to the majority of humans, she sprinted down the narrow lane he'd taken to get out onto the main road. "There!"

The bike lay smashed on the retaining wall opposite the lane, Ransom's body unmoving in the street. Going down beside him, she checked for a pulse. "Thank God."

Ransom groaned. "Ellie?"

"Can you move?" she asked, running her hands over his body. "Any broken bones, problems with your back?"

Fisting his hands he pushed himself up into a kneeling position. "I'm okay, just stunned. Wasn't going very fast when the quake hit." His eyes were dilated, huge in his face.

"You're coming with us," she said, pulling him to his feet, his arm slung over her shoulder.

"My bike." Still dazed, he glanced back at his pride and joy.

Venom took Ransom's other side. "I'll call one of the local vampires once we're in the air. He'll store it for you."

There were no more words as they half ran, half dragged Ransom back to the chopper. They'd barely gotten inside when the earth began to pitch and roll again. Not bothering to put on his headphones, Venom just said, "Hold on!" and lifted the bird.

They shook precariously under an insufficient amount of rotor action, but jaw locked and hands steady, Venom managed to get them airborne. Elena looked down as they rose. "My God." The city was literally bucking under them, parts of the road rising up in a rolling wave, buildings crumbling into newly created canyons. The only good news was that instead of shaking Boston as a whole, the quake seemed oddly localized—to an approximately fifty-meter radius around the spot where they'd parked the chopper.

Hardly a natural phenomenon.
*She is waking.*
If this was what she could do while asleep . . .


Having bullied Ransom into getting himself checked out
at the hospital, Elena refused to leave until his librarian arrived. Nyree was a surprise—because Elena had had no idea
what to expect. The woman couldn't have cleared five feet two
inches, and had curves so lethal the prim blue cardigan she
wore buttoned up to her neck was probably an attempt at cam-
ouflage. It didn't work, even paired with a full skirt straight
out of the 1950s and simple flats, both in plain black.

As Nyree neared Ransom's cubicle, Elena saw that her skin
was a light brown, her features so unusual it was difficult to
pinpoint ethnicity—but it was her eyes that stole the show.
Huge and chocolate-dark, and overflowing with worry.

She didn't even see Elena standing to the side of the cubicle, she was so focused on her man. "Ransom!" Stroking Ransom's hair off his face where he sat on the bed, she checked his
wounds with delicate, tender touches. "Baby, you're so hurt."

To Elena's surprise, tough as nails Ransom didn't shake off
his lover's hands, but instead leaned into the touch. It was the
first time in Elena's life that she'd seen him allow anyone to
tend to him—and it made her deeply curious about the woman
who'd captured his heart. That curiosity, however, would have
to wait until another day. Keeping to the shadows, she slipped
out while they were wrapped up in each other.

By the time she jumped off the chopper onto the wet green
of the grass outside the house, it was well after midnight. "You
bunking here tonight?" she asked Venom.

Shaking his head, he pulled the door shut in her face.

"Well," she muttered, "goodnight to you, too." Wings
dragging like that of an exhausted angelic child, she walked
straight into the arms of the archangel who waited for her.
Those arms clamped around her as he shifted a few degrees
to shield her from the wind generated by the rising machine.

Drawing the rain-laced scent of him into her lungs, she released a breath, then repeated the action until she felt something inside her sigh and lay down its weapons. "How was your night, Archangel? Mine was interesting."

*You carry marks on your skin, Elena.* It was a demand for an explanation.

When they'd first met, she'd probably have bristled at that. Now . . . it was kind of nice coming home to someone who bothered to notice that she'd gotten a little banged up on the job. "I'll tell you if you feed me and let me use that decadent bath of yours." The bath where they'd first touched each other in a hungry passion that still made her breath catch each time she thought about it.

"Come."

Feeling a frisson of awareness at the sexual edge in that command, she slipped her hand into his as he drew her inside the house and toward their room. That was when she saw the blood on his shirt. "Hey!" She stopped. Or tried to.

When he kept going, she decided to beard him in the bedroom.

Soon as the door closed, she broke away and put her hands on her hips, the cuts on her palms no longer tender, though they didn't look pretty. "Take off your shirt."

Raising an eyebrow, he pulled the shirt over the top of his head, the wing slots sliding over the glory of his wings with a soft hush of sound. A second later, he dropped the shirt to the side, his expression moody in a way that made her want to push him to the bed and ride him until both their brains were scrambled. Fighting the temptation, she circled around to his back. "You're hurt!"

Three massive gouges marked his skin.

Blinking, she looked closer, felt her mouth fall open. "They're healing right before my eyes." Which either meant the injury was recent, or the damage had been worse before. She glanced at his shirt, measured the blood, decided the injury had been worse.

"I'm an archangel, Elena. It is but a scratch." Turning, he slammed her body to his. "Take off your top."

It was suddenly difficult to think, but she sucked in a breath, found the will. "How did you get so badly hurt?"

Placing his hand on the shoulder of her long-sleeved black top, he gripped . . . and tore. Her top was in shreds around her a second later, her breasts bare to his gaze since the bra had been built in. Abdomen taut with need, chest rising and falling in an uneven rhythm, she licked her lips. "Feel better?"

His answer was to dip his head, bend her over his arm, and suck one tight little nipple into his mouth.

Shuddering, she thrust her hands into his hair and pulled. He used his teeth on her. She hissed out a breath. "Raphael." It was meant to be an admonishment but it turned into a moan as he covered her other breast with his hand, squeezing and caressing with a confidence that turned her knees to butter.

That was when she thought, "Hell with it," and arched her body into the voracious hunger of his mouth. It didn't surprise her in the least when he moved the hand on her breast down to the front of her jeans . . . and tore them off. Her panties were next. A second later, she was being thrown onto the massive sea of a bed, her wings spreading out on the cool softness of the comforter even as Raphael gripped her legs at the knees and pushed up and out, baring her to him.

Searing blue met her eyes when she looked up. Then his wings began to glow. She hadn't seen him get rid of his pants and cried out as his erection began to part her most delicate flesh. *"Raphael."*

A kiss that demanded, his body all golden muscle and heat above her own.

"Faster," she ordered, and when he continued to thrust into her slow and deep, she wrapped her legs around him, using her own strength to tumble him onto the bed.

"Elena!" He caught himself before he would've crushed her even as she screamed at the shock of sensation as his cock drove in all the way.

For an instant, they both lay unmoving, connected to each other with an intimacy Elena had never experienced before him.

*Did I hurt you?*

*Never.* Stroking her hands down the skin of his back, making sure to rub her knuckles along the sensitive undersides of his wings, she said, "Kiss me, Archangel." At the same instant, she squeezed her muscles around the steely part of him that was lodged so deep inside of her.

Fisting his hand in her hair, he took her mouth as he moved his other hand to pin down her hip. The first stroke made her body arch, a scream pouring into his mouth. The second had her clenching convulsively around him as pleasure broke her into a thousand iridescent pieces.

# 18

His consort, Raphael thought as Elena lay quivering below him, his mate. *Again, Hunter.* Gritting his teeth against the urge to thrust, he flexed his cock within her, had the pleasure of hearing her gasp.

But she didn't surrender. Eyes hazy, she kissed his jaw, his neck, before pushing at his chest. "My turn."

He let her reverse their positions so that he lay on his back, his wings covering the bed on either side. Palms pressed to his chest, she rose up on him, a vision of breasts flushed a silky rose with passion; pale, winter-light hair tousled from the play of his hands; wings a stunning midnight arching above her shoulders; and sleekly muscular thighs. The rest of her legs remained covered—he hadn't wanted to wait long enough to pull off what remained of her jeans. As for her feet . . .

Boots. She still wore her boots.

His consort, he thought again. Magnificent and wild, and *his.*

When she bent down to kiss him, the act lushly intimate within the cage created by the silken fall of her hair, he sur-

rendered, let her take him. Her body moved in rhythmic coun-
terpoint to the teasing strokes of her tongue, and he knew his
hunter was about to push him over the edge.

*Not without you.*

Trying something he'd never before attempted in their
lovemaking, he dropped his shields. She was a young immortal, didn't know the rules, didn't know how to keep her own
shields up at such a time. He'd never invaded her—that was
an intimacy to be given, not taken. But he allowed her mind to
sweep out, to invade his.

Her body jerked above him, her beautiful eyes turning a
pleasure-washed silver as she cried out and came in a clenching burst of damp heat. That was all it took. He fell, throwing
up his shields only because the impact of that much sensation could hurt her—and even in this extremity of passion, he
would not hurt her, this hunter with a mortal heart who held
his own in her hands.

Elena didn't say a word when Raphael scooped her up in
those powerful arms—after she'd kicked off her boots and
socks, the remainder of her jeans—and took her through to the
bath, the water set at a bone-melting temperature. Sinking into
it with a sigh, she felt her butt connect with one of the small
ledges and figuring that was enough, let her head fall back,
reasonably certain her eyes were still rolled up inside her head.

A wash of water against her skin, her archangel getting in
with her.

Temptation rose, and she opened her eyes, ran her gaze
over the muscular strength of his legs, the ridged plane of his
abdomen. It was a very private pleasure, and one she intended
to indulge in as often as possible. "How's your back?"

"Healed." He sank down into the water, bracing his arms
on the rim of the bath. "A miscalculation on my part—I flew
too close to the steel girders of a construction project in
progress."

Forcing her body to move, she floated over to sit next to him, placing her head on one of his shoulders, her palm over his heart. It was a position she'd never have taken with another man—but Raphael, in spite of the frustration he was causing her with the constant bodyguards, understood who she was, understood that a small surrender didn't equal a larger one. "You don't make miscalculations like that."

He curled his arm around her, fingers painting lazy patterns on her skin. "We had a windstorm hit perhaps an hour after the earthquake shook part of Boston. I was able to compensate for the shove of wind, but not fast enough."

That made more sense. "That quake was really weird, Raphael. It was so localized." Reaching up, she ran her fingers along the arch of his wing with delicate precision.

*Elena.*

Smiling at the warning, she tilted up her head and brushed her lips over his jaw. "The earthquake?"

The endless blue of the deepest part of the ocean held her gaze before she dipped her head to kiss the line of his throat. His fingers clenched in her hair, but that big, powerful body remained relaxed, an archangel at rest in his consort's arms.

"You say the vampires appeared to be drawn to that same general area?" His chest rose and fell in an easy rhythm underneath her touch, his heartbeat strong and certain.

"Yeah," she said, using her teeth on the tendons she'd just kissed. "Even the one we found later seemed to have been heading in that direction." Only to be overcome by a lust for blood that would allow no other thought. "But the thing is, the focus of the quake seemed to be the chopper."

*Not the chopper, you.*

She made a face. "I was trying to avoid that conclusion."

A tug from the hand fisted in her hair, her head being tipped back—but this time, there was no kiss. "Your face is severely bruised." Raising his free hand, he gripped her chin and tilted her face to the side so he could assess the damage. "You've lost more than the upper layer of skin alone."

Elena didn't protest. After all, she'd ordered him to strip so she could examine his injuries. "It doesn't feel that bad." In fact, she had the sense the skin was already beginning to regenerate—way faster than it would've on a human.

A kick to the heart, that reminder, that knowledge that she was no longer mortal.

"It'll take at least two days to heal on its own," he said, releasing her chin. "There are bruises on your ribs and hips, too."

"When did you have time to notice?" Rising to straddle him, she put her arms around his neck and nuzzled a kiss to his pulse, feeling affectionate in a way she'd never been comfortable enough to express with anyone else. "Seemed to me like you were far more interested in other parts of my anatomy."

Strong, wet hands on her waist. "How much does it hurt?" Sensual lips, eyes full of a dark male promise, but his expression made it clear they'd be doing nothing interesting until she came clean.

Blowing out a breath, she pointed to a rib. "That one hurts but not so much that it bothered me while we were engaging in gymnastics in the bedroom." The near-painful hunger to touch, to take and be taken had wiped out every other sensation, every other need. "My left wing is tender—I might've strained something." She held up her palms. "The cuts seem to be healing."

Raphael raised his hand, blue fire licking over his palm. Her stomach went taut at the reminder of the sheer power he carried within. But this flame, it was nothing that would harm. When he placed his hand against her ribs, all she felt was a warmth so deep it infiltrated her very bones.

"Oh!" The soft cry escaped her lips as the sensation spread in a burst of electric heat, arrowing to the places where she hurt the most—but a hint of it pulsed in every vein and artery . . . and there was a whisper of sex to it that had nothing to do with healing. "Archangel, if you make everyone feel like this when you heal," she said in a husky tone, "I'm going to have a problem with it."

His lips didn't curve, and yet there was a sinful amusement in the voice that came into her mind. *It is a special blend, Elena. For you.*

The last time he'd said that to her, he'd covered her in angel-dust. Erotic, exotic, and designed to kiss every inch of her skin with shimmering arousal. "Good," she replied, leaning forward to nip at his lower lip. "Then you may heal others."

*I appreciate the permission.*

Her lips kicked up at the solemn statement paired with the wicked sensuality she glimpsed in his gaze. That look . . . it was still new. Raphael didn't often allow the young angel he'd once been—reckless and wild and cocky—to rise to the surface. But when he did . . . "Are you done?" she murmured against his mouth.

His answer was to slide his hands to her hips and tug her forward, over the steely hunger of his body. "Come, hunter," he said, using his teeth on the sensitive curve where her neck flowed into her shoulder, "take me."

And she did.

Elena wandered into the dining room the next morning to find it set with a delicious array from which to choose. Grabbing two croissants and a large cup of black coffee, she walked out into the crisp air, following her instincts until she found Raphael standing on the very edge of the cliff that plunged down into the Hudson. "Here," she said, passing over a croissant. "Eat or Montgomery's feelings will be hurt."

He took the offering but didn't put it to his lips. "Look at the water, Elena. What do you see?"

Glancing down at the river that had been, in one way or another, a part of her life since she was born, she saw churned up silt, sullen waves. "It's in a bad mood today."

"Yes." He stole her coffee, took a sip. "It appears water is in a bad mood across the world. A massive tsunami just hit the east coast of Africa, with no apparent link to an earthquake."

Stealing back her coffee, she bit into her croissant, savored the buttery texture before swallowing. "Any definite word yet on where she might be Sleeping?"

"No. However, Lijuan may have something—we will see." Finishing off the croissant she'd given him, he took the coffee. "You visit your father again today."

The food she'd eaten curdled in her stomach. "No, not him. I visit my sister, Eve. She needs me." She would not allow Jeffrey to treat Evelyn as he'd treated Elena—as something ugly, something worthless. "I still can't believe he lied to me for so long about the hunting bloodline." It had been a lie of omission, but that made it no less terrible.

"Your father has never been a man who values honesty." A cutting denunciation before he turned to her. "Five days hence, your presence is required here. Tell the Guild you will be unavailable."

Spine stiffening at what was unquestionably an order, she grabbed her coffee from him, not amused to find it all gone. "Do I get to know the reason for the royal summons?"

A raised eyebrow, her archangel's night black hair whipping off his face in the breeze coming off the churning waters of the Hudson. "The Hummingbird has asked to meet my consort."

All her snippiness disappeared under a surge of near-painful emotion. After Beijing, when she'd been forced to rest so her body could recover, she'd often curled up in an armchair in Raphael's office at the Refuge. But instead of reading the history books Jessamy had assigned her, she'd ended up speaking to him about so many things.

Sometime during that period, he'd told her pieces of what Illium's mother had done for him when he'd been at his most vulnerable. As a result, Elena felt a deep sense of allegiance toward the angel she'd never met. "I've wondered—is that why you took Illium into your service?" she asked. "Because he was hers?"

"At first, yes." He closed his fingers over the back of her

neck, tugging her to him. "The Hummingbird has my loyalty, and it was a small thing to accept her son into the ranks of my people when he came of age."

In spite of everything he'd shared, Elena had always had the feeling that she was missing a vital detail when Raphael spoke of the Hummingbird, and today was no different. There was something in his tone, a hidden shadow she couldn't quite discern—added to Illium's subdued presence the day before yesterday, it made her wonder . . . but some secrets, she'd learned, belonged to others.

"However, Illium soon proved himself," Raphael continued. "Now, my bond with the Hummingbird is a separate thing."

Having seen Illium in action, Elena could well believe that. "I'll be home. Do I need to dress up?"

"Yes. The Hummingbird is an angel of old."

"How old?"

"She knew my mother. She knew Caliane."

The waves at their feet rose up, crashing in savage fury, as if Caliane was attempting once more to claim her son.


Half an hour later, Elena found herself watching Raphael fly out over the Hudson to Archangel Tower to begin what was surely going to be one hell of a complicated day.

"The angels across my territory have been ordered to send in reports of all recent disturbances and losses," he'd told her before he rose into the sky. "Boston was neither the first, nor the only casualty, simply the biggest."

"Anything I can do to help?"

"Not today, but I have a feeling we'll need your skills again before long."

It was an ominous prediction, but since worrying would get her nowhere, and this was the first real lull—for her at least—since her arrival in New York, Elena decided to use some of the time to settle in. The first place she headed to was the greenhouse, the glass sparkling under the blade-sharp sunlight today.

Waterfalls of color and fragrance filled the glass enclosure, so many things to explore, but she headed to the corner occupied by her favorite begonias. A twinge of sadness pinched her as she touched her finger to one perfect red gold blossom, thinking of the plants at her former apartment, all of which had no doubt perished after she fell broken and bloody into an archangel's embrace. "But plants grow again," she murmured, focusing on the verdant beauty around her. "They put down new roots, create room for themselves in foreign soil."

*And so would she.*

Feeling good about making a conscious choice, she picked out the smallest, weakest begonia plant, took her time repotting it in richer soil, then cradled the pot carefully in her hands as she walked back to the house. Montgomery gave her a smile when she entered through the front door. "The solar on the third floor gets the best sunlight," he said.

*They had a solar?* "Thanks." Walking up the stairs, she wandered around the second floor until she found the neatly concealed flight to the third, and began climbing.

Her breath escaped in a hush of sound the instant she entered the room at the end of the corridor. Light poured in through two glass walls and a huge skylight to drench the room in sunshine. One of those walls, she realized, seeing the window seat, was actually latched. "Of course." An angel wouldn't worry about the danger of falling from such a height. And, the hunter in her murmured, it would also act as another exit, ensuring she'd never be trapped.

There wasn't much in the room in terms of furnishings. A rug in a rich cream patterned with tiny golden leaves; a delicate little wooden table, its legs carved in graceful commas; a number of jewel-toned silk cushions on the window seat, that was it. Placing her plant on the ledge above the seat, she made her way down to the second floor. "Montgomery," she called out over the railing when she spotted him below.

The butler glanced up, doing his best not to appear scandalized by the fact that she was acting in a most uncivilized fashion. "Guild Hunter?"

"Does the solar belong to anyone?"

"I believe you have just claimed it."

Grinning, she blew him a kiss and was almost sure he blushed. She was about to head back upstairs when she frowned, catching the unexpected caress of fur and chocolate and all things a little bit bad. "Why is Dmitri here?"

The vampire materialized out of the woodwork at the mention of his name, dressed in a black suit paired with a deep emerald green shirt, a sheaf of papers in hand. "No time to play today, Elena." Yet a tendril of smoke and champagne wrapped around her. "I have to get back to the Tower."

Seeing that Montgomery had left, Elena fought the urge to bury a dagger in the wall by Dmitri's head, quite certain he was provoking her on purpose. "Don't let the door hit you on your way out."

That tendril of smoke whispered into places it had no business going. "If you want to confirm the scent of Neha's assassin," he said, "they're holding the body as is in the morgue till eleven."

The kiss of musk on her senses, thick and drugging.

"Fuck!" The scent snapped off as Dmitri stared at the thin, silver knife that quivered in the wooden wall a bare centimeter from that sensual face with its Slavic cheekbones. Then, unexpectedly, he began to laugh, and it was perhaps the first time she'd heard the genuine thing from him.

It was potent. More sexy than any of his scent tricks.

Looking up, he gave her a strangely old-world bow, laughter still creasing his cheeks. "I go now, Guild Hunter." But he stopped at the door, his expression turning solemn. "I left a copy of the latest report on Holly Chang in the library."

Elena clenched her hand on the railing at the mention of the only one of Uram's victims to have survived. The woman— girl really—had been tainted by the dead archangel's toxic blood . . . an innocent, who in the ultimate insult, might turn monstrous. "How is she?" The last time Elena had seen Holly, the girl had been naked and covered in the blood of Uram's other victims, her mind broken.

Dmitri's answer was a long time coming. "She appears to be in a stable relationship, but she is . . . different. I may yet have to execute her."

# 19

Dmitri's chilling words continued to circle in Elena's head as she dropped by the morgue to ensure the dead woman had indeed been the one who'd murdered the vampire in the park. All it took was a single deep breath—the sweet poison of oleander was embedded in the assassin's skin. That done, Elena snuck into the Tower to take a quick shower. It felt wrong to meet Evelyn straight after having come from the house of the dead.

"Here we go," she said twenty minutes later as she led her sister through the solid steel doors of Guild Academy, conscious of the tension in that small, sturdy body. "You're too young to join as a full member, and no one expects you to live here, but you'll be set a schedule of after-school classes to help you hone and control your abilities."

Evelyn glanced over her shoulder, to where Amethyst walked stiff-backed beside Gwendolyn. "Amy can come with me?"

"Yes, if you want." Unexpectedly, though it was Eve who was hunter-born, it was Amy with her fiercely nurtured anger and keen distrust who reminded Elena most of herself. Eve, she thought, was still young enough to see the world as she wanted to see it. Amy had had the rose-colored lenses ripped off long ago, likely understood the painful truth of the relationship that seemed to exist between Gwendolyn and Jeffrey.

The ghost of Marguerite haunted them both.

Shaking off that thought as they reached the glass door to the waiting area, Elena pushed through. To her surprise, the man who met them inside was in a high-tech wheelchair. That wasn't the surprise, however. "Vivek!" Closing the distance between them, she cupped his face, kissed him on both cheeks, having not realized how much she'd missed him until this moment.

He blushed but didn't shove back his wheelchair. "Wow, look at those wings. I thought everyone was pulling my leg even after I saw the news reports." Moving his chair using a pressure control, he ignored Evelyn, Amethyst, and Gwendolyn as he peered at her feathers. "Would you be willing to let me—"

"Later," she said, putting her hand gently between Eve's shoulder blades, compelled by a sense of responsibility to *get this right*, to make sure her youngest sister would never ever think herself cursed rather than gifted. "I've brought the Guild a new student."

Vivek's attention shifted at once, his brown eyes hard, incisive. "Hunter-born," he said with curt assurance. "Nowhere near as strong as you, but strong enough to get herself in trouble if she's not careful."

Evelyn shifted closer to Elena at that harsh, almost cold summation. Elena tugged on her ponytail. "Don't mind him. Vivek talks to computers most of the time—humans are too much trouble as far as he's concerned." It was highly atypical to see him away from the subterranean tunnels that were his usual milieu.

Now, grumbling, the Guild's resident computer genius nodded toward the busy office area beyond. "Go over there; they'll do the paperwork."

Elena went in with Evelyn, but when it became clear that

Gwendolyn was capable and ready to shepherd her daughter through the process, she stepped out to talk to Vivek. "It's good to see you, V."

"Did you get that gun I sent with Sara?" he asked, eyes touched with a trace of envy when they landed on her wings.

She didn't begrudge him that. He was hunter-born, too, but had been paralyzed in an accident as a child, losing all feeling below the shoulders. His wheelchair, built for wireless capability, was a cutting-edge piece of technology from which he ruled his domain—the Cellars.

She'd always understood why he preferred to stay in the secret hideaway and information clearinghouse beneath the Guild's main building—it had to be a sensory nightmare for him to be up in the world when he had no outlet for his hunting instincts. That he had managed not only to retain his sanity in the face of that pressure, but to become an invaluable part of the Guild, was a testament to his incredible will.

"You mean this gun?" She retrieved it from an inner thigh holster, then put it back before she got told off for flashing a weapon.

Vivek smiled, and it turned his face striking. He was too thin, his bones too sharp against skin a shade darker than Venom's, but he was a handsome man. Yet he never made anything of it— as long as she'd known him, he'd been asexual. Intentionally so, she thought. "So what do you want to do with my wings?"

Lines on his forehead. "I was going to ask you to come in for a scan so we could get a better idea of their internal structure, but . . . that might make you vulnerable." Moving his wheelchair with a minute shift of his head, he rolled away from the office and out to the porch that ran the length of the front of the building.

Following, she leaned against the railing. "Yeah." She folded her arms, thought about loyalties. "He holds my heart, V. I'd never do anything to betray him."

Vivek stared at her for a long time. "I always wondered who'd break through that armor—figures it'd be a scary-ass archangel." Crooked smile creasing his face, he angled his head toward the office. "So . . ."

"Yep." Vivek knew more about her tangled relationship with her family than anyone else aside from Sara. Having been rejected by his own family after his accident, perhaps he understood even better.

Now, he looked out over the paved drive and to the massive iron gates that guarded the entrance to Guild Academy. "I was watching the surveillance monitor before you landed. Your father drove your sisters here. He's outside, sitting in his Mercedes."

Elena felt her shoulders lock, and it was an instinctive response, one she couldn't fight. She understood without being told that Gwendolyn was the reason Jeffrey had come. Somehow, the beautiful woman who had always seemed nothing but a decorative fixture had found the will to force her intractable husband into supporting her children.

*"I'm not strong enough. Forgive me, my babies."*

The memory of her own mother's voice, so taut with pain, so lost, tangled through her mind, making her hand fist. Unlike Gwendolyn, Marguerite hadn't been there to stand for her daughters against a Jeffrey who'd slowly turned into a stranger. But then Gwendolyn hadn't been forced to listen to two of her daughters being tortured to death, hadn't had her arms and legs broken so she couldn't go to them, hadn't suffered such degradation that she'd screamed for days afterward.

"Ellie."

Blinking at Vivek's sharp tone, she straightened and glanced back toward the office. "Will you watch over her, Vivek?" Paralyzed or not, he had eyes everywhere. "While she's here at the Academy, will you watch over her—over them both?"

"You know you don't have to ask." His gaze was liquid-dark with pain when she met it again. "Does it ever go away? The hurt?"

Her immediate answer was to say no, but she hesitated, thought about it. "No," she finally replied, gripping his shoulder with her hand. "But it can be . . . muted by the strength of other emotions." Like the blinding fury that tied a hunter to an archangel.

"Are you ever afraid? That it'll all be taken way?" *Again.*

"Yes," she admitted, because he'd had the courage to ask the question. "But I'm not a helpless child anymore. If for some reason Raphael wants to leave me, I'll fight for him to my last breath." Because he was hers now.

Vivek's smile was small, solemn. "I hope you make it, Ellie. For all of us."

Her phone rang in the silence that followed the quiet, heartfelt wish. Checking the display, she said, "Sara," to Vivek before answering. "Hey, boss."

"I just got a request for assistance from the police." Sara's tone was crisp, what Ransom liked to call "directorial." Only once had he used the word "dictatorial"—and been assigned a hunt in the wilds of some boondock town where the locals took one look at his hair and leather jacket and termed him a "fancy boy."

Lips twitching at the memory of how he'd had to make a run for it after the hunt ended—to avoid the local beauties and their shotgun-toting daddies—she said, "Yeah?"

"I know you had a tough day yesterday, but you're the only one not on assignment today, so haul ass."

Elena was more than happy to get back into the rhythm of work, but—"Am I really the only one you've got?" Sara had access to a large network of hunters across the five boroughs.

"I want to rest Ransom up after the spill he took," Sara replied, as Vivek whispered that he was off. "Several others suffered similar injuries in the chaos yesterday. Ashwini's around, but she dragged herself down to the Cellars at five this morning, so she's out like a light."

Hunters slept in the Cellars for any number of reasons, but one of the biggest was that they needed a place to hide. "Do I need to ask?" She waved at Vivek as he headed down the ramp to his transport.

"It involves Janvier, a handwritten sign, and large quantities of honey. That's all I'm permitted to say."

Snickering at the images that sprang into her mind at the mention of the Cajun vamp Ashwini seemed to spend half her life hunting, Elena said, "So, where do you need me?"

"Delancey Street, right under the Williamsburg Bridge. DB, might've been vampire-bit multiple times, but cops say there's so much damage they can't really tell. Should be a simple assignment."

Her spine turned into a steel rod. "I don't need to be coddled, Sara."

"Don't give me lip." Snapped-out words. "You're not back to full hunting strength, and if I'd had anyone else, I wouldn't have sent you into Boston yesterday. Use the downtime you have to get back into shape, or I'll be putting you on penny-ante assignments involving idiots who think they can break their Contracts after a measly year or two."

Elena winced. "Mean."

"That's why I earn the big bucks."

Glancing into the office area, Elena saw that Gwendolyn and the girls seemed to be finishing up. "I'll probably be about twenty-five minutes."

"Cops'll hold the scene."


The cops had not only held the scene, they'd quarantined it behind so much yellow crime-scene tape it might as well have been a fence.

"Fuck me." The uniform closest to Elena shoved back his cap and stared as she landed on the lush green of the parklike area beneath the bridge. "They real?"

She couldn't help it. "Nah, costume-shop rejects."

He narrowed his eyes, stared some more before a big-shouldered plainclothes detective came between him and Elena. "Welcome back, Ms. Deveraux."

"Nice to be back, Detective Santiago." Shooting the veteran cop a genuine smile, she nodded at the crime-scene tape. "Slight overkill don't you think?"

Santiago rubbed his jaw, solid as a boxer's and bristly with salt-and-pepper stubble that was even more apparent against skin the color of dry tobacco leaves. "Rookie." He lifted up a section that had enough leeway that she could duck under even with her wings. "He freaked—first DB. It's not as bad as some I've seen though."

Elena had to fight not to let the detective's words kick her into a past that refused to stay buried. She'd freaked at her first dead body, too. The only difference was, she'd been ten years old, and the body had been that of her sister Mirabelle. Long-legged Belle, who'd played ball and danced with the same athletic grace. Belle, whose legs Slater had shattered into so many pieces that she'd never have been able to do either again even if she'd lived.

"Could be a human psycho"—Santiago's deep voice jerked her back into the present—"but after the things I've seen in my career, I've learned to check."

Walking carefully down the slight slope, Elena followed the scent of blood almost to the water's edge. She'd half expected the victim to be wet or semisubmerged, but the teenage girl lay dry in the long grasses in a shadowy corner beneath the bridge. Dry except for the blood. It coated her from head to toe, leaving bare glimpses of skin of such a pale hue, it appeared made of tissue.

Santiago, having navigated the slope with a little less grace, his black loafers slipping on the grass, blew out a breath. "Just a kid."

Elena tried not to let the girl's youth matter, tried not to see her sisters Belle and Ariel in the victim's coltish form. It was hard. With her thick, dark hair and summer dress patterned with forget-me-nots, she looked like a pagan sacrifice lying there caressed by the waving strands of grass. Then the wind shifted, bringing with it the scent of death, and the illusion shattered. "Yeah."

"Ready to do your bloodhound thing?"

"Yes." Finding her footing in work, she took a deep breath. Frowned. "Unusual number of vampiric scents in the area." The entire section was drenched in notes as diverse as cottonwood and lime, to bitter black tea with sprinkles of sea salt, and sticky strands of taffy. Those weren't the only things she caught in the air. *Oh.* "If I didn't know better, I'd say this was a make out spot."

Santiago raised his head. "Hey, Brent! You owe me ten bucks!"

"Aw, shit."

Elena felt her lips quirk. Guilt threatened. How dare she smile while a girl lay dead at her feet? Elena fought that voice—fact was, you had to distance yourself somehow at these scenes or they'd eat away at you until there was nothing left. "You betting on me now?"

Santiago winked. "Another rookie. Like taking candy from a baby." Putting his hands on his hips, he pushed back his jacket in that way men had of doing, and said, "Lot of the young vamps hang out here, along with their human partners. We keep an eye on things, but they're harmless for the most part—like to party a bit and, yeah, make out."

"Huh." Elena realized she hadn't been around any vampires that young since she woke from the coma. "Well, that's going to cause a problem unless the perpetrator—if he was a vampire—left enough of a trace behind on her that I can conclusively separate out his scent."

Pulling on the latex gloves she'd grabbed from a kit at Guild Academy—because while she might be immune to disease, she didn't much enjoy dipping her fingers in blood and other bodily fluids—she hunkered down beside the body. Not a young girl who liked forget-me-nots and wore a pretty summer dress in spite of the nip in the air. Not someone with the long legs of a dancer. Just a body. "Can I touch?" she asked, fighting to maintain the emotional distance.

"Go ahead. I cleared it with the crime-scene folks."

The grass prickling the underside of her wings, she placed one hand beside the dead girl's head to brace herself, and bent down to sniff at her ravaged neck.

*Iron. Old. Dry.*

*Soap.*

*Synthetic perfume.*

Her heart skipped a beat.

*Lush, lyrical, sensual, a scent so extraordinary it was beyond unique.* "Black orchids," she whispered under her breath, but there was something . . . She was sure she'd caught hints of a subtle underlying note when the wind smashed into her and Raphael outside the house, but this scent was pure, so, so pure. However, given the erratic nature of her angel-sensing abilities, that wasn't conclusive of anything.

"What?" Santiago came down beside her. "You think it might've been a pack of vamps?"

Swallowing against the near-certain knowledge that this was much, much worse, Elena held up a finger, then—going to her knees—bent close enough to the body that she could examine some of the wounds that weren't crusted over with blood. "Not bite marks," she said in surprise. "Slices. Tiny, tiny slices." All over the victim's body. Done by someone holding a blade, but the real question was, what or *who* had driven that hand?

"Yeah. Tortured." The big detective rose to his feet with a groan. "Guild case or us?"

"Guild." It wasn't quite the truth. "No human did this." Stripping off her gloves and holding them in one hand, she took the one Santiago held out to pull herself to her feet. "Thanks."

"No problem. Biohazard bin's up there." He jerked his thumb over his shoulder.

Walking back with him, she got rid of the gloves, then used her cell phone to call Raphael. "There's something you need to see."

# 20

Raphael took one look at the body and went very, very still. "It has been called the death of a thousand cuts."

Even as Elena's rational mind considered the implications of that, her eye kept going to those pretty forget-me-nots, to the old-fashioned friendship bracelet on the girl's slender wrist. It seemed obscene to talk of ancient methods of torture while she lay so strangely innocent in the grass—but that, of course, was a mirage. "Didn't that involve dismemberment?"

"Not when Caliane performed it."

A chill kiss on the back of her neck, that confirmation. "I can't be certain about the origin of the scent," she said, having told him of the presence of black orchids. "I've only brushed up against your mother's scent a couple of times, and never in a situation where I had the opportunity to tease out the notes."

Raphael's response wasn't anything she might have expected. "I was speaking with Michaela when you called me."

Elena fisted her hand at the mention of the female archangel. Beautiful in the most sensual of ways, Michaela had taken an instant dislike to Elena. The feeling was mutual. Except . . .

it was no longer so easy to treat Michaela as the "Bitch Queen" and nothing more, not now that Elena knew the archangel had once lost a child. Elena would never forget the heartbreak she'd witnessed that terrible night at Michaela's gracious home in the Refuge. "What did she say?"

"I hear compassion in your voice, Elena." Raphael's eyes were dark with warning when they met hers. "You must never make the mistake of weakening when it comes to Michaela. She chose the path she walks, and it is a path that may well have led to the death of another archangel."

He'd said that to her before, and despite the fact that her human heart wanted to see something better in Michaela, she knew he was right. "I won't ever lower my guard around her, don't worry."

Seemingly satisfied with her promise, he returned his attention to the body. "Another kill such as this was found in her territory last night."

And if there were two . . . "Damn."

"The killer was caught in that case, raving with madness."

"That seems to be the pattern." She looked up at the sound of the forensic investigators, waved them down. "Body's all yours."

As they came nearer, trying not to stare at Raphael while doing exactly that, the Archangel of New York moved a small distance from the body, choosing to stand right on the water's edge.

"I can't pinpoint the scent of the killer here." Frustration churned through her as she followed him. "The area's—"

"It may not signify," Raphael said. "Dmitri spoke to me earlier today of a vampire who, from the evidence, appears to have set himself alight last night then stood in place as he burned. That is not the act of a sane man."

Elena blew out a breath. "Yeah, good chance it was him. If Dmitri has a name, I can check his apartment, get the scent there, see if he was in this area at least."

"Identification may take weeks, depending on whether anyone reports him missing—the fire turned the body to ash."

He flared out his wings and beyond them, the cops went motionless.

Elena could well understand their fascination. She'd touched those wings, felt that powerful body hot and demanding above her own, and still her chest went tight.

"I will speak to Jason," Raphael said, not noticing the reaction of the humans, "have him check with his informants about other murders that may be connected." Wings spread to their breathtaking widest, he rose into the sky. *Contact me the instant you sense any hint of her presence—she would crush you, Elena, and think nothing of it.*

*I know.* With that, she let him go. Some nightmares, she knew all too well, couldn't be cured in a day or even a year.


Given the viciousness of the girl's murder, the grisly suicide of her probable killer, and the other outbreaks of violence that had been her welcome to the city, Elena was almost surprised four days later to discover that they'd passed in peace—though it was a peace strung taut as a bow as everyone waited for the other shoe to drop.

Deciding not to look a gift horse in the mouth, she'd spent a few hours one day placing several more plants in the solar, along with a selection of her other treasures—the delicately carved mask from Indonesia went on the wall beside the door, the tiny glass candy ornaments from Murano in a crystal bowl atop the small writing desk, and the swathe of hand-embroidered silk from Kashmir she hung up on the other wall like a tapestry. Midnight blue shot with gold, it glowed in the sunlight.

"Setting up a nest, Guild Hunter?" Raphael had asked only last night as he stood leaning against the doorjamb.

She'd looked up from where she was arranging her favorite books in a gorgeous little bookshelf made of reclaimed lumber that Montgomery had found for her, caught by how very male Raphael was—especially here, in a place she'd turned exquisitely feminine. "It's what hunters do." She had a feeling that deep-rooted sense of home would be even more crucial in this new life. "But," she'd added, "you've already created the nest." This house, for all its size, was nothing like the cold elegance of the Tower. Here was warmth and beauty, a place where she could collapse in bed and snuggle into the blankets.

"Then what is this?"

"I'm marking out a piece of the house as my own territory."

A cool pause. "I will not allow you to put distance between us, Elena."

She'd seen that one coming, was more than ready to handle it. "I need a place where I can slam the door in your face when I'm mad. I'm pretty sure both of us would prefer that place be here and not elsewhere."

"And will I be invited into this part of the nest?"

"Perhaps." The tease had gotten her a less than amused look. Smiling, she'd reached for a small box about the size of a memo cube that she'd kept to the side. "I have something for you."

As with the last time she'd given him a present—the ring that burned with amber fire—he'd appeared both surprised and delighted. "What do you give me?"

"It's for your suite at the Tower." Hoping he'd understand, she'd handed over the box.

He'd opened it to remove a chunk of black rock glittering with what looked like deposits of gold. "Pyrite," he'd murmured, identifying the mineral as it flashed fire in the sunlight. "*Shokran*, Elena."

He'd stolen her heart all over again with the way he handled the gift with such care. "There's a second part," she'd added. "Tonight, I'll tell you about the strange, haunted mine where I picked up that hunk of rock. There might be a former voodoo priest turned vampire involved."

Raphael's expression had shifted, the intimacy in those eyes stealing her breath. *You give me a memory, Consort mine. I am honored.* A bow of that dark head, the rock being placed carefully back into the box.

Of course then, she'd had to go into his arms, this man

who treated her memories as if they were precious jewels. She hadn't realized until much later, as she fell asleep covered by the heavy warmth of his wing, that Raphael had never challenged her right to claim partial ownership over a home he had to have lived in for centuries. It had made something in her settle, dig another root into this new life, this new existence.

But fussing with her solar was something she did in her spare time—usually, when her muscles felt like jelly. Because most of the past four days she'd spent either in the gym she'd discovered in the sprawling basement under the house, up in the air with a number of angelic instructors, or out on the makeshift practice circle, sparring against Raphael and, occasionally, Dmitri.

Today, her opponent was neither her archangel nor his second.

"Last time we fought, you ended up unconscious." Slitted green eyes watched her without blinking.

Elena bared her teeth. "I also almost took your balls off."

"They would've grown back."

"You sure didn't seem keen to lose them at the time." Raising her short sword, she said, "Shall we play?"

A small nod, Venom's upper body gleamed a warm, inviting brown in the sun, his legs covered by those flowing black pants most of the males seemed to prefer to work out in. "Since you ask with such sweetness."

As they stabbed and darted out at each other, Venom attempting to go for her wings, while she tried to take him to the ground, she ensured her gaze never met his full on. She'd learned her lesson the last time, when he'd almost entranced her. That lesson had saved her life in Beijing, but she hadn't much liked the learning of it and had no intention of repeating the experience. Her short sword hit hard against the curved blade he used, and she felt the vibration all the way up her arm and in her teeth.

He brought up his second blade to block the knife she'd been about to put to his abdomen. "Stalemate." A viper's eyes tried to catch her gaze as his muscles locked in place.

Elena wasn't stupid. Venom was somewhere around the three-hundred-year-old mark by her guess. That meant that physically, he had a massive advantage. "Don't hold back." It was a gritted-out command as she broke the deadlock and danced out of reach.

"I have to," he said, circling those blades as if they weighed nothing, the sun glancing off them in a pattern that could quickly turn hypnotic. "Face it, Ellie, you can't win if it comes down to brute strength."

"Don't call me Ellie." That was reserved for her friends.

He hissed at her, spitting poison.

Elena dived and rolled, kicking his feet out from under him before he could shift position in one of those reptilian bursts of speed.

"Stop!" Illium's voice as he strode into the circle. She'd been surprised to see him this morning, as the Hummingbird was meant to have arrived last night. However, according to Illium, his mother had been delayed by a storm and wouldn't be landing for a few hours. "Both of you, up."

Rising to a standing position, Elena watched as Venom flowed up, just itching to kick him flat again. "You could've blinded me."

A liquid shrug. "You would've recovered, but it would've hurt like a bitch. And next time, you'd remember."

Elena closed her eyes and counted to ten. "Yeah, you're right," she said, raising her lids.

Venom blinked, those slitted eyes contracting when he lifted his lashes back up. "You leave me at a loss for words." But not for actions it seemed, because he bent to give her the most elegant of bows before rising to blow her a kiss. "Another round?"

Illium, his expression subdued as it had been for too many days, turned to her. "Mind if I have a go?"

"Kick his ass."

Stripping off his shirt and boots, Illium held out his hand for one of Venom's blades. Lips curving, Venom passed it over. "Sure you can handle me, pretty, pretty Bluebell?"

"Did I ever tell you about my snakeskin boots?" A savage grin, and she knew Venom was about to bear the brunt of whatever haunted the blue-winged angel.

Venom swirled his blade in hand. "I do think I need some new feathers for my pillow."

Illium shifted into a combat stance. "Call the winner, Ellie."

Stepping out to the side of the circle, where she'd placed a bottle of water, she put down her weapons and took a seat on the grass. "Ready? Go!"

Her heart was in her throat within ten seconds, the water forgotten. Because neither Venom nor Illium was holding back now, and they moved at the speed of death. The tip of a blade a bare millimeter from an eye, a foot about to snap a spine, an edge about to sever a head. It was like watching a fight in fast-forward, Illium's wings brilliant splashes of blue, his hair a wild sweep of black dipped in sapphires, Venom's skin shimmering golden brown as sweat glimmered and caught the light.

Rising to her feet, she kept her eyes glued on them, trying to catch moves, figure out vulnerabilities. "Stop!"

They broke apart to glance at her, chests heaving—two half-naked males covered in sweat and holding wicked-sharp blades by their sides. Illium was beautiful, Venom so *other* as to be strangely compelling. Together, she thought with one part of her mind, they created a damn nice view. Sara would call them eminently lickable.

"Venom took it," she said.

That slight English accent of Illium's was very apparent as he said, "Hell he did."

"He had his teeth on your jugular." She knew enough to know that while Venom's poison wasn't lethal to angels, it would've hurt like hell, breaking Illium's concentration.

Venom rocked back on the balls of his feet, a slow taunting smile on his face that had Illium threatening him with dismemberment. That only made the vampire's grin widen and then they were at it again, moving with a fluidity and grace that turned them into living pieces of art.

It was tempting to simply watch, but she began to note down moves and countermoves she thought she could utilize—because one way or another, she was getting her name back on the Guild roster as a fully functioning hunter.

Raphael stood on the very edge of the Tower roof, looking out over Manhattan. The city bore few scars from the destruction caused during his battle with Uram. It had stood firm and proud against the quakes and the storm winds that hit a week ago, and now sparkled bright beneath the sun's rays.

*"Shh, my darling, shh."*

Images of the young girl's bloodied body surrounded by long, green grass intertwined with his mother's voice, but the memories didn't suck him under. Not today. This was his city. He had built it, and he would hold it, no matter if his mother thought to wrench it from him. "Boston?" he asked Dmitri. "Any further problems?"

"No," the vampire answered from beside him. "The calm has held since the earthquake."

No calm, this, Raphael thought. It was more akin to the unnatural quiet that settled over an area before all hell broke loose. "I—" He halted as his senses picked up something so unexpected as to seem impossible. "Dmitri, we'll have to continue this later."

Most others, even in his Seven, would have retreated, but Dmitri looked up to the sheet blue clarity of the sky. "Who is it?"

"Lijuan."

The Archangel of China . . . and of Death.

# 21

Dmitri hissed out a breath. "I'll put the Tower on alert."

Spreading his wings, Raphael rose into the air above this chaotic, beautiful city of steel and glass and humanity that had been the center from which he'd claimed all the territory he now held. Lijuan was waiting for him in the high reaches, where the air was thin enough to kill a mortal—backlit by the cutting intensity of the sun, she was as eerily inhuman as ever, with those strange pearlescent eyes and hair of purest white.

He came to a stop across from her, noting that she wore flesh today. "I'm honored." After the destruction of Beijing and Lijuan's "evolution," no one had seen her except in the pools of water she seemed to enjoy utilizing for contact.

"Of course I would come to you," she murmured in that voice that screamed the truth of her descent. "None of the others are of any interest."

*Elena, where are you?*

*On my way to Guild Academy to see Eve. Do you need me?*

*Stay away from the house until I say otherwise. I don't want you in Lijuan's line of sight.*

A pause, but she didn't argue—though he knew very well she didn't like him anywhere near the Archangel of China. *Be careful, Archangel.*

Having handled the conversation at the same time that he exchanged meaningless pleasantries with Lijuan, he angled his body toward the serene waters of the Hudson, light refracting off its surface in a thousand broken shards. "Come, we will speak at my home."

"So very civilized of you, Raphael." She laughed, the sound incongruously sweet for a woman who had made the dead rise, whose power was tinged with a putrid darkness. "Is it any surprise I prefer you above the others?"

Raphael said nothing, and neither did she, not until Montgomery closed the library doors behind himself after serving the tea. Lijuan had chosen one of the armchairs in front of the fireplace, and Raphael sat opposite, acting the host—with Lijuan, the small courtesies must always be observed. If they were, she would follow her own peculiar code. There would be no bloodshed, not while she was a guest in his home.

Sipping her tea, Lijuan let out a sigh. "There is something to be said for the physical form."

When they had last met in Beijing, she'd told him she no longer needed food for sustenance. "Have your needs changed?"

A soft smile that appeared innocent . . . if you did not see the twisted shadows that lingered beneath. "Not my needs. My wants." Another sip. "Some things power alone cannot duplicate." Holding the teacup in an elegant hand, she met his gaze. "How do you stand it, Raphael?"

Raising an eyebrow, he waited.

"These mortals." She flicked a hand in the direction of Manhattan. "All around you, everywhere you go. Like ants."

Where Aodhan had asked a smiliar question with a deep, hungry curiosity in his tone, there was only contempt in the voice of the Archangel of China. "I have always lived in the world, Lijuan."

A sigh. "I forget. You have not yet seen the millennia I have. I, too, once lived among mortals."

He thought of the stories Jason had uncovered about Li-juan's past, the horrors the other archangel had perpetuated. "You were a goddess always."

A regal nod. "Will you kill her?"

The question didn't throw him. He'd known the reason for Lijuan's appearance the instant he saw her. "If my mother remains mad, she must be stopped." Given the reports he'd received from Nazarach, Andreas, and Nimra this morning, telling of young vampires going murderously insane and kill-ing in a way that bore Caliane's stamp, that madness seemed a more and more a certain truth.

"Would it not be better to kill her where she Sleeps?" Lijuan put down her teacup with a sigh of pleasure. "She is not yet at her full strength. Once awake, she may well be unstoppable."

The idea of Caliane raining pain and fire upon the world was a nightmare. But . . . "That is not our way." Angelkind had very few laws. The only one that mattered most of the time was the absolute prohibition against harming angelic children. Neha's daughter, Anoushka, had lost her life for breaking that law.

But there was a second, even more ancient law. To kill an angel in Sleep was considered an act of murder so heinous that the penalty was instantaneous and total death. Because even an archangel could die—but only at the hand of another archangel. "I will not be a coward and strike her while she is helpless."

"Your mother is hardly helpless," Lijuan argued. "You see the effects of her power all around—death drenches the land-scape and even now, the molten core begins to boil with rage."

Raphael thought of the bloodrage that had gripped him as Caliane's power rippled around the world, of Astaad beating his concubine and—according to Jason's most recent report—Titus executing the innocent. "Yes." His mother had never been helpless.

"Then you agree. She must be killed before she wakes and terrorizes the world."

"No, she must be woken." Perhaps there remained within

him a piece of the child he'd once been, but his decision was that of an archangel—this law could not be defiled, no matter the target. For once done, it could not be taken back. The slope would turn ever more slippery, as all those who Slept became fair game. "If we can rouse her before she is ready, she will rise weak. It'll give us the advantage as we seek to learn whether or not she is sane." Whether or not she would have to die.

Lijuan's expression remained serene, but a ring of black appeared around her irises, a thick, oily color Raphael had never before glimpsed. Something in it whispered of the reborn, the corpses Lijuan had animated to mute, hungry life. "She escaped all those years ago," the Archangel of China pointed out, the black ring shifting with an almost living awareness, "because the combined power of the Cadre wasn't enough to keep her contained."

"But they did not have you." Raphael deliberately played to Lijuan's vanity.

The other archangel's gaze turned distant. "Yes. Caliane did not evolve as I have." A small, satisfied smile. "You will walk me to the door, Raphael."

"I am not your pet, Lijuan"—a soft reminder—"and never will be."

Lijuan's hair flew back in that eerie breeze that seemed to affect only her. "Pets are so easily disposable, Raphael. I have something far more permanent in mind for you." A whisper of power licking around his face. "You could rule the world."

All he'd have to do, he thought as he watched her take flight into the blue skies above his city, was give up his soul.

Rain drenched the city again that night, coming down so hard and fast that Elena wrapped her arms around herself as she stood by the flames of the fireplace in Raphael's private study, staring out at the bleak landscape beyond. "Illium's mother arrived safely?"

"Yes. We dine with her tomorrow eve."

"I figured she'd want to rest tonight." She shivered as a particularly brutal burst of rain hit the windows, but wasn't sure it had anything to do with the rainstorm. Her skin had been creeping ever since Raphael told her of his meeting with Lijuan. "Could you fly in this?"

The archangel who stood looking at papers at a solid desk set in the center of the room, his wings sheened with amber light, nodded. "You could do it, too, but only for a short period. Your feathers are designed so as not to become waterlogged, but the pressure of the rain and wind would mean you'd have to push harder with every wingbeat to keep yourself aloft."

Before, when she'd watched angels taking flight from the high balconies that ringed the Tower, she'd been filled with a quiet awe. Not the sickening and worshipful adoration that gripped the angelstruck, but a simple, deep appreciation for their otherworldly beauty and grace. "I never considered the mechanics behind flight until I grew wings." Wings that gave her a freedom beyond anything so many people would ever know.

The Archangel of New York watched her as she walked to stand beside him in front of the desk, his eyes a crystalline blue licked with the yellow orange of the flames in the fireplace. "What is on your mind, Elena?"

"Does vampirism cure paralysis?" Blinded by the entitled idiots she hunted on the job, she'd never been able to figure out why anyone would want to sign up for a hundred years of slavery just to live longer. But Venom's flip remark about his balls growing back had gotten the wheels turning enough that she'd done a bit of research at the Academy library. "I know the process heals a lot of other illnesses, but what about spinal damage?"

"It is not an instantaneous process," Raphael said. "Depending on the severity of the injury, it can take up to five years for the vampirism to advance far enough in the cells to repair the damage. Not many angels are willing to wait that long."

Elena bit her lower lip.

"You need to get his blood."

She'd known he wouldn't say no, but still . . . her heart

clenched. "I'll have to steal it. I won't give him the option unless he qualifies as a Candidate." Vivek had been hurt quite enough. "Give me a while to figure out how to do it."

Raphael's hair caught the firelight as he nodded. "I heard you talking to Sam earlier."

"He's a chatterbox." The kid had a way of getting to her. "He said Jessamy made him write an extra essay because he did something naughty, but he wouldn't tell me what it was." It had delighted her to hear him sounding so very much like himself. His memories of the trauma he'd suffered, she'd been told, would resurface slowly, giving him time to adapt.

"Have his parents begun speaking to him of it yet?" Raphael asked, following the train of her thoughts with piercing accuracy.

She leaned into the muscular warmth of his body. "He asks me the odd question at times, but mostly he's interested in how everyone in the Refuge was looking for him. He thinks that's amazing."

"Clever of his mother and father," Raphael murmured, his wings heavy against her own as he spread them out. "Even when the memories do rise, that search, the fact that he is so loved, is what will remain at the forefront, not the pain and terror."

"Yes." At that moment, her eye caught on the papers on his desk. "What's this?" She picked up what appeared to be some kind of an expensive invitation, the paper heavy, embossed with an *E* and an *H* intertwined.

"Open it."

Conscious of him watching with an enigmatic expression on his face, she lifted the flap and removed a card—to read words written in the most delicate calligraphy, the rich silver-black ink flowing faultlessly across the page.

*We invite you and your consort to our home, Raphael. It will be a delight to have a meal with another couple who understand that love is not a weakness. Do come.*

It was signed with a graceful signature, the *H* in the name curlicued with great care until it was a work of art. Elena smiled in delight when she found herself tracing the sinuous from of a mythical serpent. "Hannah," she murmured, bringing the page closer to her eye so she could see the fine detail hidden within the single letter. "Amazing."

"Hannah is an artist." And the consort of the Archangel Elijah.

Elena looked up at him, her eyes shimmering dawn in this light. "Are there any other long-term couples in the Cadre I don't know about?"

"Eris is Neha's husband, but not consort." Raphael had not seen him for three hundred years, and even before that, Eris had never been anything but Neha's creature.

Elena placed the invitation back in the envelope and set it down. "I'd like to meet Hannah."

"Elijah is the one archangel," he said, sliding the papers on his desk aside and putting his hands on her waist to lift her onto the solid surface, "who I might one day trust." Making a space for himself between her thighs, he placed his hands on either side of her hips on the desk. "But I will not take you into the heart of his territory. Not yet."

His hunter's expression shifted, became contemplative. "No," she murmured. "Not yet. I'd make you too vulnerable. But I assume Hannah is powerful enough by now that Elijah doesn't mind bringing her into your territory?"

Raphael closed one hand over the sleek muscle of her thigh. "I have never asked." As the only archangelic consort before Elena, Hannah had always been considered off-limits, protected. It was a courtesy that hadn't been extended to Elena, not just because she'd once been mortal—but because she was hunter-born . . . warrior-born.

Elena wrapped her arms around his neck. "Send the invitation. I want to talk to her—there's so much I could learn from her."

Settling his free hand on her rib cage, just below the curve of her breast, he spoke against her parted lips. "I cannot ask, Elena. The invitation was sent by Elijah's consort, and must be responded to by mine. It is protocol."

Elena scowled, brows pulling together. "How can it be protocol when there are only two consorts around?"

"Do you call me a liar?" He'd never enjoyed teasing anyone before he met his hunter.

Stroking her fingers through the hair at his nape, she used her teeth on his jaw. "I don't know how to do all that fancy stuff."

"You are my consort." A kiss placed on her cheekbone. "You may do things any way you wish."

Gray eyes rimmed with a very, very thin circle of purest silver met his as her fingers pressed on the back of his head. "Yeah? In that case, I think I'd like to distract you."

He allowed her to bring them closer, angling his head so he could take that stubborn mouth, those soft lips. She tasted of wildness barely contained, a brilliant, blinding mortal fire. Ready for the blaze, he was startled to feel her hands move to cup his face, her hold tender in a way that leveled his defenses as she whispered, "Let me love you tonight."

Enchained, he made no protest when she slid off the desk, switched off the lights, and turned to tug him to the warm glow of the fireplace. As he watched, she undid the straps that held her black top snug to her body and dropped it to the rug—to reveal lush breasts he'd marked with his kiss more than once. Tonight, it was the fire that marked her, flickering over her skin and burnishing her in red gold, creating sultry shadows he wanted to explore with his mouth, his body.

She sighed in pleasure when he slid his hand over the curve of her waist, but her fingers were on the buttons of his shirt. He shrugged it to the floor the instant it was open, wanting her hands on him. She gave him exactly that. Palms flat on his chest, she stroked over his pectorals, his rib cage, his abdomen. "I could do this," she mumured, exploring the ridges and dips of his body with a slow intensity that made his cock throb, "for hours."

Palming the erotic weight of her breasts, he bent to press a kiss to her shoulder. "I'm afraid your consort does not have such patience." He used his thumbs to tease her nipples as she twined her fingers through his hair, as she tugged him up, as she seduced his mouth with her own.

When she drew back to kiss her way down his neck to his chest and lower, he permitted it. The night was yet young and he'd discovered he had a weakness for being loved by Elena. *What wicked things are you planning to do tonight, Guild Hunter?*

Kneeling in front of him, her wings spread behind her in an extraordinary display—gleaming midnight shading to indigo, to a deep, haunting blue before whispering into dawn and a shimmering white gold kissed by the firelight—she tilted up her head to give him a provocative smile. "You'll just have to wait and see." Reaching up, she undid the fastenings on his pants, brushing the rigid push of his cock with her fingertips as she did so. He had no compunction in helping her strip off the remainder of his clothing, in standing naked and aroused before her.

So proud, Elena thought, so beautiful. Fisting him with her hand, she stroked once, tight and smooth. His hand clenched in her hair, and when she looked up, she saw he'd thrown back his head, the cords of his neck standing out so strong and taut that she wanted to rise up, bite down on them. Then there were his wings, magnificent in their power.

He was pure addiction. And he was hers. To take. To pleasure.

Placing the palm of her free hand flat on the thick muscle of his thigh, she leaned in to lick at the head of his cock.

*Elena.* A warning not to tease.

Another night, she might have done just that, but tonight, she wanted to love him hot and sweet. Sliding her grip to the base of his arousal, she closed her mouth over the head. His shout was gritted out, those muscular thighs unyielding as rock as his hand pulled at her hair. And the taste of him . . . Moaning around the rigid length covered by velvet-soft skin, she took an inch more. Sucked wet and deep.

A harder tug on her hair. *Now, Elena.*

She hadn't had her fill, nowhere near close, but there were

other ways to satiate her hunger. Releasing him after laving her tongue over the thick vein that ran along his arousal, she rose up and nudged him backward until his knees hit the back of one of the chairs not far from the fire. "Sit."

A raised eyebrow, pure masculine arrogance.

Lips curving even as things low in her body pulsed with the darkest of sexual cravings, she stepped back to pull off her jeans and panties. This time, when she pushed at the muscled silk of his chest, he went down into a sitting position, his hands sliding over her rib cage to settle on her hips. Instead of tugging her forward as she'd expected, he leaned down to press a kiss to the dip of her navel. *Hunter mine.*

Heart aching under the rush of emotion, she weaved her fingers through his hair. "I love you, Archangel." Her body trembled at the intimacy of his breath against her skin, the rough caress of his jaw. When he lifted his head, she didn't wait, couldn't wait. Shifting to straddle him, she fitted him to the ultrasensitive entrance to her body, sliding down that hard heat oh-so-slowly, his hands possessive brands on her hips.

A shudder rippled through her as she succeeded in sheathing him. Holding him within her, caressing him with intimate muscles until he whispered promises of retribution, she put her own hands on his shoulders, squeezed. "Brace me, Archangel."

*Would you ride tonight, hbeebti?* Strong hands moving down over her thighs to grip her just below the knees as he sucked on her lower lip before inciting a languorous tangling of their mouths.

*Oh, yes.* Then, as the storm continued to rage outside, she took her archangel, slow and deep, and again, until the crashing wildness of pleasure swept them both under.

# 22

The next day, having received a message early that morning, Elena found herself flying down to land in front of a gated home in the Palisades area. Set back from the street and shaded with perfectly manicured greenery, it shrieked of money. Even the architecture—old, elegant, timeless—told her she was looking at something that had cost in the millions.

*I could afford this.*

It was a startling thought. She kept forgetting that she was rich now, that the Cadre—through Raphael—had paid her the fee they'd agreed on when she had "accepted" the Uram mission. Snorting at the memory of exactly how she'd been dragged into the whole bloody mess, she folded back her wings and stared at the glossy black door of the home only a few feet away.

Narrow. Too narrow for angelic wings.

It was stupid to feel rejected. Her sister Beth had lived here with her husband, Harrison, since the day they had married—both had been human at the time. Then Harrison had applied to be Made a vampire, been accepted . . . and broken the century-long contract of service he'd signed on for as a condition of being Made. Elena was the hunter who'd brought him back to face his punishment. Harrison didn't understand that he couldn't hide for eternity, that the longer it took for his angel to track him down, the worse the price he'd have had to pay.

As a result of Harrison's antipathy, Elena had never been invited inside Beth's home. She didn't begrudge her sister for standing by her husband, had done her best to make sure Beth knew that. However, by the same token, she refused to disappear from Beth's life. No matter what, her sister knew she could pick up the phone and Elena would come.

The door flew open at that instant, revealing a gorgeous strawberry blonde dressed in what appeared to be a cashmere sweater in cream paired with a polka-dotted knee-length skirt, the shape full and feminine. "Ellie!" Her sister ran. "Ellie!"

As she caught Beth's smaller, softer body, Elena felt time unravel, scrolling backward until they were children again. Beth had always been the baby, and she'd toddled around after Elena as Elena had in her turn toddled around after Ari and Belle. Now, of the four children Marguerite had borne, only two remained—and Elena had become the big sister. "Hey, Bethie."

Beth's arms remained locked around Elena, her face damp against Elena's neck. "You didn't come see me first. You're supposed to come see me first!"

Another bittersweet reminder of childhood, Beth's insistence that she come first in Elena's life. "I thought you just got back today? Weren't you in the Caymans?"

A sniffle. "You have wings. You could've flown to me." Pulling away at last, Beth reached out and touched the upper curve of Elena's wing.

It was a sensitive spot, a place she allowed Raphael alone to caress. "Lower, Beth," she said with conscious gentleness.

Beth shifted her hold at once—forever the younger sister, used to taking orders. "They're so pretty, Ellie." Sweet words, shining eyes of a translucent turquoise that had come from Marguerite, a single moment uncolored by the choices they'd both made. "I'm glad you have wings. You always wanted to fly."

A flash of memory, Elena in her homemade cape, "flying" after a giggling Beth. It was impossible not to smile. "How are you?"

A shrug, her hand falling away. "Okay."

Worried by the muted response from a sister who'd always been vibrant, if not a little high-strung, Elena brushed Beth's hair away from her face. "You know you can talk to me. Have I ever let you down?"

"You turned my husband in to his angel." Open petulance.

*"Beth."* Harry had chosen his fate when he asked to be Made—and unlike Vivek, he'd been healthy as a human, could well have lived the full span of a mortal life. If the servitude he'd signed on for now grated, he had no one to blame but himself.

Beth's sullen expression broke, her face seeming to collapse in on itself as she began to cry in great, gulping sobs. Shattered by her sister's pain, Elena took Beth into her arms and rocked her. "Talk to me, Bethie. Tell me what's wrong." *So I can fix it.*

It was what she did, a self-imposed duty.

Even after Jeffrey had thrown her out of the Big House, Elena had checked in every week with Beth, made sure her sister was okay. Beth, too, had stuck by Elena in her own way. When Jeffrey had dumped Elena's things out on the street, it had been sweet, compliant Beth who'd gone out and saved Elena's most important treasures from the elements. She'd done it in secret, but she had done it.

*"I'm not as strong as you, Ellie." Whispered words as they stood hidden in the shadow of the Big House. "I'm sorry."*

*"Don't cry, sweetheart." Taking her sister into her arms, holding her tight. "It's okay. I'm strong enough for both of us."*

Now, Elena pressed her lips to her sister's temple. "Beth?"

"Oh, Ellie." Beth pulled away with a hiccup. Using a handkerchief to dab at her face, she managed to look beautiful even with eyes rimmed in red and a nose that had gone raw at the tip. "They won't Make me, Ellie. That was always the plan, that Harry and I, we'd both become immortal and then we'd be together forever, but they said they won't Make me."

Elena's blood ran cold. She'd asked Raphael about Beth, been told that her sister wasn't biologically compatible. If they tried to infuse her with the toxin that turned human to vampire, she'd either die or go incurably insane. "I'm sorry—"

"You're an angel now, Ellie." Beth gripped her upper arms, hope a shining beacon in her eyes. "You can Make me. Or you can ask your archangel to. Please, Ellie. *Please.*"

Feeling bruised and battered after the argument that had resulted when she told Beth there was nothing she could do, Elena was in no frame of mind to undertake the next task on her list. But—"I've been a coward long enough." She put the key into the heavy yellow lock and twisted. The first time she'd seen that key, she'd assumed Jeffrey had hired a small locker to store the pieces of her childhood . . . of her mother—but this was the size of an entire room, complete with a metal rolling door.

Sara, leaning against the neighboring storage unit, arms crossed over the rich plum of her trim suit, shook her head. "It's not about being a coward, Ellie. You know that. This has to hurt like hell."

Yeah, it hurt. So bad.

*"Forgive me, my babies."*

Anger and sadness and love mixed in a caustic brew inside of her. It was a familiar feeling—her emotions toward Marguerite would never be simple. "Thanks for coming with me. I know how busy you are."

"Thank me again, and I'll have to kick your ass." Sara reached down to fix the thin strap that arched over the top of her three-inch heels. "Though I'm surprised tall, omnipotent, and dangerous isn't with you."

"I needed you." The woman who'd become more family to her than the people with whom she shared blood. "Raphael understands friendship, even if he doesn't think so." He'd forged bonds of steel with his Seven, Dmitri in particular.

Lock undone, she held it in one hand as she reached down to push up the door. Light hit the floor within, and then the box nearest the door.

A frayed orange blanket hung over the edge.

Heart in her throat, she tried to continue pushing up the door, but she couldn't. Her entire body just froze. "Sara."

Her best friend put her hand on the door. "Which way, Ellie? Up or down?"

*"Come on, bébé." Laughing words in that husky voice with its pretty accent. "Climb on board."*

*Struggling onto the big bed, her blanket around her shoulders, she squirmed between Ari and her mom.*

*"Hey!" Ari's protesting voice before she peppered Elena's giggling face with kisses. "Little grease monkey."*

"Ellie."

Jerking herself back into the present, Elena pushed down the door, relocking it with fingers that trembled. "I can't do it." Her heart was thunder in her throat, her palms damp. "God, I can't." She collapsed onto the ground, back to the door.

Sara sank down beside her, uncaring of the damage to her hose. "It's waited all this time. It'll wait a while longer." Putting her hand on Elena's arm, she squeezed. "You've had a hell of a lot to process over the past year and a half. Nothing says you have to rush this."

"I don't know why it's affecting me like this. There are good memories in there." Except sometimes, she suddenly realized, even the best memories could cut like knives. "Sara," she said, the words tumbling out, "I need to tell you something about my past."

"I'm here."

At that simple statement of support, Elena took a deep breath . . . and finally told her best friend about the monster who had broken Ari and Belle until they were macabre dolls in a blood-soaked kitchen; until her mother was a woman who screamed and screamed and screamed; until her father was a stranger who hated his eldest surviving daughter. "I couldn't tell you before," she whispered. "I couldn't even bring myself to think about it."

Tears streaked Sara's face. "This is why you used to wake up screaming."

They'd been roommates at Guild Academy, and after they graduated. "Yes." Some part of her hadn't stopped screaming since that murderous day almost two decades in the past.

In spite of Sara's rock-solid friendship, in spite of the physical release of the intense flying drills she did later that day, Elena couldn't shake the melancholy that draped her in emotional black. As she stood in the shower prior to getting dressed for dinner, the events of the day came crashing down on her, an unforgiving rain. Even worse than her effective breakdown at the storage unit was the memory of the look of betrayal on Beth's face as her sister turned away from her.

*"I'll die, Ellie. I'll die and you'll still be alive."*

She tried to wash away the pain that twisted through her heart, but it refused to leave. When her eyes smarted, she told herself she'd gotten some shampoo into them and turned her face into the spray. She couldn't so easily ignore the knowledge that as the years passed, she'd have to watch wrinkles mark a face that had always been younger, and one day, she'd stand over Beth's grave.

Unable to bear the thought, she wrenched off the water and stepped out . . . into the arms of an archangel. "I'm wet." The words were snapped out.

He tugged her water-slick body even closer to his. *I feel the echo of your pain, Elena.*

Distressed as she was, she knew he could've taken the reason for that pain from her mind without her being aware of it, was likely battling the compulsion to do exactly that. "It's nothing," she said, the hurt too raw to share. "Nothing new."

A wave of rain and wind inside her mind, the fury of a leashed storm. *Your father again?*

"No." That was all she could say without breaking into a thousand splintered pieces. "I can't talk about it yet, Raphael."

A pause, heavy with power.

It was an unintended reminder that the man she called her
lover, her consort, was nothing even close to human. Still,
she didn't move away, didn't raise her guard. That, too, was
hard . . . but Raphael had held her when she fell, prepared
to give up his immortal life for her, a hunter, an unwanted
daughter . . . and right now, a hated sister.

The stroke of a big, warm hand on her lower back. "Then
we will talk at another time. But we will be talking."

Feeling her instincts shake off the pain that had gutted her,
she raised her head. "I thought we discussed the whole you-
giving-me-orders thing?"

Endless, relentless blue. "Did we?" Plush softness around
her as he wrapped her in a towel, wings and all. "I had a visi-
tor today."

"You're changing the subject." And he looked so very un-
apologetic doing it that she knew she was about to let herself
get suckered.

A slow smile. "Lijuan."

Steel-edged worry wiped away every other emotion.
"Again?" Ice crawled up her spine at the memory of the devotion and pain she'd seen on the face of one of the reborn who had
loved his mistress, thought, too, of how he'd torn a man apart
with his bare hands, until the viscera steamed in the open air.

"I knew she remained in my territory," Raphael said, "but it
was still an unexpected visit."

Letting him rub at her hair with a second towel while she
gripped the first between her breasts, she touched her fingers to the warmth of his chest. "So? What did she want this
time?"

Raphael dropped the other towel to the floor and ran his
fingers through the damp strands of her hair, his gaze turning
a deep, impenetrable cobalt. "The same—to convince me to
murder my mother."


Still blinking in shock half an hour later as she finished
drying her hair and turned to pick up the dress that had ap-

peared on the bed, she stared at Raphael. "We have to find your mother before she does, don't we?"

"Yes." Wearing nothing but black dress pants, he leaned against the wall, arms folded, his eyes taking a leisurely tour of her body. "You do not ask the obvious question, Elena. You did not ask after Lijuan's previous visit, either."

She'd shrugged off her robe in preparation for putting on the dress—in a brilliant shade of blue, of course—and was wearing only a pair of gossamer panties in mint green, a small white silk flower sitting below one hip. It was clear what her archangel thought of her current state of undress. "I think," she murmured, "you need to turn up the air-conditioning."

A slow smile laced with pure seduction. "Come here, Hunter."

Shaking her head, she picked up the dress and stepped into it. Unlike the gown she'd worn for Lijuan's ball, this one wasn't ankle-length but came to a few inches above the knee, the material fitting snugly over her hips before flaring out in a playful skirt. The pretty halter neck not only provided adequate support for her breasts—always a consideration for a hunter—but closed with a glittering crystal button.

She'd never, in a million years, have chosen the dress for herself, but had to admit it looked both elegant and sexy. "What obvious question?" she asked after slipping the button into its hole.

"Whether it would not be better to join with Lijuan to find Caliane, execute her in her Sleep."

"She's your mother, Raphael. Of course you can't destroy her without knowing if she *has* healed, become sane." Turning to the vanity, she raised her hair off her neck and twisted it up into a sleek knot Sara had taught her. "Your laws exist for a reason—other angels must've come out of the Sleep in better condition than when they went in."

Looking down to grab a hairpin, she wasn't ready for the burn of an archangel's kiss on her nape, the heavy weight of his hands on her hips. "Most of me is convinced she'll rise as viciously insane as when she went to ground. But—"

"She is your mother." Elena, more than anyone, understood the opposing emotions that had to be tearing him apart.

"Yes."

Teeth scraped over her skin, making her shiver. "We'll be late."

Stroking up with his hands, he cupped her breasts. Squeezed. Another kiss on that sensitive spot along the curve of her neck before he drew back. "You are right to remind me, Elena. I owe the Hummingbird my respect."

Hair done, she put on some lipstick, then turned to watch Raphael as he picked up his shirt. A pure white, the fabric on either side of the wing slots embroidered with curling designs in black that echoed the pattern of his wings, it threw the harsh purity of his masculine beauty into cutting focus.

"I know the Hummingbird was the one who eventually found you," she said, heart twisting at the thought of him lying hurt and broken on that desolate field where his mother had left him. "But the ties between you . . . there's more to it, isn't there?"

The evening sunlight turned his wings to amber as he answered. "She didn't only save me, she mothered me as much as I would allow."

Elena walked over to finish buttoning his shirt. "You didn't allow her much did you?"

"No."

The earth trembled at that instant, just enough to make her close her hand over his shoulder to steady herself.

"A minor quake," Raphael said when it passed. "Reports indicate weather is calming across the world."

She fell into the wild blue of his eyes when he lifted his head from his unhidden visual exploration of her skin, her body. "Is that good news or bad?"

"It means she is almost awake."

# 23

Elena took one look at the Hummingbird as the angel stepped into the living room on Illium's arm and stopped breathing.

Michaela was beautiful, perhaps the most beautiful woman who had ever lived, but this woman was . . . radiant. It was the only word Elena could come up with to describe her. Eyes of sparkling champagne, hair of purest black tipped with gold, skin stroked by the sun . . . and wings of a wild, unexpected indigo, each feather bearing streaks of shimmering gold so pale as to be sunlight.

When she smiled, her lashes came down for a second and Elena saw that they were black tipped with gold. "Hello," the angel said. "They call me the Hummingbird, but you may call me Sharine."

Elena took the hands Sharine held out, unable to refuse. They were small, delicate, in perfect proportion to the Hummingbird's bare five feet of height. "I'm Elena."

"Oh, I know." A laugh that was pure diamond sparkles glittering in the air. "My baby's told me all about you."

Looking up at Illium, she expected to see a playful scowl, but the blue-winged angel watched his mother with a mute sadness that made Elena's own laughter fade. "Your baby," she said at last, "is very beautiful."

"Yes, I have to have a care—the girls will be after him once he grows up a little more." Her gaze shifted to behind Elena. "Raphael." Smiling with such love that it made Elena's heart hurt, the Hummingbird walked into Raphael's arms. "How's my other boy? Never my baby, not you. But still my son."

Elena watched in fascination as Raphael dipped his head and let Sharine straighten first his hair, then his shirt. She'd never seen him bow his head before any other being, male or female, but he treated the Hummingbird with the greatest respect . . . and care. Such care that it spoke of handling something broken.

When Elena glanced at Illium again, she couldn't stand what she saw on that face that was a dream of beauty. Closing the distance between them, she curled her hand around one muscled arm—as in the Refuge, his upper body was bare. Except tonight, his chest bore a painting of a huge bird in flight. "That's stunning." It didn't take more than a cursory study to realize the bird was a stylized version of Illium.

"My mother," he said, his voice more solemn than she'd ever heard it, "is the one who taught Aodhan to draw, to sculpt. To act as her canvas is considered a great honor among angelkind."

As Elena watched, Sharine put her hand on Raphael's chest, smoothing out a nonexistent wrinkle. "We have not met for many days," she said. "Five or six at least."

Elena frowned. She knew Raphael hadn't had physical contact with the Hummingbird for over a year, and yet Sharine's words held nothing of humor, nothing that said she was gently chiding him for the time that had passed. Suddenly her earlier words, calling Illium her "baby," cast a far more somber shadow.

"Yes," Raphael said with a slow smile. "I knew you would come see me before the seventh."

Sharine laughed then, and it felt like warm raindrops against Elena's skin.

"She's . . ."

"I know." Illium's muscles tightened under her hold. "Ellie . . ."

"Hush." She leaned into him, allowing her wing to brush over his. "She loves you, loves Raphael. That's what matters."

"Yes." Smiling at his mother when the Hummingbird turned and held out a hand, he went to help her get seated.

The dinner was magical. Elena had heard Raphael use his voice in that way—until it felt like a tactile caress, but Sharine had honed it into an art form. Listening to her was like being surrounded by a thousand streamers of sensation, all of them sparkling with brilliance.

And the stories she told—of Raphael's and Illium's youth, such wonderful stories of bravery and folly, all told with a mother's pride in her sons. Sharine had not borne Raphael, Elena thought as she stood on their private balcony later that night, watching the Hummingbird take flight with Illium by her side, but she had cared for him just the same. "She reminds me of some gorgeous hothouse flower."

"One that's been crumpled," Raphael said, his hands on her shoulders as he pulled her back against his chest, one arm sliding around to hold her pressed to him. "For the rest, you must ask Illium."

Placing her hand over his forearm, she shook her head. "I can't. Not when I see how much it hurts him." She'd believed she knew the greatest tragedy of the blue-winged angel's life. He'd loved a mortal, lost her to angelic law and her human life span. But the pain she'd seen tonight, it was older, deeper . . . raw and aged and angry. "How long is she staying in the city?"

"She will leave within the hour—she finds it difficult to linger far from home."

As they stood there in silence, there was a spark of fire in the sky. Then another, and another.

The stars were falling.


There was no magic the next day. Even the spring sunshine promised by a stunning dawn was subsumed by bone-chilling horror as the calm broke in the most decisive of ways.

Flying down, then up toward the bottom of Manhattan Bridge, Elena hooked her fingers in the massive metal structure and stared at the five bodies that hung from its belly. They'd been spotted at daybreak by one of the craft that used this section of the East River—the witness was apparently still puking his guts out.

Elena swallowed her own gorge as the bodies swung from the ropes.

*Swinging so gently. One foot bare, one clad in a shiny high-heeled shoe.*

"No shadows," she said, fighting the nightmare. "There are no shadows." It was too early in the day, and for that mercy, she could only be grateful. "One, two, three." Her fingers refused to release their grip.

Another river-borne wind. The bodies swayed.

Her stomach bucked, bile burning the back of her throat.

"Hey, you see anything useful?" Santiago's distinctive voice came from the wireless device tucked over her ear.

"No," she said, forcing the word out through gritted teeth. "Let me get closer." *And do my job.* She would not let the past steal her future from her.

Taking a deep breath, she let go of the bridge finger by finger, then dropped low enough that she could spiral over the water before beating her way to a closer position. As she rose up over the choppy waves, she kept her eyes resolutely on the spot underneath the bridge where she intended to hook her arms in an effort to brace herself. "This would be easier if I was human," she muttered.

"Yeah?"

She jerked, having forgotten Santiago could hear everything. "Harness would be useful," she said. "Impossible to get wings into one though."

"We'll have to get a special set made for you."

Nothing in his tone said he was joking.

"Thanks." For accepting her wings in as straightforward a fashion as he'd accept a new coat.

*There.*

Grabbing the metal in a secure grip, she held on with one arm as she hooked her leg over the beam. Only when she was in a stable position did she look down at the rope, thick and brown, where it had been tied to the beam. Her eyes skimmed forward—each of the five bodies hung from the bridge the same way, the ropes the same length.

"Someone took their time." It wasn't the broken necks alone that had killed them—most vampires over a decade old could survive that unless the break was close to decapitation, and hunter instincts whispered that these men were all over fifty, though not by too much. No, it was the fact that it looked like their hearts had been removed, too, their shirts plastered to their fronts by stains that could've come from only one thing. At this age, the dual shock would've been enough even without total separation of the head from the body.

"Had to be fucking what's-his-name? The guy in the red and blue suit with the spider thing."

"Not a movie buff, Santiago?"

"I'm a man. I watch football and hockey as I should."

Even as she responded to his dry humor, Elena thought of the vampires she'd seen skittering over walls with the strength and speed of arachnids, and knew the answer had to be both more prosaic than a comic-book superhero—and possibly more terrifying, if the hint of scent Elena could taste in the air was to be believed.

*Lush. Sensual. Exotic. Whispers of a rain-dark forest, a hidden glade.*

Keeping her wings tight to her back in an effort to avoid the rusted metal all around, she shifted along her perch until she was directly above the first vampire. It wasn't so bad from that position, she realized, because she'd never been on the mezzanine when her mother had chosen to—

Slamming the door shut on that memory, she took a deep, steady breath, drawing in the scents. Salt, the sea, it was a constant, so she took that out of the equation straight away. She also put aside the puzzlingly pristine fragrance of Caliane's signature black orchids.

*Sweetgrass, cut on a summer's day.*

It was one of the most delicate scents she'd ever sensed on a vampire, and it belonged to the one who hung on this rope. Which meant the killer's scent was either much more faint or not present. Knowing she had to get closer to the victim, she twisted, managing to drop down into a hanging position with both arms hooked over the metal beam for support, her wings spread wide for balance.

The body was only inches away . . . but too far down.

Gritting her teeth, she shifted her hold until she was gripping the metal with her fingers. Still not close enough. "There's nothing I can do here," she said at last, frustration gnawing at her temper. "I'll have to do the final scent track when the bodies are—Fuck!"

"Elena! Talk to me!"

Heart thudding triple-time, she reached out and managed to just graze the vampire's forehead with her fingertips. Plasticky, frigid from the air. Except . . . "Oh God." She'd definitely seen it this time—the flicker of an eyelid, as if he was struggling to raise it. "He's alive! Get Rescue down here now!"

"Shit! I'm on it."

Santiago was efficient but she knew it would take time. If this vampire—Jesus, maybe all the vamps—were in any way conscious, then what they were suffering right now had to be torture. Dropping and sweeping out from under the bridge, she rose into the air, twisting her head in every direction.

"Looking for someone, Ellie?"

Startled, she fell several feet before getting her momentum under control. Illium came to hover beside her when she rose back up and caught the edge of the bridge once again, holding herself in place so she could talk to him. "At least one of them is alive. Can you get them down?" He was the single angel she knew who might have a hope of maneuvering in the cramped conditions.

He held out a hand. "Dagger."

Glad he no longer looked as tormented as he had the previous evening, she slapped one of her knives in his hand and watched as he flew in, somehow executing the tightest of turns before reaching over and cutting the rope. The vampire dropped. But Illium was faster. He scooped the male up before the vampire's dead weight of a body could touch the water. Elena followed him up onto the bridge itself—which the cops had cordoned off at both ends, making themselves real popular with commuters—and landed.

Soon as Illium placed the male on the road and dove off to get the rest of the victims, she took out another knife and began to cut through the vampire's shirt, pulling away the matted fabric and wincing at the chunks of skin that came with it. But she had to see the damage. Santiago, having come down on his haunches beside her, watched in silence as she succeeded in revealing the ruin of the vampire's chest.

It sure as hell looked like he'd suffered major damage to the region around his heart, but there was so much dried blood tangled up in thick curls of black chest hair that she couldn't tell for sure. Unhooking the wireless device over her ear, she gave it to Santiago before reaching into one of the pockets of the fleece-lined vest she'd put on as protection against the wind, and pulling out a pair of latex gloves.

Santiago took the chance to lean forward and hold the screen of his cell phone a scant inch from the vampire's mouth. "Shit," he muttered when the screen began to mist with steam. "For a minute, I thought you'd lost it down there. But shit." He glanced over her shoulder to where Illium was landing a second time.

Elena was ninety-nine-percent certain she might actually *have* lost it if she hadn't been so fucking shocked out of her mind. "I need something with which to wash off the blood." The irony of the fact that the East River churned below wasn't lost on her.

"Wait." Santiago returned moments later with two water bottles as well as a pack of tissues. "From the squad cars. Medics are on their way."

Vampires didn't need medics to heal, but during the regeneration process, their bodies hurt the same as a mortal's. The paramedics could at least give them drugs, knock them out for a while. "Good." Dampening a wad of tissue, she cleaned the male's chest with quick, careful motions as Santiago went to check the other bodies.

Great gouges marked the vampire's flesh beneath the clotted black of his blood, as if someone had tried to dig through his skin.

*A flash of memory, Raphael's hand punching through a vampire's sternum to remove his still-beating heart.*

"But that," she muttered, trying to keep things practical, logical, "was a single strike." Quick, brutal, efficient. This, by contrast, had been done by someone who didn't have Raphael's strength—because while the male's chest looked as if it had been through the shredder, his heart beat safe behind his rib cage.

"They're all alive." Santiago sounded shaken. "Christ, it's like someone fucking clawed this guy."

That was what Elena was thinking. "The question is, who?"

A strange silence.

Following the detective's gaze as he came down on his haunches again, the wind flipping his tie over his shoulder, she watched as he put a gloved hand under the victim's. The vampire's fingers and nails were encrusted with blood and what might well have been bits of flesh. "He did it to himself." A cold far deeper than the winds that buffeted the bridge slid through her veins.

Santiago glanced at the row of bodies Illium had laid out. "They all did."

Elena knew from her lessons at the Refuge that very, very few angels had the power to compel a man to savage himself. To kill, yes. But to mutilate and torture? No, that power was reserved for the Cadre . . . and the Sleepers who had once been Cadre.

# 24

Having been away from the city when he received Elena's call, Raphael now landed beside the Central Park pond where she stood watching the ducks. "We have been here before." She'd been mortal then, a hunter he intended to bend to his will.

No smile on that expressive face; the rustle of the leaves were secret whispers in the air. "I wondered if you'd remember."

"Tell me what you found."

Elena glanced around the quiet but not deserted area. "Not here."

Taking her into his arms, he rose up into the sky. The flight across the Hudson took only minutes, and then he was landing near the house of glass his consort so loved, his gaze on her as she flared out her wings to descend. *Your control is improving.*

"I'm nowhere near the level I need to be if I'm going to be effective in a hunt." Tucking her hair behind her ears, she walked into the warm humidity of the greenhouse. "I sensed black orchids. It's such a unique scent, it's impossible to mistake." Touching her fingers to a blush pink bloom, she shook her head. "The purity of it bothers me for some reason—my perfumes contact is trying to get me a sample so I can figure out why." Gray eyes solemn with concern met his as he closed the door behind them.

Instinct and experience told him to reject her worry, her care. An archangel did not survive by being weak. He survived by being more lethal than any other. *Come here, Elena.*

When she shifted to stand bare inches from him, he curved his hand around the back of her neck, rubbing his thumb over her pulse. "Not many know of this particular punishment." But he did. He'd been there, a young child who'd understood even then that justice had to be served. "My mother did not wish to be a goddess like Lijuan or Neha. Neither did she wish to rule empires like my father."

Elena's hair fell in a silken waterfall over his arm as she raised her head so she could watch him as he spoke. She didn't ask questions, but every part of her stood with him, unflinching against the darkness coming inexorably closer.

"But she was treated as a goddess, and she did rule," he murmured, "as I rule." He had learned about ruling from his mother, learned that there was a way to do it that would inspire both respect and awe without the debilitating fear that surrounded so many archangels. "She ruled Sumeria, but there was one particular city she treated as home. It was called Amanat."

His hunter's hand came to rest on his waist as lines formed on her brow. "I've heard about it. On a TV special about lost cities."

"Amanat and its people disappeared when Caliane vanished." *Some say she took her people into Sleep with her, so that they would be there to welcome her when she woke. Most believe she murdered them all before she took her own life, for she loved them too well to leave them under another's rule, and that Amanat is her grave.*

Elena brushed the fingers of her free hand over the edge of one of his wings. He spread them wider, giving her easier access. A drop of water from a disturbed cluster of tiny white blossoms trickled along his feathers as, taking the invitation, she touched him with a firmer stroke. "Which do you believe?"

He settled her into the vee of his thighs, bracing her so both her hands would be free. "My mother," he said, "loved things of beauty. Do you recall the ruby on the shelf in my Tower office?" The priceless gemstone was flawless in its faceted splendor. "She gave it to me for my tenth birthday."

"She had impeccable taste."

"Amanat," Raphael continued, "was her jewel of jewels. She loved that city, truly loved it. I spent many of the happiest years of my childhood running wild above its paved streets."

"Angels are so protective of their young," Elena murmured, continuing to caress the insides of his wings with those hands that bore calluses from weapons training—a warrior's hands. He wanted none other on him.

"My mother," he began, speaking of the dawn of his existence, "trusted the people of Amanat in a way an archangel seldom trusts anyone." Memories of hot summer days spent flying above ancient buildings carved out of rock; of playing with mortal friends and being petted and adored by adults. "And they loved her. It was not the kind of worship Lijuan or even Neha inspires. It was . . . untainted in a way I cannot describe."

"You just did," Elena murmured. "Love. What they felt was love."

He bent his head a fraction, bringing one hand up to play with the curling tendrils of hair that licked at her temple. "She was a good ruler. Before the madness, she was what an archangel should be."

His consort's eyes softened to a warm, liquid mercury. "The histories Jessamy gave me to read, they said the same. That she was the most beloved of the archangels, that even the rest of the Cadre gave her their respect."

He widened his stance, tucking her close enough that she nuzzled her face into his neck, one hand closing around his nape, the other continuing to caress the sensitive arch of his left wing. "The reason the people of Amanat loved her so"—he breathed in the spring and steel scent of his hunter—"was that she loved them in turn."

Faded echoes of his mother laughing with the maidens who served in her temple, the sunshine of her smile as she gifted a maid about to marry with a dowry of gold and precious silks. "So when a group of vampires from outside came in and hurt two of Amanat's women, she did not look the other way because the women were mortal and the vampires over four hundred years old."

Elena's body turned rigid, her breath warm against the hollow of his neck.

He tightened his hold against the nightmare memories that stalked her. *Elena*.

"It's okay, Archangel. Tell me."

He had never spoken of these events, but they had shaped him as much as Caliane's disappearance. "The vampires kept the women for three days. Three days in the span of a mortal lifetime can feel like three decades." His mother's words. "Since the women were returned alive, she decided not to execute the vampires. Instead, she sentenced them to the same kind of terror they'd inflicted."

Elena sucked in a breath. "She hung them, in a way calculated to ensure they wouldn't die."

"No, Elena. She did not hang them. She made them hang themselves."

Elena flexed her hand on his nape, the bite of her nails tiny kisses. "That explains why I couldn't pick up any other scents on the rope or on the bodies on the bridge. They were compelled to do what they did."

"Yes."

"Those vampires in Amanat, the three days must've—"

"No, Guild Hunter. Remember . . . three days of terror in a mortal lifetime can feel like three decades." He spoke with his lips against her skin, the warmth of her, the *life* of her, shoving away the cold that had been inside him for so long. "Vampires live far beyond a human lifetime."

"Three decades?" A disbelieving whisper. "How did they stay alive?"

"They were fed enough to ensure they lived, and left hanging from a specially constructed gallows in a field where crows liked to rest."

Elena shuddered at the image that bloomed fully formed in her mind. "The birds would've plucked out the eyes, other soft flesh," she whispered. "The parts would have grown back, and the crows would've come again." An endless cycle. "How long did they survive?"

"The entire three decades. My mother made sure of it."

"Your mother was a scary-ass woman," she said. "But if those men did what I'm guessing they did, then the sentence was just." Three days would've meant nothing to a four-hundred-year-old vampire. Sure, it would've hurt at the time but it would've been soon forgotten. Those women would've been scarred forever.

"Yes. They became as they'd left their victims."

She nuzzled at him, realizing they were completely intertwined, her arms around his neck, his legs on either side of hers, one of his hands in her hair, the other on her lower back, his mouth against her temple, his chest hard and solid and real against hers. She'd never felt more centered, more safe, though they were speaking of a cold, deadly horror. "I understand justice. The vampires on the bridge today—do you know anything about them?"

"Dmitri tells me they are young, less than seventy. Not one has done anything that would merit such a punishment—two are steady family men, one is a writer who prefers his own company when not in service as part of his Contract, while two work in the lowest level of Tower business."

"Under a hundred—weak, easy to control." Especially for an archangel rising from a millennia of Sleep. She didn't say that last aloud, couldn't hurt him in that way.

*It is all right, Elena. If my mother did this, and there is every reason to believe that she did, she has lost all that made her the once beloved ruler of Amanat.*

A bleak silence.

Elena held him to her, close enough that their heartbeats melded. It was the only thing she knew to do, the only thing she could give him. If he had to draw his mother's blood, she'd stand with him, no matter if he ordered her to keep her distance. Because they were linked, she and her archangel, two parts slowly become a whole.

The rest of the day passed by without incident, with Elena spending a good chunk of time with Evelyn. Her sister's innocent enthusiasm, her growing confidence in her skills, was a welcome respite against the darkness on the horizon. She was feeling pretty good about things—until an out of the blue run-in with Santiago back at the house.

"Are you going to tell me what's going on?" the cop asked her. "That, on the bridge this morning?"

Gut going tight, Elena folded her arms. "You already know I can't tell you everything."

Eyes shrewd, Santiago echoed her stance, leaning back against the squad car that had brought him over the bridge and into the Angel Enclave. "So you're not one of us now, Ellie?"

"That's a low blow." She'd known it would come, just hadn't expected it so soon and from *him*. Never from Santiago. "But yeah, if you want to draw a line in the sand—I'm not simply a hunter anymore. I'm an archangel's consort." It felt strange to hear the words fall from her lips, but she'd made her choices, would stand by them.

Straightening from his slouched position, the detective dropped his arms. "Guess that puts me in my place."

She wanted to shake him. "Why are you being so unreasonable? You've always been happy to let the Guild handle vampiric incidents."

"Something about this smells." A stubborn line to his jaw, that salt-and-pepper stubble catching the light. "I don't want the city to become a battleground like it did last time."

"You think I do?"

"You're not human anymore, Ellie. I don't know your priorities."

It hurt worse not just because they'd been friends for years, but because he'd been so accepting of her since her return. Clenching her fists, she gave him a deliberately expressionless face. "I guess that makes us even—I don't know who you are anymore either."

She thought he flinched and was almost certain he was about to say something, but then he got in the squad car, slamming the door shut. Only after he'd driven off did she double over, feeling as if she'd taken a punch to the gut. Breathing past it, she rose back to her full height and walked into the house to call Venom. She needed to pound her aggression out on someone, and the vampire had a way of provoking her past all reason—it was exactly what she needed today.

Venom wasn't only free, he was in a hell of a temper. As a result, she fell into bed that night bruised and battered and exhausted. Raphael raised an eyebrow at her condition when he came to join her. "Why was the mortal here?"

Of course he knew. "He wanted to talk about the case."

An ominous silence that spoke louder than words.

Thumping her fist into the pillow, she turned onto her side. "It's not important, not with everything else that's going on."

"I could always ask the mortal."

She scowled and turned to stare down at him where he lay on his back on the bed. "Blackmail doesn't work well with me."

Arms folded behind his head, he looked at her with blue eyes gone dangerously quiet. "I'm not making a threat."

Her hands curled into tight, bloodless fists. "It's nothing!"

An unblinking gaze.

"Fine." Slamming down on her back, she stared at the ceiling. "It's just . . . hard being torn between two worlds." With the words out, her anger disappeared, to be replaced by a far more hurtful emotion—tight and hot and abrasive in her chest.

Raphael rose up to lean on his elbow beside her, his hair falling over his forehead. It was impossible to resist the temp-

tation to lift her hand, run her fingers through the midnight silk
of it. "I didn't tell you before," she said, the words wanting
out, "but Beth, she said something to me. That she'd die and
I'd still be alive." Emotion burned at the backs of her eyes.
"I'm not supposed to outlive my baby sister, Raphael."

"No." A solemn answer. "But would you change this?
Would you change us?"

"No. Never." An absolute truth. "It still hurts to know that
I'll stand over her grave one day." A single tear escaped her
control to trickle down the side of her face.

Raphael leaned down until their lips brushed. "Your mortal
heart causes you much pain, Elena—but it makes you who
you are." A kiss that stole her breath. "It will give you the
strength to bear the costs of immortality."

He had touched her in so many ways, but that night, he
touched her with a tenderness that broke her heart. He kissed
the salt of her tears away, his lips so firm, so gentle on her
cheek, her jaw, her mouth. And his hands, those powerful,
dangerous hands . . .

Never had she been handled with such exquisite care.
Never had she felt so cherished.

Yet, at the end, he called her, "Warrior mine," this archangel who had seen her at her weakest. Those were the words
she took into a deep, dreamless sleep, Raphael's heartbeat
strong and steady beneath her palm.

*Raphael.*

Elena jerked awake at the whisper, glancing over to see her
archangel asleep on his front, his magnificent wings spread
out until they covered her, too. He had a habit of doing that in
bed, she thought, heart aching at the memory of his tenderness
earlier. But even as she stroked the white-gold of his feathers
with one hand, she retrieved the dagger she'd secreted down
the side of the bed with the other.

If that was Lijuan whispering into the inky dark of the bedroom, then a dagger wouldn't do much good, but Elena felt

better with the kiss of steel against her skin. Pushing tangled hair off her face with her free hand, she searched the room with her gaze. There were no intruders, nothing that shouldn't be there. But her heart continued to pound, as if—

*Raphael.*

Ice in her bloodstream, her eyes arrowed toward a rippling pocket of air at the bottom of the bed. Almost a mirage, but not quite. It was as if the fabric of the world itself was being twisted as something tried to take shape and failed. Throat dry, she reached out without taking her eyes off that thing and shook Raphael's muscular shoulder. It amazed her that he'd slept through this—he tended to wake the instant she did, because the fact was, he didn't *need* to sleep.

Solid muscle under her hand. But Raphael didn't wake.

*Archangel,* she said into his mind, *wake up. There's something in the room.*

Silence. Emptiness.

Her entire body went stiff, hand clenching on his shoulder. Nothing, but nothing, had ever stopped Raphael from responding to a mental plea from her. He'd found her in the middle of New York when Uram had held her captive in a charnel house of a room. He'd tracked her across the Refuge when Michaela went nuclear at the Medica. He'd broken a meeting of the Cadre itself to save her life in Beijing. There was no way he'd sleep through a call from her when she was sitting right next to him.

Staring at the strange near mirage, she set her jaw and lifted the steel in her hand. "Go to hell." A soft whisper as she threw.

# 25

The knife sliced through the air to dig home in the opposite wall, the hilt quivering at the impact. The mirage, though it didn't disappear . . . sort of fractured. That was when she caught the whisper of a scent that shouldn't have been there.

*Lush, sensual, exotic.*

Black orchids, but it was somehow different from what she'd sensed on the murdered girl's body, on the men hanging from the bridge.

But there was no time for her to process the notes, because a split second after the fracture, a wing was rising under her touch. Moving so fast she couldn't track him with her eyes, Raphael was up and standing beside the bed, the white-hot glow of him so vivid as to erase the lines of his form, to turn him into a blazing torch. Stunned, Elena threw a hand over her eyes and ducked her head in preparation for crawling out of bed so she could retrieve the weapons she'd hidden underneath, do what she could to assist.

But one blink and the blinding heat of his power was gone.

Looking up, hand itching for a weapon, she saw that the *thing* in the center of the room had disappeared, no hint of black orchids in the air. But she didn't drop her guard until Raphael said, "My mother is no longer here, Elena." There was a remoteness to his voice she didn't like.

Pushing off the blankets, she began to slide out.

Raphael was already pulling on a pair of pants over that magnificent body. "I'll be back before dawn. She will not return tonight."

"Wait!"

He didn't even pause at the balcony doors, pushing them wide open. She managed to cover the distance just in time to see him disappear into the starry night sky, flying so far and fast that she lost track of him in the space of a few piercing seconds. Anger stabbed through her, hot and determined. Damn if he was going to do this—especially after the intimacy of the moments they'd shared not only tonight, but since she'd woken from the coma, after the bonds they'd forged.

Stalking back into the bedroom, she pulled on her own pants, slapped on one of the supportive tank tops that had been designed to fit around her wings using straps, then slid on the warm, lined sleeves that fit snugly over her upper arms and left her hands free. She was back on the balcony bare minutes after he'd taken off, very conscious of the tendrils of dark chocolate and fur curling beneath the bedroom door as the male behind the scents got ever closer—Dmitri had come over for a late meeting with Raphael, opted to stay the night in one of the rooms reserved for the Seven.

Now, it was clear Raphael had told him to watch over Elena.

That, too, she thought with teeth-gritting focus, was going to stop.

Looking down, she realized she had no hope of making a flight from her current position, not with her concentration shot to smithereens. So instead, she jumped over the balcony, using her wings to slow her descent. Then she ran through the trees at the edge of the cliff to dive out over the Hudson, beating her wings—stronger, more resilient—hard and fast to sweep herself up off the choppy water and into the clear beauty of the night sky, the stars sparkling ice on black velvet.

The wind was cool against her skin, liquid soft over her wings. Below her, Manhattan was a midnight sea scattered with glittering jewels. New York. It could be a hard place, a hard city. Just like the archangel who ruled it.

But it was home.

As the archangel was hers.

*Raphael.*

She made the effort to arrow the thought only to him, having worked with him over the past few days to fine-tune what mental abilities she already seemed to have. According to Raphael, she'd gain other abilities with time, and she was happy with that—she had more than enough on her plate right now without having to deal with some unexpected superpower.

No response, but some tug in her soul made her turn, head roughly in the direction of Camden, New Jersey. Raphael had bonded to her on some level deeper than the heart. The hunter she'd once been would've scoffed at such thoughts, but that was before she'd tasted the golden pleasure of ambrosia as Raphael fed it into her mouth, as he kissed immortal life into her dying body.

Who was to say that such an act wouldn't have even deeper consequences?

*Go home, Elena.*

Startled, she dipped and glanced over her shoulder to see Raphael in the sky high above her. *We'll be going home together.*

*You can't hope to keep up with me.* Such arrogance in those words, but that made them no less true.

Instead of answering, she continued to fly, riding the night winds to give herself a break when she could. Some time later, they left the last edges of the cityscape behind, the streetlights below them speaking of quiet neighborhoods locked up in the arms of sleep.

A sweep of air against her face as her archangel shot down

in front of her before rising with heart-stopping speed. He'd shown off for her before. But this wasn't play. This was an archangel pointing out how very puny she was in the scheme of things. *Newsflash, Archangel. I already know I'm as weak as a baby compared to you. Hasn't stopped me from dancing with you anytime yet.*

As the words left her mouth, she remembered something else, a sensual promise he'd made to her at the Refuge. *You said you would show me how angels dance.*

*I am in no mood to be gentle, Guild Hunter.*

She raised an eyebrow. *Consort.*

*You're tiring. I can see your wings beginning to falter.*

Cursing under her breath because he was right, she looked for a place to land. When her eyes lit on a thick branch high above the ground, the tree situated in what looked like a deserted local park, she dropped without hesitation. Maybe she'd break some bones, but hell, she was training so freaking hard for a reason—playing it safe wasn't it.

At the last minute, right when she knew she *was* assuredly going to break some bones, Raphael slipped into her mind and corrected her angle of descent so that she was able to grab the branch and pull herself up to straddle it without damage. She glared in his direction. *Stop taking over whenever you feel like it.*

A dangerous pause. *Would you have preferred to spend the next few weeks in a cast?*

*I'd prefer to learn to do this myself.*

*Yet you attempt to pierce the clouds when you can barely fly in a straight line.*

Anger bubbled through her bloodstream. *Come down here and say that to my face.*

Her hair whipped back in a gust of wind an instant later, and then Raphael was hovering next to her branch, the angles of his face starkly masculine, his eyes blazing that metallic chrome that never augured anything good. "You shouldn't be flying such long distances, much less hunting," he said with the arrogance of an immortal who had lived well over a thousand years. "You need to spend another few years at the Refuge at the very least."

She snorted. "Angels spend that time at the Refuge because they're literally babies. I'm very much an adult."

"Are you certain?" A cold question. "Attempting to break bones making a landing you couldn't hope to realize sounds like something a five-year-old would do."

Changing position so that she sat with both legs hanging over the branch, her wings spread out behind her for balance, she curled her fingers around the living wood in an effort to calm herself. "You know something, Raphael?" she said, fingernails digging into the bark, "I think you're spoiling for a fight."

No words from the immortal in front of her, his face so austere she could almost believe they'd never loved, never laughed together.

"So," she said, leaning forward, "am I."

A glow around his wings, something she'd learned to expect when he was pissed. She held her ground. Because this was who he was, and she either took all of him or she walked away. The latter was not an option.

"You're going home. I'll call Illium to guide you there."

"No more babysitters," she said, her anger a honed blade. "I won't allow it. Neither am I about to toddle off home like a good little girl."

*You will do as I say.*

"Yeah, how's that working for you so far?"

Shifting forward, he braced his hands on the branch on either side of her, his big body pushing between her thighs. *You obey very sweetly.*

Oooh, she thought, he didn't only want a fight, he wanted a *fight*. "I am," she said, trying to remain rational, "one of the strongest hunters in the Guild. Not only that, I survived an archangel and a psycho-would-be-archangel. I've earned my stripes."

*Anoushka almost killed you.*

She thought of the poison Neha's daughter had pumped into her body, of the panic that had made her heart stutter, her blood run cold. "Do you know how many people have 'almost' killed me over the years?" When his eyes iced over with a blue so pure it was unlike any color seen on this earth, she realized that might not have been the best thing to bring up. Then again . . . "I take you as you are," she said, unwilling—unable—to back down. "I do that."

The fierce intensity of that statement cut through the storm of fury riding Raphael, and he heard her, heard, too, the words she didn't say.

*I take you as you are. Take me as I am.*

"I've never seen you as anything but a warrior." Even when she came into his arms, he never forgot that it was a very conscious surrender on her part, a choice she made to let herself be vulnerable.

Her lips tightened, and she shook her head, the fine strands of her hair sliding wild over her shoulders. "It's not enough, Raphael. Just the words aren't enough."

In the Refuge, she'd asked him to stop shadowing her mind. That had been a difficult choice for an archangel to make when keeping a mental watch on her was the best way he had to ensure her safety. "I have given you unparalleled freedom."

"Who are you comparing us with, Archangel?" she asked, watching him with those pale eyes that glimmered witch-bright in the darkness.

A sign of her growing immortality, he realized, wondering if she'd noticed an improvement in her night-vision yet. That would be a trait a hunter would value—for the kiss of immortality could only build on the bones of what was already present.

"We're making our own rules," she continued. "There is no template for us to follow."

His mind flashed to her broken in his arms, her life bleeding out of her a drop at a time. Then had come the silence. Endless, merciless silence as she slept. "Elijah and Hannah have been together hundreds of years," he said. "She follows his lead."

A shaky smile from his hunter with her mortal heart. "Is that what you truly want?" It was a husky whisper.

He knew then that he could hurt her terribly at this moment. Like her father, he could tell her that she wasn't what she should be, that who and what she was, was a cause for shame. In doing so, he'd hit at her biggest vulnerability and win this war between them.

He was an archangel. He'd made ruthless decision after ruthless decision.

"No," he said, for she was exactly who she should be. His mate, his consort. "But it would be easier if you were like Hannah."

A laugh that sounded wet. "And it would be easier if you followed my every command."

They looked at each other for a long, long moment . . . then Raphael reached forward, cupped her cheek. "I will give you your freedom," he said, fighting every instinct he had, "on one condition."

Lines formed between her brows. "What condition?"

"Do you not trust me, hunter?"

"Not a bit, not when you're trying to get your own way." But she leaned her cheek into his touch, stroking her own fingers through his hair.

He shifted his grip to her jaw, firmed his hold. "You will call me. No hesitations, no thinking, no waiting until the last possible moment. If you're in danger, *you will call me*."

"Within reason," she bargained. "A vamp hopped up on bloodlust coming after me is a different case from a power-crazed angel."

"I'm not used to negotiating." Most people gave him everything he demanded.

A slow, slow smile that melted away the lingering tendrils

of the cold rage within him. "I guess the next several hundred years are going to be an education then, huh?"

He could not help it. He kissed her, took that warmth, that laughter inside of him, where it could warm him, too. *You tease an archangel at your peril.*

Strong arms around his neck, fingers playing over the arches of his wings. *I dunno, I kinda like what it gets me.*

Her lips parted beneath his, and he surged in, claiming her with a hunger that no longer startled him. It was as if the bond between them grew ever deeper with every hour that passed. *You will call me.*

*Within reason.*

He considered it, smiled in satisfaction. *Very well. But you will explain each and every injury each time you do not call me.*

Breaking the openmouthed intimacy of the kiss, she glared at him. "That is a ridiculous stipulation for a hunter!"

He put his arms around her and pulled her off the branch, using his power and strength to take them high up into the star-studded skies.

"Raphael," she said when he released her far above the night clouds, "I'm serious. You can't expect me to, to—"

He shifted direction. "Answer to me?"

"Yes!" she said, changing her angle of flight to follow.

"And am I not answerable to my consort?"

The words Elena had been about to say died in her throat. "Well," she murmured, letting him catch her around the waist, "if you put it like that, I can't exactly argue, can I?" It was an unexpected, breath-stealing gift, his open acceptance of her claim.

Blue fire licked in his eyes, his mouth brushing over hers in tiny, teasing bites. *Then, will you dance with me, Elena?*

She felt her eyes widen, her stomach fill with butterflies. "Now? Here?"

Raphael's hands played over her ribs, his thumbs brushing the lower curves of her breasts. *Now. Here.*

"But—" The air left her throat as he bit at her lower lip at the same time that he rolled one of her nipples through the fabric of her tank. *Wait. Wait.* She had to ask him something before her brain turned to mush.

Rain and wind around her, fresh and wild and open, the archangel's hand closing with open possession over her breast. *I do not wish to wait.*

# 26

God, she was sunk, putty in his hands. Only her discomfort at the question circling in her mind gave her the will to break the kiss, to suck in a breath . . . while the angel dipped his head to close his teeth over the frantically beating pulse in her neck.

"Surveillance!" she blurted out. "There are satellites everywhere! Won't someone see?" She was too private, too possessive, to share this moment with anyone.

One hand stroking down over her back, to her bottom. *I am an archangel, Elena. I have enough power to blow out every satellite in the world.*

"That's not what I—" She cried out as he bit down on her pulse then licked the small sensual hurt, her hands fisting in the thick silk of his hair.

*No one will see us.* A kiss that took over her mouth. *I used my power to shield us from view as soon as we flew out of Manhattan.*

She bit down on his lip this time. "Thanks for telling me."

One strong hand clenched on her hip. "Biting is not nice, Elena."

*Oh, dear God.* When he started teasing . . . Forget about
the putty. She was melting into a big old pile of goo. Pushing
away in self-defense, she tried valiantly to hover and failed.
But she managed to turn her drop into a sweep that drew up
into a vertical climb. *Show me how angels dance, Raphael.*

A second later, he was there with her, his body spiral-
ing around her own as she climbed, his speed and agility so
stunning that everything female in her resonated in response.
Mine, she thought, this magnificent creature with his wings of
gold and eyes of relentless blue is mine.

A shimmer in her peripheral vision and then . . . sex.
Pure sex and temptation and passion on her tongue. *Dusting me again, Archangel?* Licking the delicious, decadent
taste of Raphael's special blend of angel-dust off her lips,
she flew through the fine, fine particles, feeling the wicked
caress of it cover every exposed inch of her body—including
her wings.

*Next time, I will do it when you are clothed in nothing but
skin.*

She clenched her thighs at the sensual impact of that image. It would drive her mad, she thought, that level of sensation. But she'd always known that loving an archangel would
be no easy matter. Smiling, she dropped without warning,
simply folding her wings and plummeting to the earth.

She flared them out again at the midpoint, sweeping away
in a different direction. Raphael was nowhere to be seen.
Feeling smug at having evaded him, she was startled to see
angel-dust raining down around her, streaking the night sky in
shimmers of brilliant gold. Pushing back her hair, she glanced
over her shoulder.

Her archangel was flying perfectly above her, his wings
bigger, a midnight shadow over her body. *Not fair*, she complained. *You've had a millennium and a half to learn these
tricks.* She tugged at the neck of her tank top, suddenly far too
hot as the angel-dust worked its way through the material and
into her pores to her bloodstream, the erotic kiss of it concentrated on the pulse between her thighs.

A light touch at her neck and the tank, then the sleeves, literally fell apart in her hands. "Raphael!" *I can't go about having my clothes scattered all over the state!*

Even as she spoke, she saw tiny flickers of blue light up the night and realized he'd destroyed the fragments of her clothing. But that wasn't at the forefront of her mind. It was the fact that she was nude above the waist. It made her feel painfully vulnerable.

*No one can see, Elena. I promise you this.*

Only Raphael could've made her believe that, made her trust. Taking a deep breath, she dropped the arms she'd crossed over her chest and looked around. She had no idea where they were, but it was pitch-dark below, so dark that it had to be—

"The sea." While they'd been flying above the clouds, Raphael had taken them out into the Atlantic, so far out that no matter which direction she turned, she couldn't see any sign of light, of human civilization.

Exhilaration burst through her bloodstream, and she thought, what the hell. *Do your magic, Archangel.* She kicked off her shoes, somehow managed to get off her pants and underwear—though her flight path probably looked like that of a drunken bumblebee. Her clothing disappeared in flashes of blue, her skin sighing at the release. Flaring out her wings to their greatest width, she gave in to the hunger inside of her and rode the air currents with an untamed, open joy.

She'd never felt as carefree.

Raphael winged over her, slow and easy, almost lazily, and she got the feeling he was letting her play. It made her lips kick upward . . . and then she tasted the angel-dust glittering in the air. *Pure sex.* The damn sneaky archangel had flown circles around her, until there was nowhere she could go to escape the exotic, aphrodisiac stuff. *You realize this is war?* she said, licking the dust off her lips, vividly conscious of it caressing every secret corner of her body.

No answer.

Her instincts kicked in.

Utilizing her recent flight training, she did a hard turn to her left and went up. Raphael shot by a bare millisecond later, missing her by a fraction of a feather. As he caught himself and turned to head back up, she swept right . . . diving just when he'd come too far to stop. But this was an archangel she played with. He managed to run his fingers over her wings in teasing promise as she plummeted.

Strong, warm hands closing on the naked skin of her waist. *Too fast, hunter.* A kiss pressed to the side of her neck as he rose up before releasing her. But when she would've turned to fly in another direction, he gripped her again, holding her naked body flush against his semiclothed one.

Every tiny inch of her skin crawling with sensation, she wrapped her arms around his neck and pressed her breasts to the muscled plane of his chest as he propelled them ever higher. "Kiss me, Archangel."

*Later.*

Too hungry to listen to the order, she nipped at his throat, sucked and kissed until the hands on her waist squeezed, his erection a pulsing brand between them. *Not yet, Elena.* There was a hoarse quality to his mental tone, the glow coming off his wings sparking electric blue.

The sight threw a switch inside her—she wrapped her legs around Raphael's waist, her wings tight to her back as she trusted him to hold her up. Then she concentrated on getting him to lower his head.

Bites along his jaw, nips over his throat, suckling kisses on his pulse. When that didn't work, she ran a hand down to circle one flat male nipple. He gripped her hand, his hold shifting to her lower back, and for a moment, she thought she had him. Then his jaw firmed.

And he flew higher.

Higher.

Until they were well above the cloud layer, at an altitude where it should've been freezing cold. Except that the blaze coming off Raphael seemed to have created a cocoon around her—not that she needed the heat, not with angel-dust in every pore and every cell. She could feel herself lushly damp against his abdomen, wanted only to ride him until he begged for surrender.

"Raphael. Now." It was a demand fueled by near-painful need.

He stopped.

High, high, *high* above the earth. Then, his mouth was on her own, stealing her breath. *Ready?*

*Yes!*

Clamping his arms tight around her, he angled them so they faced down toward the water, and then he . . . dropped.

She screamed into the kiss even as she felt an electric burn of heat against her and then the warm muscle of his suddenly unclothed body. He tumbled them over and over as they fell, and she would've been lost at the first tumble, but he held her in unyielding arms until there was no fear . . . only the feel of him—hard and demanding sliding into the melting heat of her body.

Tiny shocks of pleasure radiated out from that most intimate of joinings.

Breaking the kiss to gasp in a breath, she saw the water coming at them at overwhelming speed. "Raphael!" A single pulse of fear before he executed a turn so sharp it thrust him soul-deep inside of her.

An overload of sensation. Crackling electricity across her skin.

Not fighting the agonizing bite of pleasure, she reclaimed his lips as he pushed them both through the clouds again, his body shifting with each wingbeat to caress her with excruciating intimacy. Clenching her fingers in his hair, she rubbed herself against the solid heat of his chest, needing, wanting, hungering.

*Dance with me, Elena.*

He bit at her lips when she squeezed her inner muscles in a sexual caress, kissing his way across her cheek and down her neck before he took her mouth again.

Then they fell once more.

She came apart on a scream halfway through the dive, every nerve in her body igniting with pleasure, with sensation, with the wild exhilaration of dancing with an archangel. Lights exploded behind her eyes, blue and gold and filled with the wicked, wicked glimmer of angel-dust. And all around her, she felt sleek, warm muscle, until she didn't know where she ended and he began. *With me, Archangel.* A demand saturated in pleasure.

*But I am not finished with you, Hunter.*

He rose again, skimming so close to the water that she felt the spray cool and wet against her overheated skin.

Thigh muscles quivering like jelly, she locked her ankles at his lower back, resting her head in the curve of his neck. *Too bad. I think I'm dead.*

A laugh, husky and male in a way that shouted sex. It did something to her, that sound, blew air onto the embers of a passion so recently satisfied. Her skin stretched taut in anticipation, and she found herself kissing his neck again, caressing him every way she could. With her mouth, with her fingers, with the most secret parts of her body.

*Elena.* His hold tightened. *Once more.*

"Once more." With that, she locked her mouth to his as they plummeted in a dizzying spiral awash in the erotic gold of angel-dust.

She was so focused on the male who owned her heart, her soul, that she didn't see the sea rushing up at them until it was too late. *Raphael!* she screamed as they hit . . . except there was no pain, and she was tumbling, tumbling down with her archangel, the water held at bay by a shield of shimmering light streaked with blue.

Heart thudding triple-time, she gripped his face. "Scaring me out of my wits is not good foreplay."

Reaching between them as they came to a lazy stop, he touched the hot, slick bundle of nerves at the apex of her thighs . . . and she threatened to fracture. Clenching her inner muscles, she met those eyes so much bluer than the Atlantic. *Move.*

One hand under her butt, the other on her back, the archangel decided to obey an order for once.

Then there was no more thought.

Raphael leaned on his forearm the next morning as he lay watching his consort sleep. Exhaustion had her limp, her arms curled around her pillow as she lay on her front. He smiled, running a single finger down the centerline of her back.

She made a sound, but it wasn't a complaint, so he continued to explore.

Last night . . . She'd been magnificent. Stronger, faster, more willing than he'd ever expected. He hadn't meant for her introduction to that most intimate of dances to be so sensually rough, but when she'd ridden every wave with him without flinching, he'd given in to temptation and taken her in a way he'd never have chanced with another woman.

Because immortal or not, they would've been terrified.

"Hey." A sleepy grumble as she shifted closer to him, until his knee brushed against her body, her wings spreading till one lay across his hip and thighs.

He ran a hand over the sleek indigo of her primary covert feathers with proprietary pleasure. "Good morning."

Her hand came to rest on his thigh below the sheets, perilously close to the part of him that had the most unquenchable hunger for her. "Careful, Guild Hunter."

A drowsy curve of her lips, but her eyes were very much alert. "So, you going to tell me what happened last night?"

He'd known she'd push. That was who she was. As he'd said, it would have been easier were she malleable—but he'd never have taken her for his consort then. "I told you my mother and I always shared a strong mental bond." He fought the pull of memory, of a time when Caliane had been exactly that—his mother. "It seems that bond did survive. She can reach me even through the vestiges of Sleep."

Elena stroked her hand over his thigh, anchoring him to the earth, to the present. "What did you see?"

"The past and the future."

*"Raphael."* A whisper so quiet it was almost not sound. *"Raphael."*

*A prick of consciousness, of awareness. "Mother?" Eyes opening, he found himself standing on a verdant green field, the sky above him the brilliant shade of a blue jay's wings, the air perfumed with a thousand unnamed flowers.*

*He frowned. This place, it was hauntingly familiar . . . right down to the droplets of dew that sparkled like gemstones against the jade green stalks of grass. But his mind, it was playing games with him, refusing to divulge the name of the field where he stood.*

*Crouching down, he broke off one of the stalks, touched his finger to the dew.*

*A sigh on the wind . . . and her fine, delicate feet walking across the grass, the edge of a long white gown flirting with her ankles.*

*His heart stopped beating as he watched her come toward him, an archangel of such piercing beauty that she'd spawned legends and caused empires to fall. Her hair was a waterfall of ebony down her back, thick and wild with silken curls his father had loved to fist in his hands as he kissed her, her eyes a piercing hue that he saw in the mirror every single day of his life.*

*Caliane had given him her eyes, her power . . . perhaps her madness.*

*But his height he'd gained from his father.*

*Rising to his feet, he saw her smile as she came to a halt before him, a woman who barely reached his breastbone. "My Raphael," she whispered. "My darling boy. How you've grown."*

*He towered above her, but even now, he felt the child. When she put her fingers on his chest, he couldn't move away, his heart aching with a sense of loss that had followed him through time. "You broke me on this field." He'd remembered at last, remembered the blood and the agony. Remembered the sight of her walking away.*

*Sorrow in her gaze, the blue turning to midnight. "I was mad, Raphael." Said with a clarity that reminded him of the stunning power of a song that had once held the world in thrall. "But I fought for you."*

*He thought of his shattered bones, his body crushed and broken into so many pieces that it had taken a long, long time for him to become whole again. "Did you?"*

*Raising her hand, she touched her fingers to his jaw in a maternal caress that threatened to send him back to his youth. "The madness whispered that I should kill you, that you carried within you the potential to transcend my power."*

*Raphael knew his own strength, but he also knew that the archangel in front of him was millennia older, her abilities unparalleled. "You are an Ancient, mother. I am yet young."*

*"The youngest angel to ever become an archangel." There was a pride in her tone that cut him to the quick. "I watched over you even as I Slept, my darling boy. And I see a future in which you will fly far higher than either I or Nadiel ever dared to dream."*

*He was her son. He'd mourned who she'd once been even as he'd tried to execute her. It was impossible for him not to step forward and take her slender body into his arms, to bury his face in her hair and inhale the sweet woodsmoke of home. "You are Sleeping."*

*"No, I am Waking." Damp against his cheek, a mother's tears as she stroked her hand over his hair. "I sense a vein of mortality in you, Raphael."*

*He blinked, pulled away, shook his head. Elena. He'd forgotten Elena. How was that possible when she was the most important element of his life? "What are you doing to me, Mother?"*

*Her eyes blazed the color at the heart of the sun, so pure it burned. "Reminding you of who you are. The son of two archangels. The most powerful child ever born."*

*Shaking his head, he met that brilliant, blinding gaze. "I have made myself. I will never be your creature."*

*The fire flickered with searing blue. "I will not permit you to be hers, either. You are far too magnificent to belong to an immortal with a weak mortal heart."*

*He knew then that Caliane would kill Elena if she could.*

# 27

Elena couldn't pretend every hair on her body wasn't standing up on end by the time Raphael finished, but she had other priorities right now. "You broke her hold," she said, knowing he needed to hear it said aloud. "She couldn't keep you in that dream or vision or whatever it was."

Midnight shadows crossed his face. "It was difficult— perhaps would've been impossible if I hadn't had you to draw me back. She is my mother, and as such, has known me since I was born. She understands how to circumvent my every shield."

"Maybe she did once," Elena rose to her knees, shoving her hair impatiently off her face, "but she's been asleep for over a thousand years. She might've known the boy you were, but she doesn't know the man you've become. And she has no concept of the bonds that tie us together."

Raphael's expression shifted again, and she knew he was calculating matters with that inhuman logic he sometimes displayed. "Yes," he said at last. "That may be her only weakness."

Elena had to fight her instinctive negative response to his

expression, his words. He'd never be human and to expect it of him was to lie to herself. "Do you need to know her weakness?" she asked.

"She threatened you, Elena."

He didn't have to say anything else. She knew very well what Raphael would do to protect her—and if her hunter instincts scowled at the idea of being protected, the heart of her understood that to love this male was to accept his need to hold her safe.

"A lot of women have trouble with their mothers-in-law."

Raphael's look was priceless. "My mother is an insane archangel."

She almost laughed—or perhaps that was hysteria rising to the surface. "She *was*. Maybe these bursts of violence were a result of her being in a half-dream state. It may still be that Sleep has cured her—from what you've told me, she acted normal in the dream, or as normal as someone of her power and age can be."

*You do not know how much I wish that to be true.*

"I know it down to the last heartbreaking glimmer of hope," she whispered, swallowing the knot of emotion in her throat. "Every day, I wish I could've somehow reached through my own mother's sorrow and convinced her that life was worth living. *Every day.*"

Raphael tugged her down into his arms. "You speak rarely of those events, and yet you call out to her in your nightmares."

In the kitchen, Elena thought, they were always in the kitchen in the dreams. She was fooled into hope every single time—and then the blood would begin to seep down the walls, across the floor. Her mother always remained trapped in the room, no matter how much Elena begged her to run.

"I found her," she said, speaking of a nightmare that continued to leave her trembling in panic in the coldest depths of the night. "I got home from school, and I walked inside the house." That was when she'd seen it, that single high-heeled shoe lying on its side on the gleaming shine of the checkerboard tiles.

She should've walked back out that same instant, but she'd been happy. Mama hadn't worn high heels for a long time—the child in her had thought that maybe it meant Marguerite was better now, that maybe she'd have her mother back. The illusion had lasted a few precious seconds.

"The shadow," she said, her breath coming in short, shallow gasps. "On the wall. I could see it swinging so gently. I didn't want to look up, didn't want to see." Even now, terror pulsed in her blood. "I could feel my heart freeze into a small, hard ball, and then I looked up and it just . . . shattered." Sharp, vicious shards, they had cut into her, made her bleed. "I kept looking up at her, at the way she . . ." The words wouldn't come, wouldn't be formed. "The shadow," she said instead, "it just kept swinging. The whole time my heart was bleeding out below her, the shadow just kept swinging."

Raphael could feel his hunter breaking all over again in his arms, and it was unbearable. "Hers was a selfish act."

"No, she—"

"She lost two daughters," Raphael said. "She was tortured. But so were you. You saw your sisters murdered before your eyes, saw your mother suffer."

"Not the same."

"No. Because you were a child." He crushed her to him, wishing he could turn back time, shake Marguerite Deveraux until she came out of the fog of her grief and saw the treasures she was about to throw away. "It is permissible to be angry with her, Elena. It does not make you disloyal."

A ragged sob, so harsh that it sounded torn out of her, before a clenched fist pounded on his chest. "Why didn't she love us as much as she loved Ari and Belle?" A child's question. "Why did she leave us when she saw how Jeffrey was becoming? Why?" Wet against his chest, that fist halting as she whispered, "Why?"

L̲ater, she asked him to spar with her, and he did, letting her work out her anguish, her pain, through hard physical combat. But she was distracted, not fighting at her best. Instead of letting up, he gave no quarter.

"If you won't accept the protection I assign you," he said when he put her on her back for the second time in as many minutes, "then you must be better than the best."

A snarl that he far preferred over the haunted pain that had crumpled her spirit. "Beating me into the ground isn't helping matters." She flowed back to her feet.

He slammed at her again.

This time, she came at him like a fury, sorrow shifting into the most lethal anger.

Dancing with her, their blades moving like streaks of white fire, he couldn't stop the smile of pride from spreading across his face. "Magnificent," he said as she almost grazed his wing with those short swords of hers.

Hissing out something under her breath, she sliced out her arm in a move he hadn't taught her—he had to lunge out of the way or he'd have been nursing an impressive cut in his side. *That is more like it.* A kiss pressed to her cheek as he disarmed her left hand and moved out of range of her right.

Eyes narrowed, she used her foot to kick up her lost sword. Then she circled him, much like Venom had a way of doing. She learned, he thought, very, very fast. Now, she made a move he only avoided because he'd sparred with the vampire more than once. Even then, her blade passed a bare quarter of an inch from his nose.

But she'd left herself open. He was behind her, his knife held to her throat the next instant. "That was foolish," he snapped, furious that she'd let anger drive her into making a move that left her exposed and vulnerable. "You're now dead."

Reaching up, she gripped his wrist. "You made me angry on purpose."

He drew back. "But you fell into it too far."

Elena turned, chest heaving. "Yeah, I did." She rubbed her face with one hand. "I won't make the same mistake again."

Raphael gave a short nod. "We will finish this later. I'm needed at the Tower."

As they walked side by side, their wings brushing, she drew in a long, steadying breath. "Any further intel on where your mother might be?" Picking up her cell phone from where she'd placed it while they were sparring, she saw that she had a text message.

"Not as yet." Tense words. "If we do not rouse her before she is ready, she'll wake on her own and at full strength."

There was no need to spell out what would happen if she awakened as insane as when she lay down to Sleep.

"Will you tell me more about her?" Caliane's disappearance had marked him as surely as she'd been marked by her own mother's death.

"The memories are old, will surface in their own time." He ran the back of his hand over her cheek. "What do you do today?"

"I'm going to visit the perfumer I mentioned to you earlier." She had no intention of letting her archangel handle those memories alone when they did rise, but they'd both had a tough morning already, so she let it go for now. "Do you know how difficult it is to track down that particular black orchid? I asked him right after I got back from Boston, but he only just received it." She held up her cell phone.

"Ah. You seek the essence."

"I want to know all the notes, make sure I'm not missing anything," she said as they cleaned and stowed their weapons in a locker at the back of the house. "Archangel?"

His eyes were a clear, crystalline blue when he turned to her. "What would you have of me, Guild Hunter?"

"A good-bye kiss."

An hour and a half later, Elena walked out of the outwardly disreputable shop that housed the best perfumer in the city—the tiny vial of essence wrapped in multiple layers of cushioning material and packed into a small box—to find that half of New York suddenly had something to do in the Bronx. No one approached her as she walked down the street, but she could hear the whispers gathering like a shock wave behind her.

This was, she realized all at once, the first instance where she'd spent any extended amount of time on the streets. No wonder everyone was staring. The scrutiny discomfited her, but it was understandable—people needed time to get used to her, and she had to be visible for that to happen. As long as they kept their distance, she wasn't too fussed.

However, she hadn't factored one simple thing into the equation—the awe that kept most individuals from approaching an angel was muted almost to nonexistence in her case. She'd once been mortal, once been just like them. So they followed her, a growing press of humanity. "Damn," she muttered under her breath.

*You will call me. No hesitations, no thinking, no waiting until the last possible moment. If you're in danger, you will call me.*

She assessed the situation with her peripheral vision, saw the wonder on those shining faces, and knew no one meant her harm. But there were too many of them. If one tried to touch her wings, so would another and another and another. They'd stampede her to death in their eagerness. *Archangel*, she said, hoping Raphael would be able to hear her. *I need you.*

The wind and the rain against her senses. *Where are you, Elena?* When she gave him the location, he said, *I'm only minutes from you.*

An edgy mix of relief and frustration churned in her abdomen. *I'm probably overreacting.* This was her home, these were her people—she *hated* the realization that they both might be lost to her now. Even as that horrible, painful thought passed through her mind, she dropped a knife into her free hand and began to play it over and through her fingers in an apparently absentminded motion.

The crowd hesitated, fell back a step as light glinted off the steel.

Good, she thought. They needed to remember that she wasn't simply a woman with wings. She was hunter-born, could handle vampires twice her size without blinking. The crowd might overpower her, but not before she took down a significant percentage of their number.

Noting that the walls of humanity had blocked all other traffic on both ends of the street, she walked to stand in the middle . . . and looked up at the sky. And there he was, his wingspan creating a massive shadow as he swept down to land in front of her. "Are you well, Consort?"

Silence held their audience in thrall, their awe now licked with dread.

"They're only curious." She saw the danger in his eyes, knew he had the capacity to execute every human on the street. "I should've considered it. I just . . . forgot that nothing's the same anymore."

Raphael's hair lifted in the wind as he put his hands on her hips. Sliding away her knife, she placed one hand on his shoulder, holding the box in her other arm. She expected him to rise, but instead he turned his head to run his gaze over the assembled crowd. From the whimpers and the rapid urge everyone had to disperse, she had a good idea of what they'd glimpsed.

When Raphael and Elena did lift, it was with a slow, powerful grace meant to stun.

Only when they were high in the air did she say, "This is going to sound so ungrateful—but I hate that you had to rescue me." Her sense of loss was acid in her gut, harsh and corrosive. "I'm not a woman who needs rescue. That's not who I am." Not who he'd taken as his consort.

"I'll speak to Illium—your vertical takeoff training must take priority over all else." Pragmatic words, his hands warm on her. "Once you master that, it will be impossible to trap you in such a way."

A painful burst of sensation inside her chest. Unable to say anything, she let him see her heart in her eyes. *Thank you.* Not just for giving her city, her home, back to her . . . but for stilling her hidden terror that he wouldn't want her anymore.

The tender ferocity of Elena's parting kiss imprinted in his skin, Raphael was on his way to the Tower when Dmitri's mind touched his. *Sire, Favashi wishes to speak to you.* It was a toneless statement.

*I'll be there in a few minutes.*

The Persian archangel's face was on the view-screen when he entered, and for the first time, he glimpsed a crack in the serenity of her countenance. "Favashi. Does this concern Neha?"

"No. She appears busy within her own territory at present." Favashi's tone was distracted, her attention clearly on another topic. "We have a problem, Raphael."

Unlike some of the others on the Cadre, he'd never underestimated the Archangel of Persia. Though she ruled with a velvet glove, there was still a steel hand within it. "Who?"

"Elijah. His behavior has turned erratic."

That was a development he'd never expected. "How erratic?" Elijah was one of the most stable members of the Cadre.

"Reports are, he's become violent. That would be no surprise with Charisemnon or Titus, but Elijah?"

Raphael frowned. "Has he harmed Hannah?" Elijah hurting Hannah was as impossible a thought as Raphael laying a hand on Elena. If the archangel had crossed that line, then Caliane had to be even closer to waking than anyone believed—her power, too, was stretching awake. The impact on the rest of the Cadre could be an unintended consequence, her immense abilities not yet under conscious control . . . or it could be an insane archangel's vicious game.

"There are no reports of him touching Hannah," Favashi said, her elegant voice breaking into his thoughts. "But all I have are rumors and innuendo. Your sources are better than mine."

It was an implied request. "Jockeying for power, Favashi?"

"In all honesty, Raphael, I enjoy being queen of my territory. It's large and I am treated as a goddess." A thick fringe of lashes came down over her soft brown eyes as she shook her head. "More land would, at present, cause me nothing but problems."

Raphael wasn't certain he believed her, but he gave a small nod. "I'll let you know if I hear anything of note about Elijah." Ending the call, he turned to the vampire who'd stood out of sight in the corner. "What do you think?"

"I think she is sweet poison." Dmitri stepped closer, his face set in brutal lines. "Power is what she is and what she knows."

"You are hardly an impartial judge when it comes to Favashi."

A tic beat in Dmitri's jaw. "I was a young fool and she played me. But you can't say I don't learn my lessons."

"She's a beautiful woman. And apparently you are a great lover."

The vampire shot him a dark glance. "I believe your hunter is rubbing off on you. It is not a compliment."

Raphael felt his lips curve. "Find out if any of Jason's people know what's happening with Elijah." Raphael intended to talk to the other archangel himself, but honorable as he seemed, Elijah was Cadre, well tutored in the art of deception.

Dmitri was already pulling out his cell phone. "Favashi . . . I once saw her rip a vampire's still-beating heart out of his chest and hold it in front of him until he died because the male dared disobey an order. She's no vulnerable princess, for all she likes to use that image to her advantage."

"The vampire challenged her power, Dmitri. You know as well as I that she could not let it go."

Dmitri's phone rang at that moment, and he brought it to his ear. Like all men, the leader of his Seven had a past. Even Raphael did not know everything of what had passed between

Favashi and the vampire just over five hundred years ago, centuries before Favashi became Cadre.

What he did know was that Dmitri had come to him with a request that he be released from Raphael's service. Raphael, a new archangel himself, hadn't been able to afford to lose him at that stage and had asked the male to wait another year. He had not decreed it so—Dmitri had earned what he asked for—but the vampire had been agreeable.

"Favashi," he'd said with a smile that had been rare before he met the Persian angel, "is too sweet to cast curses on your name, but I've been told that the instant the year is over, I am hers."

Yet when that time came, Dmitri's smile had long disappeared and aside from a single discussion where Raphael had asked Dmitri if he wished to leave, and Dmitri had replied with a curt "no," they'd never spoken of it again.

Now, the vampire finished his conversation and closed the cell phone. "We may have a situation—Elijah was spotted flying into your territory. He is currently over Georgia."

# 28

Coming on the heels of Favashi's words, there could be only one response. Raphael contacted Nazarach and asked him to intercept the other archangel, invite Elijah to his home in Atlanta. "I will join you." While he could and had flown such distances with ease, he decided to conserve his power in case Elijah had more than conversation in mind. "Tell Venom to prepare the plane," he said to Dmitri after hanging up.

"Sire."

"Dmitri." He waited until the vampire turned, to say, "You will watch over her."

"I made a vow. I won't break it." But Dmitri's expression said he still wasn't convinced—not when it had become clear after Beijing that Raphael's bond with Elena had somehow made him weaker. He healed slower, was easier to wound. Such a flaw could be deadly for an archangel.

"Perhaps," Raphael said to his second, "an archangel needs a weakness."

Dmitri shook his head. "Not if he is to survive the Cadre."

* * *

Sara was chatting with another hunter when Elena, the box containing the essence held to her side, poked her head around the open door of the Guild Director's office. "Ash!"

The dark-eyed hunter looked up, a smile lighting up that face that wouldn't have looked out of place on the silver screen. "Hey, Ellie."

"So, it's safe for you to venture out of the Cellars?"

Long jean-clad legs sprawled out in front of her, Ashwini buffed her nails on her white T-shirt. "No comment."

Across the desk, Sara made an inelegant sound. "They're flirting."

Elena's mouth fell open. *"No."* She turned to Ashwini. "You and Janvier? I don't believe it."

"Janvier, who?" An angelic look that was so fake Elena burst out laughing.

"Did you really do what I think you did to him?" she asked, any remaining shreds of her earlier frustrated distress drifting away. Because this place, these people, they were hers, too.

Ashwini's lips curved into a feral grin. "All I'll say is that damn vamp will think twice about messing with me now."

Sara's phone rang at that moment. As she took the call, Ashwini lowered her voice and said, "Those wings are wicked awesome." She wiggled her fingers. "Can I touch, or is that too weird?"

Elena knew Ashwini wouldn't be offended if she said no—the other hunter had her own gifts, carried her own nightmares. "Quick touch of the primaries is okay."

Ashwini ran a gentle finger over the large feathers of white-gold at the edges of her wings. "Wow. They're alive—warm. I guess I never really thought about that."

"You wouldn't believe how much I have to learn," Elena said as Sara hung up.

"Ash," Sara said. "I have a job for you." A slow smile.

Ashwini's eyes narrowed. "No effing way."

"Language." Sara's eyes were dancing. "Seems like Janvier's got himself in trouble again. Florida—somewhere in the Everglades."

"There are swamps there." Ashwini gritted her teeth. "I hate swamps. He knows I hate swamps. That's it—I'm going to kill him this time. I don't care if I lose my bonus." Snatching the piece of paper Sara was holding out, she stalked out of the room.

Elena grinned. "You know that's just what I needed after the morning I've had." She told Sara what had happened in the Bronx.

Her best friend flapped a hand. "The fascination won't last, Ellie. You're not pretty enough."

"Gee, thanks."

"Hey, not my fault you hang around with gorgeous man-flesh." A more solemn expression. "No matter what, you've got every hunter in the Guild behind you. Never forget that."

"I won't." Raphael was her rock, but Sara and the Guild, Elena thought, were the foundation on which she'd built her adult life, found her footing. "How did you get to be so wise and all-knowing?"

"I hope Zoe thinks the same when she's fifteen and wants to date some moronic senior." Sara raised an eyebrow. "You want to talk about something else, I can tell."

"Do you have Vivek's blood stored?" The Guild did that for its hunters, for use in a medical emergency—however, Vivek wasn't an active hunter.

Sara gave her a penetrating look. "No, but he's up for his yearly physical next month." A pause. "How much do you need?"

"A vial."

"I'll make sure you get it."


Ten minutes later, having successfully navigated the obstacle course of the subterranean Cellars below the Guild—and Vivek's snippiness that she hadn't visited earlier—Elena walked into the scent chamber.

Empty of furniture, the room was painted a stark white. It was also about the size of a shoebox. Gritting her teeth against the edge of claustrophobia, she drew in a breath to establish that the room was free of outside scents—other than those on Elena herself—before unstopping the bottle of liquid night that had cost her a considerable chunk of change.

*Lush, sensual, rich . . . addictive.*

She blinked, took a mental step back, tried again.

*Dark, hidden notes of sunlight . . . of a very feminine compulsion. Not dangerous to a woman.*

An intricate scent, Elena thought, fitting for an archangel.

But, while she was now certain she'd detected this exact combination of notes on the swinging bodies on the bridge and on the girl with the forget-me-not dress, it wasn't quite what had hit her above the Hudson, or what she'd sensed in the bedroom when Caliane had whispered her son's name.

Her brow furrowed.

It was highly possible, she admitted, that her memory was at fault, given that her adrenaline had been through the roof on both of those latter occasions. The other fact was that both the girl's mutilated form and the vampires on the bridge had been exposed to the elements—a more subtle note could've been lost long before Elena arrived on the scene.

Still . . .

Elijah was standing by the river that ran behind the plantation house from where Nazarach controlled Atlanta when Raphael arrived. Landing a short distance away, he moved through the shade of the leafy trees that lined the bank, and to the edge of the quiet current. The fingers of a weeping willow touched the clarity of it on the other side, and he could hear the calls of the birds hidden in the foliage.

It was a beautiful place, and it spoke to none of the violence that Nazarach had done. Each angel had his own way of ruling. Nazarach used fear. But it wasn't the amber-winged angel Raphael had come to see. "Why are you in my territory, Elijah?"

The archangel who ruled South America looked up, his golden brown eyes haunted, his hair disordered as if he'd been thrusting his hands through it. "I come to ask you for sanctuary, Raphael."

"Not for you." Elijah was older than Raphael, powerful in his own right.

The other male looked unseeing into the water, his wings trailing on the mossy earth. "For Hannah."

"You think you will harm her?" Raphael had faced the same fear after he'd executed Ignatius, taken Elena so roughly.

"I would never hurt her," Elijah said in a hollow voice, "but I am not always myself."

"A rage, red across your vision?"

Elijah jerked up his head. "You've felt it?"

Raphael considered his answer as the heavy-limbed trees above them, around them, sighed into the silence. This could well be an act, Elijah probing for a weakness. But the South American archangel was also the one who had always stood behind Raphael in the Cadre, the one who had told him he had the potential to lead. "Yes, but not in the past week." He examined Elijah's tortured face. "Has it touched you in that time?"

A quick negative shake of that golden head that had inspired sculptors and played muse to poets. "But once was enough. I do not trust myself—I acted with a cruelty that will haunt me for centuries to come. The vampires in question survived only because of Hannah's intervention." Elijah fisted his hands. "I could've hurt her with the same violence."

Raphael had learned to spot and exploit the chinks in an opponent's armor long ago. He'd had to, to survive the Cadre. But he'd also known Dmitri for almost a thousand years, understood something of friendship. "Yet you did not, Elijah. That is the line. You did not cross it."

Elijah was silent for a long time, the water passing with serene patience over pebble and rock as they stood unmoving on the riverbank. Across from them, the fronds of the weeping willow swayed in a gentle motion, pulled by the tug of the water. But the birds had gone silent, and suddenly the world was a much darker place.

"If she can do this to us in her Sleep, Raphael," Elijah said at last, "what will she do when she wakes?"

Having showered and changed after training with Illium— every one of the drills geared to give her the strength to achieve a vertical takeoff—Elena walked into the library where Montgomery had laid out an informal dinner, and came to a complete halt. "Aodhan." He stood next to the window, looking out over the storm lashing Manhattan once more. The dark beyond threw the piercing brilliance of him into cutting focus.

The fact was, Aodhan would never, ever blend in, not among angelkind and certainly not in the mortal world. His eyes were shattered from the pupil outward in shards of vivid green and translucent blue, his wings fractured light, his hair glittering strands encrusted with diamonds. The whole of it should've made him appear a cold being of marble and ice, but his skin held an undertone of gold, warm and inviting.

"Elena." He inclined his head in a slight bow, his voice still unfamiliar, she'd heard it so infrequently.

"Raphael should be here soon." Walking to the table, she poured herself a steaming cup of coffee—wine would put her to sleep after the workout she'd had. "He returned from Atlanta ten minutes ago." From the territory of an angel who would've given Elena the creeps even if Ashwini hadn't warned her before she ever met him. *Screams*, Ash had said of Nazarach's home, *the walls are full of screams.*

Aodhan said nothing, simply turned to look at the rain-drenched dark once more, a remoteness to him that she knew was deliberate. The angel fascinated her. He was akin to some great work of art, something you admired without understanding in truth. Except . . . there was far more to him. Pain, suffering, and a hurt that had made him withdraw into himself like the most wounded of animals.

Elena didn't know the details of what had been done to him, but she knew how it felt to hurt that bad. Putting down her coffee, she poured a glass of wine. "Aodhan."

He closed the distance between them to take the wineglass, his wings tight to his back. "Thank you."

"No problem." Ensuring she didn't touch him, she grabbed a seat at the table and began to slap together a sandwich. Montgomery would surely be horrified at the use to which she was putting the dishes on the table, but a good, hearty sandwich sounded perfect at that moment. She made one for Raphael, too, just to see the look on his face.

After almost a minute of silence, Aodhan moved to take the chair across from hers, his wings draping gracefully over the back designed for angels. He didn't eat but drank the wine, and when she looked up, she found those strange, beautiful eyes on her.

"You're an artist," she said, wondering what he saw. "Did you notice my vase in the front hall?"

A spark of interest. "Yes."

Swallowing the bite she'd taken, Elena said, "You can't have it," with a straight face. "Montgomery would only steal it back."

Aodhan tilted his head a few degrees to the side, as if he was trying to understand her. But he didn't say anything, and she decided not to tease him anymore. He wasn't Illium, who'd fire back something wicked. Aodhan needed more careful handling—which wasn't to say he wasn't as lethal. She'd seen him fight, knew he could be as dangerous as the two blades he wore in parallel sheaths on his back—there was a reason he was part of Raphael's Seven. But he was broken, too, on the deepest of levels.

A rustle of wings at her back, the scent of the sea lapping against her senses. "Hello, Archangel." *That was a quick shower.*

*There was no temptation to linger.* A firm touch along the

upper curve of her wing, making her entire body tingle. In front of her, Aodhan rose to his feet.

"Sire."

"What do you have for me, Aodhan?" Nodding at the other angel to sit, Raphael took his own place. Lips kicking up at the corners when he saw what she'd put on his plate, he said, "I do not think this is what Montgomery had in mind for the bread rolls." But he took a bite.

"It's made with love," she quipped, saw Aodhan's eyes flicker with . . . surprise?

His voice, however, betrayed nothing. "As you know, the entire world has been wracked by rain and wind and snow. The Far East suffered considerable damage from floods, typhoons, and quakes. Japan, too, was hit . . . except for one region that has remained untouched by even a quake that shook the rest of the island."

Hairs rising on her nape, Elena put down her empty coffee cup as Raphael abandoned his meal and stood. "No disturbances at all?" he said, moving to stand by the unlit fireplace.

"None." Aodhan rose, too, those wings of light and shattered glass unfolding a little, as if he'd grown comfortable enough to trust that they wouldn't make any attempts to touch him.

"Where?"

"A specific area within a mountainous prefecture called Kagoshima."

Getting up herself, Elena moved to lean against one of the bookshelves, so she could more easily talk to both men, though her next words were directed at Raphael. "You're planning to head there."

"I must." Face expressionless, he glanced toward the storm-dark window. "Now that we may have narrowed the search to such a specific locale, I may be able to sense her place of Sleep."

Elena made her next question private. *What will you do when you find her?*

*What I must.*

Her chest grew tight at the ice in those words—because she knew what lay beneath. She'd felt the power of his heart, knew how much he'd bleed if it turned out Caliane *was* still mad. "I'll come with you."

Midnight blue pierced her. "You have responsibilities here."

"Your people are watching over my family, and as for any possible repeat of Boston—better to go to the source of the problem and sort it out." She couldn't take the task from him, didn't have the power to kill an archangel, but she could, *would*, stand by him.

"She is worse than Uram, Elena."

Her gut went taut, her heart seizing into a hard, fast rhythm. The bloodborn archangel, his body riddled with poison, had killed hundreds, would've slaughtered thousands more if they hadn't halted his rampage. "We stopped him," she said, speaking to herself as well as to him, "and we're stronger than we were then."

*Perhaps.* He turned to Aodhan before she could question him on that ambivalent assessment. "Speak to Dmitri. Organize the transport. We'll fly out with the first break in the storm."

Waiting only until Aodhan had left the library, Elena closed the distance between them. "Raphael," she said, stomach twisted into painful knots, "your strength . . . are you still more susceptible to injury, less quick to recover?"

"Yes."

Guilt clamped steel claws around her. It was her. Somehow, she'd done this to him. "How bad is it?"

"My ability to heal others continues to grow, Guild Hunter. It is not a bad trade."

Not in the Cadre. Not if he was going to survive. *"Tell me."*

A small curve to his lips, an immortal's dangerous amusement. "It matters little, Elena. Even were I at the peak of my strength, my mother would be a lethal adversary. She may well be a hundred times more powerful than Lijuan."

Frigid cold in her veins. "I—"

"Stay here, Elena. This is no hunt for an immortal barely-Made."

She knew that. But she also knew something else. "Logic doesn't have anything to do with this, Archangel. To ask me to sit in safety while you walk into a nightmare. No." A shake of her head. "I can't do it. It's not the way I'm built."

"If I leave you behind?"

"You know the answer." She would simply follow.

Brushing back her hair with one hand, he curved his lips in the faintest of smiles. "Are you sure you do not wish to be more like Hannah?"

"If you ask nicely, I might be up for learning some calligraphy." But the laughter faded all too soon. "Will the others in the Cadre help you against her?"

"Elijah and Favashi, yes, but as to the others—uncertain. Astaad's behavior has remained erratic, Michaela is no longer answering anyone, and I've just had word that Titus and Charisemnon are both showing violent outbursts of temper. Favashi says Neha is stable, but the Queen of Poisons has the ability to strike without warning." His next words were in her mind. *My mother is the monster that scares other monsters.*

# 29

The storm continued to be a wild squall the next morning but was forecast to pass within two hours. "I need to go speak to Evelyn," Elena said as they landed on the Tower roof, the rain driving their clothing into their skin. Raphael could've protected them using his abilities, but she'd argued for him to conserve as much of his strength as possible for the battle that might well await.

"Your sister lives at the family home," he said, raising his wings to shelter her from the needlelike stabs of rain. "It is inevitable you'll meet your father."

"I know," she said, pitching her voice so it would carry above the pounding sound of the water hitting the metal and concrete of Manhattan.

"You will not go alone."

"I need to." Her father would try to crush and demoralize her, and she didn't want her archangel to see her hurt and broken.

Raphael caught the pain in his consort's eyes before she could hide it, felt his anger turn into an unsheathed blade. "No."

Shaking her head, Elena pressed her hand against his chest. "You'll hurt him when he hurts me," she said with blunt honesty, blinking the rain from her lashes. "You won't be able to stop yourself. And no matter everything else, he's still my father."

Raphael closed his hand around the side of her head, tangling his fingers in the wet silk of her hair. "He doesn't deserve your protection." Jeffrey deserved nothing from his oldest living daughter but her contempt.

"Maybe not." Elena acknowledged, leaning into his touch. "But he's also Beth, Evelyn, and Amethyst's father—and they seem to love him."

"You ask the impossible."

"No, I ask for what I need." She held her ground where even other angels would've backed down. "What I *need*, Archangel."

He had allowed her freedom beyond anything he might've imagined, but this he would not do. "I will come with you." He gripped her chin when she would've argued. "I will not land. That is the only concession I'm willing to make."

She folded her arms, her eyes silver in the storm-light. "It's not much of a concession, but we don't have time to argue."

He spoke into her mind as they flew out into the tempest of wind and rain once more. *Hear this, Elena—if he crosses the line, I will break him. I do not have that much patience.*

Less than fifteen minutes later, and very aware of Raphael sweeping across the sky above, Elena turned and walked up the steps to her father's house. Again, it wasn't a maid who opened the door. "Gwendolyn," she said, shaking off the rain from her wings. "I just came to have a chat with Eve before I head out of the city." She didn't want her youngest sister to believe she'd been forgotten. It was a hurt she'd never inflict on anyone of her own.

"Come inside," Gwendolyn said, concern on that discreetly made-up face. "You must be so cold."

Elena stood dripping in the hallway. "I'm sorry, I'm wet."

"Give me a moment." Gwendolyn disappeared and returned with a towel, handing it to her.

Elena wiped off her face and did the best she could to squeeze the water out of her ponytail. "I'll stay in the hallway—don't want to ruin your carpet."

"It can be cleaned."

Somewhere in the midst of patting down the parts of her wings she could reach, Elena became aware that Gwendolyn was staring at her. "I must look a sight," she said with a laugh, expecting a polite response.

What she got was nothing she could've predicted.

"I always wondered," the other woman said in a husky voice, "what was so wonderful about her that he couldn't let go, that he had to keep a mistress who reminded him of her."

Elena felt the ground open up beneath her feet. She did not want to be having this conversation with her father's second wife. "Gw—"

"I see it now," Gwendolyn continued, deep white grooves around her mouth. "There's something in you, something she must've given you—and it's something I'll never have. That's why he married me."

Acutely uncomfortable, Elena nonetheless couldn't just stand by in the face of such raw pain. "You know how he reacted when I wanted to attend Guild Academy." It was her enrolling at the Academy without his permission, permission he'd never have given, that had led to the fight in which he'd called her an "abomination" before throwning her out of his life. "Yet he allows Eve to go. That's because of you—he listens to you."

Gwendolyn hugged herself, tiny lines flaring out at the corners of her eyes. "The worst thing is—I love him. I always have." Turning, she began to walk down the hallway. "He's in the study."

"Wait, I just want to talk to Eve."

The slender woman tucked a wing of raven hair behind her ear as she glanced back. "I'll bring her down, but you can't avoid speaking to him, you know that."

Maybe not, but she could delay it as long as possible. So she waited for Eve to come down and spent a good half an hour with her sister, answering the questions on hunting that Eve had built up since their last meeting—and letting her know she could call Elena anytime.

Afterward, they spoke of other, more painful things.

"I miss Betsy," Evelyn whispered, her hand a rigid little fist. "She was my *best* friend."

"I know, baby."

Eve's eyes shone wet as she threw herself into Elena's arms, seeming far younger than her years, the acknowledged baby of the family. "Mom thinks I don't know, but I do. We looked the same. Everyone said so."

Elena didn't know what to say, how to heal that hurt, so she just held Evelyn tight and rocked her until the tears passed. "Shh, sweetheart. I don't think Betsy would've wanted you to make yourself sick like this."

"She was so nice, Ellie." A gulping sob. "I miss her every day."

Elena understood to the deepest core of her soul. She missed Ari and Belle and Marguerite every second of every day. "Why don't you tell me about her?"

It took a while for Evelyn to find the words past her tears, but when she did, it was a dam breaking open. She spoke not only about Betsy, but about Celia, too, the girl who had "played the clarinet the best out of everyone" and who hadn't laughed when Eve made a mistake during class.

Elena sat still and listened, coming to the sobering realization that Eve hadn't spoken to anyone else about this, damming up her pain. She could understand why when it came to Jeffrey, but Gwendolyn's love for her daughters was palpable. "Why didn't you talk to your mom about Betsy and Celia?"

"She's sad all the time anyway." Wise words from a child with solemn gray eyes. "Do you mind if I talk to you?"

"No, of course not."

A direct look, clear of tears now. "I used to think you must be mean, and that's why Father didn't ever invite you to stay with us."

Elena's heart stabbed with pain. "Yeah?"

"Yeah. But you're not. You're nice." A fierce hug from those solid little arms. "You can come stay at my house when I have one." It was whispered in her ear.

Elena held the unexpected emotional gift to her heart a few minutes later as she pushed through the door to her father's study without knocking. She found him standing at the open French doors, staring out into the rain. Not knowing why she didn't turn around and leave, she closed the door behind herself and crossed the room to stand against the opposite doorjamb, three feet of space between them.

Outside, the rain fell down in silver sheets, blotting out the world. She didn't know if it was the conversation she'd had with Gwendolyn or something else, but she found her lips parting. "Mama loved the rain."

*"Come, chérie, dance with your mama."*

*The damp, squishy feel of earth between her feet, her chest bursting with giggles as she ran outside with Beth by her side. "Mama!"*

*Laughter, sweet and carefree as Marguerite twirled in the rain, her skirts flying out around her in an unruliness of color.*

*"Mama. Pretty." Beth's soft voice, her hand curling into Elena's as they jumped in the puddles around their mother's spinning figure.*

"Yes." The word was clipped. "She was happy in the rain, but she couldn't survive the storm."

Stunned that Jeffrey had actually replied, she didn't know what to do, what to say. She found herself rubbing a fisted hand over her chest, as if she could brush away the years-old hurt. "She wasn't strong. Not like you." Marguerite had been the light and the laughter, the wildfire in their life.

A bitter laugh. "She wouldn't have needed to be if I'd been there that day."

This conversation wasn't going as she'd predicted, and she felt scared, lost, a child again. Gripping at the doorjamb, she thought back to that fateful day when everything had fractured, remembered that her daddy had been missing. "You went to pick Beth up from her sleepover." She'd always been grateful for the kindness of fate that meant her sister had been spared the butcher's attention.

A cold gray glance from behind those clear spectacles. "I had a fight with Marguerite, went off to clear my head, picked your sister up later than I should have."

Elena's whole world began to spin.

"We fought because I thought she was too flighty. I wanted her to be a businessman's wife . . ."

"When she was a butterfly," Elena whispered, knowing that in spite of his harsh words, her father had *loved* his first wife, loved her in a way that he'd never again loved anyone else.

*"Sweetheart, this cake looks delicious."*

*Marguerite laughing and tugging on Jeffrey's sedate tie to pull him down for a passionate kiss. "The cake looks atrocious and you know it, mon mari."*

*A smile that turned her father into the most handsome man in the world. "Ah, but the cook is definitely delicious."*

Even as the fragment of memory tumbled unbidden into her mind from some secret hiding place, Jeffrey straightened, thrusting his hands into the pockets of his suit pants. She knew the moment was gone before he spoke. "Have you come to tell me that more of your new friends will be coming to harm your sisters?"

She flinched. "They're under constant protection."

Jeffrey didn't look at her. "I'll make sure word gets out that you're not a welcome member of this family."

It was a good precaution, but it also burned like a poker searing through her heart. "All right." Her voice caught, but she didn't let it break, refusing to crumble in front of this man who couldn't be the same one who'd held her hand in that hospital morgue almost two decades in the past. "I'll make sure any meetings I have with Eve are at the Guild from now on. No reason for anyone to question my presence there."

Jeffrey said nothing.

Turning, Elena went to leave.

"Elieanora."

She froze with her hand on the doorknob. "Yes?"

"Of all my children, you have always been the most like me."

Repudiating the thought with every part of her, she walked out of the house without looking back. Raphael was there to pull her up into the sky until she'd gained enough altitude to fly. And fly they did, as she tried to bury her father's words deep under a mountain of truth.

*Elena.*

*I'm nothing like him! I would never do to my child what he did to his.*

Raphael didn't immediately agree, and his words, when they came, were not what she wanted to hear. *You are both survivors, Elena. You chose different methods to do it, but you both did it.*

Her lower lip quivered, and she was so frustrated at the sign of weakness that she bit down hard enough to draw blood. *He survived by destroying all memory of our family. I hold them here.* She slammed a fist to her heart, blinking the rain out of her eyes.

*I am not your father's champion. I would kill him if you would only not hate me afterward, but the fact of his mistress, it argues against your belief.*

Dashing away more of the rain . . . and realizing the salty droplets weren't falling from the sky after all, Elena thought of the poor woman Uram had brutalized in his rampage through New York. That light blond hair and golden skin, it had been a pale imitation of her mother's butterfly beauty . . . but an imitation nonetheless. *I can't,* she said, a painful lump in the center of her chest, *I can't see him that way.*

They'd reached the Tower, and Raphael waited to speak until they'd landed. Taking her into his arms, wings raised to protect her from the driving rain once more, he spoke against her ear. "You may be Jeffrey's daughter, but you are also Marguerite's."

Elena clutched at his back, her fingers digging into him as she buried her face against his chest. "That's the thing," she whispered, almost hoping he wouldn't hear her above the storm. "I hate him for what he is . . . but at least he stuck around."

A lonely red high-heeled shoe on the cold black-and-white tile. A thin shadow swinging against the wall of the Big House. Those were her last memories of her mother. "At least he didn't give up when it got too fucking hard. It was hard for all of us! But she left; she *chose* to leave!"

Her archangel said nothing, simply enfolded her in the circle of his arms and the protection of his wings as the storm raged with relentless fury around them.

Raphael knew his hunter needed time, but he couldn't give it to her, not today. *We must go, Elena*, he said too soon. *The sky is beginning to clear.*

A nod against his chest. "Don't worry, Archangel. I'm okay."

No, he thought, she wasn't. But she would survive, as she'd survived the losses of her childhood, Uram's evil, the staggering change from mortal to immortal. *Come.*

The flight over the Hudson was relatively quick, the wind no longer against them. Once there and in dry clothes, Elena said, "I'll see if my hunter friends in Japan were able to dig up any more intel."

While she did that, Raphael spoke to the leader of his Seven in the library. "Do you foresee any problems in my absence?" Lijuan wasn't the only one who'd noticed that he'd become more vulnerable to injury—it might well be the incentive another angel needed to attempt conquest.

Dmitri shook his head. "The fact that I'm here will deter anyone who might have ideas. They know I'm no new-Made vampire."

"If there is an attack, go for the kill." Only the most ruthless will would keep the city safe. "I'm leaving Venom with you, with Jason ready to fly in if necessary, while Galen holds the

Refuge territory. Illium comes with me, and Naasir is already in Tokyo." The vampire would meet them in Kagoshima.

"What about Aodhan?"

"I'm sending him back to the Refuge." The angel had already pinpointed Caliane's possible location on a satellite map. "I don't want Galen alone." He didn't trust the others in the Cadre not to strike at him through eliminating one of his Seven.

"He would've been my choice as well," Dmitri said. "Other than Galen, Aodhan is the one most used to handling your affairs in the Refuge." The vampire turned a fraction as Elena walked into the room, and Raphael knew he'd likely curled out a tendril of scent in an effort to get a rise from her. About to tell Dmitri that today was not the time, he saw Elena's lips curve.

"That hard up for a date, Dmitri darling?" she purred. "I have a number you can call."

Dmitri's eyes narrowed, and at that instant, there was nothing of the sophisticated male who was Raphael's second. Instead, it was the warrior honed in fire who spoke. "You look weak." It was a condemnation. "You're in no shape to go into battle beside Raphael."

*Dmitri, take care.* A soft warning—Raphael allowed Dmitri to push Elena, because the inescapable fact was, Elena needed to be able to hold her own against vampires and angels alike. Dmitri was the perfect testing ground. But there were some lines he would not allow even Dmitri to cross. *It is my consort to whom you speak.*

Jaw set, Dmitri parted his lips to reply, but Elena beat him to it. "I might look like shit, but I'm feeling plenty bloodthirsty." Her voice was a razor. "I'd be happy to demonstrate if you'd like to step outside for a while."

"I would not damage the Sire's consort." Arctic politeness.

Elena put fisted hands on her hips, cheeks filling with color. "Raphael, tell him you won't do anything to him if I get 'damaged.'"

"That would be a lie, Elena. I would tear out his throat."

Dmitri's smile was loaded with provocation. "Too bad, I guess. You'll have to wait for my touch another day."

Elena glared at both of them. "No wonder the two of you get along. I'm going to go finish my calls—I just wanted to let you know that a hunter who was in that part of Kagoshima a week ago said he got the creeps the entire time he was there. As if something was telling him to leave *or else*."

Raphael met the gaze of the leader of his Seven after Elena left. "You will go too far one day." Dmitri had proven his loyalty, but Elena was Raphael's heart. There was no contest.

The vampire shrugged. "She fights better when she's angry than when she's hurt."

*The fact that you enjoy baiting her had nothing to do with it?*

"Side benefit." Dmitri's smile faded the next second. "Sire, if your mother wakes, what do you want me to do?"

Raphael understood what his second was asking. "If she wakes and she is as before, there will be nothing anyone can do."

# 30

The last time Elena had set foot in Japan, it had been on the trail of an investment executive—a vampire who'd decided that having served ten years of his hundred-year Contract, he'd now live a life of leisure using the money he'd siphoned from the accounts of his more trusting vampiric clients.

The angel who held the Contract had been "severely angered" by the fact that not only had the vampire broken the agreement, but that he'd used his position in the angel's employ to swindle others. Elena had been given a "kill if unable to retrieve" order, but she'd brought the idiot back to his angel alive if petrified.

"Thank you, Guild Hunter," the angel had said in a calm tone that held pure death when she delivered the package. "I will take care of the punishment."

Elena had pitied the vampire, but the man had dug his own grave when he'd stolen that money. "He's not dead, you know," she said to Illium—who stood by her shoulder, listening to the story of the hunt. The fourth member of their party, Naasir, had stayed behind at a small settlement about an hour's flight from here, hoping to mine further information from the locals. "His angel preferred to punish him in other ways."

Illium's face was clean and beautiful in the breeze that swept across the mountaintop where they stood, the blue-tipped black strands of his hair silken against his skin. "Sometimes, death is too merciful."

"Yeah, but I felt sorry for him anyway. It was a white-collar crime."

Illium gave her an odd look. "In the human world, such crimes are lightly punished, though they harm hundreds, leading some to choose death out of despair, while the man who beats a single person is considered the worse criminal."

"*Huh.*" She stared out at the endless spread of mountain and forest in front of her. "I never thought of it that way." Frowning, she realized the dark green of the forest wasn't totally uninhabited—she could just glimpse the distinctively tiled roof of what might have been a temple.

*Raphael?* She tried to keep the worry out of her mental question. Raphael had landed with her and Illium, told them to wait while he did a preliminary survey, then disappeared into the clouds. That had been over fifteen minutes ago, and no matter how hard she tried, she couldn't sense the familiar rain of his scent. *Archangel?*

A glint of gold in the clear blue sky. Shading her eyes, she looked up and felt her heart sigh. *Hey, what's with the silent treatment?*

Still no response. Deciding to hold her peace, she watched with aching wonder as he made his way down toward the canopy—his movements powerful, precise, making the act of flying appear effortless. "He's the most magnificent male I've ever seen." The words just spilled out.

"You wound me, Ellie."

Her lips curved, but she didn't take her eyes off Raphael as he circled around the temple before turning to head back to them. "Ah, but you are surely the prettiest." All eyes of gold and wings of blue, Illium should have been too beautiful, and sometimes she thought he was. What woman would dare walk beside him?

"Prettier than Ransom?" His wing brushed hers as he shifted to nudge at her shoulder with his own.

"Well now, depends if a woman likes eyes the color of ancient Venetian coins, or hair that's a sheet of ebony silk." She razzed Ransom about his hair, but it really was gorgeous.

A wash of wind against her face as Raphael backwinged to a landing in front of her. "You prefer the crashing hue of the sea, do you not, Elena?"

"Heard that, did you?" But she wasn't smiling. "Why didn't you reply when I was talking to you?" She tapped her head to make sure he understood.

His expression grew watchful. "I heard nothing." Glancing at Illium, he said, "Did you attempt contact?"

"Once, Sire. I thought you preoccupied when you didn't answer." Illium's face was suddenly that of the man Elena had seen amputate the wings of his foes with pitiless efficiency. "Something in this place attempts to break you away from us."

Elena stared down at the mountainous terrain. "She can try, but she won't succeed." It was a challenge, and when lightning shattered the sheet blue of the sky, she knew the challenge had been heard.

Raphael touched the back of her neck. "Stay close, Elena. You are the easiest to hurt. And this entire region . . . sings to me. She is here, somewhere."

In response, Elena pulled down his head and took his mouth with fierce, possessive hunger. "You're mine," she whispered. "I won't let anyone take you from me, not that creepy Lijuan and not *her*."

Raphael's bones stood out sharply against his skin, that skin holding a faint glow as he spoke against her mouth. "Come, warrior mine. Let us find her wherever she may Sleep."

Diving off the mountain with him, Illium on her other side, she kept her senses wide open as they flew to the old tiled roof she'd seen from a distance. As they came close enough to look

down at it, she glimpsed the remains of what could well have
been the curving arch of a *torii* guarding the entrance, con-
firming her supposition that it had been a temple. Or perhaps
shrine was the correct word. Now, it stood abandoned.

The forest had encroached over and through it to the extent
that vines crawled into windows that had long lost their cov-
erings, while fallen leaves and other debris lay at least a foot
deep in the doorway. Most of the roof, too, was covered by
vines and mossy growth, while below, the roots of an ancient
*sakura* tree appeared to have slipped under and buckled what
might've once been a small courtyard.

"Elena, collapse your wings." Raphael dropped just below
her and went vertical, as Illium did the same on her other
side.

Realizing what they intended to do, she snapped back her
wings. One strong masculine hand closed on each of her upper
arms at the same instant—as they came in for a tight landing
in the courtyard where people might once have waited to enter
the shrine. Or maybe . . . Bending down when Illium and Raphael released her, she brushed away the leaves and dirt to un-
cover traces of a gritty white substance. "I think this might've
been a sand garden."

Neither of the men spoke, moving away toward the building. Looking up, she glanced around. Given the size of the
shrine, it was possible that the sand garden may have been part
of a larger garden—complete with velvet green grass and trees
planted after the utmost thought and care alongside a small
bubbling stream, perhaps a tiny Japanese maple or two with
leaves that would turn a brilliant orange red come autumn.

So quickly nature takes over, she thought, rising to her feet
and dusting off her hands. Now, though enough light came in
through the canopy that they could see what they were doing,
it was soft and shaded by the time it hit the ground, and the
roots of several forest giants had not only overwhelmed the
sand garden, they appeared to have gone under then cracked
upward through the floors of the shrine itself.

Walking to one huge root, she put her hands on the wood

and vaulted over, her wings trailing across the knotted surface as she did so. "Find anything?" she called out to Raphael, unable to see Illium.

He glanced over at her from where he stood by the entrance. She took a startled step back. His eyes . . . "Raphael, talk to me."

That unearthly glow continued to shine unabated as he held out his hand. "Come here, Elena."

Walking carefully over the twisted and broken remains of two low steps, she reached out to take his hand, let him pull her up beside him. "What do you see?"

That inhuman gaze focused on something in the forest. "I see nothing, but I hear her."

*Raphael.*

Elena shivered. "I heard that, too." Looking down at their clasped hands, she realized the glow from his skin was traveling over hers in a glittering wave. "What's happening?"

Raphael shook his head, silken strands of midnight black hair sliding across his forehead. "I do not know. But I know that my mind is clearer when you stand beside me." His eyes continued to smolder with that preternatural fire, as if he was burning huge amounts of power . . . to keep Caliane at bay, she realized.

She dropped one of the knives from her arm sheath down into the palm of her free hand. "Do you still want to look inside the shrine? The debris in front of the door isn't too bad." What little she knew about Japanese shrines said this was unlikely to have been the main entrance—but from what she'd seen in the air, the front was inaccessible.

"Yes." He returned his attention to the ruins. "My mother was Cadre. She is adept at games, may well be trying to lure me away from here because it is her resting place."

Glancing around, Elena frowned. "Where's Illium? Inside already?"

"I cannot hear him." Raphael's tone was sharp.

"That doesn't mean anything," Elena said, hand tightening on the hilt of her dagger. "Not here, with the static." But her heart thudded double-time. Not Illium, she thought, not the angel who'd become one of her closest friends.

"Wait." Raphael held her back when she would've headed down to where she'd last seen the blue-winged angel. "I will go first—there are things here you have no hope of defeating."

"Go." She wasn't stupid, no matter that worry for Illium had her frantic. The angel had become one of *her* people, someone she'd fight to the death to save. "Be careful Archangel." Because if she loved Illium, what she felt for Raphael was beyond words, beyond her ability to describe. A huge, powerful, near-painful emotion, it simply was.

"Death holds no allure for me, Elena." The power of him cut against his skin, a cold white fire. "Not when I have yet to sate my hunger for you." Turning, he walked not to where she'd last glimpsed Illium, but into the bowels of the shrine. "He came in here."

Following, her entire body on alert, she paused by a long, pitted column that bore flecks of what appeared to be rust-colored pigment and checked in the shadows around its side. Seeing nothing, she continued on, the rustle of her and Raphael's wings the only— "Wait." Gripping Raphael's arm, she stopped him when he would've gone farther into the depths of the building.

When he glanced back at her, she leaned forward to brush the dirt off a cracked but still-standing column using her fingers. "Do you see?" It was a whisper.

Raphael reached out to trace the shape of the dragon carved into the eroded surface. "This should not be part of this shrine. Everything about it is wrong."

"Do you think . . . ?"

"Perhaps. Or perhaps she is simply remembered as legend in these parts." Turning again, he walked a few steps into what had been the main room—the roof of which was now almost entirely gone, the sky covered with a filigree of green—and stopped three feet in. "Illium." Bending, he picked up one startling blue feather edged in silver.

There was a drop of crimson on the very tip.

\* \* \*

Half an hour later, they'd combed every single inch of the shrine and the surrounding area and found no further sign of Illium. "You said your mother liked beautiful things," she said to Raphael as they stood beside the gnarled old root she'd vaulted over not long ago.

Raphael gave a slow nod. "And Illium is very much a man many have desired to collect over the years."

"He's not helpless despite the fact that he appears decorative, so that'll be a surprise." Folding her arms, she turned toward the being for whom she would walk into hell itself. "You're also far stronger than you were when she last saw you—you can reach Illium."

Raphael looked at her for a long, long moment before raising his hand to touch her cheek. "Such faith in me, Elena."

She closed her fingers over his wrist, his pulse strong and steady under her touch. "I know your heart, Archangel. It gives you more power than you believe."

Raphael felt a tug of urgency at Elena's words, a flare of understanding that he couldn't quite grasp. It was tempting to chase, but experience told him that would only send the whisper of thought further into hiding. Allowing it to fade away for the moment, he focused on the facts at hand. "She took Illium for a reason."

Elena's eyes glittered with intelligence, that thin ring of silver luminous in the muted forest light. "A warning."

"That may be." However, his mother wasn't like other mothers. "Or it may be that she grows impatient."

"She wants you to find her?" Elena frowned and parted her lips . . . but the words never came, blades gleaming in her hands even as Raphael sensed the intruder at his back and turned.

A shift in the air, as if something was trying to take shape. For a fraction of a second, he thought it was Caliane, but then the formless being turned into an angel with hair of ice and irises of a strange pearlescent shade that almost melded into

the whites of her eyes, giving her the look of an eerie blind-
ness. Her wings were the last part of her body to appear, a
silken dove gray that was as exquisite as Lijuan was dangerous.

"Raphael." Her voice held the same faint echo he'd sensed
before, as if there were other voices within her, ghosts trying
to reach out. Trying to scream.

"What are you doing here, Lijuan?"

The Archangel of China smiled, and it was nothing even
remotely of the world. What Lijuan had become, what she'd
"evolved" into, was a nightmare even the Cadre couldn't quite
comprehend. But Raphael understood. Because he'd looked
into the face of madness as a child, felt it touch him with featherlight fingers . . . and knew it might one day crash over him
in an overwhelming wave.

Elena's wing brushed his in a silent caress, as if she'd read
his thoughts. As if she was reminding him of her promise.

*"I won't let you fall."*

Lijuan's eyes flickered over Elena's wings, and there was a
faint avarice in her gaze. The most ancient of archangels had a
fondness for the exotic and unusual—unfortunately, she liked
to pin them up as trophies on her walls. "Your hunter's wings
are exceptional. Unique. Did you know that, Raphael? In all
my millennia of existence, I've never seen wings like hers . . .
or like the young one's."

The "young one" was Illium—and Lijuan's fascination
with him was such that Raphael made sure Illium was rarely
in her vicinity, and never, ever alone. "You did not come here
to talk of wings."

"In a sense." Settling her own wings, Lijuan looked around
with those eyes that appeared blind. "I remember this place.
It was an ancient shrine known only to its disciples. Legend
said they worshipped a sleeping dragon." A shake of her head,
her hair blowing back in a wind that touched nothing else. "I
didn't pay it much mind."

Because a goddess, Raphael thought, had little to fear from
small mortal gods. But now, he thought, looking at that ageless visage, she did know fear. Lijuan had evolved . . . but Ca-

liane had been millennia upon millennia older than her when she lay down to Sleep. Who was to say that his mother could not vanquish the nightmare that was the Archangel of China?

Lijuan's eyes settled on Raphael once more. "You always loved your mother," she said in a sweetness of words that did nothing to hide the death that clung to her like a putrid shade. "So it is unfair of us to expect you to find and eliminate the problem."

"You are here to kill my mother." It was no surprise, but he wondered at her speaking to him of it again.

"I am here to kill a monster."

# 31

Elena had been certain where she stood on the whole Caliane situation the instant the archangel took Illium, but now, looking at Lijuan, she reassessed. *Did your mother ever reanimate the dead?*

Raphael didn't betray even by the barest flicker of an eyelash that he'd heard her, but his response was instant. *No.*

An absolute answer, but she heard the things Raphael didn't say, felt the tendrils of an ancient darkness curl around her heart. Because whatever form Caliane's madness had taken, it had turned her own son against her. *What did she do?* It was the one thing she'd never asked, for she understood that mothers could be hated and loved at the same time.

*She sang thousands upon thousands into slavery, until they saw nothing but her, until they would have slit their own children's throats and walked over their bruised and battered bodies if she asked.*

Elena swallowed, watching Lijuan as she turned to walk across the remnants of the sand garden, her wings so flawless in color and formation that it was impossible not to admire them even knowing that their purity was a lie, hiding the truth of Lijuan's nature. *Did she give that order?*

*No. My mother was once the Guardian of the Innocent and some part of her remembered that responsibility. But she gave other orders.*

For a moment, she thought that was all he was going to say on the subject, but then the sea slammed against her senses. She almost staggered under the force of it, only then realizing how rigidly he was holding on to his control.

*She sang the adult populations of two thriving cities into walking into the Mediterranean until they drowned, because they were about to go to war. In her mind, it was a better option than the death and devastation war would've caused.*

*I have never heard such quiet as I heard in those cities. The children were shocked and mute, and in spite of the care we gave them, many died of inexplicable sicknesses over the next year. Keir has always maintained that they died of such heart-sorrow as immortals would never know.*

Lijuan finished her exploring at that instant and turned to face them again. "She does not Sleep here." It was a definitive statement.

"You will forgive me if I do not take your word for that." Raphael's response held the same chill Elena had sensed in his mental voice.

Lijuan smiled that damn creepy smile that made spidery fingers crawl up Elena's back. "You think I covet your mother's power, but you are wrong. Caliane's"—a massive gust of wind that pushed Elena's hair off her face—"power drove her mad. I enjoy my sanity."

Whether Lijuan was sane was a question of interpretation, but one thing was clear. "She can hear us."

Lijuan's eyes shifted to Elena. "Michaela doesn't understand what you see in your hunter, Raphael." She drifted closer, too close for Elena's comfort. "But I do."

Elena held her ground. Lijuan was batshit crazy as far as she was concerned, but according to Raphael, the oldest of the archangels also had a weird code of honor. She wouldn't kill Elena for speaking as other archangels might—but she'd strike out if she thought Elena wasn't treating her with the respect demanded by her status. "To be honest, I'm not sure half the time myself," she said, keeping her voice steady, though her every instinct screamed at her to get the fuck away from the creature in front of her.

*Elena.*

*Hush, let me talk to the crazy lady.*

A flicker of his wing and she wondered if she'd almost surprised her archangel into a smile.

"Life," Lijuan whispered, reaching out a hand as if to touch Elena's face.

Elena took a step back just as Raphael moved to stand slightly in front of her.

Laughing, Lijuan dropped her hand. "As I said, life. There is a flame within you, hunter, one that is rare. So he keeps you close, though you weaken him more with every day that passes."

Elena felt the heart-blow slice home, piercing her through and through. She knew Raphael thought it a fair trade, but she didn't think so. If he was hurt because of her, she'd never forgive herself. Even the possibility terrified her. But there was no room for self-pity here, in front of an archangel who'd let her reborn feast on the flesh of the newly dead. "Do you know where she's taken Illium?" she asked, stepping up to stand beside Raphael once again. *I'm your consort, remember?* she said when he shot her a hard glance.

*I would never forget, Guild Hunter.* Cool words, but they were as good as a caress to her.

"I sense a hum of power here," Lijuan said, "but Caliane is strong. Her tentacles pervade this entire region."

The leaves on the ground rose up in miniature tornadoes as Lijuan spread out her wings. "I search for her, Raphael."

"As do I, Lijuan."

"You will call me." It was an order as the oldest of the

Cadre twisted into a pillar of dark smoke that spiraled up into the sky and disappeared.

Turning her face away from the rush of leaves and dirt stirred up by Lijuan's departure, Elena felt Raphael's hands lock on her waist. Used to the drill by now, she clamped her wings tight to her back and held on to his shoulders as he took them above the canopy, high enough that she could fly on her own.

But she didn't let go. Instead, wrapping her arms around him, she pressed her cheek to the warmth of his neck. "Together, Archangel," she said in his ear, a preemptive strike against any attempt he might make to distance himself. "Always. Remember?"

His hands tightened on her hips. *I know where my mother Sleeps.*

Jerking in surprise, she looked up. "You do?"

*She underestimated Illium's strength as you predicted. He is rising to consciousness and attempting to lead me to him.*

Shuddering at the confirmation that Illium was safe, she met eyes gone a stormy midnight. *Will you call Lijuan?* It seemed safer not to say the name aloud.

*I should. She is the only one who may be able to battle Caliane and win.*

"She's your mother." A knot formed in her own heart. "If I had the chance to speak to my mother again, I would grab it with both hands." No matter how angry she was at Marguerite, no matter how much her mother's betrayal continued to burn like acid, she would walk into Marguerite's arms and hold on . . . and hold on.

*Caliane is likely to arise a horror, Elena. Far worse than Lijuan, for Caliane does not look monstrous in any way. Even her madness is a thing of impossible beauty.*

*If that's true, Lijuan will sniff her out soon enough.* Perhaps it would only take her minutes, but that time would be Raphael's. *You deserve the chance to talk to your mother alone, to see her one more time.*

Raphael leaned down to claim her lips in a slow, potent kiss as the sky rolled with a wave of thunder, lightning spiking in vivid bursts of color on the horizon. *I would leave you in a safe place.*

*I would just break out of it.*

He looked at her then, and she knew he was well aware he had the power to trap her in ways that would allow no escape. A cage of protection . . . but still a cage. Instead of arguing with him, she waited.

Wind whipped that midnight-dark hair off his face as he touched his fingers to her cheek. *Not alone, Elena.*

Her heart caught at the emotion in that simple statement. *Never.*

With those words, they turned and flew into the heart of the storm.

Two hours later, the muscles that supported Elena's wings had gone beyond protest and into an almost numb state that she knew would get her through the next few hours—but would leave her whimpering in the days that followed. She had a feeling that wouldn't be a problem. Whatever was going to happen would happen today. Either she'd survive—or she wouldn't. Anything else was a peripheral concern.

Raphael flew ahead of her, a blaze of white-gold against the roiling turmoil of the clouds that seemed ready to devour them both, the rain a freezing constant. According to her watch, it was a few minutes after four in the afternoon, but the skies were so black that had they been flying over a city, the entire area would've been lit up by thousands of tiny lights—in office windows, along the streets, blinking high up on the towers.

However, the land below them was composed of mountain and forest broken up only by the occasional isolated hamlet of farmers and their kin. They'd also seen a village even smaller than the one where they'd left Naasir. The glow of warmth from that village had been too small to penetrate the stormy dark, so when Elena caught a glimpse of light a bit farther on, she wiped the rain from her eyes and focused—it was odd, but she could've sworn her vision grew sharper, more crisp, as if her eyes were compensating for the conditions.

Shrugging off the sensation, she continued to concentrate. The light was diffuse, covering a wider area than could be accounted for by a farm or other small settlement. Guessing it to be a larger village, she dropped just far enough below the clouds to get a closer look. At first, she couldn't quite understand what it was she was seeing, her mind unable to process the impossibility of it.

Because below her spread the gracious lines of what appeared to be a city of sparkling gray stone, all of it shrouded in an iridescent glow the color of the Aegean. Not only were the buildings utterly dissimilar to the accepted architecture of this region—heck, this country!—according to the satellite images Elena had accessed, that city hadn't existed this morning. *Raphael!*

No response, and she thought Caliane might have succeeded in blocking their communication again, but then she saw him sweep down below her, his wings spread to their widest as he held his own against the surging winds. *Wait above, Elena.* He flew toward that stunning shimmer of color.

Elena knew that would be the safest option—but every part of her said it would be a very, very bad idea to let him go into that strange city alone. Dropping in a steep, scarcely controlled dive, she reached him just before he would've gone through the . . . whatever the hell it was.

Raphael's gaze was almost impossible to hold, it burned with such power when he glanced at her. *Elena.* It was an order.

Her hackles rose, but she bit back the reaction, blinking away the tears caused by the momentary contact with his eyes. *I have to come with you. Trust me.*

*It's not a question of trust. I would not lose you to my mother's madness.*

Flying a fraction below him, so their wings wouldn't tangle, she reached up with her hand. *I won't lose you to her, either. This feels like a trap, Raphael.*

Raphael curled his fingers around hers, holding her in position. *It may well be. And you would fly into it with me?*

She infused her voice with wickedness. *Trouble's not only my middle name, it's my first and last, too.*

A blaze of electric heat as Raphael's power swept out to cover her. She'd been shielded by it when they'd danced that most intimate of dances, felt it cut across her when he was angry, but never had it enfolded her with such brutal completeness, until her eyes streamed tears from the shocking force of it. Shutting them tight, she squeezed his hand. *I can't see.*

*It won't be for long. If the shield around the city is the trap, it'll give us enough time to get back out.*

With that, he flew, pulling her with him.

She knew the instant they hit the cool energy of the shield. The shock wave rocked through her entire body, but it was concentrated on where her fingers intertwined with Raphael's, a wrenching pull that attempted to separate them. She knew if it succeeded, she'd be thrown out while Raphael disappeared inside the city she wasn't sure wasn't just a fancy mirage, a snare created by an archangel so old, it made her bones ache to even think about it.

*Hold on.*

She didn't know which one of them said that, her body battered by icy rain that had turned brutal, her wrist bones threatening to break—Caliane was determined to smash them apart. *Not on your fucking life,* she thought, and set her teeth against the pain of tendons that felt like they'd snap the next second.

An instant and an eternity later, they were tumbling out of the rain and toward the strange city at high velocity. A few months ago, she would've been helpless to stop her descent. But a few months ago, she'd been an angel newly fledged. Releasing Raphael's hand so she wouldn't drag him down with her, she stretched out her wings and began to beat upward in strong, fast movements, fighting the speed of her own tumbling body.

It became clear very quickly that her velocity was terminal. Four seconds tops and she was going to find herself smashed to jagged fragments against the flat gray stone of the roof below her.

*Elena.*

She shoved up her shields when Raphael would've taken over. *Conserve your strength.* Then she poured every ounce of her own strength into averting what might well be a fatal fall given her age. Lose enough pieces and she was toast, but she'd been training hard. She had the skill. She just had to—*Got it!*

Her wings brushed the coarse stone of a building as she managed to shift her trajectory enough that she missed the roof and fell into the gap between two of the graceful gray structures. It gave her enough time to stabilize and get herself back up into the sky. She more than half expected Raphael to be furious with her for her defiance, but when she reached him, he was staring down at the city, his wet hair shoved off his face.

"What is it?" she asked, thrusting a hand through her own hair . . . and realizing that no storm raged here. Rain lashed with unremitting force against the shield, but inside, the whole area was bathed in a golden light that almost succeeded in softening the stark edges of the buildings. "It needs flowers," she found herself saying. "It doesn't look quite right." Unable to hold the hover, she made a controlled descent onto the roof she'd almost crashed into only a minute ago.

Raphael followed her down with far more grace. "It was once overrun with them."

"With what?"

"Flowers."

Walking to the edge of the roof, she looked down and saw an amazing array of carvings on the wall of the opposite building, the stone sparkling with hidden flecks of color that would turn this city into a brilliantly cut diamond in sunlight. Her heart slammed against her ribs. "What is this place?"

"The jewel in my mother's crown. Though it is far from where it should be."

"You know, most archaeologists believe Amanat never existed," she said, staggered by the awareness of just how much power it would've taken to not only disappear, but *move* an entire city. "That it's nothing more than a legend."

A faint smile on Raphael's face that didn't reach his eyes. "I wonder at human archaeologists who do not speak to those of us who lived in these times of legend."

Elena snorted. "As if any of you angels would answer their questions."

*You know us too well, Elena.* Light words, but the way he stood, the way he looked at this strange city of stone and shadow, it spoke of lethal alertness.

Her own guard up, she continued to scan the area for any sign of Illium. They stood on one roof, but other roofs stacked up to her right, lodged directly into the mountains, as if they'd been carved out of rock, had stood there for centuries. Which was impossible. Except of course, she was dealing with an immortal of such power that she scared Lijuan.

And that scared the bejesus out of Elena. "Illium?"

"He's dropping in and out of consciousness, but I can sense him." Stepping off the roof, he flew down to the ground with a grace and strength that made her wonder what he'd become in another thousand years. Something extraordinary, of that she was certain. Unless . . . whatever it was that their relationship was doing to him ended up stealing his immortal life.

*No.* She repudiated the thought as her own feet touched the ground but knew it wasn't a truth she could ignore.

"What do you see, Guild Hunter?"

For a moment, she thought he'd guessed the direction of her thoughts, but then she followed his gaze. This lost city, its stone walls carved with ethereal, delicate art she recognized as so ancient as to have no modern equivalent, slumbered around them, an elegant lady perfectly preserved. "It should be crumbling into pieces, but everything's . . ."

"As if the city is simply sleeping through a long night," Raphael murmured.

Elena nodded. "Yeah." Followed the thought through to its

logical conclusion. "Raphael, what happened to the people who lived in Amanat at the time it went to sleep?"

Without discussion, they walked through the first doorway wide enough to accommodate wings, and found themselves in some sort of a temple full of light despite being carved into a mountainside. Elena didn't know what she'd expected to see, but it wasn't what they found.

# 32

They lay in peaceful repose, small groups of women curved around each other, faint smiles on their faces, as if they were having the most pleasant of dreams. "My God." Stunned, she kept watch as Raphael walked across the stone floor inlaid with precious gems of sparkling fire and dazzling brilliance, his wings leaving droplets of water in their wake.

When he bent to touch his fingers to the neck of a maiden—the word fit better than any other given the woman's gauzy, flowing garment of softest peach, her tumble of curls laced with ribbon—who lay in graceful repose on a silk cushion of gold-shot ivory, she walked to join him.

"We're right below the dais," she murmured.

Because that dais was set only a few feet above the rest of the floor, coming to just below her breasts, she could see across the sweeping breadth of it, see, too, the square of stone that was a different color from the rest. It was, she knew without being told, the place where the statue of a goddess—not a god, not in this place that sang of feminine power—had once stood.

"She is warm." Raphael rose to his feet. "The Cadre of my mother's time was wrong—she took her people into Sleep, not into death."

Elena shoved her hands through hair that was frizzy with damp. "Raphael, this kind of power . . ."

"Yes." Walking up the steps cut into the side of the dais and to the empty space she'd already noted, he stared down at the square imprint. "The populace of Amanat once had their own gods and goddesses, but when Caliane claimed it as her home, they became her people, their devotion complete."

"Did she sing them to that devotion?" Elena asked, able to hear the soft breaths of the sleepers now that she was listening for it. It raised the hairs on the back of her neck and nothing was going to get those hairs to go back down—not until they were out of the unnatural grasp of this city frozen in time.

Raphael shook his head. "No. Amanat was hers from long before I was born."

Elena thought of all she'd read about Caliane in the history texts, all Raphael had told her, remembered, too, that his mother had been called the Archangel of Grace, of Beauty. "The love always went in both directions."

"Yes." Crouching down, he touched his fingers to the square of stone that spoke of absence. "Illium."

Elena began to circle the stone walls below the dais, searching for an entrance. Nothing, the gray walls seamless. Then . . . a tiny blue feather lying at her feet. *Illium*. Tucking the feather into a pocket, she focused on the wall directly in front of where she'd found it. She felt nothing under her palms on the first pass. Or the second. But on the third . . . "Raphael, I think there might be a seam here."

He was beside her an instant later. "I played in this temple as a young boy—I may remember how it opens."

"Here." She stepped away to stand guard while he ran his fingers over the spot.

As she watched, he appeared to press down on specific areas of the stone, though she couldn't differentiate any one section of the wall from another. But the instant after he lifted his hand, the stone cracked open with a groan that spoke of great age, releasing a puff of dust that had Elena coughing as she ducked to poke her head inside.

At first, she saw nothing, the area beneath the altar was so dark.

Then her nose picked up the wicked bite of some exotic liqueur. Lime, she thought, it had the tart sweetness of lime, kissed with a richer, more languid flavor. It was a scent she hadn't realized she associated with Illium until that second. "He's here."

"Be ready." A brightness of blue.

In the lingering flash, she saw Illium's crumpled form in the corner, his head tipped against the stone wall, his wings crushed under his body. "What's she done to him?"

"Go, Elena." Taut words. "I need to remain here to ensure the door does not close."

Blinking against the aftereffects of the blaze of light, she stepped down into the cavern—it went deeper than the floor outside, until even Raphael could've stood upright—and made her way through the dark space by feel, stumbling over Illium when she miscalculated. *Please be okay.* Crouching, she touched his leg, his thigh, his chest, then finally, found her fingers on his face.

"Come on, Sleeping Beauty. I can't carry you out of here." He was too heavy with muscle, and under no circumstances did she want Raphael to leave the doorway—it would snap shut the instant he did, of that she was as sure as she was of her own name.

No response from Illium.

Leaning closer, she gave in to the urge to press her cheek against his, trembling in relief at the warmth of his skin. "Illium, you have to wake up. I need you to protect me against Dmitri."

A change in his breathing, fingers brushing against her hip, then . . . "Liar."

*Thank God.* She got to her feet, one of her hands around his. "Up, Sunshine, now."

Illium mumbled something, but she could tell he was attempting to obey. He got himself on his feet after a few tries, but then all but collapsed against her. Bracing his front against her own, she let out an *oomph* before managing to manhandle him enough that she could wrap an arm around his waist, pull his own muscular arm over her shoulders.

"Walk," she ordered, gripping at the wrist of the arm around her shoulders.

His wings lay heavy against her own as he spread them in an instinctive attempt to find his balance. The intimate slide was not something she'd have allowed even Illium under normal circumstances. Today, she held him even tighter, muttering orders in the voice of a drill sergeant in an effort to keep him conscious as she hauled him out of the pit where he'd been dumped, her back and shoulders straining against his muscled weight.

"Elena."

Only when she heard Raphael's voice did she realize she'd reached the doorway. "He's dazed," she told her archangel.

Illium lost consciousness again right then, becoming a dead weight.

"I've got him." As Raphael reached in to haul the blue-winged angel up out into the light, Elena made a mistake. She put her hand on the wall and took a moment to catch her breath. At the same instant, Raphael shifted just out of the doorway, turning to set Illium down against the outside wall.

The door slammed shut.

The shock of the absolute pitch-dark was so sudden and unexpected that Elena didn't scream, didn't cry out, didn't do anything but stare at the door that she *knew* was there, though she couldn't even see her own fingers in the extremity of the blackness. There was no light. None. *Raphael?* she tried after a couple of seconds, her brain kicking itself back into gear.

Silence.

It didn't scare her—she knew he was on the other side, working with single-minded focus to get her out. All she had to do was stay in place and fight the disorientation caused by the utter lack of sensory cues to aid perception. "Nice and easy," she told herself, shifting very carefully to lean against the wall, her wings tucked neatly to her back. The quiet within the stone room was . . . tomblike.

That was when she heard them.

Whispers. So many whispers. Around her. Inside her.

*Drip. Drip. Drip.*

*Come here, little hunter. Taste.*

*Get on your knees and beg, and maybe I'll let you back into this family.*

*Run, Ellie. Run.*

*She won't run. She likes it, you see.*

*Ah, chérie, you know I never left this room.*

*Mama?*

*Ari's having a nice nap—*

"Stop it!" she screamed, clapping her hands over her ears. But the voices continued to torment her, her nightmares boiling over to trap her in a prison far more terrible than the stygian gloom that surrounded her on every side.

*Little hunter, little hunter, where aaaaaarre you?*

*Perhaps I'll tie you to Bobby, let him feed.*

*You disgust me.*

*Dead, they're all dead.*

*Because of you.* Her sister's voice. Ari's voice.

*Monster.* Belle, whispering so low and mean. *You're a monster.*

"I'm sorry," Elena whimpered. "I'm sorry."

*Monster.*

"I didn't know. I swear I didn't!"

*Better that you die here in this tomb, than lead others to their deaths.*

Ari would never say that to her. Belle had never spoken to her in that vicious tone. The wrongness of it snapped the snare of nightmare. Shoving up the mental shields she'd been working on since she woke from the coma, she slammed herself against the wall, only then realizing she'd taken several steps forward. "I'm not playing this game!"

The instant her back met the wall, she became aware of the rush of cold air at her feet. Horror uncurling within her, she reached out with a foot, scooting forward an inch at a time. Her leg was almost fully extended when she felt a "lip" of stone—as if there was nothing beyond except a deadly crevice.

Shaking, she pulled back her leg, dropping her knives into the palms of her hands at the same time. Sweat trickled down her temples, stuck her hair to the sides of her face, made the air chill against her skin—she welcomed the rush of sensation, even as she decided to gamble with what might very well be her life. *Wish me luck, Archangel.*

There was no response, but she knew he had to be blasting the rock with angelfire by now. He'd get her out. She just had to keep herself alive in the interim.

Right on cue, she heard the slither of something on the stone, something heavy and scaly and reptilian. Shivering, she switched one of her daggers for the short sword Galen had drilled her in until she *could* fight in the dark—so long as she avoided that gaping pit in the center—and she opened her mouth. "Games," she said, speaking to the alien intelligence behind this trap, "are beneath you."

The slithering didn't cease, but she felt the sense of something, some*one* watching and listening, the heavy weight of that presence pressing down on her as she drew in long, slow breaths and tried to pinpoint the location of whatever it was that had crawled out of the pit to join her.

*Musk. Dirt. Moss.*

It was the last that gave her the anchor she needed—the stone room had been bare of living plants when she'd retrieved Illium. The creature was in the left-hand corner, she thought, heading toward her. So she began to inch to her right a fraction at a time, always testing ahead before she moved. She didn't trust the hole to remain in the center of the room.

"You were a goddess," she said as she moved. "Intelligent and beautiful, and worshipped by people not out of fear, but out of love. I am nothing but an angel new-Made, no real challenge to someone of your power." It was the unvarnished truth, and that, Elena thought, might just save her. Unless Caliane *was* still utterly insane. "To torment me serves no purpose but to lessen you."

A sudden cold that made her heart stutter in shock. The thing in the room with her hissed in rage at the same instant, and she knew she was skirting the edge of what would be tolerated. But she had to keep talking, had to keep Caliane from ordering the creature to attack. "Do you know what Raphael told me?" she said, hope flaming anew as she felt a vibration in the wall. *Archangel.*

The moment's distraction almost cost her everything as the serpent or whatever the fuck it was spit something in her direction. She caught the scent of acid a fraction of an instant before it would've been too late and slammed herself down and to her right, breaking what felt like a rib in the process. That pain, however, was nothing to the searing agony on the very tip of her left wing. Swallowing the scream that wanted to escape, she blinked back tears and crawled another foot out of range. "He told me," she said through the agonizing hurt, "that you had a voice like the heavens, so pure and strong and imbued with love that the world itself stood still to listen."

The cold retreated with such unexpected swiftness that Elena wondered if she'd surprised Caliane. But it was too late. She was trapped in a corner, with the floor falling away in a steep drop to her right, solid stone walls to her back and left . . . and the creature coming straight for her. She could see glowing slivers of swirling yellow and green that she guessed were its eyes, and from the sound it made as it slithered across the floor, it was massive.

There was no way in hell she'd be able to fight that thing trapped like this, but there wasn't any time to do—"Idiot, shit." She was moving even as the thought entered her head, rolling off to her right and into the pit, wings flared wide to control her descent. She had a feeling she did not want to drop down to the bottom—who the fuck knew what waited below, but she could use this space to maneuver. She didn't let herself consider the fact that the whole thing might snap shut, crushing the life out of her—maybe, just maybe, Caliane had heard enough to decide to give her a chance.

Twisting so that she faced the last known position of the creature, she beat her wings up and sliced out with the short sword. A scream of rage and the thick, pungent odor of body fluids told her she'd scored a hit. Her elation lasted only an instant—before agony blazed down her left side and she realized the creature had spit at her again.

It felt like her flesh was being peeled off her bones. Tears streamed down her face though she tried to fight them, knowing she couldn't give in to any vulnerability. Then her left wing began to drag, and she knew the acid had hit something vital. Fighting to keep herself afloat, she slammed into a wall inside the hole, felt the roughness of it scrape away the skin on her arms, her face, to expose her flesh to the air.

A second after that, she heard the slithering below.

*Jesus.* Swallowing, she beat her good wing faster in an effort to rise, but only succeeded in slowing her momentum a little. *Archangel, if you have something up your sleeve, now would be the time.*

A slam of crashing noise and then light, so bright that it made her cry out, shade her eyes with her uninjured arm as rocks and stone . . . and wetter, slimier things, rained down from above. Ducking to the side, she scrabbled at the coarseness of unfinished stone as one wing collapsed completely. "Raphael! Down here!"

A nail tore off her finger, another, blood slicking over her skin. *Hurry!*

Strong hands clamping over her shoulders. Two seconds later, she was being hauled out through a gaping hole where there had once been a door. Blinking against the sudden light, she tried to speak but couldn't get the words out past gritted teeth, the agony on her left side starting to crawl to the right.

Raphael brushed the hair off her face. "I have you, Elena. I have you." The warmth from his hands began to soak into her skin, chasing out the vicious pain that made her feel as if her organs were caught in a massive grinder.

Giving in to the need, she buried her face against his chest and fisted her hand in his damp shirt as he used his power to heal her. He was big and strong and warm, and she wanted to strip him to the skin and wrap herself around him until nothing could touch either of them. Sucking in a breath when his hand brushed her still-burning hip, she set her jaw, holding on with a white-knuckled grip.

Sooner than she'd expected, the pain was nothing but a memory.

"How bad is it?" she asked against his chest. "My wing?" It felt dead, gone. *No, please no.*

# 33

His arms around her. "The creature's poison was not as bad as Anoushka's."

"Not reassuring, Archangel."

"Your wing was paralyzed, not damaged—the acid didn't have time to eat through the tendon and bone. You'll be able to fly again in a few minutes."

So relieved that she was shaking, she pulled away to sit up—and got a good look at her side. Her clothing had been eaten away in spots large and small to expose her flesh. And it *was* flesh, the skin having been burned to nothingness by the acid. Bone gleamed white through one section and the sight of it made her want to retch.

Tensing her stomach against the urge, she wiped off her tears and blew out a breath. "Not as bad as it could've been."

"They go for the eyes," Illium said, sounding coherent and functional as he stood guarding the gaping hole in the stone below the dais, his sword in hand. "Good thing it was dark in there or your eyeballs would've been leaking down your face by now."

Elena stared at him. "Thank you for that cheerful thought."

The damn blue-winged idiot winked at her, those astonishing lashes closing over one golden eye.

"Raphael, can we kill him now?" she muttered, trying not to think about the fact that she had holes seared into her flesh.

Raphael's bones cut against his skin as he helped her to her feet. "Not yet, Elena. We may have need of him." It was said with such frigid calm that for a moment, she thought he'd taken her seriously.

Then she followed the direction of his gaze into the dark maw of the chamber where she'd been trapped. "No." She gripped his arm. "You're not going in there."

A glance so arrogant, she knew most beings—mortals and immortals both—would've fallen to their knees in submission. "Leave me, Guild Hunter. Illium will take you to the roof, to safety."

"Sire—" Illium began, no hint of laughter in his expression now.

"Illium." A single word. A command.

Illium looked as if he wanted to argue, but in the end, he bowed his head. However, Elena wasn't one of Raphael's Seven. She didn't have to obey his orders. Moving around to face him, she folded her arms. "If your mother is so powerful," she said, "then she can meet us out here just as well as in that pit."

"Caliane is not used to coming to anyone."

She raised an eyebrow and hoped like hell her next words wouldn't get them killed. "Or maybe she's only powerful when she has her prey trapped and alone. You've never had trouble facing anyone down in the full light of day."

The temple shook at her feet, trembling so hard she almost tumbled into Raphael. For a moment, she was afraid the entire structure would collapse, burying them. But she'd forgotten that Caliane was a goddess in Amanat—and that her people slept vulnerable beneath the stone roof.

When the trembling stopped, everything was as it had always been. Except that Raphael and Illium had their eyes trained on the dais. On what had appeared atop the stone.

* * *

Raphael strode up to what he now realized was an altar, aware of his consort and Illium coming to stand beside him, their swords drawn. But his attention was on the stone slab before him. Six feet long and three feet wide, perhaps as deep, it was a cool pale grey and free of ornamentation. Like the door below, the slab appeared seamless, but unlike the door, he didn't know how to unlock this puzzle.

*Raphael.*

Placing his palm on the stone that should've been cold but instead held a lingering warmth, he dropped his shields a fraction. *Mother.*

There was no answer, but he knew . . . "She is awake." It was too late to kill her while she lay weak and vulnerable.

*Could you have done such a thing, Raphael?*

Her voice, that beautiful, haunting voice, it penetrated to his very bones, stripped him bare. *I am an archangel.*

*Yes.* Such pride in that single word, a wonder of words unsaid. *You are the son of two archangels.*

He spread his fingers over the stone. *Are you sane, Mother?*

Laughter in his mind, painful in its familiarity. *Is any immortal ever truly sane?*

The temple shuddered again, but this time, it was different, dust and rock raining down from the ceiling. Raphael felt the touch of death an instant before he sensed the power of another archangel. "Lijuan is here."

*"Wait!"* Elena grabbed his arm when he would've turned, headed out. "I can taste your mother's scent in the air—exotic and rich and sensual. Black orchids."

"I must go, Elena."

"But it's leavened with a strange, unexpected note of sunflowers." Her fingers clenched on his arm. "There were no sunflowers on the body of the tortured girl, on the bridge, on the vampires who went mad in Boston. The scent was too pure, too much the essence. *Do you see?*"

*Thank you, Guild Hunter.* He was already moving, Elena and Illium running across the temple floor behind him.

They exited out into the streets of Amanat to see the Archangel of China in physical form, throwing arrows of power at the temple building. Each bolt was black. There was nothing inherently evil in black—all of Jason's abilities manifested in that midnight shade—but Lijuan's power was riddled through with a rotten core that made Raphael recoil.

Rising to face her in the air above the temple, he blocked one of her shots with the vivid blue that was the manifestation of his own power. "I did not ask for your assistance, Lijuan."

Her hair whipped off her face. "She cannot rise, Raphael. You must not let your emotions blind you to the truth of her madness."

He knew Lijuan spoke the truth—to a point. Blocking another arrow of power, one that slammed him back several feet through the air, he gathered angelfire in his palms. It might no longer do her mortal harm, but with her in her physical form, a direct hit would still cause significant damage. "The question of her insanity remains unanswered."

"She took the young one," Lijuan said, her hair electric with black strands that Raphael realized were streamers of pure dark energy. "And your consort looks injured. Those are not acts of sanity."

Perhaps not, Raphael thought, but most archangels walked a fine line between sanity and insanity. "Any one of us may have done the same." He spoke not to defend Caliane, but to oppose Lijuan—and because his mother, while she had acted with the cold arrogance of power, had done nothing as yet to speak of madness. Lijuan on the other hand . . .

"What of the people she murdered around the world? The ones hanging from the bridge in your city?" A hail of black rain designed to gouge and kill.

He swept out of the way, throwing back a volley of angelfire that she swamped in black. "Those acts did not bear her touch, Lijuan. They bore yours." It was a guess. The murders and torture could well have been orchestrated by Neha, but Lijuan was the one with the most to lose if Caliane rose.

A pause in the rain of black fire. Then a soft, girlish laugh. "You always were clever."

He attacked her with angelfire while she was distracted. Lijuan raised a wall of black flame to block him, her power incomprehensible. And her voice, when it came next, was nothing the least bit human. "Good-bye, Raphael."

There was no way to avoid it. The bolts came from everywhere.

He heard Elena scream as he took a direct hit to the chest. It was not angelfire, for Lijuan had never had that ability, but that didn't matter. Bloated with her toxic power, it was a killing blow, even for an archangel. The blackness invaded his blood, spread through his cells until he could see his veins turn black under his skin, feel the crawling of it across his irises.

"I am sorry, Raphael." Lijuan's voice. "I always did like you. But you would protect her."

He tried to speak to Elena, to tell her that she would be safe. Even after his death, his Seven would not break their vows. They would protect her. But Lijuan's poison spread throughout his system, blocking his efforts to fight it with the cutting blue of his own power. And he fought. He fought with every ounce of will in his immortal heart, every ounce of the unnamable, unending emotion he felt for Elena.

Even dying, he managed to throw a final ball of angelfire, using his fading vision. It made Lijuan scream. That high-pitched sound ringing in his ears, he fell to earth, coming down hard on the temple roof, his wings crushed but not broken, his fall cushioned by a power that felt akin to that which had once been the standard against which he judged himself.

*My son! My Raphael.*

Too late, he thought, it was too late. Caliane had never been a healer, and his entire body was riddled with Lijuan's black poison. Shoving outward with his own newborn gift, he tried to heal himself, but his ability was young, scarcely formed. It stood no chance against Lijuan's brand of evil.

"Raphael!" Hands cupping his face, fierce determination in his hunter's voice.

He wanted to order her to leave, to warn her that the infection that was Lijuan's power could spread, as it had with the reborn, but he knew she'd never leave, his consort with her mortal heart. *Elena mine.*

Elena swallowed the tears and panic that threatened to take her over when she saw Raphael's beautiful eyes overrun with tendrils of Lijuan's evil, obscuring those irises of a haunting shade found in the deepest part of the ocean, intense and absolute. "No," she said. "No!"

Above her, the sky fractured in a cataclysm of light, and when she looked up, Lijuan was no longer alone. An archangel with hair of tumbling raven black and wings of purest white faced her, her hands ringed by blue flame.

*The template from which I was cast.*

Snapping back her head, she squeezed Raphael's hand, his golden skin pale above veins turned black and rigid. *Archangel, can you hear me?*

*These words hold the last remnants of my power.*

Focusing on the fact that he was still alive and refusing to consider anything else, Elena ducked as a piece of rock went flying past—spreading her body and her wings above Raphael.

*Go, Elena! They will fight to the death.*

*Ordering me around even now, Archangel?* She wouldn't leave him. She'd never leave him. Looking up, she saw that Illium continued to stand guard, his face streaked with anguished fury. *Bluebell will tell us when to duck.*

A moment's silence, and her heart almost stopped.

*I should be dead.*

Trembling, she pressed her forehead to his. *Don't say that. You survived Lijuan once. You'll do it again.* Except that his golden skin had turned cold and pale, his eyes now eerie blocks of black, and his wings . . . She lifted a fisted hand to her mouth, biting down hard on her knuckles.

The evil was spreading out over his wings in a slow creep, turning the gold and white to an oily darkness that brought out every one of her most aggressive instincts. She wanted to fight it, to cut at it, but knives wouldn't work here. Not when the canvas was Raphael's body.

"Elena, cover!"

She moved with Illium's first syllable, spreading her wings out over Raphael's vulnerable body. Something hit her shoulder hard enough to bruise, but she held her position until Illium gave the all clear.

"What the fuck are they doing?"

*I would like to know the answer to that question.*

Realizing her archangel no longer had his sight, his beautiful eyes blinded by black, she looked up and felt the air leave her body. "Dear God, Raphael. They're . . ." Swallowing to wet her throat, she focused on the two immortals in the sky. "Your mother's managed to damage Lijuan's wings, and it looks like she's flickering in and out of her physical form."

*Then it must take power for her to maintain her other form. That, we did not know.*

"Your mother doesn't look injured, but she's not avoiding Lijuan's bolts fast enough." Caliane was moving at phenomenal speed, but—"Next to Lijuan, she looks almost sluggish."

*I was wrong. She was not yet ready to awaken.*

And Elena understood, her heart twisting. Caliane had woken for her son. "She's holding her own." But now that she was searching for it, she could see Caliane's weakness and so, clearly, could Lijuan.

Looking down into Raphael's face, she wanted to lie to him, to give him peace, but that wasn't what they were. "I think your mother's going to lose, Raphael."

Raphael's body shuddered, his wings pure black, his skin without life.

*Archangel!*

Raphael heard Elena, but he couldn't answer her, his mind overrun with a searing burn so hot, it flared incandescent white against his vision, turning his world from cold black to a piercing conflagration.

The instincts of over a thousand years of survival urged him to fight the rage of flame . . . but then he saw what it was doing. Eating away at the black, obliterating it in a fury as wild as angelfire. As it did so, it left a lingering "taste" on his senses, one he couldn't quite define, and yet knew to the depths of his soul.

*Raphael, don't you dare leave me. Together! Your promised me if we fell, it would be together!*

Even in the midst of the brutal fight taking place in his body, her demand made him want to claim her lips with his own, to stroke his hand over those warrior's wings in open possession.

A spear of lightning scored down his spinal cord and spread in a nuclear burst through his wings, blistering with such heat that he half expected his body to turn to ash. But when the burn faded to a dull, throbbing hum, when he lifted his lashes, he saw Elena's face staring down at him, determination in every line of her. *I won't let you go, Archangel. I won't!* Then, heartbreakingly quiet, "I can't do this without you, Raphael."

Raising his hand, he cupped her cheek. "I am not so easy to kill, Elena." Except he should be dead. He was an archangel, but Lijuan had evolved to another plane of existence. Her power was beyond that which was known, which could be fought. It tasted only of death to mortal and immortal alike.

Elena's entire frame shuddered, and she pressed her forehead to his for a long, broken second. A single, painful droplet splashed against his cheek before she raised her head and he flowed to his feet beside her. Every part of his body ached, but he'd fought feeling far worse—even the violent heat that continued to spark within him, searching out and eradicating the final traces of Lijuan's taint, was no longer the overwhelming inferno it had been.

*Raphael. My son.*

Looking up, he saw Caliane's right wing crumple as Lijuan managed to slam her against the side of a building.

# 34

"Go," he said to Elena. "My mother's people will be waking. Get them moved to safer locations."

Elena didn't fight him, stepping back so he could take flight. *Take care, Raphael. You belong to a hunter.*

With her words circling his heart, he flew up and caught his mother's falling form, protecting them from Lijuan by throwing out a spray of angelfire that made her swerve and lose concentration. He took the opportunity to lower Caliane gently onto a rooftop. She would heal, he thought, having seen the damage. It had not been a heart-blow like his . . . and it did not seem to affect her as it had him. But then, his mother was far older.

Her eyes shimmered an aching blue as he rose to meet Lijuan once more. *You fight for me.*

*I fight against Lijuan.* His mother might yet act the monster once she regained her strength, but there was no question that Lijuan already was one. If she wasn't brought under control, her brand of death would soon crawl across the world—Caliane at full strength might be the only one capable of keeping her in check.

*So you would use one monster to cage another?* A voice that still held its haunting magic.

*All archangels carry the threat of darkness within.*

Lijuan rained a fury of black down on him. Throwing up a shield, he slammed the bolts into another wall, crumbling an edifice that had stood for centuries upon centuries. Sensing movement below, he saw Elena's distinctive wings as she half carried, half dragged a dazed citizen of Amanat to another area of the city. *Elena, stay out of sight*, he ordered, knowing Lijuan would go after her if she saw the chance.

*Focus on keeping your neck in one piece, Archangel. I'm not the one Lijuan's got a hard-on for.*

Laughing at the acerbic reply, he threw several balls of angelfire, positioning himself just above Lijuan. She weaved out of the way, but he had her on the defensive, and using that, he maneuvered her to the edges of the city, where the buildings were more apt to be empty of mortals.

Lijuan's wings had turned black during the course of the battle, as had her hair. That wasn't as important as the fact that she no longer seemed to be able to shift to her noncorporeal form. It made her vulnerable in a way she hadn't been since Beijing, but she was far from easy prey.

Flinching as she managed to singe one of his wings again, he felt a renewed burn as that incandescent fire arced through his veins to neutralize the black. It made him wonder . . . Reaching deep within, he coaxed the near-uncontrollable wildness of it to his hands, then released it as he would angelfire. In every other way, his power manifested as either blue or a blinding blaze, but this was a luminous white-gold with iridescent edges of midnight and dawn . . . and when it hit Lijuan, she bled.

Her shock obvious, she stared at him as the dark red stain spread across her front. Capitalizing on her disbelief, he hit her again, but the fire within him was already fading, and this hit was nowhere near as potent as the first. But, it was enough. It caught one of her wings, and she shrieked in rage before changing direction and slamming through Amanat's shield, out into the rain-lashed night.

Raphael went after her, the rain slicing at his face like so many sharp knives . . . but the Archangel of China was gone. Hovering to a standstill, he searched the forested landscape, thinking her wing might've collapsed, crumpling her to the earth. But the forest lay undisturbed, the storm-dark skies empty.

She'd had a reservoir of power, he realized, had used it to escape by taking her other form for a short period. There was no way to track her—but she was vanquished for now and would think twice before attacking him or his own again. Now . . . now he had to face the monster who had given birth to him.

Elena, having moved the last of the men and women of Amanat to safety, away from the damaged buildings, ran up to a small rooftop, then took flight, Illium at her side. It didn't take long to spot Raphael's mother on another, much higher rooftop. Caliane's white gown was streaked with black, that face of impossible beauty burned on one side, but all that was superficial to an archangel.

Landing, Elena looked for signs of the blackness that had overtaken Raphael like a creeping poison. Caliane's wings bore scars of the oily slickness, but . . . "I think she's got it contained," she said to Illium.

"I am the most powerful of archangels," said a voice of such faultless clarity that it almost hurt to hear it. "Lijuan is yet weak."

Raphael's mother's eyes were as pristine a hue as his, a shade no mortal would ever possess, but there was something in them . . . something unknown and old, so very, very old. Stepping back, Elena stood, watching as Caliane flowed to her feet, elegant in spite of her injuries and torn clothing. Already, the scars of black were noticeably smaller.

The archangel's eyes bored into her. "My son calls you his consort."

"I am his consort," she said, holding her ground. Caliane didn't have the creepy Lijuan factor, and neither did she put out the bitch vibe like Michaela, but there was an alien quality to her, something Elena had never felt with any other archangel, no matter how old—as if Caliane had lived so very long, she'd become something truly *other* in spite of the fact that she continued to maintain a physical form unlike Lijuan.

Caliane raised a hand, flames of unexpected yellow green licking over her fingers, and Elena heard Illium unsheathe his sword in a shush of sound, knew he was going to move in front of her. "Illium, no."

The blue-winged angel didn't obey. "You told me to choose my loyalty, Elena. It is to Raphael, and you are his heart."

Knowing she'd never be able to budge him, she instead took a step to the side so she could meet Caliane's gaze. "He doesn't want you to be mad." She more than half expected a whiplash of temper—archangels did not like being spoken to in such a way by mortals, or angels newly-Made.

But Caliane turned her head, her hair lifting in the breeze. "My son." Unbridled pride. "He is of Nadiel and I, but he is better than both of us."

Raphael winged in to land in front of Caliane then, and Illium shifted aside enough that Elena was able to watch mother and son come face-to-face for the first time in more a thousand years.


Raphael's heart, a heart he'd thought had turned to stone before he met Elena, stabbed with daggers of pain at the expression of love on his mother's face. It brought back memories that usually broke through only during *anshara*, the deepest of healing sleeps.

He remembered not simply that she'd left him broken on that forsaken field, but that she'd held him when he'd cried as a child, wiping away his tears with long, elegant fingers before kissing his face with tenderness that had made him throw his arms around her, hold her tight. "Mother," he said, and it came out quiet, husky with memory.

Her responding smile was shaky. Reaching forward, she raised her hand to his cheek, her fingers cool against his skin, as if her blood had not yet begun to truly pump through her veins. "You've grown so strong."

It was an echo of the dream, and it made him wonder what she remembered of it. "I cannot allow you freedom, Mother." It had to be said, no matter that the boy in him was reeling in stunned wonder at having her so close, so very near.

Her hand fell off his cheek and to his shoulder. "I do not seek freedom. Not yet."

Giving in to the need within him, a need that had survived over a millennium, he reached out and drew her into his arms. She wrapped her own around him, laying her head against his heart, and for a frozen instant, they were nothing but mother and son standing beneath an impossible sky.

*I was not meant to survive your father, Raphael. We were two halves of a whole.*

The sorrow in her tone made him tighten his hold. *He could not live.*

His mother said nothing for a long, long moment. When she drew back, her expression was different, more formal. *So, you have a mortal consort.*

"Elena," he said out loud, refusing to allow Caliane to shut out the woman who made the idea of eternity a breathtaking promise. He placed a hand at the curve of her back when she came to stand beside him, "She is no longer mortal."

Caliane's eyes moved from him to Elena and back again. "Perhaps, but she is no mate for an archangel."

Elena spoke before Raphael. "Maybe not," she said, "but he's mine and I'm not giving him up."

Caliane blinked. "Well, at least she has spirit." Folding away wings she'd spread out after his embrace, she looked back at Raphael. "Even your blood carries the taint of your mortal." With that, she turned and walked to the edge of the roof. "I must look after my people."

"Your awakening changes the balance of the Cadre." Lijuan was no longer the strongest of them all—and after her Sleep, Caliane was a complete unknown.

"Later." She raised a fine-boned hand. "I have no wish for politics at present. However, make it known that this region is now mine."

Since Lijuan wasn't likely to return to face Caliane anytime soon, that claim would, Raphael knew, remain unchallenged. *There is no way to know what she will do*, he said to his consort. *If I am to have any chance of killing her, it must be now.*

Elena curled her hand around his. *She's done nothing as yet that another member of the Cadre might not have. The impact on you, Elijah, and the others was an unconscious effect, so you can't blame her for that.*

*She attempted to harm you more than once.*

*I rest my case—even your Seven isn't sold on me. I never expected your mother to welcome me with open arms.*

Raphael looked down at his hunter, at the piercing ring of silver around her eyes and knew that Elena would do anything to have another moment with her own mother; that her pain, her need, might blind her to the brutal truth. *If this choice is wrong, thousands could die.*

*We won't let that happen.* Her voice was resolute.

Even as she spoke, silver blue flashed on her other side and then Illium was standing beside her, his wing touching Elena's in an intimacy that made Raphael raise an eyebrow. Illium's lips curved in a wicked smile that did little to hide the intensity of his emotions. *I would not watch you die again, Sire.* His veins stood out against his skin as he gripped the wrist of one hand with the other.

Raphael met those eyes of gold that had stood beside him for centuries. *If I had done so, I would have gone knowing you would keep my heart safe.*

Illium's gaze went to Elena. *Always.* "I will remain behind with your mother."

"No, Illium." Stroking his hand down Elena's hair, he shook his head. "I will send Naasir."

The blue-winged angel's jawline turned knife-blade sharp. "Naasir has no wings should he need to follow Caliane."

"Jason will take care of that part of the equation." Shaking his head when Illium went to argue, he said, "I need you in the city when Aodhan arrives."

When both his hunter and Illium gave him intrigued looks, he said, "Later. For now, we will leave Caliane. She told the truth in that much at least—she has always cared for the people of this place and will not venture from it until they are thriving once more." Taking a last look at the lost city of Amanat—lost no more—he rose with his consort into the skies, through the shield of power and into the rain-dark night beyond.

Standing in the huge bathroom of the penthouse apartment in Kagoshima-shi, the capital of the prefecture, Elena looked at her side in the mirror, saw that she no longer had holes in her flesh. Raphael had sent healing warmth racing through her before she walked into the shower, insisting on it though she was more worried about him.

Relieved nonetheless, she wrapped a plush white towel as firmly as possible around her body and padded out into the bedroom, heading to the windows. There was no angelic tower in this city, but the striking building across from this one seemed to be the center of operations, with angels flying in and out on a regular basis.

As she watched their silhouettes arc against the glittering skyline now clear of rain, she thought over the events of the day. What would it do to her if Marguerite suddenly rose from the grave and took flesh and blood form?

*Pain. Need. Guilt. Love. Anger.*

It was such a tumultuous blend that she took a shuddering breath in an effort to control herself, then another and another until she could shake it off. Tonight, this, it wasn't about her. It was about her archangel. *Raphael.* He'd taken a quick shower

of his own, then gone out to speak to the angel who ran this
city. She hadn't wanted to let him go, the terror that had torn
through her as Lijuan's evil spread through his veins a living,
breathing entity, but as she was a hunter, he was an archangel.

*I can see you, Guild Hunter.*

Smiling, she pressed her fingers to the glass and looked out
at the angels flying away from the ultramodern high-rise, its
balconies asymmetrical—almost seeming to hang in midair. It
took her less than a second. Less than a fraction of a second.
He was the strongest, most compelling of them all, his wingspan magnificent. *Are wings proportional to body size?*

A glow of silver on his feathers as they were hit by the
lights from a nearby billboard, the Japanese nightscape a tech-
nological wonderland. *You know what they say about men and
their wings.*

She laughed, and it was a sweet, unexpected gift. *Yeah?
Come here and show me.*

Instead of landing, he dipped and dived far enough away
that she could see him—admire him—before changing direction to come straight to the balcony outside the suite. Walking
out to meet him, she shook her head. "Show-off." Before he
could say anything in response, she wrapped her arms around
the muscular heat of his body and pressed her lips to his pulse,
needing to feel the living, beating heat of him.

His hands tightened on her hips. "I would kill anyone who
saw you this way."

She nipped at his jaw as he walked her backward into the
suite. The instant he reached back to pull the doors closed, she
jumped up to wrap her legs around his waist, the towel falling
to the floor. "Windows," she muttered against his throat, kissing her way up the strong column.

Carrying her without effort, his heartbeat ragged against
her lips, his skin hot, he reached out and flipped the switch
that turned the windows opaque. Then his hands moved up
the backs of her thighs and up over her butt, his hold raw and
possessive. When he turned to pin her against the wall, she

instinctively spread out her wings on either side, clamping her hands on his shoulders.

His mouth was on hers before she could draw breath, his hand closing over her bare breast. She tried to meet the kiss, but he was so wild that she had to give in—to his mouth, to his kiss, to the hand he shoved between them to stroke at her damp heat with firm, demanding strokes that had her arching into him.

He removed his hand much too soon, and she would've protested if he hadn't claimed her lips for another deep kiss. Gasping in air when he released her mouth for a second, she moaned as he bit at her lower lip hard enough to sting before taking her again, his tongue stroking against her own. An instant later, she felt his cock nudging at her core.

A single, powerful thrust and he was buried to the hilt inside of her.

She screamed, her back arching off the wall, her nails digging into his shoulders as pleasure short-circuited her system, inner muscles clenching and unclenching over and over again. If she'd had any hope of holding on to even a hint of rational thought, it went out the window when he bent his head and bit down on her pulse. Hard enough that she knew she'd be wearing his mark.

After that, there was only touch and taste and the hotly intimate friction of skin against skin.

# 35

Elena lay sprawled on top of Raphael, a surely stupid smile on her face. "Wow," she murmured into the warm curve of his neck. "That was . . ."

He ran his hand over her back, fingers brushing the sensitive inner curves of her wings. "I was rough."

"That you were." Nuzzling into him, she licked at the salt of his skin. "It was perfect." That he'd trusted her with the full fury of his emotions . . . Smile growing deeper, she stroked her hand down the ridged musculature of his chest. "When did you get rid of your clothes?"

"Hmm?"

He sounded so lazy and sated that laughter bubbled out of her. "Hey." She slapped his chest. "No going to sleep."

*I'm the archangel. I give the orders.*

Her laugh turned into a startled grin. He had a sense of humor, her archangel, but not long ago, he'd have meant it when he said that. Placing her hand over his heart, she listened to the deep beat that wasn't yet steady. She should've felt sleepy, but all she wanted to do was stroke him, kiss him, feel him warm and alive under her hands. "What happened, Raphael?"

He understood without further explanation. "It was a fatal blow. Even had Keir been beside me the instant after I took it, he wouldn't have been able to heal me."

The words chilled the embers of passion. "Lijuan's that powerful?"

*Yes.* "But her power has twisted and changed from our last confrontation. It now carries total death, even for immortals."

"You were scored on your wings and shoulders before the chest hit."

"I think that type of a glancing blow would've killed a weaker, young angel." His hand closed around the back of her neck, gave a little squeeze. "I'm old enough and strong enough that she needed to strike me either in the head or in the heart."

"God, Raphael." The idea of his death made her scrabble inside in panic. "I can't lose you." She'd lost two of her sisters, her mother, and in every way that mattered, her father. If she lost Raphael, that would be it. She wouldn't make it.

"I live Elena." Quiet words, his arms holding her close. "Because of you."

She jerked up her head. "What?"

"My mother said even my blood carries your mark." Reaching up, he ran his finger down the shell of her ear.

"I thought she was being insulting."

"No." Raphael thought back to when he'd first met Elena, when he'd first begun to feel the impact of the nascent bond between them. "Lijuan told me you would make me a little mortal and, in so doing, kill me."

Guilt colored her expression. "I *have* made you weaker, Raphael. You heal slower—"

He pressed a finger to her lips. "I should've considered the source. Everything came from Lijuan."

"I don't understand." Lines formed on her brow as she

spoke. "You're saying she somehow twisted the truth? Tried to sabotage you from the get-go?"

"I don't think she would have thought of it in that fashion." Moving his hand down to curve around her throat, he rubbed his thumb over her pulse . . . over the mark he'd put on her.

Elena arched into the touch. "She does seem to like you in that weird, creepy way of hers."

"Such flattery will go to my head, Guild Hunter."

"Someone's got to keep you humble."

"Lijuan deals in death," he told her, her laughter sinking into his skin, an invisible mark of her own. "A mortal is very much alive and of the moment." Humans didn't have the luxury of wasting years or decades, their lives beginning and ending in a firefly flicker.

Elena's eyes went wide, that thin ring of silver not apparent in this light, but he knew it was there, a silent meter of how deep immortality had grown into her cells. "The change in you," she said, "whatever it is, means you have the ability to resist her powers?"

"Not only resist, but neutralize." Giving him an incredible advantage against the most powerful member of the Cadre, barring his mother. So long as he managed to get to safety long enough to recover from a strike, Lijuan *could not* kill him.

Elena whistled. "She knew. She knew that might happen."

Raphael wasn't so sure. "I think she had an idea of it, but I also believe part of what she told me was the truth—she did once have a lover who threatened to make her mortal."

"And," Elena completed, "she chose to kill him because he endangered her power. He scared her."

"Yes." He watched the expressions fly across her face. Such passion in that mortal heart, such a hunger for life. "Come here, Elena."

She leaned down until her hair created a soft intimacy around their faces. "You worry that you have the seeds of madness in you"—a soft whisper husky with passion—"but you'll never become what she is. *Never.*" Because Raphael had chosen to love when it had seemed the worst possible option.

His gaze was a cold mountain lake and the cool heart of a gemstone. "We may have unleashed a horror, Elena."

She knew they were no longer talking about Lijuan. "If we'd killed her in cold blood as she Slept, or as she stood weakened before us, we'd be no better than monsters ourselves."

"Then we wait."

# Epilogue

Three days later, Raphael looked across the semicircle of the Cadre at a glowing Michaela. Whatever the nature of her relationship with Astaad's second, it seemed to be making her happy—for the time being at least. Flanking her sensual beauty were Charisemnon and Astaad himself.

Elijah had taken the seat to Raphael's left, while Favashi sat next to the South American archangel. Neha reclined with regal grace beside her, Titus on her other side. Then there was Lijuan . . . on Raphael's right. It was the first official meeting of the Cadre the Archangel of China had attended in over a year.

Elena had asked him if Lijuan would be held to account for Caliane's attempted murder, had been stunned when he explained that because the Sleeper lived, there had been no crime. Such was the ruthless world of the most powerful immortals.

"There has," Favashi now began in her serene voice, "been a shift in the power structure of the world."

Michaela, dressed in a corset that spoke of bygone times,

skintight black pants, and boots that skimmed over her thighs, crossed her legs one over the other. "The Queen of Under-statements as always, Favi." For once, there was no bitchiness in her tone when she spoke to the other archangel.

Favashi's lips curved upward in a slight smile, her own dress an ankle-length gown in palest green that left her arms bare and reminded Raphael of the maidens in Amanat. "You aren't worried about this change?"

"Raphael's mother is powerful," Michaela said, "so power-ful that she probably won't bother with day-to-day politics." Her gaze went to Lijuan. "It's what we expected of you."

Lijuan, her body not as solid as it should've been, didn't deign to reply, turning her attention to Raphael instead. "You should have killed her," she murmured, her skin stretched so thin over her bones that he could almost see the white of her skeletal structure shining through. "It's too late now."

Raphael remembered the choice she'd urged him to make when he'd met Elena, thought of the consequences if he had listened then. "You are no longer the strongest archangel in the world. It seems to have clouded your judgment."

Those eerie eyes swam with gleaming black. "I have al-ways liked you, Raphael." Caressing words against his cheek, though she made no move to raise her hand.

Ignoring the silent invitation, he looked to Astaad. "You have not spoken."

"What is there to say?" Astaad spread his hands in a grace-ful gesture, rings of finest gold flashing on his fingers. "Ca-liane appears to want nothing beyond what she already has at this stage."

"Are we certain?" Neha's words carried an undertone of a sibilant hiss. "There were strange reports from your court, Astaad."

Raphael, his gaze on Astaad, saw the male's eyes flame with rage for a flashing second before he gave a lazy smile. "There are always reports. Be careful what you believe."

Lijuan's shoulder brushed Raphael's—and it felt akin to being touched by a solid illusion. "Do you think he is taking

Uram's path?" Her voice was pitched low, meant to reach his ears alone.

Raphael hadn't considered that. But if Astaad was continuing to behave in an erratic fashion, then Caliane's awakening was not to blame. "If he is, he's a fool." Letting the toxin build up in your system until madness encroached was a gamble no one ever won. *I stood in your way,* he said to Lijuan. *I tried to kill you.* It was an implied question.

*You are young, Raphael. You have not yet learned to choose your battles.*

He wondered if Lijuan truly believed he would one day stand by her side, if her insanity was that deep, that true. But he said nothing, for her calm was necessary at this moment. Caliane might be powerful, but Lijuan remained a force who could destroy the world. "Neha," he murmured under his breath. "What do you know?"

"She has been visiting her mate more often of late," Lijuan murmured as Charisemnon and Titus exchanged stinging comments. "Perhaps she wishes to conceive another child."

"Raphael," Titus said, turning away from the archangel who always seemed to rub him the wrong way. "You and your people are the only ones who are being allowed through her shields and into her city."

"I will keep watch," he said, knowing that responsibility could be no one else's. After what he'd learned in Amanat, he knew he held within him the potential to do what he hadn't been able to as a youth—this time, if Caliane rose a monster, her son would be the one to bring her down.

When he returned home, it was to the embrace of a woman who reminded him that no matter what happened, he'd tasted life, such life as no other archangel would ever know.

"Raphael," she said to him as they stood on the highest balcony of their home. "Will you come with me somewhere?"

"Anywhere."

A jerky nod. Not saying another word, she flared out

those wings of midnight and dawn, and they flew out toward Brooklyn, landing beside a quiet row of storage units. She'd come here with the Guild Director earlier, and now she came with him. When they'd first met, he may well have taken that choice as an insult. Now he understood that Elena needed her friendships if she was going to survive and thrive in this new life into which she'd been thrown. "I'll do that." He pushed up the door for her when she unsnapped the lock.

Taking a deep breath, she took a single step inside, and he could almost touch the conflicting emotions tearing at her. When she turned and held out her hand, he allowed her to tug him into the small space, nothing an angel would normally even countenance entering. And when she asked him to close the door, he did so without argument.

She switched on the single yellow bulb an instant later. "See this?" Her fingers lingered on a faded orange blanket. "It was my blankie." A tremulous smile. "I wouldn't go *anywhere* without it." Sinking to the floor, she let her wings trail on the cold concrete.

He went down on his haunches beside her, listening and watching as she carefully folded the blanket, put it on her lap and opened a cardboard box overflowing with her childhood. She showed him drawings she'd made in school, toys she'd played with as a babe.

"We will keep this for our child," he murmured, holding a solid wooden bee meant to be pulled along on wheels.

Elena gave a shaky laugh. "We're having children are we?"

He'd never asked her before, but now, he raised his head. "Would you wish for a babe, Elena?"

"I'd be afraid for him or her all the time." Nightmares whispered in her eyes. "I can't imagine the terror."

He thought of her childhood, thought of the blood that had christened her. However, when he would've spoken, she surprised him. "But you're the one man I could see myself having rug rats with—you're bad-ass enough to reassure me."

Cupping her cheek as she rose to her feet, he rubbed a thumb over her cheekbone. "It will likely take a long time."

Angels were nowhere near as fertile as humans. "We will have a chance to get used to the idea."

"I'll practice on Zoe. Poor kid." With that laughing comment, she walked to another box, opened it.

And froze.

Coming to stand by her side, he saw her lift up an intricately patterned quilt to her nose, breathe in deep. "If I think hard enough, I can still remember her scent as she used to kiss me goodnight." A whisper so quiet, he almost missed it. "Gardenias stroked with a hint of a richer, more sensual fragrance."

Reaching out, he touched the quilt, felt a quiet hum of power. "Elena."

Elena looked up at the strange tone in Raphael's voice, the heavy weight of memory easing for a fraction of a second. "What is it?"

His eyes turned a stunning cobalt as he rubbed his fingers across the soft old cotton. "There is power in this, the kind of power that comes only with blood."

"This was on my bed," she said with a frown. "Until Jeffrey packed away everything of my mother's one winter while I was away at boarding school, this quilt covered my bed. Slater never went into that room. There can't be blood on here." She didn't want the evil to have defiled this, too.

"No, not his blood." Dropping his fingers from the quilt, he touched her wing. "It is the blood of the maker."

Elena ran a finger over the fine stitching. "She created it by hand, probably pricked herself." That scent was long gone, buried under the ghosts of the gardenias she wanted to keep fresh.

When Raphael said nothing, a warning sensation skittered up the back of her spine. "Archangel? Talk to me."

"This kind of blood," Raphael murmured, "this kind of lingering power . . . it is not a mortal thing."

"My mother was very much mortal." Elena had seen her dead, her face bleached of color, those beautiful, laughing eyes turned forever dull.

Raphael closed his hand over her nape. "As a human, you

once pushed me out of your mind. It should've been an impossible task."

"Raphael, she wasn't an angel, or a vampire. Only one thing left."

"Not quite." Eyes on the quilt, he said, "Vampires under two hundred years old can sire children. Those children are mortal."

Elena blinked, stared at the quilt, back at him. Her life shifted on its axis with a grinding screech. "You're saying I'm part vamp?"

"No, Elena. You were mortal before you became an angel. But your mother carried within her blood something powerful enough that it survived her passing. There is a vampire somewhere in your lineage."

"I need to sit down." But what she did was lean against Raphael, the quilt clutched to her chest. "My father . . . he can't know." Jeffrey hated vampires, only put up with Beth's Harrison because of business ties with Harry's family. "I think it might break him."

"There is no reason he should know." Raphael stroked her hair off her face. "I would see more of your childhood—there is time enough for other things."

"Yes."

Then, as the most powerful being in the city, in the country, knelt by her side, one of his wings spreading over hers with heavy warmth, she showed him shining, laughing pieces of her life before Slater Patalis broke it into a thousand bloody pieces. Along the way, he told her how he'd run wild through the flower-lined streets of Amanat, how he'd been the pet of an entire city. "Tell me more," she said, enchanted.

Raphael had never spoken of these memories to any living being, but he told Elena all she wanted to know. In turn, she shared with him the joy she'd found in being the third daughter of four, the one who was young enough to get away with everything, and old enough to be allowed privileges her youngest sister was denied.

Much later, as they stood on the cliffs by their home, looking across at the stark beauty of the Manhattan skyline after nightfall, she kissed his jaw and gave him another gift. "She lives, Raphael. There's hope."

Hope. Such a mortal concept. *For you, Elena, I will accept that this hope might not be a foolish thing.*

"Ah, you know us mortals—or recent-mortals—have a tendency to be foolish." A heartbreaking smile. "It makes life interesting."

"Then come, Guild Hunter." Putting his arms around her, he lifted them into the crisp night air. *It is time to make your life very interesting.*

She laughed, played, and later sighed as he took them into the ocean. *Knhebek, Raphael.*

And he knew no matter what happened when the pale rays of dawn hit the earth, it would not defeat them. *Knhebek, hbeebti.*

Turn the page for a special preview of
Nalini Singh's next book in the
Psy-Changeling Series

# Kiss of Snow

Coming June 2011 in hardcover from Berkley
Sensation!

# X

1979.

The year the Psy race became Silent.

Became cold, without emotion, without mercy.

Hearts were broken, families torn apart.

But far more were saved.

From insanity.

From murder.

From viciousness such as unseen in the world today.

For the X-Psy, Silence was a gift beyond price, a gift that allowed at least some of their number to survive childhood, have a life. Yet over a hundred years after the icy wave of the Silence Protocol washed away violence and despair, madness and love, the X-Psy are, and remain, living weapons. Silence is their safety switch. Without it . . .

There are some nightmares the world will never be ready to face.

# 1

Hawke folded his arms and leaned back against the solid bulk of his desk, eyes on the two young females in front of him. Hands clasped behind themselves and legs slightly spread in the "resting" stance, Sienna and Maria looked like the SnowDancer soldiers they were—except for the fact that their hair straggled in a wild mess around their faces, matted with mud, crushed leaves, and other forest debris. Then there was the torn clothing and the sharp, acrid scent of blood.

His wolf bared its teeth.

"Let me get this straight," he said in a calm tone that had Maria turning pale under skin that was a warm, smooth brown where it wasn't bruised and bloody. "Instead of staying on watch and protecting the pack's defensive border, you two decided to have your own personal dominance battle."

Sienna, of course, met his gaze—something no wolf would've done in the circumstances. "It w—"

"Be quiet," he snapped. "If you open your mouth again without permission, I'm putting both of you in the pen with the two-year-olds."

Those amazing cardinal eyes—white stars on a background of vivid black—went a pure ebony that he knew full well indicated fury, but she clenched her jaw. Maria, on the other hand, had gone even paler. Good.

"Maria," he said, focusing on the petite changeling whose size belied her skill and strength in both human and wolf form. "How old are you?"

Maria swallowed. "Twenty."

"Not a juvenile."

Maria's thick black curls, heavy with mud, bounced dully as she shook her head.

"Then explain this to me."

"I can't, sir."

"Right answer." No reason they could offer up would be a good enough excuse for the bullshit fight. "Who threw the first punch?"

Silence.

His wolf approved. It mattered little who'd incited the exchange when neither had walked away from it, and the fact of the matter was, they'd been meant to be working as a team, so they'd take their punishment as a team—with one caveat.

"Seven days," he said to Maria. "Confined to quarters except for an hour each day. No contact with anyone while you're inside." It was a harsh punishment—wolves were creatures of pack, of family, and Maria was one of the most bubbly, social wolves in the den. To force her to spend all that time alone was an indication of just how badly she'd blundered. "The next time you decide to step off watch, I won't be so lenient."

Maria chanced meeting his gaze for a fleeting second before those rich brown eyes skated away, her dominance no match for his. "May I attend Lake's twenty-first?"

"If that's the use you want to make of your hour on the day." Yeah, it made him a bastard to force her to miss most of her boyfriend's big party, especially when the two were taking the first careful steps into a relationship, but she'd known exactly what she was doing when she decided to engage in a pissing contest with a fellow soldier.

SnowDancer was strong as a pack because they watched one another's backs. Hawke would not allow stupidity or arrogance to eat away at a foundation he'd rebuilt from the ground up after the bloody events that had stolen both his parents and savaged SnowDancer so badly it had taken over a decade of tight isolation for them to recover.

He turned his attention to Sienna—holding on to his temper by a very thin thread. "You were," he said, the wolf very much in his voice, "specifically ordered not to get into any physical altercations."

Sienna said nothing in response. It didn't matter—her rage was a hot pulse against his skin, as raw and stormy as Sienna herself. When she was like this, the wildness of her contained by the thinnest of barriers, it was hard to believe she'd come into his pack Silent, her emotions blockaded behind so much ice, it had infuriated his wolf.

Maria shifted on her feet when he didn't immediately continue.

"You have something to say?" he asked the woman, who was one of the best novice soldiers in the pack when she didn't let her temper get in the way.

"I started it." Color high on her cheekbones, shoulders tight. "She was just defending—"

"No." Sienna's tone was steady, resolute, the anger buried under a wall of frigid control. "I'll take my share of the blame. I could've walked away."

Hawke narrowed his eyes. "Maria, go."

The novice soldier hesitated for a second, but she was a subordinate wolf, her natural instinct to obey her alpha too powerful to resist—even though it was clear she wanted to remain behind to support Sienna. Hawke noted and approved of the display of loyalty enough that he didn't rebuke her for that hesitation.

The door closed behind her with a quiet snick that seemed shotgun-loud in the heavy silence inside the office. Hawke waited to see what Sienna would do now that they were alone. To his surprise, she maintained her position.

Reaching forward, he gripped her chin, turning her face to the side so that the light fell on the smooth lines of it. "You're lucky you don't have a broken cheekbone." The flesh around her eye was going to turn all shades of purple as it was. "Where else are you hurt?"

"I'm fine."

His fingers tightened on her jaw. "Where *else* are you hurt?"

"You didn't ask Maria." Stubborn will in every word.

"Maria is a wolf, able to take five times the damage of a Psy female and keep going." Which was the reason Sienna had been ordered not to get into physical confrontations with the wolves. That and the fact that she didn't have her lethal abilities under total control. "Either you answer the question or I swear to God I really will put you in the pen." It would be the most humiliating of experiences, and she knew it, every muscle in her body taut with viciously withheld anger.

"Bruised ribs," she gritted out at last, "bruised abdomen, wrenched shoulder. Nothing's broken. It should all heal within the next week."

Dropping his grip on her chin, he said, "Hold out your arms."

A hesitation.

The wolf growled, loud enough that she flinched. "Sienna, I've given you a long leash since you came into the pack, but that ends today." Insubordination from a juvenile could be punished and forgiven. In an adult, in a *soldier*, it was a far more serious matter. Sienna was nineteen-going-on-twenty, a ranked novice—letting her actions slide wasn't even an option. "Hold out your fucking arms."

Something in his tone must've gotten through to her because she did as ordered. A few small cuts on that creamy skin kissed gold by the sun, but no gouges that would've spoken of claws. "So Maria managed to rein in the wolf." If she hadn't, he'd have kicked her right back into training. Losing control of your temper was one thing; losing control of your wolf was far more dangerous.

Sienna's hands fisted as she dropped them to her sides.

Looking up, he met those eyes of absolute, unbroken black. It was clear she was fighting the elemental impulse to go at him, but she continued to hold her position. "How far did you go?" Her control was impressive—and it irritated him in a way it shouldn't have. But then, nothing about Sienna Lauren had ever been easy.

"I didn't use my abilities." The tendons in her neck stood out against the dirt-encrusted hue of her skin. "If I had, she'd be dead."

"Which is why you're in far more trouble than Maria." When he'd given the Lauren family sanctuary after their defection from the cold sterility of the PsyNet, it had been under a number of strict conditions. One of those conditions had been a prohibition against using Psy abilities on packmates.

A significant number of things had changed since that time, and the Laurens were now an integral and accepted part of SnowDancer. Sienna's uncle, Judd, was one of Hawke's lieutenants, and often used his telepathic and telekinetic abilities in defense of the pack. Hawke had also never tied the hands of the two youngest Laurens, knowing Marlee and Toby would need their mental claws to defend themselves against their rambunctious wolf playmates.

But that freedom didn't extend to Sienna, because Hawke knew exactly what she could do. The instant Judd accepted the lieutenant blood bond, keeping secrets from his alpha had become a question of loyalty and trust.

"Why?" Sienna lifted her chin. "I didn't disobey the rule about using my abilities."

Naturally, she'd challenge him. "But," he said, reining in the wolf's snarling response to her defiance, "you did disobey a direct order in engaging in the fight—you said it yourself, you could've walked away."

White lines bracketed her mouth. "Would you have?"

"This isn't about me." He'd been a young hothead once upon a time, and he'd had his ass kicked for it . . . until everything had changed, his childhood wiped out in a surge of blood and pain and piercing sorrow. "We both know your lack of control could've led to a far more serious outcome." The hell of it was, she knew that, too—and still she'd let herself cross the line. That angered Hawke more than anything else.

"I could be confined to DarkRiver land," Sienna said while he was still considering how to deal with her, "if you don't want me in the den."

Hawke snorted at her reference to the leopard pack that was SnowDancer's most trusted ally. "So you can hang out with your boyfriend? Nice try."

Sienna's skin flushed a dull red. "Kit isn't my boyfriend."

Hawke wasn't going to get into that conversation. Not now. Not ever. "You don't get to have a say in your punishment." He'd spoiled her. It was his own damn fault it was coming back to bite him in the ass. "One week confined to quarters in the soldiers area, one hour out per day." Psy were much better at handling isolation than changelings, but he knew Sienna had changed since defecting from the PsyNet, become far more intertwined in the bonds of family, of pack. "Second week spent working with the babies in the nursery since that's the age you've been acting recently. No duty rotations until you can be trusted to stick to your task."

"I—" She snapped her mouth shut when he raised an eyebrow.

"Three weeks," he said softly. "Third week you'll spend in the kitchens as a dish hand."

Her cheeks burned a hotter shade but she didn't interrupt again.

"Dismissed."

It was only after she'd gone—the autumn and spice of her scent lingering in the air in a silent rebellion she would've no doubt enjoyed had she known about it—that he loosened his hold on the wolf who was his more feral half.

It lunged for her scent.

Sucking in a harsh breath, Hawke fought the primal urge to go after her. He'd been battling the instinct for months, ever since the wolf decided that she was now an adult and, therefore, fair prey. The human half of him wasn't having much success in changing the wolf's mind, not when he had to fight the hunger to claim the most intimate of skin privileges every time she was in his presence.

"Christ." Picking up the sleek new sat phone the techs had issued him four weeks ago, he put through a call to Dark-River's alpha.

Lucas answered on the second ring. "What is it?"

"Sienna won't be heading down to spend time with you cats for a while." Aside from the distance Sienna apparently needed from the den, from *him*, she'd been working with Lucas's Psy mate, Sascha, to understand and gain control of her abilities. But—"I can't let it go. Not this time."

"Understood." The answer of a fellow alpha.

Hawke sat on the edge of his desk, shoving a hand through his hair. "Can she handle it?" He knew she wouldn't break—Sienna was too strong for that, a strength that acted like a drug on his wolf—but the power that lived within her was so vast, it had to be treated as the wildest of beasts.

"Last time she was down," Lucas responded, "Sascha said she displayed an exceptional level of stability, nothing like when they first began to work together. They're not having regular meetings anymore, so that's not an issue."

Mind at rest on that score at least, Hawke said, "I'll make sure Judd keeps a psychic eye on her just in case." Sienna wouldn't appreciate the oversight, but fact was fact—she was dangerous, and he had to consider the safety of the pack as a whole. As for the ferocity of his protective instincts when it came to her, he wasn't about to lie and pretend they didn't exist.

"Can I ask what happened?" Lucas's tone was curious.

Hawke gave the cat a quick rundown. "She's been worse this past month." Prior to that, her newfound stability *had* been noticed—and approved of—by all the senior members of the pack. "I've got to start coming down hard on her or it'll cause discontent in the den." Hierarchy was the glue that held a wolf pack together. As alpha, Hawke was at the top of that hierarchy. He could not, would not, accept rebellion from a subordinate.

"Yeah, I get it," Lucas replied. "Surprises me though. She's the perfect soldier down here, doesn't ever give me lip. Got a mind as sharp as a razor."

Hawke flexed and unflexed his claws. "Yeah, well, she's not yours."

A long, quiet pause. "I heard you were seeing someone."

"You want to gossip?" He made no attempt to hide his irritation.

"Kit and the other novices saw you with some drop-dead gorgeous blonde a few weeks ago. At a restaurant down by Pier 39."

He thought back. "She's a media consultant with CTX." SnowDancer and DarkRiver held majority shares in the communications company, an investment that was paying off big-time as even Psy began to search for news reports free of the crushing influence of their dictatorial ruling Council. "Wanted to talk to me about doing an interview."

"When's it going to be on?"

"Next time you see a pig flying past the window." Hawke didn't play for the cameras, and he'd made damn sure Ms. Consultant understood that SnowDancer wasn't planning to change its mean and carnivorous image to pretty and fluffy anytime soon. She could work with that or find another posi— A sudden thought sliced clean through his remembered annoyance, had his hand tightening on the phone. "Was Sienna with the novices?"

"Yep."

It was Hawke who paused this time, his wolf taking a watchful stance, caught between two competing needs. "There's nothing I can do about that, Luc," he said at last, every muscle in his body taut to the point of pain.

"That was what Nate said."

The leopard sentinel was now happily mated with two cubs.

"Not the same." It wasn't simply a question of age—the

brutal fact was that Hawke's mate was dead. Had died as a child. Sienna didn't understand what that meant, how little he had to give her, give any woman. If he was selfish enough to succumb to the unnamed but powerful pull between them, he knew full well he'd destroy her.

"Doesn't mean you can't be happy. Think about it." Luc hung up.

*She hasn't slept with him, you know . . . Don't leave it too late, Hawke, or you might just lose her.*

Indigo's words just over two months ago, speaking about Sienna and that cub who was stuck to her like glue whenever Hawke turned around. Aside from the fact the boy was a leopard, there was nothing wrong with Kit. He'd make the perfect ma—

A crunching sound.

His new sat phone bore a jagged crack through the screen.

# NALINI SINGH

## *Play of Passion*

As Tracker for the SnowDancer pack, it's up to Drew Kincaid to rein in rogue changelings who have lost control of their animal halves. But nothing in his life has prepared him for the battle he must now wage to win the heart of a woman who makes his body ignite...and who threatens to enslave his wolf.

Lieutenant Indigo Riviere doesn't easily allow skin privileges, especially of the sensual kind—and the last person she expects to find herself craving is the most wickedly playful male in the den. Everything she knows tells her to pull back...but she hasn't counted on Drew's will.

Now, two of SnowDancer's most stubborn wolves find themselves playing a hotly sexy game even as lethal danger stalks the very place they call home...

penguin.com

ALSO IN THE GUILD HUNTER SERIES FROM
*NEW YORK TIMES* BESTSELLING AUTHOR

# NALINI SINGH

# ARCHANGEL'S KISS

Waking from a yearlong coma, vampire hunter Elena
Deveraux finds herself thrust into a darkly seductive
new life alongside her stunningly dangerous lover, the
archangel Raphael.

But another archangel has been waiting for Elena to
wake. Ancient and without conscience, Lijuan's power
lies with the reawakening of the dead—and she has
prepared the most perfect and most vicious of wel-
comes for Elena . . .

penguin.com

First in the Guild Hunters series from
*New York Times* bestselling author

# Nalini Singh

## ANGELS' BLOOD

Vampire hunter Elena Deveraux
is hired by the dangerously beautiful
archangel Raphael. But this time, it's
not a wayward vamp she has to track.
It's an archangel gone bad.

**"NALINI SINGH IS A
MAJOR NEW TALENT."**
**—Christine Feehan**

M415T0209

First in the Psy-Changeling series from
*New York Times* bestselling author

# Nalini Singh

# SLAVE TO SENSATION

In a world that denies emotions and where the
ruling Psy punish any sign of desire, Sascha
Duncan must hide the emotions that mark
her as flawed. Both human and animal, Lucas
Hunter is a changeling hungry for the very sensations the Psy disdain. When the two meet,
the passion in Lucas will tempt Sascha to reveal
everything—but the consequence could be the
loss of her very soul.

**"I love this book! It's a must read for all of my
fans. Nalini Singh is a major new talent."**

—*New York Times* bestselling author
Christine Feehan

M350T1008